PRAISE FOR

"Andrea Mara's tight plotti[ng]
make her books both
– Liz Nugent, author of *Our Little Cruelties*

"Andrea Mara writes twisty mysteries that keep me turning pages"
– Jo Spain, author of *Six Wicked Reasons*

PRAISE FOR *ONE CLICK*

"Mara is a master of the red herring and there are lots of plot twists to keep the reader guessing until the terrifying end ... Once again, Mara has produced a gripping story of suspense that will have you on the edge of your seat to the last" *The Independent*

"This is a cracking read"
– Liz Nugent, author of *Unravelling Oliver* and *Skin Deep*

"*One Click* is the best psych thriller I've read in quite a while.
Great end, but more importantly, the journey was wonderful too"
– Sinéad Crowley, author of *One Bad Turn*

"[Mara's] latest offering will doubtless embellish her reputation
as a grip-lit author of note" – *Sunday Independent*

"Flew through *One Click*, fantastic read, hours of pleasure"
– Jo Spain, author of *The Confession*

"A well-plotted novel, with a lot of red herrings and false leads. I was convinced many times that I had guessed the denouement, but the author outsmarted me . . . the dramatic revelation shocked me to the core, yet made perfect sense of all that had gone before" – Sue Leonard, *The Examiner*

"The perfect poolside read with twists and turns that kept me guessing right to the end" – Carmel Harrington, author of *The Woman at 72 Derry Lane*

"*One Click* pulls you in and won't let go – be prepared to read it in one sitting. It's a page-turner that will hook you from page one, and will make you stop and think before you make one click online again"
– Patricia Gibney, author of *No Safe Place*

THE
SLEEPER
LIES

ANDREA MARA

POOLBEG
CRIMSON

Published 2020 by Crimson
an imprint of Poolbeg Press Ltd
123 Grange Hill, Baldoyle
Dublin 13, Ireland
E-mail: poolbeg@poolbeg.com
www.poolbeg.com

3

A catalogue record for this book is available from the British Library.

ISBN 978-1-78199-766-6

Author back cover photo by Nessa Robinson.

Typeset by Poolbeg Press Ltd

www.poolbeg.com

FSC
MIX
Paper | Supporting
responsible forestry
www.fsc.org
FSC® C013604

ABOUT THE AUTHOR

Andrea Mara lives in Dublin with her husband and three children. She blogs about balancing work and home at *OfficeMum.ie*.

The Sleeper Lies is her third book. Her first book, *The Other Side of the Wall*, was shortlisted for the Kate O'Brien Award 2018, and her second book, *One Click*, was shortlisted for Irish Crime Novel of the Year at the 2018 An Post Irish Book Awards.

Also by Andrea Mara

The Other Side of the Wall

One Click

Published by Poolbeg

To Dad, for everything

CHAPTER 1

2018

I don't know what a dead body looks like. I've seen them in coffins in tidy funeral homes, but not like this – not in this maybe-state, flat on the frozen ground.

Dead. Or not dead, just waiting for me to come closer.

One or the other.

It's too dark to see, and I understand now that it's always been too dark – for me, and for Hanne. Spinning blindly in the wind while other people pulled the strings.

And I feel it even now, the snap of the string, pulling me forward. Towards the body.

Dead. Or not dead.

One or the other.

My breath comes fast. Another step. A closer look. A movement. Slight, but enough.

And I think about all of it, all of the deaths and all of the accidents and all of the pain. And it's not dark anymore. I know what I need to do.

24 days earlier

The day it all began started out, in many respects, just like any other. I woke up on my own, in my own bed, in my very old cottage, in the Wicklow hills. So far, so normal. I checked the time, noted I had thirty minutes until my first conference call, and got up to make coffee. Still all very normal. Then I walked through to the kitchen and saw that it would not, in fact, be a normal day – outside, my back garden was covered in a blanket of white. Just as the weatherman had predicted. I couldn't remember the last time I'd seen so much snow. I'd been away for the big freeze of 2010, and before that . . . maybe back when my dad was alive? A memory surfaced – a snowman, a pipe in his mouth, pebbles for eyes, and my dad's scarf around his neck. We didn't have a carrot and my dad made up some story about snowmen not needing noses, because they always had colds. I was probably four or five at the time, although – I realised with a sudden pang – there was no way to check. Not now, with nobody left but me.

Still mesmerised by snow and memories, I made a coffee, went back through the living room, and opened the front door to get a better look. I wasn't fully awake, and maybe I was dazzled by the brightness, but for whatever reason, in those first moments, I didn't notice the footprints.

And even when I did, I still didn't register that there was anything strange about them – about their very existence in my garden in the middle of nowhere. I stood in the doorway, cradling the coffee, as my eyes followed the trail, tracing their journey from the garden gate all the way up to the cottage. I shook myself, suddenly wide awake. Someone had been here. While I was asleep.

I pulled on boots and stepped outside, my feet sinking into powdery white, and squinted to see where the prints went. That's when the first prickle of unease hit. The footprints led right up to my bedroom window.

I stared at the indentations, deeper under the window, as though they – he? – had stood there, watching me, while I was asleep.

My stomach lurched. I didn't want my coffee anymore. Putting the cup on the snowy ground, I stepped towards the window. Two deep, wide prints, side by side, just inches from the front wall of the cottage. Directly under my bedroom window. I leaned forward and, with my hands on the windowsill, peered into my room. Through the muslin curtain, I could make out my bed, duvet thrown back just moments before. Who on earth had been spying on me? And why?

An icy wind whipped at my hair, reminding me I was wearing pyjamas in zero-degree temperatures. Inside, I shut the door and stood with my back against it, staring around the living room. Could he be in the house? The front door was closed when I woke. It could only be opened from outside with a key. What about the back door? In a haze, I crossed the living room and walked through to the quiet, shadowy kitchen. On my left, the door to the boot room stood ajar – had I left it open last night? Stepping towards it, I pushed it wide. Empty, save for my jacket on its hook.

The bathroom door beyond the coat-hook was closed. Wishing it was already open, I pushed down the handle. Cold air and shadows greeted me, but nothing looked out of place. The shower curtain was pulled around the bath, just as I'd left it yesterday morning. My toothbrush stood in the mug, exactly where I'd left it last night. About to turn away, I stopped, and looked again at the shower curtain. Dark green, to match the bath, I wished now it was lighter. Transparent. Unmoving, I listened. Nothing. Not even the sound of my own breath. The silence was cold and heavy and suddenly false – a trick – someone else

3

listening, not moving, not breathing. Before I could change my mind, I stepped forward, grabbed the curtain and wrenched it back.

Empty.

Lightheaded with foolishness, or maybe relief, I half-ran out of the bathroom, and pulled the door behind me.

Now the back door. I stared at it, the chipped wood and spotted glass reminding me it needed replacing. The key was in the keyhole, just as it always was. I had turned it when I came in last night. Steeling myself, I pulled down the handle.

Nothing. Still locked. Turning the key, I pulled it open, letting in an icy blast. A foot-high snowdrift swooped upwards against the house, and some of it fell inside onto the floor. Kicking it out, I closed the back door and locked it again.

The kitchen was quiet save for the ticking of the wall clock – twenty to eight, and my first conference call was at eight. An eerie half-light rested on counter-tops and pale green cupboards, gloomy and bright all at once. The small kitchen table, littered with files and chewed biros, sat quietly in the centre of the room. Nothing stirred. Nobody here.

I made my way back to the living room, and stood in the centre, my eyes roaming across every detail. The Aztec-print throw lay on the dark-red couch, exactly where I left it when I put down my book last night. My laptop and the TV remote sat side by side on the coffee table, my book had slipped to the floor. Agatha Christie's *A Murder Is Announced*. I picked it up and put it back on the coffee table. Nothing out of place, nobody here but me.

Unless there was someone in one of the bedrooms.

I swallowed, wishing for the first time in a long time that I didn't live on my own, and moved towards my dad's old room, on the far side of the living room from mine. The door creaked, loud in the silence. Inside, dust particles danced in weak morning light but, apart from my dad's old bed, Ray's old desk and a mahogany wardrobe, the room was bare.

Only my room left. The one he'd looked into.

Crossing the living room in quick strides, I pushed the door and burst into my bedroom with forced ferocity. I scanned the room, taking in the overstuffed bookshelves, the narrow wardrobe in the far corner, the waxed-pine dresser, the Oriental rug. The muslin curtain, and the window through which he'd looked.

My eyes went to the bed. The duvet dipped low on the side nearest me, almost but not quite touching the floor. From where I stood, I couldn't see underneath. Biting my lip, I stepped back towards the door and bent down. Just a little. I could see between the duvet and the floor now – the empty space and the light beyond. Nobody there.

I stood again, looking at the wardrobe in the far corner. A single wardrobe with a single door and one scant rail of clothes, but still big enough to fit a crouching human. *Christ*. Checking it was impossible. But not knowing was impossible too. With every childhood bogeyman story running through my head, I made a decision. In three long steps, I was at the wardrobe, my finger looped through the metal ring, ready to pull it towards me. I stopped, but only for a second, then yanked it. I jumped back, letting out a yell, not at all ready for whoever or whatever was in there.

There was nothing. No-one.

There was nobody in my house.

But it was comfort of a cold sort – who was looking in my window while I was asleep?

CHAPTER 2

The French office didn't care that it was an hour earlier here in Ireland – the world of banking had no time for easing into a new week, and the Zorian IT Programmers' call signalled the start of business at eight every Monday morning. Today would be no different, inexplicable footprints or not.

"Marianne here," I said as I dialled in, still staring out the window.

I needed to look around outside. What if he was still out there? Could I do the call on mute and check the garden at the same time? My gut said no. I'd need my wits about me to search, not project managers mumbling in my ear. Or maybe I just didn't want to go outside.

Distracted and on edge, I waited as participants announced their names and locations.

My boss was up next. "Clare in Dublin here – morning, everyone – Marianne, are you snowed in? I heard on the news that Wicklow is bad – they're calling in the army to clear the roads?"

"It's not too bad," I told her. "I'd get down to the village in the jeep if I needed to."

The jeep. Could that be what he was after? Holding my phone to my ear, I slipped into boots, opened the front door and stepped out into the snow. The jeep was always parked around the side of the house, and I readied myself for empty space when I turned the corner. But it was still there. I wondered why I didn't feel more relief.

Back inside, I put the chain on the door, just as fresh snow began to fall. I hit the light switch, and the bulb flickered unconvincingly to life. I sat but couldn't sit still. *There's nobody here, you've checked*, I reminded myself over and over, as my eyes flitted from window to door. A creak from the bedroom gave me a jolt. *There's nobody here*. The creak of an old house. Nothing more.

As the meeting rumbled on, I picked up a pen and notebook. Writing things down would help, it always did. Calm, cool, unemotional words. Black and white. Reliable. Like computers. Unlike humans.

Footprints: Man's boots/large boots = male, not female
Alan? Jamie? Bert checking on me? Someone lost/drunk?
Kids from village (footprints too large for kid?)
Burglar checking if someone in house?

I put down the pen and stood, pacing the living-room floor as the meeting meandered. Catching my reflection in the mirror above the couch, I shook my head, glad none of my colleagues could see me this morning. With my uncombed hair and unwashed face, I looked nothing like the groomed version of myself on the Zorian staff website. That photo was five or six years old – my hair was golden-blonde then, warmer than the natural pale colour I have today, and I wore make-up then too, an unnecessary step now that I was spending most of my days on my own. Something flickered in the top corner of the mirror and I

7

spun around. Through the window, I could see the branches of the old hawthorn tree at the bottom of the garden swaying in the wind. That's all it was.

There's nobody here.

"Marianne?"

Clare was asking me something.

"Sorry, I just dropped my notes – would you mind repeating?" I said, sitting back down. I opened my laptop and prepared to talk.

The meeting ended just after nine and, with it, my excuse to stay indoors – I'd have to go outside for a proper look around. Jesus, I wasn't cut out for this. People on TV were always racing into danger – I just wanted to stay locked in my living room until . . . well, until what? That was the problem. Nobody was coming to rescue me.

I pulled on my jacket, reminding myself that if someone was spying on me in the middle of the night, they were hardly still out there, hanging around in the cold. The snow was coming down heavily as I walked out into the front garden and down to the gate. No footprints now – the fresh snow had covered them. At the gate, I stared down towards the bend in the road that led to Alan's house. Could it have been Alan? If he was in my garden last night, it certainly wasn't to check if I was okay. But I couldn't think of any other reason either – despite all that had happened and everything he did to us back then, I didn't take Alan for a prowler.

I trudged up the driveway and around to the back of the cottage. The garden stretched, long and white and empty, the trees and bushes that lined both sides covered in snow. Through the blur of swirling flakes, the wall at the end was only just visible. I thought about going down there but decided against it – whoever was at my window last night was long gone, not hiding in the undergrowth in my garden.

As I rounded the corner to the front of the house, I found Bert Quinn trying to push post through the letterbox, his task hampered by thick leather gloves.

"Are you *mad* coming out in this weather," I said, rushing to take the post from him. "I could have waited a few more days for my credit-card bill or whatever it is."

"Ah, us oul' fellas are made of hardier stuff than you young ones," he said with a wink. His grey moustache had flecks of snow in it, despite the huge navy poncho-type thing that covered him head to toe.

"Will you come in to dry off a bit? You surely didn't walk up, did you?"

"Didn't think the van would make it up the hill to you in the snow, so left it outside Alan's. A little birdie told me he was three sheets to the wind in Delaneys' on Saturday night – it's worse he's getting. I don't know how young Jamie puts up with him. D'ya see much of him?"

"Alan?"

A smile. "Jamie."

"No, not at all. But, sure, I'm either in here working or up in Dublin working – that's all I do."

"It's Wednesday you go to Dublin, isn't it? Not sure you'll make it this week to be honest, the forecast isn't great. Your boss is decent though, isn't she?"

"Is there anything you don't know about anyone in Carrickderg, Bert?"

"Says Ms Amateur Detective herself," he said, winking again.

I squirmed, wishing I'd never told him that bit.

"How're you getting on with the cold anyway?" he continued. "You didn't freeze to death last night, I see."

"Still here, just about."

"I shouldn't be joking, it can happen. You'd be worried about the old folks, wouldn't you, and anyone out on their own in the countryside? No harm to check in on people."

As he tramped down the driveway, I looked down at my post – a flyer advertising insurance and a promotional mailing from a car dealer. I smiled. Every village needs someone like Bert.

Back inside, I sat cross-legged on the couch, a blanket across my lap. Warmer. Calmer. There was nobody in the house, and nobody in the garden, and though the footprints made no sense, they were gone, deleted by freshly falling snow. Time to move on.

My phone beeped, showing a Facebook notification from the Armchair Detective group and I wondered who was posting so early – most of the members had day-jobs like me, scattered across cities and towns in the UK. There was only one other Irish member in the group – amateur sleuthing hadn't really taken off here, and in my experience people greeted it with ridicule or confusion: *Why on earth would you spend your time reading articles about serial killers?* I used to try to explain – I'd say it's not so different to reading a newspaper or watching a true crime documentary. But, yeah, I understood why people thought it was a little odd, and mostly I didn't talk about it.

I clicked into Facebook to check who was posting – Judith, sharing a new article on the Blackwood Strangler.

It was our common interest in the Blackwood Strangler that prompted us to set up the Armchair Detective Facebook group, and really the group existed solely for swapping information and theories about him. Every now and then someone posted an article on another serial killer, but the unspoken rule was clear – our primary interest was in the man responsible for at least eight murders, the first of which had taken place in the small village of Blackwood Heath, near Leicester in England, some fifteen years earlier. There was always speculation about the gaps between the murders – was he in and out of prison, or in and out of relationships, or maybe serving overseas in the Armed Forces, taking him away from the UK for chunks of time? But that the eight murders were the work of one man didn't seem to be in question, at least not according to the dozens of articles we'd read and shared in the group.

What are you doing up so early? When I'm retired I'm going to lie in every morning till midday! I typed in response to Judith's post, glad of the distraction.

I'll sleep when I'm dead ☺ she replied.

Judith was almost eighty and battling a litany of worsening health problems – her response made me wince. I changed the subject.

So what's in the article – want to save me a click?

And she did, summarising the story – an old victim, a new theory, a suggestion that a family member had been responsible. I didn't buy it. It had all the hallmarks of the Blackwood Strangler – the way he scoped out her house in advance, the neighbour who saw someone in her garden, the missing gold pendant that fit with the killer's habit of taking souvenirs.

Judith said she was going to do some digging anyway, some online research on the family member. That's what we did most of the time – online searches and looking at old crime scenes on Google Maps. We all knew of amateur sleuths who had tracked down lost witnesses and missing persons, but even when we found nothing the research was addictive.

Some of the group would be sceptical of Judith's plan – it would be hard to find much on the new suspect after so many years. But, like Judith, I figured every avenue was worth a shot – not all cold cases are solved because of advances in forensics. I looked over at the photo on my living-room shelf, at her long blonde hair and long-gone smile. I knew that better than anyone.

CHAPTER 3

At two o'clock, tired from bashing keys, I came up for air. I'd typed up an unnecessarily long report to distract myself from the footprints and to create noise – the clacking of laptop keys was preferable to silence. My stomach growled as I made my way through to the kitchen, still unnerved. Gurgles and creaks I'd never noticed clanged loud as I put my last two slices of bread in the toaster and inspected the lonely shelves in the fridge. Unless I wanted yogurt for dinner, I'd have to brave the outdoors. The only question was whether or not I could drive.

Outside, banishing thoughts of watching eyes, I trudged to the jeep to take stock. Snow piled against tyres, snow covering the roof, snow completely obscuring the windscreen. Would heat and wipers help? Would it even start? I opened the driver's door to sit in, but something stopped me. I stumbled back, heart hammering.

Jesus Christ. There was something sitting on the seat.

The jeep door was half open, half closed, and from where I stood I couldn't make out what was on the seat. Sweating despite the cold, I edged closer. With my right hand I pulled the door open wider, and peered in.

It was a doll. A rag doll. About two feet long, sitting in the driver's seat, staring straight ahead with button eyes. Dark woollen hair sprouting from its head, its mouth sewn shut with tight, jagged stitches. I stepped closer. The doll was wearing a brown overall-type thing – a homemade dress or some kind of sackcloth, I couldn't tell. And it was sitting in my jeep, as though it was the most normal thing in the world, only I'd never seen it in my life. How the hell did it get there? Someone playing a joke? A really weird, unfunny joke. I reached out to pick up the doll, but changed my mind. Somehow, though it was just a harmless bundle of rags, I didn't want to touch it. Instead, I closed the door.

Back inside, too jittery to work, I buttered cold toast and clicked into Armchair Detectives. There were dozens of comments on Judith's earlier post, and most were in agreement – this was the work of the Blackwood Strangler. Only one person gave the new theory any credence at all – Barry. Of course it was Barry.

But what if it was someone the victim knew, and he made it *look* like the Blackwood Strangler? It's not hard to copy his MO. What do you think, Marianne? he asked, tagging me on his comment.

Barry lived in Dun Laoghaire in Dublin, and he and I were the only Irish members of the UK-based group. Barry had discovered the group a month earlier and, realising I was Irish, decided that made us best pals. Mostly he got on my nerves. He had far too much time on his hands and posted about twice as often as anyone else – he was like a needy puppy, bringing titbits of information and waiting for a pat on the head. Sometimes I felt sorry for him, but mostly he drove me mad. I closed Facebook without replying, and sat, listening to the silence.

At twenty to four, when my final call finished, I heaved on my heaviest jacket, locked the front door and, ignoring the jeep with its uninvited guest, plodded through the garden out onto the road. The sky was heavy, a grey blanket signalling what was to come, but for now there was no fresh snow falling. As I followed the narrow road around the first bend, something made me glance back at the house. A movement, a flicker under the hawthorn tree. A blur, there, and just as quickly, gone. I stopped and waited, focussing on the tree. There it was again – a fox. Just a fox, a regular visitor to my garden. I turned towards the village.

Half a mile farther, I passed Alan's farmhouse, noticing it in a way I didn't usually when I was driving. The old white paintwork was looking worse for wear, and the tin roofs of the sheds and outhouses were rusty and jagged. The yard was littered with broken machinery, and the Land Rover parked outside the house was covered in muck.

As I looked over, I spotted him standing at an upstairs window. He turned away when he saw me and I shook my head. He was never going to let it go. This was the kind of thing that could go on for generations, until people lost track of what had started it in the first place. I wondered if Alan was disappointed that I didn't have children – nobody for his son or future grandkids to feud with in years to come. I smiled. Jamie wasn't as bad as Alan. I got the feeling on more than one occasion he thought the whole thing was daft. Then again, he wasn't about to go against his dad.

Another mile and a half farther, I rounded the corner and the Carrickderg Arms came into view. An old-school hotel, with a wagon wheel fixed to the gable wall, and a rusty plough beside the front door. Tourists loved it. I thought it was twee.

As I made my way along the slushy footpath towards what Carrickderg locals optimistically called "the supermarket", I found Mrs O'Shea from the Post Office standing outside on the street, staring at a broken window.

"Marianne, did you walk down? Shockin' weather for March, isn't it? God, you must be freezing." She looked up at the sky, and pulled a purple woolly hat further down over her dark-grey perm. "Out for supplies?"

"Yep, didn't listen to any of the warnings to stock up, so it's my own fault. What happened to the window?"

Mrs O'Shea shook her head. "Some gurrier thought it'd be great craic to fling a brick through it last night. I didn't open up this morning with the snow, so only found it now. Patrick's on his way."

Patrick Maguire was a local young garda, and always looked like he was dreaming of solving crimes CSI-style, instead of dealing with speeding tickets and the odd drunken argument in a sleepy Wicklow village. His boss at the station, Geraldine, twenty years older than him, seemed happily resigned to the lack of excitement in Carrickderg and I wondered if it was just a matter of time before the village sucked the soul out of Patrick, replacing it with middle-age spread and apathy. I suspected a brick through the Post Office window might be just the thing to liven up his Monday afternoon.

"Actually," said Mrs O'Shea, squinting at me through tiny rimless glasses, "you're a bit of a detective yourself, aren't you? Would you have any thoughts on who did it?"

For the hundredth time, I wished I'd never told Bert

about my hobby. Because Bert told everybody everything. And when it came to my particular pastime, people either misunderstood it completely – as Mrs O'Shea was doing now – or teased me with one-liners from *Columbo* and *Murder She Wrote*.

"Well, it's a bit different," I explained. "I'm not any kind of real detective. I just look up information about old cases online and try to piece them together."

She shrugged. "It can't be that different – though why you'd want to be solving old crimes in other countries instead of real crimes like this," she nodded at her window, "I don't know."

"Ah, what I do is just a hobby – I'd be useless at it in real life," I told her.

"Here's the real guard anyway, and about time too," Mrs O'Shea said, looking over my shoulder. "It's twenty minutes since I called it in."

I smiled at her straight-from-TV "called it in" and waited as the tall, gangly guard approached.

"How'ya, Mrs O'Shea, what have we here?" Patrick asked, nodding hello at me as he inspected the damage.

Even to a layperson, it was pretty self-evident what "we" had – there was a brick-sized hole in the glass, a brick in the middle of the window display, and bits of glass on the ground.

"I don't know what took you so long to get here, Patrick. An old woman like me, home alone when Mick's out driving the cab – it's not right for me to be worrying about thugs targeting me."

Patrick placated her with a nod of agreement. This was about as far as he could get from a CSI-style crime.

"There was a bit of trouble up at the Arms last night,"

he said. "An American fella who'd had a few too many flinging glasses around the place. I wonder if it was him? He stormed out of the bar when they told him they were calling us, and had to slink back two hours later when he remembered he was staying there. That's where I was just now – taking a statement at the hotel. Yer man has fecked off though – he was gone before breakfast this morning. Good riddance."

"That's all very well but who's going to pay for my window?"

"I know it's a pain, Mrs O'Shea, but I'd say he's halfway back to America at this stage, or at least Dublin. Have you insurance?"

Mrs O'Shea was shaking her head but it wasn't clear if it was an answer to the question or general distaste for marauding tourists wreaking havoc in Carrickderg.

"You don't think he'd have gone anywhere else last night, do you?" I asked Patrick. "Like up as far as my place?"

"I suppose he could have, though I don't know if he'd have made it all the way up to yours and back within two hours in that snow. Why, do you think you saw him?"

Now Patrick was interested – this was a bit more exciting.

I told him about the footprints under the window and, for the first time, he took out his notebook and wrote down some details. I could feel Mrs O'Shea bristling behind me – my footprints were stealing her thunder. I told him about the rag doll, and Mrs O'Shea made a *tsk* sound with her tongue – a rag doll wasn't something to worry about, not compared to a brick through a window. I could see her point, but then she hadn't seen its creepy button eyes and stitched-up mouth.

Patrick suggested he come up to have a look around

outside the house and I was tempted to say no – it all seemed a bit "damsel in distress" – but common sense won.

"I don't think the car will make it up the hill to your place," he said. "I'll walk back up with you."

The thought of making small talk with Patrick Maguire all the way up the hill didn't spark much joy, but I couldn't back out now. He was about twenty-five, I reckoned, a good decade younger than me, but somehow seemed even younger than that. Or maybe I was feeling old – nothing like chatting to a young guard to make you feel older than your years, especially one with cheeks like a sun-bleached peach.

We went our separate ways for half an hour – me to stock up on supplies and him to write up details of Carrickderg's crime spree – then met back at the Carrickderg Arms to set off up the hill to my house.

The small talk wasn't as awful as I imagined and it distracted me, at least for a short time, from the footprints. He told a few funny stories about his training years in Templemore, and a few more about some Carrickderg locals – he didn't name names but he didn't have to, you never do in small Irish villages. When he smiled, he seemed even younger, and his clean, shiny face made me think of soap and aftershave. As he talked, I tried to work out what colour his hair was. It was so short I couldn't tell, but it looked kind of beige. In contrast, his eyes were a deep ocean-blue. Intelligent too, and full of enthusiasm. God love him, but Carrickderg would soon knock that out of him.

Up at the house, I showed him where the footprints – now long covered with fresh snow – had been. With nothing to see, I could sense he was wondering if I'd imagined it, and I could understand why. It was highly unlikely the drunk tourist or anyone else had trekked up through the snow in the middle of the night to look through my window. Yet even as I thought about it, a shiver ran across my shoulders and up the back of my neck. I didn't imagine the footprints. Someone had been there, and that someone had left a doll in the jeep.

I brought him around the side of the house and opened the driver's door to show him, standing back to give him space.

"What am I looking at?" he asked.

"I know, weird, right?"

"What though?"

He stepped back to show me. There was nothing there. Just empty space on the seat, where earlier the doll had been sitting.

My breath quickened. "Jesus. Where the hell's it gone?" I looked down in the footwell, and on the other side too, though it could hardly have moved by itself.

"Are you sure it was there – could it have been something you thought you saw, a shadow, or a bag or something?"

"No, I was right up here beside it, as close as I am now."

"Did you have the jeep locked?"

"No, I never bother – I'm so far away from everyone up here."

"*Ah.*"

He didn't need to say anything else – I heard the admonishment in that one *ah*.

I shut the jeep door and clicked the key-fob to lock it, stable doors and bolting horses dancing through my head.

"Right, I'll take a look around the premises," Patrick said, walking towards the back of the house.

I followed, because it was preferable to waiting on my own as darkness slipped across the snow.

A few minutes and no stalkers later, he asked if I'd like him to check inside too.

"I searched it this morning and was there most of the day working – there's nothing out of place. I'm certain he wasn't inside." Almost certain. "You go on back down – it's getting dark out now and the snow is on its way again. I'll be fine."

He nodded. "If you're sure. Give us a call if there's anything else, won't you?" He handed me a card, though like every other person in Carrickderg I had the Garda Station number saved in my phone.

"Will do, but what are you going to do without the car – cycle up here to rescue me?"

He laughed and I waved him off.

I went inside and shut and locked the door.

That night, once I'd eaten, I checked all the windows and doors again, and perched on the edge of the couch, listening. The house was far too quiet. The living-room light bulb flickered, reminding me to get the wiring checked – my dad had been brilliant with all that stuff, but now it was just me. And someone creeping up to my house at night. *Fuck*.

Suddenly, more than anything, I wanted to talk to Linda.

I picked up my phone and clicked into Favourites to pull up her number, but at the last second something stopped me. It was seven o'clock in the evening – peak getting-the-kids-to-bed time from what she'd told me. The last thing she needed was a phone call from me and, admittedly, the last thing I needed was a distracted, one-sided conversation. I'd try her mid-morning instead.

Still on edge, I pulled my laptop onto my knee, and clicked into the Armchair Detective group where I found a discussion that came up at least once a month. Neil, a particularly prickly member, had been asked why he investigates old cases, and how on earth he thinks he can solve something if the police can't.

It's not as if I tease someone about their hobbies – why do people feel it's ok to question mine? Neil was typing, still smarting over his encounter.

I know! My mum spends her entire day watching crime on TV, but thinks I'm wasting my time with web-sleuthing, answered Cheryl, a perennially cheerful university student. **I spent an hour last week telling her about that case we solved but then I realised she wasn't listening at all – too busy watching Inspector Morse!**

"That case" – a missing person who'd been found via online detective work – was our poster child for winning any argument about the value of armchair-detecting, though to say "we" solved it was an overstatement – it was solved by a member of iSleuth, the US forum on which we'd all originally met. But it summed up how we felt – armchair-detecting was a virtual hobby that could yield real-life results.

Whatever about the UK, I don't think the Irish would get it at all – would they, Marianne? Barry said, tagging me. Again.

Ah, I think most people here are very "live and let live", I replied, though it wasn't strictly true – I'd had my fair share of raised eyebrows.

Ignore them, Judith said to Neil. **It's not hard to understand**

if people really think about it. Most of us grew up reading detective novels and watching TV shows about fictional murders – now we're looking into real murders, something we could never have done before the internet.

I glanced at the photo of my parents on the living-room shelf – him smiling like I never remember in real life, her laughing, her blue eyes sparkling, her blonde hair so like mine, but faded by the decades since the photo was taken. I'd grown up reading detective novels too, but my interest in true crime came from somewhere else entirely. Suddenly chilled, I closed the laptop.

CHAPTER 4

I woke with a jolt. Eyes wide open. White noise in my head shouting at me, telling something was wrong. Black all around. Middle of the night. Middle of nowhere. My breath stayed stuck in my chest, my limbs deadweight on the bed. A creak. The house moving. I waited, still no breath, lying motionless. My head fixed on the pillow, eyes to the ceiling. Slowly, I moved my eyes around the room, adjusting to the darkness. The bright green digits on my clock radio showed 4:11, the screen casting a tiny glow from my bedside table. The bedroom door tightly shut, just as I left it. The window, covered in black plastic sacks, pinned up with thumbtacks. Nobody would see in tonight.

A creak. Not the house moving. Coming from outside. Coming from the window. A fox. My friend the fox. Had to be. Stomach churning, nails digging into numb palms, I forced myself up. Slipping from bed to ice-cold floor, I pushed one foot in front of the other. *Don't think about it. It's a fox*.

At the window, my hand out. *Keep going. It's just a fox*. Another creak. *It's just a fox*. My fingers fumbled, unpicking tacks. One, and another, and another. *Enough now, enough to see. To see the fox*.

Fingers wrapped around the edge, I pulled it back. *Sharp. Quick. Rip off the plaster.*

But there was no fox.

There was a face.

A white face, pressed to the glass.

Staring in. Staring at me.

I screamed and tripped, falling backwards onto the floor. Scrambling, crawling. Not looking at the window. Yanking open the bedroom door, I threw myself into the living room. Slammed the bedroom door shut. Curled in a ball, in the corner, because brave people get up and fight, but I am not brave.

CHAPTER 5

When the alarm went off I was confused – it sounded far away, like a distant church bell. I shifted in the bed, and suddenly realised I wasn't in bed at all – I was on the couch, under a throw. Wearing my jacket.

With a rush, it all came back. The bin bag tacked to my bedroom window, the white face outside looking in. Jesus Christ, how had I managed to sleep at all? Sitting up and swinging my feet to the floor, I put my head in my hands. Groggy and sick. I felt like I'd fallen into a deep sleep two minutes before the alarm went off. The alarm that was still going off. Christ, I'd have to go in there. I wasn't cut out for this.

At the bedroom door I reached out and grasped the handle, ready for another pull-of-the-plaster but I was too slow. The what-ifs seeped in. *What if he's in there. What if he's waiting for me behind the door. What if he's still at the window staring in. Breathe. Deep breaths. Listen. No sound. Nothing. No breathing but mine. And it's daylight. There's nobody there. Pull the plaster.*

I pulled.

Inside, it was dark but not quite black. And empty. I hit

the button to make the alarm stop and stood, staring at the window. The bin bag had flapped down where I'd pulled it aside but I knew in a million years I couldn't go over there and look out again. The memory flashed up – the porcelain-white face, no expression, no colour. Staring. Close to the glass. Not a face, but a mask. No way to see who or what was behind it. And no way to look now, no chance. Not brave.

Back in the living room, I looked in the mirror. My face was pale, almost ghostly, even my lips, the only hint of the colour the purple circles beneath my eyes. I shook myself.

Could it have been my own reflection in the window last night? Distorted by sleep and snow and unease?

I stood in the middle of the room, trying to remember. Focussing on details. But every time I brought up the image, it slipped further way.

I looked at the front door, but I wasn't ready. Instead I walked to the living-room window and, biting my lip, pulled the curtain to one side.

A blanket covered the outside world, a sea of white, drifting high against the wall at the end of the front garden. And no footprints. No human footprints. Fox prints, yes. And little birdlike indentations. But no humans. Maybe the prints had been covered by fresh snow? I let out a ragged breath. Or maybe the face was mine.

In the kitchen, I pulled my cardigan around me while I waited for the kettle to boil and stared out the window. The snow was up to a foot high in places – there would be no trip to the village today. My phone, my window to the outside world, told me a curfew would be in place from 4:30 PM. I wasn't going anywhere anyway. As the kettle rumbled on without speed or enthusiasm, I spooned coffee into the cafetière, and hugged myself for warmth. Minus two degrees according to my phone, but it felt colder in my kitchen. When it was finally ready, I drank the coffee in my marginally warmer living room and, only then, emboldened by caffeine and the certainty – the almost certainty – that I'd imagined the masked face, did I open the front door.

And there they were.

Footprints.

Just like yesterday, all the way from the gate, across the garden and up to my bedroom window. I swallowed. Only not just like yesterday – because they hadn't been there when I'd looked out fifteen minutes ago. My skin prickled and I took an instinctive step back from the door. *Jesus*. While I was in here making coffee, someone had been outside.

Locking the front door, I moved to the window and pulled back the curtain. Maybe the prints had been there all along – maybe I'd missed them when I looked out earlier? Wrong angle, too far away? But no, they were clearly visible now, tracking all the way across the garden, and ending under my bedroom window. Jesus Christ – where was he now? I stared across at the prints, and that's when I saw there were more – leading away from my window, but not back across the garden. My breath quickened as my eyes followed the trail along the front wall of the house and around to the side, out of sight. A surge of nausea swelled inside my stomach. Was he at the back of the house?

Pushing one foot in front of the other, I made my way towards the door to the kitchen. As I touched the handle, I paused, remembering something I hadn't thought of in years. I didn't stop to worry about whether it was the right decision or not – in three quick strides I was in my father's old bedroom, pulling out the drawer at the bottom of the wardrobe.

Awkwardly lifting the shotgun, I marched through to the living room and braced myself to open the kitchen door. The gun was heavier than I expected and I wasn't sure it would actually work anymore, or if it was loaded, but it might be enough to scare off an intruder. What would I do if I found someone looking in the back window? Before I could talk myself out of it, I yanked the handle and pulled open the door. Through the window above the sink, there was nothing but grey sky and white grass. No face. No mask. Nobody. I sagged against the doorjamb.

But where was he now? If he'd been here in the last twenty minutes, he couldn't be gone far. Was he somewhere on the grounds? I stepped towards the window to look out. There they were. Footprints trailing all the way across the back garden as far as I could see.

My hand shook as I scrolled for the Garda Station number. Geraldine answered, and I explained what had happened: the face at the window (mine? not mine?) and the footprints (definitely not mine). She'd send someone up to look around, she said, and in the meantime I should lock the doors and windows, and make myself tea with extra sugar. Silently I shook my head, and thanked her. How was sweet tea going to help?

My first conference call of the day was about to start and I thought about crying off, but the alternative – sitting worrying myself to death – didn't appeal either. I dialled in. As each participant announced his or her name, for the first time in a long time I wished I was in our busy city-centre office and not out here in the middle of nowhere.

ANDREA MARA

I sat cross-legged on the couch with my phone on speaker and my laptop on my knees, only half-listening as each person gave their update. My eyes were fixed on the living-room window. Who was out there? What did he want with me? It couldn't be the drunk tourist Patrick had mentioned – he was apparently on his way back to the States. Or was he? Maybe that was just an assumption the gardaí had jumped to. Maybe it was someone who lived outdoors, looking for an empty house to shelter from the cold? Years ago, Alan used to have people staying in his sheds and outhouses during the winter, though he was charging them for it, the tight-fisted git. Ray soon put an end to that.

The thought of my ex made me sit up, suddenly cold. It couldn't be anything to do with Ray, could it? As far as I knew, he was back home in New Jersey. And anyway, if Ray ever came back, he'd . . . my hand went instinctively to my cheek. I shook my head. I couldn't see him creeping and spying, no matter how much sneaking around he did back then. A memory surfaced. Dead-animal eyes, rusty, matted blood. On my doorstep, once upon a time. I closed my eyes.

Someone from the office was asking a question. I gave the answer, and slumped against the couch, staring out the window. Last time I googled, Ray was safely back in New Jersey, working on his next book. It couldn't be Ray. Then who?

CHAPTER 6

The knock, sharp and unexpected, made me jump. From my spot on the couch, I could see out the living-room window, but not who was at the front door, not without getting up to walk over. Frozen, I waited, as a familiar high-pitched whirring inside my head took hold.

A second knock, sharper now, and a voice – a familiar one.

"Marianne, it's Sergeant Breen and Garda Maguire."

Geraldine and Patrick.

Relieved, I opened the door and led them in, babbling about what had happened as I showed them through to the kitchen window. The footprints were gone, obscured by fresh snow, and the futility struck me as I turned to see Patrick exchange a look with Geraldine.

"There were prints out the front as well, as far as my bedroom window," I said, "just like yesterday. They'll be gone now too . . ."

Patrick nodded. "Sure show us anyway, no harm."

We walked out to the front of the house, and I pointed to where the footprints had been. Another look exchanged.

"You didn't take a photo of them by chance, did you,

Marianne?" Patrick asked, as Geraldine peered through my bedroom window.

"No. I will if it happens again." Christ, was it likely to happen again? Something stirred in my memory, something I'd read somewhere, but when I tried to grab hold of it, it disappeared.

"And this is the window you were at," he said, running a hand through his barely-there hair, "when you saw the face?"

The face. I shivered. "Yes. I had a bin bag tacked to the window last night, and I pulled it aside and it was just *there*. A white face, looking straight in at me."

Another look exchanged. They either thought I'd been dreaming or seeing my own reflection. Maybe I had.

"Would you think about getting a better curtain?" Geraldine asked, turning to look at me, her dark hair escaping a loose ponytail. She reached to tie it up again but was defeated by the wind. "Like, you can see straight through that net thing you have there at the moment. He'd be able to see you asleep in the bed. Why do you have something so flimsy anyway?"

Geraldine didn't go in for the soft and cuddly approach.

"I know. But I like waking with the natural light, and since there's nobody around for miles, it normally doesn't matter that you can see in."

"Well, nobody around for miles except some stranger who's been staring in at you," she said matter-of-factly.

"And what about Alan Crowley and his son?" Patrick asked. "They're not far away."

"Yeah, I thought of that but, despite everything that's gone on over the years, I can't see why Alan would suddenly start creeping up to my bedroom window."

Patrick nodded, but didn't look convinced. Geraldine was still thinking about my sub-par curtain.

"Like, you could get something nice in that new homeware shop in Arklow – doesn't have to be heavy, just enough that every Tom, Dick or Harry walking past can't see you in your nightdress."

Patrick tried to hide his smile. Geraldine was no-nonsense at the best of times, and clearly baffled at my choice of window-covering.

"You're right. I'll keep putting up bin bags for now, and I'll head into Arklow as soon as this stuff clears," I said, kicking at the snow. "But listen, what about that tourist – the guy who was causing trouble in the hotel?"

"He's well and truly gone," Geraldine said. "He's not staying in the Carrickderg Arms and nobody could stay outside in those temperatures overnight. You'd freeze to death. I'm guessing he's knocking back the contents of a minibar in some Dublin hotel."

So we were at square one. I had absolutely no idea who was sneaking up to my window and neither did Patrick or Geraldine. When they left, I locked the door. Now that I'd reported it, perhaps that would be the end of it.

But it wasn't the end, or at least, not in any way I anticipated. Logging on to iSleuth that night, hoping for distraction from the creaks and gurgles in the walls, I forced myself to read some new articles. And it worked like nothing else ever could – soon I was slipping from one post to the next, tumbling down rabbit holes, lost in a world of unsolved mysteries. At some point, oblivious now to my surroundings, I clicked into the Blackwood Strangler sub-forum and found a fresh article someone had posted. Only it wasn't fresh – it was from five years ago, and I was halfway through when I realised I'd read it before. I was about to click out, when I saw something that stopped me cold.

The Blackwood Strangler, as he's become known in the media, has a number of trademarks – the surveillance of his victims' homes in the days before he attacks, and a preference for single-storey houses. But sources suggest there are some lesser-known trademarks too that have been withheld by police. At some of his crime scenes, markings such as crosses and drawings have been found, as well as footprints in the victims' gardens, with deeper indentations under windows, as though the killer stood outside to watch before attacking.

I knew all this – but I'd forgotten about the footprints under the windows. I glanced over at my own living-room window. The curtains were drawn against the dark outside and all the doors and windows were locked – I'd checked a thousand times before sitting down. The red weather alert was promising a storm, and a nationwide curfew had been in place since late afternoon – surely he wouldn't be out tonight? But suddenly the house I loved and the solitude I valued so much were tainted.

In the Armchair Detective group, I shared the article I'd just read, and asked the others if they'd seen much about footprints under windows. Anne, who had an eye for detail and a strong pedantic streak, was quick to point out that it was an old article – **I know**, I replied, **but I'd forgotten about the footprints until now, and I'm wondering if they were present in just a few cases or maybe all of them?**

Cheryl said she thought she'd seen them mentioned since and went off to google.

I suppose since we know he always stalked his victims,

the shoeprints are seen as a given and not mentioned in every article? Judith typed.

Good point. I toyed with the idea of telling them about my own footprint experience and the face at the window but stopped short of doing so. It would sound like I thought the actual Blackwood Strangler had decided to abandon his UK hunting ground and chase down an armchair detective in Ireland. Taking my interest in web sleuthing just a *little* too far.

Ray could never understand my fascination with true crime. *Why do you read this stuff?* he used to say, wrinkling his nose. But then, there was a lot Ray didn't understand about me, and so much more I didn't know about him. Until it was too late.

CHAPTER 7

2005

Ray and I met under a cloud you might say – at my dad's funeral – and perhaps that should have been an omen. I'd been standing in the function room for an hour, shaking hands and wishing for escape, as another tear-stained face zeroed in on me. Before I could work out who it was, I was pulled into a woolly hug by a vaguely familiar woman in her eighties.

"Your dad was so good to me, Marianne, always checking in on me especially in the winter months. If I can return the favour in any way, you'll let me know, won't you?"

I nodded and smiled and saw the look cross her face – the same look I'd been seeing all morning. They were searching for tangible grief, and I was coming up short. I was numb. The last three days had been a flurry of grotesque activity – the knock at the apartment door late on Tuesday night, the two gardaí, hats in hand, their faces telling me nothing good was coming. The suggestion to sit. The story unfolding. A late-night walk by the lake. Slippery rocks. Deeper than anyone realised, they said. And just like that, on a normal Tuesday night, he was dead.

And then we did what we do best in Ireland – people I

hadn't seen in years appeared out of nowhere with offers of help. Help calling the funeral home, arranging the readings, meeting the priest. I'd been gone from Carrickderg for five years by then, and had lost touch with almost everyone in my bid to escape. But it didn't matter to any of them – they came in droves. At twenty-two, I had no idea how to organise a funeral but they did it all, and the flurry of activity carried me through, insulating me from the raw grief that threatened to invade through even the smallest chink and swallow me whole.

There was no question about *where* – my dad had lived in Carrickderg all his life, and he'd be buried there too, in the tiny graveyard beside the church. The "afters" – a reception with food and drinks and black-clad locals – was in the Carrickderg Arms, and for an hour now I'd been standing in the function room, enveloped in hugs and other people's tears.

The woman moved on and a man in his fifties took her place. The local butcher as far as I recalled, though everything was vague and swimming.

"What will you do, Marianne?" he was asking. "With the house, I mean. You won't sell it, will you?"

That was what they all wanted to know. *You won't sell it surely? That house has been in your family for generations.*

I didn't want to think about it. I couldn't imagine selling but there was no way I could leave my city-centre apartment and come back here – not a chance. I'd worked so hard to get the apartment, in Dublin's insane rental market, and I wasn't about to walk away.

"You could always live in it and commute to Dublin, couldn't you?" the butcher was saying. "Where is it you work again?"

"Grand Canal Dock, near the city centre," I said mechanically. "A bit far for commuting from Carrickderg."

"Doesn't that fella who moved out here last year commute – yer man who lives out on the Ramolin Road? In and out of Dublin every day, only a bit over an hour if you leave early enough. You'd be grand!"

I couldn't tell if he was waiting for me to make life-changing decisions over weak coffee in a hotel function room, or if he was just making small talk. He was joined by a tiny woman with a birdlike face – his wife, if I remembered correctly – and she caught a mixed-up version of what he said.

"Ah no, that fella out on the Ramolin Road wouldn't be suitable for Marianne at all. He's a bit of a loner – she needs someone who's a bit of craic."

"What are you on about? We're not matchmaking, we're talking about Marianne moving back here!" said her husband.

"Oh, you're going to move home! That'll be lovely for you. It's what your dad would have wanted."

"Oh no, I haven't made any decisions yet. I have an apartment in Dublin really near my work – I don't want to give that up . . ."

"But sure you must feel awfully smothered there – the traffic and the noise and everyone living on top of each other. Much better out here where you'd be left in peace."

I smiled at that, but the irony was lost on her. "We'll see. Now, sorry, I've just spotted someone I need to talk to over there . . ."

They nodded their goodbyes as I slipped past them towards the other side of the function room and the open doors to the hotel garden. Darting through, I stood outside, taking in the fresh June air and the rolling green gardens of the Carrickderg Arms. At the end of the garden, an empty wrought-iron bench sat by a small fountain. I watched the water spray high into the blue sky as I made my way down to the bench, and it was there, just minutes later, that we first met. The start of everything.

He sat beside me, jolting me from my fixation on the spray. Turning to smile, I tried to work out who he was. I'd spent the whole morning putting names on faces, but this time I drew a blank. He was mid-thirties, I reckoned, younger than most of the funeral goers, but at least a decade older than me. His dark-brown hair was flecked with grey but only just, and he was – to use an old-fashioned word – handsome in the truest sense. He was tanned and outdoorsy and tall – his long legs stretched across the grass much further than mine – and his green eyes studied me with interest but none of the pity I'd seen over and over that morning.

"Beautiful day, isn't it?" he said, his accent unmistakably American, and then it clicked – he wasn't at the funeral at all. "Are you from around here?"

"I am. How about you?"

"I'm here for work – a working vacation, I guess you'd call it. I'm writing a novel set in Ireland, and I figured I needed to come here myself to do it properly. I'm Ray, by the way." He reached out a hand to shake mine.

"I'm Marianne. So you're an author? What are the names of your books – maybe I've read them?"

He smiled. "Only if you found them in the darkest, dustiest corner of your library. They're not exactly on the bestseller lists. What kind of books do you like?"

"Crime mostly," I told him, "I've been reading crime

since I discovered *The Famous Five*, and devouring mysteries ever since."

"You'd hate my books so," he said with a grin. "No detectives, no police, though plenty of angst and death. Mostly people throwing themselves off cliffs because of unrequited love or an inability to write a perfect poem – that kind of thing." His eyes twinkled, and I decided I liked this self-deprecating author from America.

We talked, sitting on that sunny bench – I told him about my dad and the funeral and a little about my mother too, and he told me about his ex-wife and his seaside home in Cape May, New Jersey. When it was time go back inside, without stopping to think I invited him to join us for a drink. I don't know if it was because I was enjoying the conversation, or because he had no link to Carrickderg and my dad but, either way, I was glad when he said yes and walked me back inside.

The crowd had grown – people who worked locally coming in to pay lunchtime respects.

Geraldine from the Garda Station moved towards me, balancing a cup of tea on a saucer.

"Did you see who's here?" she said, nodding towards the bar.

I looked over just as Alan Crowley glanced up from his pint and caught my eye. He nodded briefly, and turned back to someone beside him. Was it Jamie? I craned my neck.

"Yeah, that's Jamie beside him," Geraldine said, reading my mind. "I hope there won't be any trouble . . . you know what Alan's like after a few pints." She turned to Ray who was hovering behind me and stuck out her hand. "Geraldine Breen, local Garda Sergeant," she said, waiting for him to respond in kind. I don't know if it was police instinct or pure nosiness, but Geraldine always wanted to know who was who and what was where.

"Ray Sedgwick," he replied, shaking her hand, and offering nothing further.

"You're not from around here then?" Geraldine went on, looking up at him – he was about a foot taller than her. Ray repeated his story as she nodded along, pushing her flyaway hair behind her ear. We had plenty of tourists in Carrickderg, but not so many handsome American authors.

Out of the corner of my eye, I saw Alan get up. Jamie glanced over, and put a hand on his father's arm.

"Oh, now, what's going on here?" Geraldine said, under her breath.

Alan started to make his way towards us, with Jamie trailing behind looking anxious.

"Do you want me to deal with him?" Geraldine whispered to me. "He's had a fair skinful at this stage."

I didn't have a chance to answer – Alan was standing in front of me, hat in hand.

"Marianne, I'm sorry for your loss," he said, his words following a cloud of Guinness breath.

"Thank you," I said, hoping that would be it.

"Even if your da and myself didn't always see eye to eye," he continued, slurring the last words, "there was never any ill-will towards you. You know that, don't you?"

I nodded. Jamie hovered behind, eyes on me.

"What Jamie did back then, that was the kind of stupid thing kids do – it wasn't his fault."

I nodded again.

"Da, leave it," Jamie said, eyes down now, one hand on his dad's arm.

"I just want to tell her there's no hard feelings. Marianne's our neighbour again, and we need a clean slate. Isn't that right, Marianne?"

I nodded a third time, willing him to go away.

"Are you moving back?" Jamie asked, looking up again.

"I don't know, but I'll be there for the next few days anyway, to organise my dad's stuff."

"And Hanne's too," Alan said. "It's like a shrine to her still, the priest was saying. Can't be a healthy way to live."

"Da, stop, that's enough."

"I'm only telling the truth," Alan said, lurching forward to shake my hand. "We'll see you soon, no doubt."

He turned and went back to his pint, followed by an apologetic-looking Jamie.

"What was all that about?" Ray asked, when they were out of earshot.

I opened my mouth to answer but couldn't work out where to start.

Geraldine jumped to the rescue. "Let's just say Alan spoke about something ten years ago that should never have been discussed publicly, much less with his twelve-year-old son, and in his clumsy attempt to make amends he's only gone and done exactly the same thing again." She shook her head. "That man is a fool and his son is no better."

As I stared after Alan and Jamie, I wondered about that – would it have been preferable if they'd never said a word? For my dad, undoubtedly. But for me? That part wasn't clear at all.

CHAPTER 8

Ray was only supposed to spend three weeks in Carrickderg but, in the end, it was three years. It started as these things often do – slow and fast all at once. As I said my goodbyes to the last lingering mourners at the funeral, Ray touched my elbow and asked if I'd like to have coffee sometime. I think that's why I said yes – it was so unobtrusive. If he'd used the word "date", I'd have said no, not at my own father's funeral. But coffee was casual. And so I said yes. Then back I went in my clapped-out old car, navigating the winding roads to the cottage.

Inside, it was cool and dark, at odds with the bright June sunlight. My dad was everywhere – his cup, half-full of cold tea, sat on the coffee table, beside his copy of the *Irish Times*. Tuesday's copy. Half-read. My throat tightened and I closed my eyes to stem the tears. Too much to do.

In his room, the bed was perfectly made, and his book, carefully bookmarked, sat on his bedside table. In the wardrobe, pressed trousers and ironed shirts hung side by side, polished shoes neatly below. His job in the hardware store in Carrickderg didn't require such attention to sartorial detail, but that was my father – how you presented yourself was important, he'd always said. All intentions to go through his clothes disappeared in one gulp of grief when I opened his dresser drawer and saw my mother's shirts neatly folded inside. More than twenty years had gone by and still, there they were, as though they'd been put there yesterday. I picked one up and smelled it, finding none of the mustiness I'd expected. Was he washing her clothes over the years? I swallowed and swiped at my eye.

On top of the dresser sat their wedding photo. My mother, laughing and radiant and so *other* with her striking Danish colouring. My father, with a rosy flush in his pale cheeks, bright-blue eyes and a mop of dark-brown hair, still unable to believe this exotic foreigner had said yes to a quiet, unassuming Irishman who worked in a hardware store.

Back in the sitting room, I lowered myself onto the small red couch, looking around as I did. Hanne was everywhere – her paintings on the walls, her photo on the shelf. Her books – a mix of Danish bestsellers and English-language art books – sat side by side with my dad's history collection. The cups she'd bought on their honeymoon in West Cork, the candle from the daytrip to Bantry. I knew this only because my dad told me, another contribution to my made-up memories. She was a patchwork sewn from my father's stories and the photos on his walls: this woman who up-ended his world, then broke his heart.

As it happened, a week went by before the coffee with Ray – he'd taken my number but hadn't phoned, and I was too busy sorting through my dad's things to think about it. The call came on Friday morning as I was about to start clearing the attic. He suggested coffee that afternoon in the Wooden Spoon, Carrickderg's one and only café. He needed a break from his typewriter, he said, and I wondered if he really used a typewriter. We agreed to meet at three, and I got back to climbing the rickety ladder to the attic, and he, presumably, got back to his typewriter.

Inside the attic was musty and dark, the single light bulb casting an anaemic glow near the hatch. I crawled along the floorboards to start at the far end – I hadn't been up there in years and didn't realise there would be quite so many boxes. What on earth had he been storing up here? I opened one and peered inside. Even in the low light, I could see it contained clothes – dresses, I realised, pulling one out. Hanne's, presumably. My God, how much of her stuff did he keep? The dress was turquoise blue as far as I could make out, long and shimmery, with thin straps. A gown for a ball, not an attic. What was it for? As far as I knew, Hanne had come here after college, met my dad, and they'd married within months. They'd never lived anywhere else, and there weren't a whole lot of black-tie balls in Carrickderg. I pulled out the next dress – a jade-green one, shorter than the first, and just as beautiful.

Beneath that was a wooden jewellery box with a carving of a bird on the lid. Carefully, I opened it. Empty. There was a little drawer below the main compartment, with a hole where the handle should have been, but it was stuck closed. I shook the box. Something moved inside the drawer but there was no tell-tale clink – perhaps she'd taken her jewellery with her when she went home. Or perhaps she never had any – a box waiting in vain to be filled.

Beneath the jewellery box was another dress – silver and

sparkly and far too beautiful for the dusty attic. Maybe she'd brought it here from Denmark, hoping for a life that was different to the one she found.

Inside the next box there were sketchbooks – charcoal drawings of unfamiliar faces, page after page. A slim, middle-aged man, with a high forehead and heavy brows and, further along, a woman of similar age, her hair and clothing changing from one page to the next, her mouth always set in a tight line. Wondering who they were, I put them to one side to take downstairs.

Deep in the corner, where the attic roof met the floor, was a smaller box, an old USA biscuit tin. I carried it under the light bulb and prised off the lid. Inside, there were postcards, letters, coins, ticket stubs and airline boarding cards – future contents for a scrapbook maybe? I set it down beside the hatch, and went back to open more boxes.

A knock on the front door stopped me before I could see what was inside the next one and part of me was glad to leave this dusty, unsettling work for now. As I climbed down the wobbly ladder, the knock came a second time, louder now. I opened the door, expecting to find Bert with a package, or a frustrated courier – it always took them ages to find the cottage – but it was Jamie.

"Hiya, Marianne, sorry to bother you, I just wanted to check in on you and see if you need any help with the house and the, eh . . ." he trailed off, gesturing with his hand. Death is awkward.

"Clearing my dad's stuff?"

He nodded.

"I'm good, thanks, I'm done except for the attic. Do you want to come in?" I asked, pulling the door wide and ushering him through.

He followed me into the kitchen.

"Will you have tea or coffee?"

"Tea'd be grand," he said, standing awkwardly by the table until I pulled out a chair for him. He hadn't been inside our house since he was twelve years old, back when he was a regular caller, doing homework here because it was nicer than sitting on his own at home while Alan was out on the farm. We had a lady looking after me – Mrs Townsend – right up until I was fourteen: meeting me from school, cooking dinner, overseeing homework. The contrast with Jamie's upbringing was stark – his mother had passed away when he was small, and because Alan was always in and out between house and farm, he didn't see the need for a housekeeper or babysitter after Jamie turned eight. So Jamie came here, and the three of us – Mrs Townsend, Jamie, and I – sat together around the kitchen table, doing sums and chatting about school.

Until the day it all fell apart.

I glanced over as I made tea, taking in what was different and what was just the same. His brown curls were cut shorter, but the slightly awkward grin hadn't changed – he always looked like he was about to smile but wasn't quite committing. He had his father's heavy brows but, unlike Alan, his blue eyes were wide and soft. Nature and nurture had both missed a trick.

"Look, I meant what I said about offering help," Jamie was saying, "but I also wanted to apologise for Alan's behaviour at the funeral. He had a few jars on him, and, well, you know yourself."

I waved away the apology as I put a mug of tea in front of him.

"It's grand. He was just trying to make peace."

"And going about it completely arseways," he said, shaking his head. "He shouldn't have brought it up last week, no more than I should have ten years ago."

His eyes met mine, and a tingle of something long forgotten fluttered inside me.

Jamie and Marianne up a tree, K.I.S.S.I.N.G. They used to sing at us all through primary school – because we were neighbours and because we were friends. And, as I looked at him now, I wondered for a second what might have been if it wasn't for that day.

"Don't worry. You were just a kid, and you were angry. And, you know, part of me feels it was the right thing."

He looked surprised.

"Not the way it happened," I went on, sitting down opposite him, "but the *knowing*. It's important to know the truth, no matter how awful, isn't it?"

He nodded, but I could tell he wasn't sure.

"Were there any of Hanne's people at the funeral?"

His question caught me off guard.

"God, no! My dad lost touch with her family back around the time it all happened. I know absolutely nothing about them actually." A fresh wave of regret washed over me. Now he was gone, I never would.

"Really? No contact at all? But you have grandparents there surely?"

As he said it, I realised how strange it seemed. But I'd grown up accepting it as normal. My family was made up of Dad, his two aunts, and a sprinkling of second cousins. Dad never talked about my Danish relatives, and rarely about Hanne. It was the no-go topic and, from a young age, I knew not to ask.

"I guess. Though I don't know if they're still alive. That

sounds weird now that I say it out loud. But I've never had any contact with her family, so I don't feel a connection to them. They're like characters in a fairy tale I heard as a kid but can hardly remember now. You know?"

Jamie tilted his head, frowning.

"But surely they'd want to meet their granddaughter? Wouldn't it be a way of helping them deal with losing their daughter?"

I shrugged. "Maybe. If it was a film, that's exactly what would happen, and I'd help them deal with their grief and we'd all live happily ever after. But life's not like that."

Jamie looked unconvinced. "I just can't understand why they wouldn't want to meet you though. Like, it's not your fault what happened – why punish you?"

"But I don't see it as a *punishment* – you can't miss what you never had."

Even as I said it, I wondered if it was true. When I was small, I didn't think about why I had just one grandparent in a nursing home, and lots of other kids had four each, as well as siblings and cousins spilling out the doors. As I got older, I started noticing the differences – the kids who got Christmas presents and Easter Eggs from grandparents or spent Sundays visiting them – but my dad had explained it all. He'd told me the story. Or at least, the sugar-coated version.

"Don't you remember that time in Mrs Griffin's class, when we had to write a story about a granny or granddad?" Jamie said. "And you were crying and eventually told Mrs Griffin you had nobody to write about?"

I stared at him. I had absolutely no idea what he was talking about.

"You don't remember?" he said, reading my blank look. "Maybe you blocked it out. You were so upset. Remember

49

Mrs Griffin sent you and Linda outside to the yard to get some air?"

"Yeah, maybe . . ." I said, though I still had no recollection.

"Do you still see Linda? You two were in UCD together, weren't you?"

I nodded. "Yep, she's off doing a year in Australia now and has fallen madly in love with a student doctor. Her parents were petrified she was going to stay in Oz, till they realised the doctor's from Kerry and only over there for two years."

"And how about you?" he asked, looking up at me from under his lashes. "Did you fall madly in love with any doctors from Kerry?"

I laughed, and shook my head. "Nope, but there are no doctors from Kerry in my office – just geeks who love data more than humans. A bit like me." I smiled to show it wasn't completely true. "And what about you?"

"Oh God no, not seeing anyone," he said. "It's not like there's anyone my age around here."

"Oh no, I just meant what are you up to?" I said, feeling my face grow hot. "Like are you working or in college or what?"

"Oh right, yeah – I'm technically working full-time on the farm now, but I talked my da into giving me time off to do a part-time course in the IADT in Dun Laoghaire. It's graphic design. Alan doesn't get it at all – says it's a course for girls, and a waste of time." He rolled his eyes. "But at least he agreed to let me have the time, so I go into Dublin two days a week for that."

"And is that what you want to do after – work in graphic design?"

He looked down at his tea, and his shoulders fell. "Nah, I'll be working on the farm – that's been the plan since day one. This is just something to do on the side."

I watched him sip his tea, eyes still down, and wondered about that – the call of home, the obligation to stay, the pull to return. The cottage drawing me back, Jamie's farm holding him here, and the faraway country that called my mother, then swallowed her whole, in one merciless bite.

CHAPTER 9

The Wooden Spoon was as busy as it ever was at three o'clock on a Friday afternoon – one man treating his son to an after-school brownie, and two teenage girls who'd just got off the bus from Dublin, judging by their A-Wear and Penneys shopping bags.

Ray was there already and stood to greet me. He'd taken a table near the back, beside the till, and ordered a black coffee. I asked for the same.

"I thought everyone here drank tea?" he said, smiling as we sat.

"Absolutely. I'm literally the only person in Ireland who drinks coffee," I told him, "and there'll be a free leprechaun to take with us when we leave to go dancing at the crossroads."

He put his hands up.

"Touché! Although, as cliché goes, the Carrickderg Arms is up there with the best of them. I mean, there's an actual wagon wheel attached to the wall."

"And I bet you're having the Full Irish breakfast there every morning," I said, "to immerse yourself in Irish culture, right?"

He smiled and patted his completely flat stomach. "I'll have to ease off next week – for my last week I'll order oatmeal."

So it was his final week already. I turned that over in my mind and realised I was disappointed.

"Did you get everything you need for your book? I don't want to rain on your parade, but I'm not sure Carrickderg is representative of the whole country . . ."

He smiled. "Don't worry – I hired a car and went to Glendalough one day, and up to Dublin city another. Actually, when I was getting gas, I met your friend from the funeral."

"My friend?"

"That guy Alan? When I stopped at the gas station yesterday, he was there too, putting gas in a jeep." He paused, a sheepish look on his face. "Okay, this is kind of embarrassing, but you look like you'd see the funny side. Alan was wearing a dark-grey polo shirt like the guys you see in gas stations, and in New Jersey where I come from, you can't fill your own tank – by law, the staff have to do it. So I subconsciously assumed Alan worked there, and I said, 'Fill 'er up, full tank, please' to him when I pulled in."

I put my hand over my mouth. "No! What did he say?"

"If looks could kill, I'd be six feet under. He told me to fill up my own effing tank and stormed off into the store." He shook his head. "It was an honest mistake! I don't know why he was so mad."

"Don't mind him, he's always cross about something. And, in fairness, he doesn't know about your New Jersey law. I've never heard of it either. We've had self-service here since the early 80s, I think."

"Even so – what's the big deal if I thought he worked there?"

"Well, first of all because he owns the biggest farm around and has been craving the social standing he thinks that warrants for as long as I can remember. And, secondly, he may have assumed you were being deliberately rude."

Ray looked perplexed.

"Don't worry, Alan takes offence like it's an Olympic sport. Forget him."

But fate had other intentions – right at that moment, the bell above the café door rang, and Alan walked in. Years later, I wondered how things might have gone if he'd never shown up that afternoon.

"Don't look now," I whispered, "but your new best friend's just arrived."

Alan walked up to the counter and said something to the girl at the till, then turned to face us while she busied herself wrapping two plates of pork-pie dinner in foil.

I nodded at him, and turned back to Ray, to ask him about his book.

But Ray was eager to make amends. He stood.

"Alan, I want to apologise for my error yesterday at the gas station – where I come from all stations are staffed and I made an incorrect assumption." He stuck out his hand.

Alan did nothing at first, staring out at Ray from under his hat, dark eyes assessing, stubborn chin firmly set. Then he seemed to make a decision, and took Ray's hand.

"No bother. No harm done," he said, and turned to pick up the two foil-wrapped plates behind him.

Ray stayed standing, his expression hard to read.

"So, listen, I'm writing a book set in Ireland, and the main character is a guy from a small town like this one. He's a legend-in-his-own-lunchtime kinda guy – the main man in town, but he's never been outside his own locality and knows nothing of the wider world. It's kind of a satirical black comedy – a departure from my usual stuff."

Alan looked blankly at him.

"And I was wondering if I could interview you – to get a better sense of what it's like to be a local farmer in a community like this?"

Ouch.

I didn't think Ray meant any harm – well, back then I didn't – but Alan heard what I heard. His mouth opened and, in deafening silence, Ray waited for an answer.

"I don't think he means *you're* like the main character, right?" I said, when neither man spoke.

Ray's eyes widened. "My God no, of course not! Sorry, that's not what I meant at all. How 'bout I buy you a drink tonight in Delaneys' – I can make up for my faux pas and interview you for research at the same time?"

Alan nodded and smiled, though there was nothing warm in it.

"Right," he said. "Eight o'clock in Delaneys' – I'll see you there."

He took his plates and left, and we sat back down.

"Doesn't he pay for his food?" Ray asked in a stage whisper as the door closed.

"He has a tab. Gets his dinner and one for his son Jamie every afternoon – has done since his wife died, years and years ago. That's if they don't actually eat here."

"And he's really the big man in town?"

"Well, his farm is the biggest. I suspect that used to mean more than it does. It comes right up to our cottage and beyond – we're surrounded on three sides by Alan's land. We're like a little pocket inside his giant coat." I paused. "I guess I should say *I* not *we*. Weird."

I took a sip of now-cold coffee to swallow the lump in my throat.

Ray cleared his. "Hey, how about you come along to Delaneys' tonight? It can't be doing you any good sitting at home on your own. Come help me interview the grouchy farmer, and I'll buy you a drink. Deal?"

An evening with Alan Crowley and a tourist I hardly knew wasn't exactly how I'd pictured Friday night, but Ray was right – I'd done enough sitting at home on my own. And, really, what harm could it do?

CHAPTER 10

A little after eight thirty, I pulled into the Carrickderg Arms car park and walked the short distance along Main Street to Delaneys'. Alan and Ray were already sitting at the bar, getting on unexpectedly well it seemed, so I slid into a booth and pulled out a paperback – glad of background noise and other humans, but happy too to be on my own for a little longer. Bursts of conversation floated my way each time Ray became animated, and Alan looked less surly than usual – he even smiled once or twice. Maybe the olive branch was working.

A girl of about sixteen came to take my order, bringing back memories of my time gathering empties in Delaneys'. Except unlike this perfectly made-up teen ("Keeley" according to her name badge) with butterscotch hair and impeccable eyebrows, I didn't know a bronzer from a hole in the ground and had no idea what contouring was. I still had no idea what contouring was. I remember working for £3.50 an hour and thinking I was rich, and I remember my dad waiting patiently outside in the car as I counted my tips, wishing I could stay on for a post-work drink like everyone else. John the barman used to offer to put a vodka

in my Coke when we were getting close to finishing time –
"on the house," he used to say, with a wink, and a flick of
his ponytail, though he had no right to be offering anyone
drinks on the house, least of all fifteen-year-old staff.

He was still there, behind the bar, his hair in rivets of
gel, pulled into the familiar low ponytail. As Keeley swirled
across the floor to bring him my order, I wondered if he
was offering her vodka in her Coke too.

She was back in minutes balancing my sparkling water
on her tray, and with Alan and Ray still engrossed in their
conversation, I got back to my book.

Half an hour later, a glass of red wine appeared in front of
me. I looked up to find Keeley nodding back towards the bar.

"John sent that over – he says you used to work here?"

I did, I told her, but I'd have to turn down the kind offer
of a drink – I had the car outside. Her beautiful eyebrows
creased in disappointment, like I'd ruined the gesture,
which I suppose in a way I had.

"Sure leave it here, I might chance half of it," I said.
"Do you like working here?"

"It's fine, usually just boring old codgers who never
tip," she said. "Bit of craic tonight though with yer man .
. ." She indicated towards Ray with her elbow. "Alan and
John are feeding him all sorts of bull about town history
and made-up traditions. They're just after telling him we
all wash our faces in cow's milk every night to ward off
evil spirits, and he's writing it down in his notebook."

Just then, the notebook fell to the ground and, as Ray
climbed off the stool to retrieve it, he stumbled a little.

"He's had a few, I see," I said to Keeley.

She smirked. "Oh, he has alright – he's getting a real

taste of Ireland tonight. So will I leave the wine with you?"

I picked it up and raised it in a salute to John who caught my eye from behind the bar, and off went the girl to serve Mrs O'Shea and her husband Mick.

Some time later, a crash of glass pulled me away from my book – I looked up to find Ray sprawled on the flagstone floor, broken glass and beer all around him. Alan reached down to help him up and, as he stood and brushed glass from his jeans, he was clearly unsteady on his feet.

"One too many," Alan said over Ray's shoulder to me. "I'll keep an eye on him."

I went back to my book, wondering a little why I was there at all, but mostly enjoying being out of the house.

Minutes later, Ray slipped off his stool again, though caught himself this time.

"Don't fade on me now. man, I still need to tell you about the excitement last year when we first got hooked up with electricity."

Surely Ray wasn't falling for all this?

My new friend Keeley sidled over to take away my empty glass of water, her expertly lined eyes dancing with conspiracy.

"They're gas!" she whispered. "This is the most fun I've had in here since I started. D'ya want another one?"

"I'm okay, thanks. He hardly believes all the stories though? He'll sober up tomorrow and see his notes and realise it was all made up."

"He'll have some headache tomorrow, that's for sure." She hesitated, then I guess decided I was in the gang. "John's putting a double shot of whiskey into every pint the writer guy is having – he's *plastered*!"

"Ah hang on, that's dangerous – he shouldn't be doing

that," I said, getting up from my seat.

Her face changed – I wasn't in the gang after all.

"It's just a bit of fun. Anyway it was Alan's idea, John's only doing what the customer asked." She flounced off, less sure of herself now.

Stuffing my book in my bag, I walked over to Ray, throwing Alan a look.

"Hey, should we get you back to your hotel?"

Bleary eyes met mine.

"Marianne, you're here!"

Alan sat back on his barstool, arms folded, smirking.

"I am, but I need to head home now. My car is in the hotel car park – I'll walk you back."

"But we didn't get to have our drink!" He turned to wave at John who was busy cleaning an already clean glass.

"I think John's done enough pouring for tonight – come on, let's get you back."

He put a hand on my shoulder to steady himself as he got off the stool, and together we walked towards the door.

"Safe home now, you two!" Alan called after us.

I shook my head but couldn't find a suitable retort.

Outside, cool night air seemed to sober Ray a little, but he kept one hand on my shoulder all the way to the hotel. Inside, we went straight to the stairs, ignoring looks from the man behind reception. Ray couldn't get the key to work, so I took over and opened the door to a room that was bigger and more modern than I'd expected. A laptop sat on the desk in the corner, a neat stack of notebooks beside it. Not a typewriter after all.

"Would you like to stay for a drink?" Ray asked, swaying in front of me.

Before I could answer, he put his hand to his mouth, but

it was too late. He threw up, all over the floor, and all over my shoes.

That was our first date. It should have been an omen.

CHAPTER 11

The knock came mid-morning on Saturday, saving me from an unappealing return trip to the attic. Ray looked surprisingly good for someone who had been comatose on his hotel bed when I left him – maybe there was a tinge of grey pallor under the tan, but his eyes were bright, his smile cheekier than ever.

I fixed him a coffee and we sat side by side on the couch. It felt awkward, but not *bad* awkward.

"So I guess your pal Alan wasn't okay with my gas-station error after all – that's some grudge he's got," Ray said, propping one ankle across his other knee. "I mean, it was an honest mistake."

"Yeah. And I'm sure it's illegal to spike someone's drink – like if he did it to a girl, there'd be murder. You could probably go to the guards?"

"The what?"

"Guards – gardaí – it's what we call police in Ireland. You could report him. He was getting John the barman to put a double shot of whiskey into every pint. It doesn't surprise me either – John's a bit of a dick."

Ray uncrossed his legs and sat forward.

"Water under the bridge. No point in making a fuss, especially now I've decided to stay."

He turned to look at me, and there was something in his expression, but I couldn't tell what.

"You're staying?"

"Yep. I'm going to take a room in the hotel for the next three months – I'll be like those artists who used to live Chateau Marmont in LA, except not so much of the drugs and debauchery."

I nodded, though I'd never heard of Chateau Marmont.

"Perhaps we can try again for a drink, since the first time didn't work out," he continued. "I don't even remember seeing you come in. I must have been drunk from the get-go."

"Yeah, I slipped in and sat on my own for a bit, but if I'd realised what was going on, I'd have said something."

He held up his hands. "Not your fault. I'm sorry you had to see me like that. I didn't . . . do anything I shouldn't have, did I?"

"God no," I said, going red. "More coffee?"

He nodded yes and I made my escape, cheeks still burning.

When I came back, he was looking at the photo of my parents.

"Your mom and dad?"

I nodded.

"Your mom was beautiful." He turned to look at me, then back to the photo. "Your dad was one lucky guy."

"It's okay, you can say it – he knew he was punching above his weight. I don't think he ever got his head around it – what someone like Hanne saw in a very ordinary man like him."

"She really was stunning. You look a little like her. You must miss her terribly."

"She's been gone a long time. I don't actually remember her at all – it's pretty much always been my dad and me."

"I guess you had a very close relationship with your dad," he said, his voice softening.

"Yeah, I did." I picked at the fringe of the throw. "And now I can't stop thinking if I'd been living here, I'd have seen more of him while he was still alive."

He reached out a hand and covered mine, jolting me with the intimacy.

"But you had to live your life too. Kids grow up and move out – it's the natural order of things. If you'd stayed, who knows, maybe you'd have been on top of each other, falling out, right?"

I nodded but wasn't convinced.

"Also, you work in IT, and I don't see a whole heap of IT firms here in Carrickderg. Don't beat yourself up, you just did what anyone your age would do."

I nodded again. That part at least was true. But still. If I'd been here, maybe I'd have gone with him for the walk by the lake, and maybe I could have pulled him out. Or we'd have both stayed home, safe inside.

Ray finished his coffee, apologised again, and suggested we grab a glass of wine Sunday night. I was due back in work Monday morning, but told him I'd meet for one quick drink.

"Are you sure you don't want to do anything about Alan – Geraldine in the Garda Station is a bit nosy but she's no-nonsense – she'd have a word with him?"

"I'm sure. And I guess in a small town like this I'm going to see him around over the next three months. I don't want any bad feeling."

He stood up and I walked with him to the door.

"Oh yeah, what made you decide to stay?" I asked, as he said goodbye from the doorstep.

"The book. Everything just clicked into place. I need to stay here and write the story."

He waved and walked down the drive towards his car, a shiny rental in much better shape than my old banger, and I wondered where it might go, this one drink we'd have on Sunday night, and if after that I'd ever see him again.

CHAPTER 12

1990

Ms Brown was pretty. She had long, wavy brown hair and brown eyes, just like her name. She was only there for a bit though, when Mrs Mulligan was in hospital. I wished she could be there all the time. She was much nicer than crabby old Mrs Mulligan. The only thing was, she didn't know our stories. So when she asked us all to make Mother's Day cards, I was stuck, and I didn't know how to tell her.

Linda looked over at me, and put up her hand.

"Teacher, Marianne doesn't have a mammy."

Ms Brown's mouth made an O shape and her cheeks went pink.

"Sweetheart, I'm so sorry, I didn't realise. Well, why don't you make a card for your daddy instead?"

I nodded, still not sure what to say. Linda spoke again.

"Her mammy went to Denmark for a holiday and she died when she was there. She died in her sleep."

I let out a breath, and picked up a colouring pencil. But Nigel Stock, who was always worrying, and a complete cry-baby, jumped in.

"You can't die in your sleep, can you?" His voice wobbled. "Is my mammy going to die if she goes to sleep?"

I looked up at Ms Brown.

"Oh no, Nigel pet, not at all – it's very, very rare. Maybe we should focus on our colouring now."

"But then how did it happen to Marianne's mammy? How do you know it isn't going to happen to somebody else?"

Ms Brown's mouth went into an O shape again and I think she was wishing Mrs Mulligan was back from hospital.

Sorcha Riordan joined in. "Actually, my dad says you can't die in your sleep – there's no such thing. It's just something people say when they don't want to explain." She folded her arms and looked at me out of the corner of her eye.

"Well, you can, but it's usually because of something going wrong, like . . . like someone's heart stopping," Ms Brown said, picking up chalk from her desk then putting it down again.

"But, Teacher, you said that it doesn't really happen?" wailed Nigel Stock, tears in his eyes.

"It doesn't happen often, I said. Look, we'd really better make these cards, the day is nearly over – I'll put on some nice music now to help you all concentrate, will I?"

As the sound of whale song filled the classroom, we set about making our cards and Ms Brown flopped down on her chair, shaking her head.

Linda nudged me. "Sorcha will be going on the Blacklist if she's not careful," she whispered.

I giggled. The Blacklist was where we put people who bothered us – Mrs Mulligan got put on there when she rapped me on the knuckles with her ruler for accidentally dropping my pencil on the floor, and Nigel was on it for telling on us when we faked a collision in yard to get out *of P.E. The Blacklist was serious – once you were on it, you couldn't get off. It wasn't just in our heads either – there was an actual written-down list in a notebook we kept hidden in our den in my garden. Linda and Jamie were worried about mice and rats eating the notebook and the biscuits we sometimes kept there too, but I told them as long as we kept everything in a tin box, they'd be okay. We had wool and candles and a big scissors in there too, from the time we were thinking of making voodoo dolls. We decided not to in the end – the den was supposed to be a good place. Linda said she wished she lived in an old cottage like mine, with a big garden and a den, but sometimes I was jealous of her smart shiny house in the new housing estate on the way into the village.*

Anyway, the Blacklist wasn't quite black – the notebook we used was dark purple – but it was as real as it could be. We weren't going to do anything to the people on the list, not in real life, but on bad days it was fun imagining. Like today.

At home that evening, when my dad was reading the paper after dinner, I sat down beside him on the couch and picked up the photo of my mum and him. When he saw what was in my hand, he put down the paper. He didn't like talking about my mum, but I needed to know.

"Dad, in school today people were saying you can't die in your sleep. Is that what happened though?"

At first he didn't answer. Then he took my hand in his.

"That's what happened, love. Your mother fell asleep one night on her holidays in Denmark, and she didn't wake up."

"Oh," I said, trying to decide if this was good or not good.

"But it's very, very unusual," he said. "It almost never happens. Your mother was very unlucky." His voice cracked in a funny way as he said the last bit. He cleared his throat. "Now, let's have a look at those spellings, will we? Test tomorrow?"

Later that night, long after my dad had turned out my light, I switched off my torch and closed my book. I needed a drink of water, but Dad would know I'd been reading under the covers if he caught me. Maybe he was already in bed. I looked at the crack between my bedroom door and the living room – no chink of light. Quietly, I opened my bedroom door. But something stopped me. A sound, coming from my father's bedroom. Worried now, I tiptoed across the living room to his door and put my hand on the handle. I stopped to listen. At first I couldn't work out what it was. Then I knew. He was crying. My dad was in his bedroom, crying. I stood for a moment, wondering if I should go in. But I didn't know what to say. So I tiptoed back across the floor to my own bedroom and climbed under the covers, wondering about Denmark and dying in your sleep.

CHAPTER 13

2018

I looked at the window, fresh black sacks tightly pinned, and wondered if I'd hear him. *I don't want to hear him.* I glanced at the shotgun, leaning against the wardrobe. There was no way I'd use it. But if he tried to get into the house, I'd have something to scare him off. In theory. The idea of actually picking it up and facing him made me feel shivery and sick.

The heating was on full blast but even with two blankets over my knees, it was still cold. I considered getting into bed for warmth – but then I might fall asleep. The chair, an old pintuck reading chair my granddad used to own, was just uncomfortable enough to keep me awake.

I turned back to my book, my eyes flitting uneasily over the words on my Kindle screen. A book on the Green River Killer – not the best choice for a night-time vigil.

At midnight, I felt myself nodding off and got up to make coffee. The kitchen was quiet and shadowy, the glow of the snow casting an eerie pink dusk through the window. I reached to close the old roller blind, creaky from lack of use. The coffee machine took an age to heat up and, when

I pressed the button to fill my cup, the volume of noise made me jump. It never sounded so loud during the day. I willed it to hurry, as the sound drowned out everything else – everything that was probably nothing, I reassured myself.

Back in my bedroom, I tucked my feet under me and started to read again, the hot coffee welcome and unfamiliar at this time of night. The black sack over the window rustled, and my head snapped up. It rustled again – just a breeze sneaking through the old window frame. I got up to pin it tighter, and sat back down to scroll through my Kindle for something – anything – that wasn't about serial killers. But everything I'd bought recently was true crime – the Boston Strangler, the Zodiac Killer, and a particularly gruesome book on the BTK Killer. *Why do you read such awful books?* Ray used to say, *I can recommend dozens of wonderful novels to you, and yet you're stuck on this trash.*

By "wonderful", he meant novels like his; his early self-deprecation soon exposed itself as faux humility. With Ray, there was no room for grey – it was all black or white. You either liked *good books*, or *trashy books* – almost everything to him was in the latter category. Right now, I could have done with one of his so-called good books or indeed a trashy book – something upbeat that didn't involve decapitation and dismemberment. I searched for a book Linda had been talking about last time we spoke – something touching about a single woman who lived on her own and never saw anyone at the weekend, Linda said, and I had wondered if she was referring to my own status. I had found the book and bought it.

Two chapters in, my eyelids began to droop. Falling, falling, snapping open. Over and over. *A little sleep might be okay.* Eyes closed, staying closed this time. Seconds turned into minutes and minutes turned into I don't know how long. That's when it came. Jolting me awake.

Firm, deliberate, loud in the silence. And far too close to where I sat.

A knock on the glass. He was at my bedroom window.

CHAPTER 14

My eyes snapped open, wide awake now. I sat up, straight as a pitchfork, white noise roaring in my ears. Staring at the window. Rigid. Paralysed. *Fuck. Fuck.*

Silence.

Did I imagine it?

As soon as the thought formed, it came again.

Three times. *Knock. Knock. Knock.*

Slow.

Deliberate.

Not banging, not urgent. This was no neighbour calling for help, no driver of a broken-down car. This was for me.

On the other side of the room, the shotgun leaned against the wardrobe, mocking me. What had I thought I was I going to do – pick it up and walk outside and challenge whoever was there? I could hardly breathe, let alone move. I stayed in the chair, staring at the window. Forcing myself to listen. Waiting. For a million years. Then a rustling. A crunch. The crunch of snow underfoot. Footsteps through snow, walking away.

Please let him be walking away.

No noise now for the longest time, but still I couldn't

move. My hands frozen to the sides of the chair. My eyes fixed on the window. At some point, my Kindle slipped off my knee and skated along the blanket, down to the bedroom floor, the clatter loud in the otherwise silence. Still I didn't move.

Shards of grey filtered through the side of the window, prodding me awake. It took a moment to understand why I was asleep upright in a chair, then with a sick feeling I remembered the vigil. And the knocking.

Pushing the blankets off my legs, I stood, my knees and shoulders stiff and sore. At the window, my hand shaking, I reached out to undo the thumbtacks holding my makeshift cover in place, but stopped. Daylight now and he was long gone. He wouldn't be there. He couldn't be. But still. What if he was?

I stepped back and walked through to the living-room window instead, and pushed the curtain a fraction of an inch to one side. Nobody. I stepped away and let out a long breath. Could I have imagined the knocking – had I fallen asleep and dreamed it, my head full of footprints and stalkers and the Green River Killer?

At the front door, I hesitated, then grabbed the handle and pulled it open.

There they were.

Just like before.

Footprints all across the garden, and deeper at my bedroom window. A wave of nausea coiled through my stomach. I hadn't imagined it. As I sat in my chair, facing the window, he was outside looking in. No more than ten feet away. He couldn't see me, I reminded myself, the black sack blocked his view. But still. He was there.

This time I took photos. Outside in wellington boots at quarter past seven in the morning, I took a dozen photos of the footprints, focusing on the ones below the window. The diagonal trail led from the gate at the bottom of the garden, across the snow-covered grass, right up to my bedroom. Then, like the previous day, it went around the side of the house. I followed the prints to the back and right around to the other side, from where they continued down the driveway and out the gate.

Back in the living room, I phoned the Garda Station. Someone I didn't know answered the phone, and said he'd pass the message to Geraldine, who'd be in any minute. He gave me an email address and, still shaking, I sent the photos.

Jagged thoughts careered like ping-pong balls inside my head – who was coming into my garden, and why? Why knock? There had to be a reason – some link between me and him. Because strangers don't just peer in random windows, do they?

My phone rang – Geraldine had seen my message.

"It could be young fellas having a laugh," she said without preamble, "but don't worry, we'll figure it out."

"During a curfew?" I said, staring out the living-room window, as fresh snow began to fall.

"Oh listen, the amount of people who didn't take that seriously! And then the storm passed over the Atlantic, so of course everyone thinks they were right to ignore it. You can't win."

"I know, but I'm in the middle of nowhere. I can't imagine 'young ones' out having a bit of craic would want to stand outside my bedroom three nights in a row, in the snow, for fun. It makes no sense."

"And did you cover that window of yours or were they looking in at you in your bed?" she asked, and I could hear her boiling a kettle in the background.

"I covered it with a black sack again. I'll get a proper curtain when the thaw comes."

"They say it's coming today, Marianne, so you should be grand. And if there's no snow, there'll be no more footprints – because you won't be able to see them!"

I had no answer to that.

"Ah sorry, that wasn't funny. But you know what I mean – someone was trying to freak you out with the snow here, and they'll lose interest when it's gone."

She promised that she or Patrick would be up later for another look around, and said goodbye.

I flopped on the couch, thinking about what she'd said. She was right – if there was no snow, there'd be no footprints. But twisting it the other way – what if it meant he'd been coming all along, and I hadn't realised until now?

Work should have been a distraction, but every few seconds I found myself looking up at the living-room window, half expecting to see a face peering in. Eventually, for diversion, I clicked into iSleuth, where I found a new update and a flurry of chatter in the Blackwood Strangler sub-forum. A newspaper had just done a big feature on him, more comprehensive than anything I'd seen before. Much of it was familiar – the stalking and the preference for single-storey homes, but the article also referenced footprints – some victims had spotted footprints in their gardens and mentioned them to neighbours, with a sense of curiosity, it seemed, more than any great concern. One woman had gone to the police, and they'd told her it was probably a neighbour taking a shortcut through her garden. She was found dead two days later. I shivered.

The next section was subtitled – rather cruelly as it turned out – *X Marks the Spot*.

A victim had been speaking to her sister by phone when she spotted an X scratched into her front door. She was furious, sure a neighbour's child had done it, and told her sister she'd call in the following morning to complain. She never had the chance – she was found dead the next day. What caught police attention was the X mark – they had another case with something similar, this time in Bournemouth, over a hundred miles from the Blackwood Strangler's usual hunting ground. There was no phone call to fill in the grey areas, but they did find an X that had been freshly scratched into the paintwork on the back door.

I clicked into the Armchair Detective Facebook group to share the article.

Barry responded immediately. **Wow, that's creepy, I wonder does he have other victims outside the East Midlands area then?**

Good question. It was the media who gave him the Blackwood Strangler name, but maybe they just hadn't joined the dots – maybe he'd spread his wings.

I've always wondered about that case in Leeds, Judith replied. **You know the couple who were killed out in the countryside? Lots of similarities with the Blackwood Strangler but I suppose if police assumed he stuck to the East Midlands, they didn't look at this one.**

I didn't know the case and went off to google. It came up quickly in multiple news reports – a couple in their thirties found dead in bed, one stabbed, one strangled. They were supposed to be away, and the incident was believed to be a burglary gone wrong. The next bit stopped me cold. They'd reported seeing footprints in soil under their bedroom window, two days before the attack. At the inquest, police presented details of that report as further evidence of a burglary gone wrong. But what kind of burglar stabs and strangles homeowners? Wouldn't he just run if he discovered they were home?

You're right, I typed in reply to Judith's comment, it's very similar. I guess they'll look at it now if they widen the scope? Have you read anywhere that they'll do that?

I have, Barry chirped up, I saw it on iSleuth. Police are looking at murders across the UK where strangulation is involved.

But why wouldn't they have made the connection already? I asked.

Strangulation's not that unusual, I suppose, Judith replied. And if the locations were widespread and separated by long periods of time, each one would be seen as a random attack.

Anne chimed in, always quick off the mark when there was a chance to educate the rest of us: To be classified as a serial case, there must be three or more killings and they must be spread out timewise. One killing in one area wouldn't stand out.

Scary to think of it that way, I typed. Anyway, I need to do some work, chat later.

I closed Facebook and went back to my work email, but something was niggling at me. I opened Google.

When was last Blackwood Strangler murder? I typed in the search bar.

The top result was a Wikipedia page, one I'd looked at many times before. He'd been active on and off for years, always with long breaks between attacks. I kept reading, until I found what I was looking for. His last suspected attack was a year earlier in Nottingham. Nothing since.

Or nothing that they knew of, I thought, as I closed the screen and swallowed, my throat suddenly dry.

I stood and walked to the window. Outside, the thaw had begun. The snow had taken on a watery sheen and the small shrubs that lined the driveway were poking through, dark against the greying slush. Towards the end of the garden, a shadow caught my attention. Not a shadow, I thought, as I squinted, but something on the ground, under the snow. Exposed by the thaw. What was it? The house was achingly quiet, holding its breath it seemed, while I stood at the window, staring. It was probably nothing, I told myself as I turned the door handle and walked outside. Probably a mound of earth I hadn't noticed before. Or a molehill. I drew closer.

It wasn't a molehill.

The bird had no injuries but was clearly dead. Small, brown, speckled, dead. Frozen under the snow, until now. Lying on something square and dark that definitely wasn't a molehill. And that was the problem. A dead bird wasn't unusual – I'd found dead birds in the garden before. But someone had placed it on top of what looked like a folded jacket. A camouflage jacket, the kind soldiers wear. A memory flickered. A long-ago photo. A fire. Ray.

"I suppose the bird might have frozen to death, poor little thing," Patrick said, licking his finger to turn the page of his notebook. "Not unusual in this weather, I imagine. Do you want me to remove it for you?"

"No, that's fine, I can do it – it's not the bird in itself

79

I'm worried about, it's that someone clearly put the jacket there, and put the bird on top."

"Well, maybe not," Patrick said, hunkering down to lift the edge of the jacket. "Couldn't the bird have just settled there and died?"

I sighed inwardly. "I suppose, but either way someone left an army jacket in my front garden. I don't know who or why or what it means. They obviously meant for it to appear once the snow melted."

Patrick looked up at me expectantly.

"Maybe it's to show me that he was here before the snow?" I suggested.

Patrick stood. "Maybe. It's not a threat in its own right, though. I mean, it looks like an Irish Defence Forces jacket to me – it's not like it's some scary despot's army coming to get you, is it?"

I said nothing.

"Listen, I'll have a look around, I'll check the window where you heard the knocking, and I'll take the jacket into evidence, in case something comes up later. How about that?"

I nodded. Evidence of what, I wasn't sure, but I knew I wanted it gone.

CHAPTER 15

By two o'clock, I couldn't bear to be in the cottage any more. I messaged my boss to say I was heading out for supplies, checked every door and window a thousand times, and set out for the village on foot. The snow was turning to slush and, as I trudged down the narrow road, I slipped and caught myself. The sky overhead was grey and heavy, but the forecast was promising no more fresh snow. All over the country, people would be digging cars out of driveways and braving slippery footpaths, desperate to reconnect with the outside world. *It wasn't as bad as this in '82,* they kept saying on radio shows and on Twitter. *At least there was no curfew back then, and the shops didn't run out of food.* But the snow had caught us all off guard, and savvy shoppers had cleared supermarket shelves of bread and milk before it became too difficult to get to shops at all. I wondered if there'd be anything to buy in the local supermarket in Carrickderg when I eventually got there, but really it didn't matter – I needed air and space.

As I passed Alan's farmhouse, I glanced over – no smoke from the chimney or sign of life around the yard – they must be out too. It couldn't be easy looking after farm animals in weather like this, I thought, with an unfamiliar pang of sympathy. However boorish Alan was with humans, he had always taken care of his animals. Back when Ray was still here, he had offered to help Alan once during lambing season but Alan had turned him down with a sneer – what would a writer from America know about lambing? At the time I felt sorry for Ray – the rebuttal of his olive branch left him looking hurt. As things turned out, Alan was probably right to steer clear.

By the time I got to the village, the road was relatively free of snow, though the car park in the Carrickderg Arms hadn't been cleared. The window of the Post Office hadn't been replaced either – duct tape covered the spot where the brick had gone through. As I passed, I could see Mrs O'Shea behind the counter, her coat buttoned up and her purple woolly hat on her head. I nodded in at her, and went on to the supermarket, where I was greeted by empty shelves and worried faces.

"The delivery trucks will be here within the hour, we've been *assured*," said the manager as I walked past, his smile reeking of hope and false promises.

I checked my watch – maybe if I had a late lunch in the Wooden Spoon, there would be something to buy by the time I was done.

The café was packed with people fixing hunger and cabin fever with towering club sandwiches and giant sausage rolls. I squeezed through to a free spot at the back and was already sitting when I realised Alan and Jamie were at the table beside me. Jamie nodded and smiled, but Alan very deliberately turned his head away – to the point where it was awkward for him to eat his soup.

Jamie locked eyes with me and gave a small shrug. I

shook my head and grinned.

It was a long time since I'd chatted to Jamie – I watched him as he ate his soup, wondering if he'd ever done anything with the Graphic Design course he was doing back when my dad died. When we were in school, we used to talk about what we'd be – Linda was going to be a fashion designer, Jamie an artist, and I was absolutely one hundred per cent sure I'd be a detective. A blonde Nancy Drew mixed with a bit of Christine from *Cagney and Lacey*. Now Linda was a doctor's wife in Kerry, Jamie was a farmer, and I was doing what everyone else was doing – basically working in an office.

I ordered lasagne and glanced over at Alan and Jamie as they ate in silence. Alan in his black wide-brim hat, something that always made him look like a lost cowboy or a slightly creepy minister. His heavy black coat and boots completed the look, utterly at odds with the usual farm attire of waterproof jacket and jeans. Jamie, thankfully, hadn't followed in his father's sartorial footsteps – he was wearing a red check shirt, snug across his wide shoulders. A swimmer's physique, wasted in a town with no swimming pool or beach. Where did he socialise these days, I wondered, or did he at all? I shook myself. Why was I wondering about Jamie's social life?

Alan got up to go to the bathroom, and after a moment Jamie leaned over.

"Are you doing okay with the snow up there on your own – is there anything you need?"

I put down my fork, surprised and unexpectedly charmed by the concern.

"I'm grand, going to the shops after this, but thank you for asking."

"Remember the last time – the bad snow when your jeep got stuck and me and Ray were trying to push it up the hill?"

I did remember. Ray didn't want Jamie's help, and it was a struggle to talk sense into him. I wondered if Jamie remembered that part. "And Ray kept asking why we didn't have snow tyres and we were trying to explain that it never snows in Ireland as this blizzard swirled around us."

Jamie laughed. "He must have thought we were awful eejits. They're so much better at dealing with bad weather in the States. Where is he living now?"

"New Jersey."

It felt abrupt. I grappled for something to add, just as Alan arrived back to the table asking Jamie about pig feed, and that was the end of that.

"Nothing like a bit of snow to bring people together," whispered an elderly lady at the table to my left. "Brings out the best in folk."

I smiled, and wondered if perhaps she was right, and if maybe it wasn't too late to patch up this thing with Alan. Ray would be furious. But Ray wasn't here.

As they got up to leave, Jamie nodded at me, and this time Alan looked over too.

"You'd want to watch yourself in the snow, Marianne – you could slip and fall up there at that cottage, and there'd be nobody to hear your screams."

Then he tipped his hat and walked out into the slushy, slippery dark.

CHAPTER 16

2005

That Sunday night glass of wine with Ray was the first of many more dates, all far less eventful than his spiked-drink incident with Alan. We drifted into a relationship, spending weekends between the hotel and the cottage, and I began to resent returning to Dublin on Monday mornings – missing Ray on my weekday evenings in my once-beloved Dublin flat. I hadn't done anything with the cottage and, as time went by, I realised I had no intention of selling it. It was more than my weekend home – it was my home full stop.

"Why don't you just tell them you're sick and stay here for the week?" Ray suggested as I was packing for Dublin one Sunday night in early August.

I laughed it off but imagined how good it would be to stay put. Ray had only three weeks left in Ireland – I hated that we'd be spending most of it apart.

"How about booking some vacation time?" he continued. "We could take off around the country for a week?"

My instinct was to give a dozen reasons why it wasn't possible, but then I stopped. Why not?

And that's how it happened. We took off on our road-trip, and somewhere between Moll's Gap and Kenmare he decided to stay on in Ireland. He didn't say for how long and I didn't ask but somehow we both knew it would be forever.

Or three years, as it turned out.

Back in Carrickderg, things progressed quickly. Ray moved into my cottage, and I joined him at weekends. He spent his days writing – filling one notebook at a time, transcribing to a newly purchased computer he installed in my dad's old bedroom. It was easier that way – he was old-school, he explained.

Carrickderg locals were shocked at how quickly Ray moved in, while my Dublin friends raised eyebrows at the age gap – Ray was thirty-five then, thirteen years older than me. My friends were spending every Saturday night drinking vodka and Red Bull in Coppers and Doyle's, falling into taxis and other people's flats. There were jobs everywhere and the country was still mid-boom, flooded with money. Dublin was buzzing, day and night, and why I'd want to escape to the Wicklow Mountains every weekend to shack up with an older man was beyond anyone's comprehension. But I didn't miss any of it – it was as though Ray had rescued me from a life I was fake-living. Or perhaps he simply swept me off my feet at a time when I was buried in grief and trying to pretend nothing was wrong at all.

We used to see Alan around town of course, and he and Ray were always civil to one another – a hat tip or the hatless equivalent. The first time I realised that Ray was not in fact over his early falling-out was when a Planning

Permission notice went up on the farmhouse grounds.

We were walking past one Sunday in early October, planning a midweek date in Dublin to see *A History of Violence*. Ray was expressing his surprise, not for the first time, that Carrickderg didn't have its own cinema, when he spotted the notice. He stopped to examine it and asked me what it was.

"If you want to do building work or an extension to your house, you have to apply for permission, and the notice must be on display so that neighbours can object."

"Ah, you mean like a building permit. So Alan wants to do some renovations and people from around here can stop him if they don't like how it sounds?"

"Yeah, like, I don't know the ins and outs of it – I doubt you can just say 'I object' without having a good reason, but that's pretty much how it works."

He moved closer and leaned in to read.

"What is it?" I asked when he shook his head.

"Alan is looking to convert his home into a guesthouse, it seems – adding extra bedrooms and bathrooms so he can cater for tourists."

"Oh my God, imagine coming on holidays to Ireland and booking into a guesthouse and discovering Alan is your host – I'd run a mile!"

I laughed. Ray didn't.

"You should be concerned about it, Marianne – this narrow road can't handle any extra traffic, and with tourists in and out of the place all the time, there'll be more noise and more trash. You should object."

"Ray, it's half a mile from my house – there's no way I'm going to be impacted!"

"But what about traffic?"

I looked left down the empty road to the village, and right, up towards my house, then back at Ray and raised my eyebrows.

"Okay sure, there's no traffic right now, but what about in the future? You need to take this seriously, Marianne."

"I'll think about it – now come on, let's keep going before it gets dark," I said, linking arms with him, and by the time we'd rounded the next corner, I'd forgotten all about it.

CHAPTER 17

The knock, when it came, was more of a hammering, and late on an October night it made both of us jump. I looked at Ray – was he expecting someone? He shook his head, answering my unspoken question. But there was something in his expression and looking back later I realised he knew exactly what was going to happen. The banging came again, accompanied now by shouting.

Alan.

I got up and opened the door, and before I could stop him he barged into the living room, his face mottled red and white.

"*Who the fuck do you think you are, sticking your nose in – you don't even live here! What's it to you if I'm doing building work?*"

He stood over Ray, who was still sitting on the couch.

"I'm just looking out for Marianne's interests," Ray said, eyes wide and innocent. "She's young and she's lost her dad and she needs someone who's been around the block looking out for her."

I looked from one to the other, trying to work out what was going on.

"*You fucker. You did it to spite me, no other reason!*" Alan shouted, poking a finger in Ray's chest.

I took a step forward.

"Wait, what's going on – what happened?"

Alan turned around. "Your *boy*-friend here objected to my planning permission and it's been turned down." His eyes flashed. "Are you going to claim you had nothing to do with it?"

Jesus, what was Ray thinking? I looked over, and he mouthed something at me. I couldn't make out what, but his expression said it all – *play along.*

"Um, I guess it's not ideal to have all that traffic and noise . . . and the countryside is so unspoilt out here . . ."

Alan looked at me, a slow smirk sliding across his face.

"You didn't know, did you? Then I wish you well. That sounds like an ideal start to a courtship." He shook his head. "Then again, you're used to lies, aren't you?" He pulled his hat down, and strode out of the house, leaving the door swinging open behind him.

I stared after him, stung more by the parting comment than any of what went before. Slowly I shut the door and sat beside Ray.

"Wow, that was dramatic – someone needs a blood-pressure check," Ray said, picking up the TV remote control.

I took it out of his hand.

"Ray. What were you thinking? You objected to his planning permission? Why? It doesn't affect you in the slightest!"

"But if affects *you*, Marianne, and without your dad here to look out for you, someone's got to."

"Excuse me, but I'm well able to look after myself, and

if I was worried about the guesthouse, *I'd* have objected."

"And now you don't have to, I've taken care of it for you. And Alan can consider that the next time he decides to make a fool of someone."

There it was.

"I see. Look, I get that you were pissed off for what he did in the pub that night, and on some level I understand why you sabotaged his plans."

Ray opened his mouth to object but I held up my hand to stop him.

"That's what it was, Ray, sabotage. But you know, apart from the fact that it's over the top, and the fact that we have to live in the same small village as Alan, and the fact that he can, if he wishes, now retaliate in some way –"

Ray opened his mouth again, but I kept talking.

"Yes, *of course* he can retaliate. But the thing that bothers me most is you didn't tell me about it. You went behind my back. You have to swear you'll never do that again, right?"

"Is this about what he said – there's something about your dad lying to you, isn't there?"

I flopped back against the cushions.

"For all the right reasons though – he was looking out for me."

Ray waited for me to say more, and when I didn't he patted my hand. "Just like I am, right?"

He picked up the remote and switched on the news, but I couldn't concentrate on any of it – my mind was back on that day ten years earlier, when everything I thought I knew came tumbling down.

CHAPTER 18

1995

Mrs Griffin said she'd only be gone five minutes but it was at least half an hour, and maybe that's where it all started to go wrong. We had finished our work and were getting bored and fidgety, and even though Mrs Griffin had said there'd be extra homework for anyone caught away from their desk, people were getting up and walking around.

Then Philip, the boy sitting behind Sorcha Riordan, started pinging her bra strap, and every time she told him to stop, he nodded, then did it again. Some of the other boys were cheering, including Jamie. I threw him a look to tell him to cop on, and Linda got up to go over to Sorcha. We weren't mad on Sorcha, but this was crossing a line.

"Leave her alone," Linda said, planting her feet firmly between Sorcha and Philip.

"Who's going to make me?" Philip said, smirking up at her.

Linda was at least three inches taller than him, and not afraid of anyone, so I'm not sure why he thought that was a good idea. He reached past her, and pulled Sorcha's bra strap again. That was enough for Linda – she smacked him across the face, a wallop that left a bright red mark. He put his hand to his cheek and looked like he was about to cry, while Sorcha sat still as a statue.

Linda was standing, staring Philip down when Mrs Griffin walked back into the classroom.

"What on earth is going on in here?"

Philip was holding back tears, massaging his cheek.

"She hit me!" he said.

"Because you wouldn't stop pulling her bra strap," Linda said, hands on hips.

"Linda, up to my desk right now," Mrs Griffin said, her mouth set in a thin line. Though Mrs Griffin looked like that ninety per cent of the time.

"But, Miss, I was just standing up for Sorcha," Linda said, as she walked up to the desk.

"Sorcha, can you tell me what happened?"

But poor Sorcha, the only girl in the class who had a bra, was too embarrassed to explain. She said nothing.

"Does anyone else want to tell me what happened?" Mrs Griffin asked, looking around.

"What Linda says is true, Miss," I said.

"No, it isn't," piped up Nigel Stokes. "He didn't do anything. You two are always on each other's side and telling lies."

"Yeah, they're always telling lies and trying to get people in trouble," said John-Paul Ryan.

And before I could say another word, half a dozen boys in the class joined in, all claiming Philip had done nothing.

I stared over at Jamie, waiting for him to speak up. But he just looked down at his hands and said nothing.

"Miss, I'm telling the truth," I said again, and some of the other girls joined in, until the room was full of battling voices.

"*Enough!*" *roared Mrs Griffin, and gave us all a page of Maths to do while she spoke to Linda, then Philip, and finally a blotchy-faced Sorcha.*

They all had to go to the principal, because slapping was so serious apparently, though it seemed to me that it was precisely the right response to bra-pinging. The principal made Linda apologise, and said she hoped Philip's parents didn't take it further. She made Philip promise he wouldn't do anything like that to Sorcha or anyone else again. She told Sorcha she needed to get used to it and not be so sensitive, and Linda was madder about that than anything else.

She flounced out of the school when the day came to an end, as Jamie and I trailed behind. She rounded on him as soon as we got to the gate.

"*What were you thinking – why didn't you speak up?*" *she yelled.* "*You're supposed to be my friend!*"

Jamie pulled up short, almost toppling over her.

"*What?*" *he said, his voice breaking over the end of the word. He cleared his throat and stood with his hands on his hips, mirroring her.*

"*You know what. Why didn't you tell Mrs Griffin I was telling the truth?*"

Jamie rolled his eyes and shrugged. Big mistake. "*What difference would it make? I'm just one person. All the girls were on your side anyway. Mrs Griffin hardly cares what I think.*"

"*That – Is – Not – The – Point,*" *Linda hissed.* "*You are my friend. Friends stick together no matter what.*"

"*Oh, for God's sake, it's only bloody Sorcha Riordan! You don't even like her. Don't get your knickers in a twist.*"

Linda stared open-mouthed.

I jumped in.

"Jamie, cop on. You know that's not the point – if it had been the other way around, me and Linda would have stood up for you. That's what friends do."

A group was gathering behind us and someone shouted, "Jamie's scared of his two girlfriends!"

Colour flared in Jamie's cheeks, but he didn't turn around.

"I don't need you to stand up for me, Marianne. Just cos we live near each other doesn't mean we're friends."

"Excuse me?" Now my hands were on my hips too. "Where do you go after school every day? At whose kitchen table do you do your homework? We were definitely friends when we were playing Scrabble with Mrs Townsend yesterday afternoon – what's changed since then?"

There were sniggers in the crowd behind us and Jamie's face went redder.

"You play Scrabble after school? In her gaff?" someone said. Nigel Stokes, I think, big man that he was all of a sudden.

"My dad makes me go there!" Jamie shouted, to me or to them, I don't know.

I shook my head.

"That's not true. You like coming over to my house, you told me that."

"I don't!" he shouted. "I only started going cos I felt sorry about your mam being murdered!"

Silence. Then a roar, but only inside my head. In the outer world, the one where his words had just fallen, there was no sound.

"Shut up, Jamie," Linda said quietly. She reached out to grab my elbow and pull me away.

95

I couldn't move.

A murmur rose in the group behind but I couldn't make out the words. Jamie stood beside me, eyes down, kicking a stone with the scuffed toe of his trainer.

I swallowed, and shaped my mouth to make words come out.

"My mother died in her sleep. Why would you say something like that?"

"Ignore him, Marianne, come with me," Linda was saying.

Jamie was silent.

"Jamie, why did you say it?" I asked again, reaching out to shake his arm and make him look at me.

But he wouldn't.

"Ask your da, he'll tell you," he muttered, turning to walk away.

He didn't come back to my house after school ever again.

Linda came with me that day and, ignoring our homework, we went straight to the den at the bottom of the garden. We wriggled under the branches that hid the entrance, and sat cross-legged on the hard soil floor, facing one another. There was more space that day than we were used to – we were rarely there without Jamie, and his absence amplified everything that had just happened. Linda reached for the tin box where we kept the torch, and pulled it out. The beam lit up the squat wooden walls and tin roof, built by my dad back when I was short enough to stand upright in there. Now we could only crawl or sit.

I pulled out a packet of Maltesers I'd stashed the week before, but I never felt less like eating.

"Are you okay, Marianne?"

"Do you know what Jamie was talking about?"

In the torchlight, I saw her shake her head but just a little.

"You need to ask your dad."

And there we sat on the damp floor of the den, sharing a bag of Maltesers and saying little, because good friends listen but best friends know when you just can't find the words.

That night, with a hot stone lodged in my stomach, I sat down beside my dad when he came in from work. His shoes were at the front door, and I remember there was a tiny hole in one of his socks. I focused on that as he switched on the TV and asked how my day was.

"Fine," I said, still not sure how to bring it up.

I remember the Six O'Clock News was on, a story about a prisoner called Fred West who'd been found hanged in his prison cell a few weeks earlier.

My dad looked at me and changed the channel.

"Dad," I said eventually, and it came out as a mumble.

"Yes, love?" he said, without looking away from the TV.

"I need to ask you something. Can you turn down the telly?"

He did, and swivelled on the couch to look at me.

"What is it, love?"

Was there a wariness in his eyes? Or did I imagine it?

"Jamie said something at school today."

My dad blinked twice. I wasn't imagining it. He knew what was coming.

"About my mother." The seal was broken, the words

flew out in a rush. "He said she didn't die in her sleep, that she was murdered. But that's just crazy, isn't it? That's just Jamie being an idiot? Isn't it?"

I waited for him to tell me Jamie was an idiot, but he didn't. Instead he took my hand in his and closed his eyes. When he opened them again, it was all laid bare. There was no going back and it hit me like a wallop from a punch bag.

"Oh my God. What happened?"

And he told me. Sitting on our little couch that night, holding my hand, he told me that she went back to Denmark to visit her parents, and that's where it happened. She went out for a walk one night, and never came home. Her parents had gone to bed, not thinking they needed to wait up and it was late the following morning when they realised something was wrong. She'd been sleeping a lot during her visit, and they hadn't gone to her room all morning, he told me. Her mother had put her head around the door at lunchtime and realised Hanne wasn't there – the bed was made. Had she got up early and gone out? But they didn't hear from her and began to wonder if she'd come back at all the night before. Hanne was twenty-three, a grown-up, free to come and go as she pleased, so the alarm wasn't immediately raised. And even when it was, the police didn't worry too much. She'd probably just gone off on a trip for a couple of days, they said. Wasn't she a wanderer? And she was. She'd gone to Ireland on her own, and she'd gone to the States during college summers, exploring the east coast with only a backpack for company. Her parents weren't convinced though, my dad said. They didn't think she'd take off without saying anything. They phoned my dad that first day to find out if she'd been in touch, but she hadn't. He was here looking after me. He sat by the phone, waiting for updates as hours turned into days, then weeks. And then came the call, he said, his face so full of pain it hurt me to look at him. They'd found a body. Hanne's body. She was buried in woodlands near Roskilde, about 40 miles from her home in Købæk on the island of Zealand.

My dad stopped then, and closed his eyes, his hand still on mine.

For a while, neither of us spoke.

"Are you okay?" he said eventually, opening his eyes.

Slowly I nodded.

"I'm so sorry, Marianne. I never wanted you to have to deal with this. It's bad enough to lose your mother, but like this . . ." He lifted his hands and dropped them again.

"Did they find out who did it?" I asked, because I couldn't think of anything else to say.

My dad's face changed. "No. There were two other women who had been . . . well, they were found a bit before Hanne disappeared. Because they were all young women, the police wondered if the same person had . . ." He stopped.

I knew what he was trying to say.

"What happened to her – how did she die?"

"She had been drowned," he said, his voice low and cracking on the words.

I sat staring at my hands, trying to take it in, trying to work out how I felt. There was horror, but distance too. Maybe it hadn't sunk in. Or maybe because I never really knew her, it was like watching a film about a fictional character.

"What happened then?" I asked, because I needed something to say. "Did you go to Denmark?"

ANDREA MARA

"No, I never went – I had you here, I needed to stay with you. And there was nothing I could do." He shook his head. "Hanne was gone."

That night, I dreamed I was being held under water by strong hands, and when I woke, panicking and sweating and crying, my dad heard me and came in. He put his arms around me, not something he often did, and rocked me until I was ready to go back to sleep.

The following morning, on his way to work, he stopped into Alan's house. I never heard exactly what was said, but Alan and my dad didn't speak again, and until I came back for my dad's funeral ten years later, neither did Jamie and I.

CHAPTER 19

2018

On Thursday morning, I woke on the couch to the low hum of a television breakfast show – I'd slept in the living room with the TV on, unable to bear another night in my bedroom, waiting for the knock.

Outside, the thaw had well and truly taken hold – I checked the ground below my bedroom window but there was nothing on the concrete path: no snow, no slush, no prints. Nothing to show if someone had been there or not.

As I stared down, with my back to the garden and the gate beyond, a sudden prickling sensation crawled across my neck. Was someone watching me? I whirled to look, my eyes skittering across the slushy grass, and down to the open gate, swinging as the wind whipped up. Blank, empty space looked back at me – the hawthorn tree, the low stone wall, the swaying gate, the deserted road. Nobody out on there looking in. Nobody anywhere.

Pulling my cardigan tighter, I went inside, and was still trying to shake the feeling of watching eyes when my phone pinged. A text from an unknown number. I clicked in, and realised it was Jamie. His text sounded formal, but then again, we weren't in regular contact – he wanted to know if I was driving to Dublin in the next few days and if I could give him a lift. The car he and Alan shared wouldn't start since the snow, and Alan needed the Land Rover. I imagined Alan's surly response, saying no for the sake of saying no. And as I looked around my silent living room, facing into another day on my own, I knew what I wanted to do.

Actually, going to work from the office today. Would need to head soon. Is that too short notice?

Jamie came back quickly.

I can be ready in ten?

Be down to you in twenty, I replied, checking the time.

One quick shower later, I found myself in front of my wardrobe, searching for something – anything – other than leggings and T-shirts. Black jeans and a print shirt would do the trick, I thought, taking out my neglected make-up bag to scrutinise the contents. Who is this for, I wondered, as I rubbed a hint of blusher on my cheeks and blow-dried my hair. Maybe it was just about breaking out – away from old habits and out of the house. *And* – I realised as I swiped on a self-conscious smear of lipstick – for a full five minutes, I'd forgotten about the footprints.

"Thanks for this, I really appreciate it. Three days with my da is enough – it was either this or throw myself off the barn roof," Jamie said, grinning, as he hopped into the jeep.

I laughed and suddenly it was like old times. He didn't have anything urgent to do in Dublin, he said, he just needed to get away – his dad had been moaning about the snow non-stop, as though the entire weather event was a conspiracy designed solely to inconvenience him.

"You have the patience of a saint," I said. "Do you ever think about moving out?"

"Nah, no chance of that. My da's been telling me for as long as I can remember that the farm is mine, my 'birthright', and there's never been a question of anything else."

We slowed behind a tractor and I glanced over at him.

"But what about being an artist?"

"Ah, same as anyone, I wanted all sorts of things when I was a kid – every child wants to be a footballer or an actor or an inventor or a spy. Then we all grow up and do exactly what our parents did – work in offices and shops and farms."

I couldn't argue with that.

The conversation with Jamie was still on my mind at lunchtime when I decided to give Linda a call – it had been a while since we'd spoken, a month or more. Actually I couldn't remember the last time I'd called her; she was usually the one who called me. When she answered, at first I didn't realise it was Linda – her voice was quieter than usual, hoarse.

"The baby's asleep," she said in an almost-whisper. "It took ages to get him down, and if he wakes again I'll cry."

"Where are the others?"

"Watching TV. I don't have it on all the time, but I just needed to get the baby down."

"God, if I had kids I'd have them watching TV the whole time – what's wrong with TV all of a sudden?"

A pause.

"Yeah, well, you can't just plonk them on front of telly all day – they need to get out and get exercise and air and all that."

She sounded off. I'd put a foot wrong somehow.

"Oh sure, of course. So how're things?"

Another sigh.

"Grand, I guess. Same ol' same ol'. How's work?"

I couldn't think of anything interesting to say about work, so I told her about the snow instead, and the footprints and the face I thought I saw and the knocking.

"Maybe a neighbour checking on you? Hang on –"

In the background I could hear her shushing someone.

"Sorry, Marianne, I'm going to have to go – the girls are starting to squabble and if they wake the baby I swear to God I'm walking out of this house."

She was gone halfway through my goodbye. I sat for a moment with the phone in my hand, wondering what had just happened. Since when did Linda end a call after five minutes? We used to chat for hours, about everything and anything. Though now that I thought about it, I couldn't remember the last time we'd done that either.

Jamie's message arrived that evening, when I was walking down to Zorian's basement car park. At first I thought he was looking for a lift home – I'd told him I'd be driving back around six, but he was already on the bus and the text had nothing to do with lifts.

Hey Marianne, just wanted to let you know I saw someone today who looked very like someone you know. I wasn't talking to him so not 100% sure. Pic to follow.

Tensing, I stood in the car park, with no idea what to expect, but somehow sure it would come to no good.

CHAPTER 20

The car park plunged into darkness as I stood halfway between the basement door and my parking space, waiting for Jamie's second message. I waved my arm to make the light come back on but I was too far past the door. Where was the damn message? The car park was underground and the phone signal sketchy – I was just about to give in and walk back to the basement when it popped up.

A photo of a man in a bookshop, taken from the side, grainy with distance and low indoor lights. But unmistakable all the same. Suddenly, I was ice-cold. The man in the photo was Ray.

As soon as I got home I started googling. Ray's author page came up first, and a list of his books, followed by various articles and features. I clicked into the News tab, but the most recent link was about a hospital he'd opened in San Francisco. That was a long way to go for a charity event – maybe this was a new, more altruistic Ray than the one I knew. Back then, nothing was ever for nothing, despite early impressions to the contrary.

I leaned back on the couch, staring at useless Google

search results – articles about his upcoming book (called *The Wanderer*, no other details), his home renovation (costing upwards of $2 million gushed one report) but nothing to suggest he was in Ireland. I let out a breath.

I shut the laptop and went into the kitchen to make a sandwich, realising as I opened the door I was tensing, bracing myself. Light flooded the room when I hit the switch, sucking up shadows. Comforting. A little. Waiting for the grill to heat, I stared out the window. Dark drifts of snow nestled against bushes that bordered both sides of the back garden, but the thaw was almost complete. There would be no more footprints. Or at least none that I could see. I shivered. Maybe I should put in one of those lights that comes on when someone moves outside? Then again, it would give me a heart-attack every time a fox set it off – perhaps we're better off not knowing what goes on outside when we're asleep.

With my cheese-and-ham sandwich deposited in the grill, I forced myself to walk through to the boot room to check the back door, making yet another mental note to replace it with something more secure. And maybe installing an alarm wasn't such a bad idea, though the thought of it going off in the middle of the night made the hairs on my skin stand up. I had a sudden flashback to my old flat in Dublin city centre – cosy, flanked by other flats, high off the ground. Safety in numbers. Smoke from the kitchen called me back to real life, and I took my charred sandwich through to the living room.

With footprints and Ray still swirling through my head, I clicked into the Armchair Detective group. Judith had posted another case she'd found – a murder in Calais in France, two years ago. A woman had reported noises in her back garden, and trampled shrubs. Police suggested urban foxes. Two days later, the woman was found dead on her living-room floor. Strangled.

What do you think of this? Judith had written. **Not unlike the Blackwood Strangler. And Calais is an easy trip from the UK, but it means the case fell into an entirely different jurisdiction. Unless the investigators from both countries are talking to one another, would they even know?**

Neil was sceptical.

But if it was that easy for you to find it, the investigators would have found it too. No doubt they have, and already ruled out a link.

Judith replied: **But isn't that the point, Neil? We're here using the Internet to search for links that may have been missed.**

I jumped in. **How did you find it, Judith? I was searching through unsolved murders one night last week, and there are just so many.**

I used "stalking" as a keyword, she replied. **There are still too many results – it will take forever to go through them all – and I definitely don't have forever ☺ Want to help?**

Sure, I could do with a distraction, I wrote, without explaining why. **I'll do some research and meet you back here in two hours?**

Thumbs-up emoji from Judith. And from Neil – who likes to be right and hates being ignored – nothing at all.

I tried "Unsolved Murders" + "Stalking" first, and soon I was lost in list after list of "10 of the Creepiest Murders of All Time". Lots of the stories I knew already – Girl Scouts who had disappeared from camp, a family who vanished on Christmas Eve, but none that fit either the time frame or the hallmarks of the Blackwood Strangler. I needed better search words.

I got up and walked to the living-room window, staring out at the inky sky. Nothing stirred. I pulled across the curtains, blocking out the blackness, and sat back down. I hesitated, wondering about rabbit holes and knowing too much, then started to type new search words.

"Unsolved Murder" + "Footprints".

CHAPTER 21

At ten o'clock, I came up for air, trying to unstick myself from all I'd just read. Jesus, the Internet was a scary place. I looked at my notebook – half a dozen pages of cases from all over Europe, all of which fit the timeframe for the Blackwood Strangler, and all involving some level of stalking and footprints.

Like the one in Austria, with a trampled rosebush under the victim's bedroom window. She thought she had a Peeping Tom and began keeping her curtains closed day and night. Two days later, there was a pink rose left on her doormat. A week later, she was dead.

There was a case from Poland: a couple found letters scratched on their windowsill. Seemingly random letters, as though drawn by a child: the letter R, the letter L, and what looked like a B. They were curious, not worried, although surprised that the footprints under the scratched windowsill looked too big to belong to a child. They were found two days later, one stabbed, one strangled.

In Rotterdam, a young woman, home alone while her parents were on holidays, had woken one morning to find a cross drawn in the condensation on her bedroom window. It was so innocuous, but made no sense. Whoever had done it had hardly meant any harm, but then who and why, she wondered to a friend she spoke to that afternoon. Her friend reportedly told her it was "probably just one of those things", and I thought about all the times in my life I'd seen things that didn't make a whole lot of sense, and heard people say exactly that. *Just one of those things*. The cross was there the following morning too, and the one after. Her parents came home from their trip to find her body on her bedroom floor, and the window wiped clean.

In Denmark, a woman came out one morning to find chalk drawings on her front driveway. Someone – kids, she assumed – had chalked out a stick drawing of a hangman, like in the word game, but with no words. She thought little of it until she realised that night that someone had removed the bulb from the light-fitting in her porch. She mentioned it to her next-door neighbour, and the following morning she was found, just like the others. But maybe they weren't linked at all? Each of them had something – a tiny detail that made no sense, but not enough to ring any serious alarm bells. The kinds of things kids do, nothing unduly threatening, and no two cases the same. Except for the footprints, of course – the common denominator. And perhaps not a real common denominator – maybe each of the murders would have involved footprints anyway.

There were more search results to go through but I was out of steam and ready to report back.

Judith, how are you getting on? I tried using "footprints" in my search and found 8 cases so far that aren't even in the UK – they're all around Europe.

She was back within a minute to crosscheck details. She'd found the same cases. But it was hardly reasonable to think the Blackwood Strangler was committing murders in other countries, was it? I said as much, only then realising a huge part of me wanted Judith to say of course not, there was no way there was a connection, no chance he'd widened his hunting ground. But she didn't get a chance to – Enthusiastic Barry jumped in.

Why don't we take a few cases each and research them further, and at the same time keep searching for more? Using "footprints" in the search seems like a good idea – well done, Marianne 😊😊

I ignored the pat on the head but agreed to the plan. And promising myself I'd be in bed by midnight, I checked the door one last time, and sat down to read about stalkers who kill.

CHAPTER 22

On Friday morning, when my alarm went off, I wanted to cry. I'd stayed up far too late reading up on murders and footprints, and my dreams had punished me for it. Outside, the garden was almost clear of snow – the thaw had transformed everything, taking the footprints with it. I wondered if the guards had found anything and as the kettle boiled I phoned the station. Patrick answered, and told me he had nothing back on the army jacket yet, other than confirmation that it looked like Irish Defence Forces, and the owner's name badge had been ripped off.

I asked him if he'd heard more on the tourist who'd caused trouble in the hotel.

"He's gone back to the States now, that's confirmed, so it's not him."

Dammit, I really wanted it to be the drunk but otherwise reasonably harmless tourist.

"If it was just the Sunday night you saw the footprints, then maybe it could have been him," Patrick went on, "but he was definitely gone the next day. Anyway, no way he could have hung around all week without us spotting him when we're out on patrol."

An image of Geraldine and Patrick in a police car, cruising up and down the mean streets of Carrickderg popped into my head.

"And we've had no other reports of prowlers or kids messing," he continued. "So maybe it was nothing."

"I guess if nobody else reported anyone though, it just means the person was focussed on me, doesn't it, as opposed to meaning it didn't happen?"

"Yeah, no, I don't mean it didn't happen – I mean, maybe it was just one of those things, something and nothing. You know?"

Just one of those things. Things we can't explain so we ignore them. I didn't say anything.

"Like, is it still going on?" he asked, filling the silence.

"I don't know. The snow is gone, so I can't tell anymore if someone has been here. Or for how long they were coming before the snow."

"Yeah, I see what you mean. Did you get a new curtain, like Geraldine was saying?"

Mother of God, they were obsessed with curtains.

"Not yet but I'm still tacking black sacks over the window every night."

"There you go then – he's hardly going to bother coming back now he can't see anything, is he?"

"But he *did* come back after I put them up – I saw a face at the window on Monday night and heard knocking on Tuesday night."

"But you said you weren't a hundred per cent sure about either of those, didn't you?"

"Well, yes, but I didn't imagine the footprints – you've seen the photos."

"*Hmm.* Would it be an idea to put in some security on

113

the house? Not even because of this, but just as a general precaution?"

He was right. I'd been putting it off for years, but it was time to put in an alarm and finally replace that back door.

I thanked him and disconnected.

With no idea where to start looking, I sat and googled home security.

I was elbow-deep in mindboggling burglar-alarm information when there was familiar rap on the door. One thing I liked about Bert was his reassuringly identifiable knock, along with the promise of a package. What had I ordered? Books, I realised, as I opened the door, delighted with the distraction from home-security research – and, I realised, with the temporary company of another human being.

"You're a great woman for the books, Marianne," Bert said, nodding towards the label on the package. "What are they this time – Agatha Christie?"

"An old Julia Land murder mystery, and a new Kate Atkinson. I have a ticket to see Julia Land being interviewed next week, so I need a refresher."

"Well, I'm glad it wasn't this week or it'd have been cancelled along with everything else. Country's gone mad for cancelling things," he said with a back-in-my-day shake of the head. "But, look, you made it through the snow in one piece, that's something."

"I sure did. What, were you expecting to find me frozen solid on my living-room floor?" I laughed.

He tilted his head to one side, and lowered his voice. "I wouldn't laugh – it can happen, you know."

"Ah, I know, but things aren't that bad yet. Still a bit of oil in the radiators."

"Remember that poor fella in Ramolin?" he went on. "Froze to death that time and nobody found him till three days later."

I vaguely remembered the details and couldn't help wondering why Bert thought this was a good time and place to bring it up.

"Well, we're out the other side of it now anyway," I said.

"Oh, that won't be the end of it," he replied, touching the side of his nose. "Watch this space. More snow on the way before the end of the month."

"Really?"

"Don't worry, Marianne – if you don't answer my knock some morning, I'll make sure to check you're okay."

I couldn't tell if he was joking or serious, but either way it was oddly reassuring. Because, realistically, if something happened to me, how would anyone know?

CHAPTER 23

2006

"Let it go, Ray," I said, staring at the scratch on the otherwise pristine dark-green paintwork. "It's a tiny mark, barely noticeable, and you don't know for sure he did it."

Ray reached out and rubbed the car, as though it were a pet dog who'd been injured.

"Of course he did it. Who else would?"

We were parked outside Delaneys' and had gone in for a bite to eat. I couldn't say for sure that the scratch wasn't there before we went in, but Ray was adamant.

"I saw him down the street when we were going into the pub – that dumb black hat of his stands out a mile. Think about how easy it would be for him to stick a key in the paintwork as he walked past."

"But that's just it – think how easy it would be for *anyone* to do it, by accident *or* on purpose. You have no way to prove it was him, so let it go. You blocked his planning permission, and if he *has* keyed your car, maybe you're even again and we can all move on. Right?"

He turned to face me.

"Are you saying that's fair? To illegally damage a car in return for an entirely legal planning-permission objection?"

"No," I said, my hand on his arm. "It's not. But sometimes it's not about whether it's strictly legal or not – if you can do it just to get at someone, rather than for more genuine reasons, does it matter that it's within the law?"

He pulled away from me, his eyes suddenly cold.

"Ray, honestly," I said, my voice softer now, "it's tiny – it's not worth tackling him – he'll just deny it anyway and then you'll feel worse."

He shook his head, and I couldn't tell if it was in resignation or opposition, but he got into the car and we drove home without discussing it again.

The following Friday, when I arrived back from work in Dublin, we dropped into Delaneys' for a pre-dinner drink, where John was behind the bar.

"Did you hear what happened up at Alan's?" John said, pouring two glasses of wine.

I stiffened and looked over at Ray, but his face was impassive.

"Someone left the henhouse door open," John went on, "and a fox got in – every one of his hens was killed. Jamie was in earlier, said he found them this morning. Blood and bits everywhere. Carnage."

I sat on my bar stool, my hand wrapped around the stem of my wineglass, unable to look at Ray.

"That's terrible," he was saying to John. "Nature can be so cruel."

John moved to the other side of the bar to serve Mick O'Shea, and I turned to Ray.

"Please, please, tell me you didn't do this," I whispered.

His eyes widened. "Jesus, Marianne, of course I didn't! You honestly think I would do that?"

117

I shook my head. "Shit, sorry, of course not. I just got a fright – I know you were pissed off about the car last week."

"Well, sure. But this is a whole other level." His green eyes searched my face. "You trust me, right?"

I touched his knee. "Of course I trust you. But, God, poor Alan."

"Poor Alan," Ray snorted, taking a swallow of wine. "He shouldn't have left the henhouse open, I guess. Outfoxed, right?"

"Ray, it's not funny. That's his livelihood. And the poor chicks . . ."

He laughed. "Now tell me this, are you the same young lady who ordered roast chicken in the hotel last Sunday?"

I shook my head. It wasn't the same thing at all, but I didn't want to keep talking about it.

"How's the book going?"

"Good, I got lots done this week. My agent called on Wednesday to ask when I'll have some chapters over to her but I want to wait until I'm finished the first draft this time. Surprise her." He grinned. "How was your week in the big bright lights of Dublin city?"

"Oh, *very* exciting," I said, "I cleaned my apartment on Monday night and watched *Desperate Housewives* on Tuesday. Living the dream." I took a sip of my wine. "Oh, actually, I went to see a film on Thursday – two of the gang from work talked me into it. It's called –"

"Who from work did you go with?" he interrupted.

"Fiona and Anne-Marie, you don't know them. Anyway, it's called *When a Stranger Calls*. It's this film about a girl who's babysitting and gets these creepy phone calls and then the phone calls are traced and they're coming from inside the house. *So* freaky."

"Oh, that's an urban legend that used to go around when we were kids – supposedly happened to a girl one town over. It's not an original story."

I sipped again, feeling unmistakably put in my place.

"Well, yes, but nothing is original, is it? We just tell the same legends and stories in different guises?"

For a beat, Ray looked affronted, and I wondered if he thought it was a dig at his chosen career. Then he smiled again.

"How's work?"

I filled him in, and he managed to look interested almost all of the way through.

"You know, exciting as all that is," he smiled, "some day I'm going to whisk you away from the bright lights of Dublin, put a gold band on your finger, and keep you here in the countryside as my muse. I'll fill your bath with champagne, bring you fresh croissants for breakfast every morning, and you'll never have to press a key on a keyboard again. Are you in?"

"I'd rather drink the champagne than bathe in it, but the rest of it sounds glorious."

"Then let's do that," Ray said, and I didn't know what he meant until he asked John for a bottle of champagne, slipped a small gold ring out of his pocket and on to my finger, and toasted Marianne McShane, his wife and muse.

That was Ray all over – grand gestures and small surprises, and I was swept up in it. At twenty-three I wasn't ready to get married, and I don't know that we were actually engaged, but it was such a *Ray* thing to do and I loved it.

From then on, we acted as though we were married – a kind of inside joke for just the two of us. I wore the gold band on my ring finger, he signed us into hotels as Mr and

Mrs Sedgwick, and when we went to events with publishers and authors in Dublin, he introduced me as his wife.

The authors and publishers didn't bat an eyelid – I have no idea if they knew we weren't really married, and I imagine nobody cared. But in Carrickderg it generated some subtle and not so subtle inquiries. Mrs O'Shea from the Post Office asked if she should buy a hat or if she'd already missed the wedding. Geraldine from the Garda station was more direct, asking were we *engaged* or actually *married*? "What's the difference really?" Ray said to her. "It's just a piece of paper." Mrs Townsend who used to look after me when I was in school hugged me and said she hoped I was happy, and I had to stop to think about it but I decided I was. For the first time since losing my dad, I was starting to feel good again.

June came, the anniversary of my dad's death and our first encounter. We marked it a week later with a dinner in Dublin, then splashed out on a taxi back to Carrickderg, and a late night with red wine when we got in.

I was groggy when I opened the living-room curtains the following morning, and at first I couldn't make out what I was seeing. When I did, I nearly threw up. Lying across the mat at the front door was a dead fox.

"*Ray!*" I yelled, and he came stumbling out of our room, misshapen and blurry after our late night.

I pointed through the window.

"Jesus Christ," he muttered, opening the front door.

The fox looked like it had been shot. Its eyes were open and glazed, its fur matted and rust-red with blood.

"Alan. That motherfucker couldn't let it go," Ray said, staring at the fox.

"Ray, don't start. It might not have been him . . ."

But even as I said it, I knew it was Alan. And I knew why.

"You left the henhouse open that time, didn't you?" I said after a moment.

He closed the front door and ran his hand through his hair. "How the hell do you get rid of a dead fox? Do you have animal control here?" he said, ignoring my question.

"I have no idea about animal control . . . Actually, I remember once years and years ago my dad found a dead fox at the end of the back garden."

"And what did he do?"

"God – I'm nearly sure he asked Alan what to do, and Alan took care of it."

A smile spread across Ray's face. "Then that's what we'll do. Play dumb, ask him if he'll help us get rid of it, and we kill two birds with one stone."

"What do you mean?"

"We get rid of the fox, and we leave Alan thinking we don't know it was him – so he won't expect us to get back at him." A shadow crossed his face, the smile suddenly gone. "He'll never see us coming."

CHAPTER 24

It was a black-tie ball just before Christmas that started it all, a sequence of events kicked off by a mission so innocuous in hindsight – the search for something long and sparkly to wear to the Shelbourne Hotel, to a charity event, with eye-watering prices, in a country still drunk on boom-time money.

I didn't think I'd get away with my go-to black dress any longer, and was gearing up for the chore of shopping when I remembered Hanne's dresses in the attic. Could I? Would it be weird? Maybe they wouldn't fit anyway, I figured, as I pulled down the attic ladder.

The box was where I'd left it a year and a half earlier, at the back of the attic. The blue dress and the green dress were at the top of the pile, and the silver dress underneath. I left the silver one behind – beautiful, but definitely not me. I pulled the other two out and made my way back towards the ladder. That's when I spotted it – the USA biscuit tin I'd left beside the hatch the last time I was up. I leaned out and dropped the dresses gently to the couch below, picked up the tin, and climbed down.

My plan was to try on the dresses while Ray was out

and have one ready to show him on his return, but instead I was drawn to the old biscuit tin.

Inside, there were bits of paper of all sizes – it looked like a mix of tickets and postcards and letters. From the top of the pile, I lifted a postcard. One of those "Welcome to Ireland" cards with sheep and a green postbox on the front. On the other side, it was blank, waiting to be inscribed. By whom, I wondered – my mother? I put it down and took out the next piece of paper – a sequence of words that looked like a shopping list, but in another language. Danish as far as I could tell, though I had never learned any. Below that I found train-ticket stubs – a journey from Dublin to Cork, and the dates coincided with the trip my parents took after they got married. I put them aside, wondering if I should buy a scrapbook and do what my parents had perhaps intended to do with their souvenirs. Next I found a photo I had never seen before – my parents on a windy beach, both of them laughing. Who took the photo, I wondered? Looking at their faces, it was hard to believe they were only a few years from tragedy. Beneath the photo, I found a folded page of lined paper. Not sure if I was prying, I opened it – maybe it was another Danish shopping list. But this time it was in English – a letter, addressed to my dad.

> Michael,
>
> I am so sorry to do this to you and to the baby, but I know it is best for you and for her and for me.
>
> I never meant for any of it to happen. I came to Ireland for all the best reasons but instead I found myself in a cage.
>
> I can't live the way I was living. I'm not the

*person I know. I need to escape from the cage. I'm
back where I belong, and it won't be a visit. I need
to stay now. I trust that in time you'll explain this to
the child, and I hope you will eventually forgive me.
I will understand if you can't.*

    Yours,
    Hanne

I sat back on the couch, the breath knocked out of me.
She'd *left* him? And me – *The baby* – she never even used
my name. What kind of mother walks away from her own
child? My God, my poor dad, how had he coped – left
alone with a baby and losing his wife?

I sat up again. *Did* he lose her – did she really die? A
sick feeling spread through my stomach. Was all of it lies?
It made no sense though. If she left us, he might say she'd
died in her sleep, not that she'd been murdered. He couldn't
have been lying that night. Could he?

In a daze, I went into my dad's old bedroom and
switched on Ray's computer. The monitor's creaks and
groans were loud in the quiet house, and I wondered for a
moment if Ray would mind me using it. Part of me wanted
to be done before he got back, mostly because I wasn't
ready to explain what I'd just found.

After what felt like forever, I managed to connect to the
Internet, and opened a Google search page. I tried Hanne
McShane first and waited while the incredibly slow Internet
tried to churn out results. In the end, there were none, there
was nobody called Hanne McShane. I tried Hanne Karlsen.
This time, there were too many. Hanne Karlsen was not an
uncommon name in Denmark it seemed. With a knot in
my stomach, I tried "Hanne Karlsen" + "Murder".

It seemed to take even longer this time, and as I waited I could hear Ray's car coming up the driveway. It really didn't matter if I was still searching when he came in, of course it didn't, but somehow it did. I needed this to be mine before it was ours. As the first halting results flickered on to the screen, his car door opened and shut again. As story after story of Hanne Karlsen filled the space in front of me, his keys were jangling outside the bedroom window. And as he opened the front door and walked inside, I reached to switch off the monitor, but not before I'd seen what I was looking for.

Body found in Roskilde, Denmark: Fears of Serial Killer.

CHAPTER 25

That's how it started. Slow, frustrating searches on Ray's PC when he was out, until I eventually wrangled a laptop of my own from work. I learned the names of the other two Danish victims and got to know them while I got to know Hanne, in the morbid context of reading reports on her death. I discovered that she had been dead for a number of months by the time she was found, and her body had been unrecognisable, a victim of the elements and wildlife. They couldn't establish time of death and although the autopsy suggested she drowned, there was nothing conclusive. It was eerily similar to the case of Maja Pedersen who was found just a few weeks before Hanne went missing, also drowned, washed up in the sea. The other victim, Frederikke Frandsen, was strangled, not drowned but, like Hanne, found in woodland. Police pointed out that her body was discovered in Odense, on a different island entirely from where Maja and Hanne were found, but the public and the media were sure there was a connection.

I found a photo of Hanne's parents, and recognised them from the sketches I'd seen in the attic – two desperately sad faces stared out at me, and no matter how hard I tried, I couldn't see them as my grandparents. I felt sorry for them, but disconnected too.

Hanne had been their only child, and in early newspaper reports their pleas for her safe return were heart-wrenching. Later, when her body was found, they retreated, begging for privacy in their grief. I searched under their names but found nothing new in the intervening years – I couldn't tell if they were still alive, but hadn't found any death notices either. It seemed the newspapers and public had respected their wishes and they'd been allowed to stay out of the spotlight.

In a weird way, as I looked at their faces, I felt like a relay baton was being passed to me.

Despite knowing that Hanne had been murdered, reading about it for the first time changed things. It made it real, it sparked something. I inhaled stories about the investigation and trawled the internet to find out more, looking for similar deaths, slipping to stories that were nothing like Hanne's but impossible to ignore. I discovered cases in other Scandinavian countries and beyond, hopping from link to link, chasing virtual paths around Europe, and across to the United States. Some stories were familiar – Ted Bundy, the Zodiac Killer, the Yorkshire Ripper. But there were so many more I'd never heard of – literally hundreds and hundreds of unsolved murders and suspected serial killers all over the world. I started bookmarking stories that seemed connected, seeing tenuous patterns and links. The stories were horrifying but oddly compelling too, and I wondered at first if there was something wrong with me – how could I spend so much time reading up on these terrifying cases? I told nobody, not even Ray, at least at first.

Then one Wednesday evening, hunched over my laptop in my Dublin apartment, I discovered iSleuth, and finally understood I was just one of thousands of people with an interest in true crime. Most of the forum members were there to toss around ideas – others were more serious about it, actively trying to investigate disappearances, and some even had police contacts with whom they shared information. It was eye-opening and jaw-dropping and, in a surreal way, it was wonderful. I'd found my gang. I wasn't the only one.

As months ticked by, I read up on the Original Night Stalker and the Green River Killer. I read about children walking out of camp, and students walking out of bars, never seen again. I read the high-profile cases on which everyone had an opinion, and the lesser-known ones that were even sadder in their obscurity.

But however far and wide I read, I was always drawn back to Denmark. To Hanne. What had happened when she left the house in Købæk that night – who had she met? She was slight in build, I knew that from photos, but surely not so small that she could be stolen from her walk without some kind of struggle or witness? I studied the photos – the ones her parents had provided to the police. A slightly younger Hanne, her hair bright, her smile less so. Or maybe I was reading too much into old pictures of ghosts I never knew. In a notebook, I pieced together everything I could though there wasn't much. The news reports had been in print and only later added to the Internet, so there was no way to know if everything was copied over – presumably not.

What I *did* gather was that Hanne had been back in Købæk for a full month by the time she disappeared, and that she had stayed close to home, sleeping late and going to bed early. A friend, not named, had told a journalist she was worried that Hanne wasn't well, and there was speculation early in the search that she had taken her own life, but her parents were quoted in the same piece saying it wasn't true. Hanne was tired and a little run down, but not ill they said. On the night she disappeared, her parents had been out for a walk, something they did after supper every Sunday evening. When they arrived back to the neat two-bedroomed house on Damtoften, Hanne was not in bed as they expected, but dressed in a warm jacket, jeans, and boots. Her parents were surprised that she was going out for a walk but pleased too they said afterwards – this first inclination to go outside was seen as a good sign. The weather was cooler than usual for April, and her mother had suggested a hat and gloves, but Hanne said she wanted to feel the wind in her hair. Another good sign, they thought. She'd left the house just as darkness fell. Her father had given her a torch.

That night, her parents went to bed early as they always did. Hanne's mother left a slice of Kiksekage on the kitchen table for her daughter, and a note to say goodnight. The following morning, the cake was still there, but this in itself was not a red flag – Hanne had not been eating much since her return. It was only when her mother went to wake her mid-morning that she realised Hanne wasn't there. Even then, it didn't strike her that her daughter hadn't been home – she thought she'd gone out for another walk. Some of the newspapers commented on that – why hadn't her parents called the police more quickly? I felt sorry for them. Relatives of missing persons don't always react as we think they should – perhaps if they anticipated future newspaper columns, they would.

As the day wore on, Hanne's mother phoned around old friends and neighbours but nobody had seen her daughter. Hanne's father came home from work and went out to look for her, soon joined by other inhabitants of Damtoften, and in the early evening one of them found the torch at the entrance to a laneway near the house. Nobody could say if it was left there deliberately as she set out on her walk, or if it fell during some kind of struggle.

Hanne's parents called the police. Hanne was formally declared missing, but the local Inspector reassured her parents that she had more than likely gone of her own free will.

What seemed strange is that there was no mention of her husband or her baby daughter. Surely that would have been taken into consideration in the early days – wouldn't the papers have wondered if she'd just gone back to Ireland?

One of the papers did pick up on the story of Maja Pedersen, the twenty-three-year-old woman who had gone missing the same year. Her body had eventually washed up near Hellerup, just north of Copenhagen. There was nothing suspicious about the drowning itself, it could have been accidental it seemed, but the fact that she had been missing for some time beforehand drew media attention. The only similarity with Hanne at that stage was the age of both women, but in a country with a small population and low crime rate, the two cases stood out.

The search for Hanne continued, widening to cover all of Zealand and then to the other islands. Hanne's parents spoke regularly to the press, begging whoever had their daughter to let her go. Some elements of the press continued to speculate that she had simply walked away, right up until the day her body was found in a forested area near Roskilde. There had been an effort made to cover her up – someone had dug a hole in the ground, and put her body in it, then covered it with a corrugated-iron sheet from a nearby derelict cabin. Branches had been put over the metal sheet so that it wouldn't be seen, but a dog-walker with a particularly tenacious dog eventually made the discovery. The newspapers stopped saying, "simply walked away".

Official reports suggested she had drowned, though the nearest lake was five miles from her burial ground. So someone had moved her body at least that far, if not further – there was no way to determine exactly where her death had taken place. Her parents shut down, buried in grief, no longer speaking to the press, or anyone it seemed. I wondered again, were they still there? Still in Købæk mourning Hanne? And I thought back to something Jamie had asked – why weren't they curious about me? The more I thought about it, the less sense it made. Why didn't they come to find me, their only living link to Hanne?

CHAPTER 26

2018

Saturday morning was bright and sunny, making it hard to believe the earlier part of the week had been punctuated with red weather alerts and snow. As a nation, we stretched our legs, like caged animals set free, ready for fresh starts. Time to take action, I told myself, as I nosed the jeep out of the driveway. I'd found a small security firm based in Arklow with a good number of testimonials on their website, and had called to make an appointment.

Sheena, the consultant who welcomed me to her small office, was exactly the kind of person I needed to meet after six days of worry. Efficient, reassuring, but not pushy. When I told her why I was there, she was sympathetic, and I waited for her to tell me that's why I needed to spend thousands on security, but she didn't.

"An alarm would be a good idea," she said, "though of course I'm going to say that – it's my business. But there are lots of other things you can do to make your house less appealing to the opportunistic intruder. Do you have a gate at the end of your driveway?"

I nodded.

"And do you keep it shut at night?"

"No," I replied. "It's only waist-high so it wouldn't keep anyone out. And until this week, it hasn't crossed my mind that I needed to."

"You're absolutely right – if someone really wants to come in, they'll easily scale a gate, but any kind of barrier can be an effective deterrent. A gate of any size, a gate that's locked, not just closed. Lights on at night, motion sensor lights, lights on timers –" She stopped and laughed. "Don't worry, I'm not going to tell you that you need all of these, I'm just giving you a picture."

I nodded again. At that point, I'd have parted with any amount of cash for some peace of mind.

"Make sure your doors look solid – nothing is more attractive to a burglar than an old, weathered door that looks like you could open it with a good shoulder to it – you know what I mean?"

"Yeah, my front door is okay but I need to replace the back door."

"Go for one that doesn't have glass near the handle – it's too easy for someone to break it and reach in. What kind of lock is it?"

I wasn't sure.

"Some locks are easier to circumvent than others – you might want to check that," she went on. "Also, if you have a nice car, keep it out of sight if possible – do you have that option?"

"I have a half-decent jeep, and I keep it round the side."

She nodded her approval.

"Don't have lots of high shrubs and hedges – they offer protection to burglars making their way towards your home. What you want is a nice open space that will put them off. Now, will we go through some alarm options?"

"Sure."

"I'm getting a sense you're *not* sure though – is it the cost? We have some good finance options?"

"No, that's fine. It's the fear really – I live on my own, and when I imagine a burglar alarm going off in the middle of the night, it freaks the hell out of me!" I laughed, but it came out high and empty. "Like, what would I actually do if it happened, other than die of fright?"

"The only thing you need to do is sit tight. The alarm isn't there so that you can get ready to take on an intruder – it's there to ward him off. As soon as it sounds, he's going to be gone like a shot. No matter how nice your laptop or your iPad or your grandmother's diamond ring, it's not worth getting caught. You see?"

I nodded. It made sense. At least if it was a burglar. But someone inexplicably looking in my bedroom window? Without knowing the why of it, it all became less predictable.

She went on to explain different options for connecting to the gardaí and I wondered which guards would make it out to my middle-of-nowhere house and how long it would take. Again I thought of my little apartment in Dublin – I hadn't had an alarm there either, but I never needed one in crowded city-centre safety, high off the ground.

I left an hour later having signed up for a monitored alarm to be installed in three weeks' time and holding brochures for motion-sensor lights and security cameras. It wouldn't help that night or the night after, but as I drove back to Arklow to buy some proper bedroom curtains, I did feel a whole lot lighter.

When I woke on Sunday morning I was confused at first – the light cast through my new blue-grey curtains was different to the recent bin-bag blackout. It had taken a ridiculous amount of time to get them up the night before, and I'd fallen asleep sitting up in bed reading the book Linda had recommended, the one about the lonely woman. Linda was never subtle in school either. Although thinking about it, it was a long time since she'd sent me a book recommendation.

There was something unexpectedly cathartic about the new curtains – perhaps this was the line in the sand, I thought, as I crumpled the black sacks and stuffed them in the bin. Outside, the sky was granite-grey and promising rain – a day to stay indoors. As the first drops began to fall, I leafed through the literature the security consultant had given me, and my scribbled notes on how to deter burglars: *Gate, doors solid, alarm, no high shrubs, lights on timers.*

Day one, and I'd already managed to leave the gate open, despite what she'd said. Shaking my head, I slipped on a raincoat, and opened the front door. Sure enough, the gate was open. So much for lines in the sand, I thought, as I stepped out into the rain. Then I stopped, my eye drawn to something on the ground. Something that hadn't been there the night before. A huge letter R, chalked on the path in front of the door. Stark and white on the grey stone beneath. My skin went cold as I stared at it. What did it mean? And who had drawn it there – who had been crouched outside my front door while I was asleep inside?

CHAPTER 27

Even as I watched, the rain was doing its work, washing the chalk off the ground. I stood, mesmerized, for a moment, then rushed indoors to get my phone. Fumbling to open the camera, I took a photo of the letter, then another, and another. As I clicked, the rain grew heavier, and the chalk outline grew lighter, until eventually it was as though it had never been there at all.

I thought about phoning the Garda Station and emailing the photo but, no matter what way I rehearsed it in my head, it sounded daft. A chalk drawing of the letter R wasn't threatening, and if someone I didn't know answered the phone, it would be hard to explain.

In the end, I drove to the station, where I was greeted by an unfamiliar face. The guard, who looked like he was still in school, seemed relieved to fetch Garda Maguire for me.

Patrick invited me through to the back, asking his young colleague to bring us two teas, and we sat in a cramped office, Patrick behind a paper-strewn desk, me in a bright-orange plastic chair. Maybe Geraldine had picked the furniture – functional, no frills.

Patrick picked up a pen, an expectant look on his face.

"More footprints?" he asked, and in that moment I gave thanks to whatever deity looks after such things that I'd already reported everything that had happened. In context, the new development might seem less silly. I passed him my phone, open on the first and clearest of the photos.

"What is it?" he asked.

"When I looked out this morning, I found this drawn on the ground outside my front door – the letter R, in chalk."

Patrick blinked. I rushed to clarify.

"Obviously not a worry in its own right – but it means someone has been at my house again during the night."

Patrick tilted his head and turned the phone sideways.

"Is it definitely a letter R?"

"Yeah. Hard to see on screen but it was clearer in real life."

"It reminds me of when we were kids," Patrick said, still looking at the photo. "We used to draw hopscotch in the front driveway and my mam would go mad because she said it looked common." He smiled at the memory, and shook his head. "Sorry, I don't mean to trivialise it. But could it have been kids? Any chance it was there yesterday and you missed it?"

"No. I'd have seen it. But, anyway, no kids are going to come all the way up to my house – it's too far from everything. And, like, what would be the point?"

"I suppose to play a prank on you or freak you out – maybe word went out about the footprints. Or maybe it was kids all along?"

"No, the footprints were big – not a kid's shoe."

"Jesus, you should see some of the kids these days,

137

Marianne. Huge. Different generation. Not so much the kids around here, but in my old station in Store Street they were all towering over me. Wouldn't have minded a bit of chalk drawings to deal with then, easier than the kind of things they were getting up to."

He looked wistful for a minute and I wondered who he was trying to convince. Poor guy – over his time in Carrickderg, my footprint case was probably about as exciting as it had been.

I threw up my hands. "Look, I know, I get it – a chalk drawing isn't exactly threatening, and it's gone now. But it's all making me really, really uneasy."

"Well, if not kids, could it have been Alan or Jamie? Playing a particularly slow game of hangman?"

Patrick laughed at his own joke, but I stiffened. Hangman. It stirred a memory – the case in Denmark, or was it Holland, where a woman found a hangman drawing in her driveway, and wound up dead a few days later.

Patrick must have seen something in my face.

"What is it?"

I started to speak then stopped to clear my throat. I tried again.

"It just reminded me of a story I read online, about a woman who found a chalked hangman in her front yard. She didn't think much of it, but she was found dead shortly afterwards."

Patrick raised his eyebrows, and I played back what I'd just said, realising how random it sounded – like an urban legend.

"I was reading up on the Blackwood Strangler, you see," I went on, "and until recently they thought all his victims were in and around the same area."

Patrick's eyebrows stayed up.

"I was looking at articles about murders like those East Midlands' ones, but outside the area. And even outside the UK." I stopped and waited.

"And?" he prompted.

"And there are some. Victims who had reported finding odd things in their gardens and on their doorsteps, and victims who had seen footprints."

The eyebrows went down. A sigh escaped.

"Marianne, I understand why you're rattled, but listen – there's absolutely no way some serial killer from England is over here stalking you in Wicklow. You're probably freaked out from reading about the cases and seeing footprints yourself, then putting two and two together and coming up with ten. Have you heard of apophenia? It's where people mistakenly see connections between random, unrelated things." If he'd reached out and patted me on the head, he couldn't have sounded more patronising. "Is there any chance the stories on the Internet made you think you saw things – like, if you fell asleep reading an article about a serial killer then dreamed you saw one at your own window? Or like with the footprints – could they have been your own prints and you just forgot?"

I stood up, wiping imaginary dust off my sleeve.

"No, definitely not my prints. I'm a size 5. Those prints looked more like an 11 or 12. You still have the photos I sent you, right?"

He nodded vehemently. "Absolutely. We're still actively investigating. But I don't think you need to worry about any serial killers from England coming over here."

Suddenly I felt like a character in an Enid Blyton book, trying to make Mr Goon the Policeman understand there was something wrong. Only I wasn't a ten-year-old kid, I was older than the bloody policeman. Forcing a smile, I agreed he was probably right, and said goodbye.

As I pushed through the door, the young guard from the front desk was coming through with two mugs of tea, his face falling as he realised he'd failed at his one job that morning.

I was still cross when I arrived at Delaneys' to get a coffee, only to find the doors locked. Bloody Sunday opening hours, I thought, looking at my watch.

"Bit early for a drink, isn't it?" said a voice behind me.

I turned to see Jamie grinning at me.

"Yeah, the double whiskey breakfast will have to wait," I said, giving him a half-smile back.

"I was going to grab a coffee in the Wooden Spoon. Want to try there? No whiskey on the menu, but their cappuccinos are alright?"

I nodded and fell into step as we made our way to the café.

"So what's up?" he asked as we took a table, and suddenly it was just like the old days, hunkered in the den in my garden.

"It's going to sound ridiculous."

"Try me."

So I did.

We ordered coffees, and I told him about the footprints and the rag doll and the chalk drawing and the face I thought I saw and the knock I was almost sure I'd heard, and I waited for him to tell me it was probably nothing.

"Wow, weird," he said, as our coffees arrived. "I mean, I'm sure there's a reasonable explanation, but it would be good to know who it was and move on."

I nodded. "That's it exactly. In one way, it's no big deal, no harm done. But for peace of mind, I'd like to know who it is. And I can't help worrying he's going to try to get into the house. Like, would I even know if he did?"

"Wouldn't your alarm go off?"

"I don't have one. It's ordered but not in yet. So if he had a way to get in . . . Jesus, I could walk into my house with no idea he was there waiting for me." My heart was thumping now.

"Okay. First, he can't get in. Your doors are locked, right?"

I nodded.

"But for peace of mind, couldn't you do something like leave things a certain way so if they're disturbed you'll notice? Or put thread across your hall or tape around your windows? If it's where it should be each time you get home, you know you're okay."

I laughed. "It sounds like something from a mystery novel."

"Well, in fairness, no better woman to solve a mystery, right?"

Did he know about the web sleuthing? My cheeks flushed.

"I remember it so well," he continued. "You were going to be a detective, I was going to be an artist, and Linda was going to be a fashion designer."

I sat back and smiled. "In a way, we all did what we set out to do – you did your graphic design course, Linda is apparently a dab hand at knitting jumpers for her kids and, honestly, working in IT feels exactly like being a detective sometimes – usually trying to work out what the hell the Ops team did this time."

Jamie smiled but there was something not quite real about it and I wondered if I'd hit a nerve.

"How many kids does Linda have?"

"Four under five – I don't know how she does it. The youngest is only a few months old."

"God, I can't imagine Linda with four kids! Is she the same as ever or has she changed much?"

Good question. I had to think for a second before answering.

"I guess now that you say it, she *has* changed. I didn't really notice it happening, but she's kind of drifted away from me in the last while. That's quite sad actually, now that I say it out loud."

"I imagine it's busy with four kids. No doubt she'll be back to her old self soon."

"I wonder . . . we don't have so much in common anymore. She's talking about sleep deprivation and I'm talking about work, and we're not really finding common ground. You remember we used to sit in the den for hours and hours – what the hell did we talk about?"

"Usually how annoying Sorcha Riordan was, who was going in your little black book, and how you were going to be the greatest detective since Hercule Poirot."

"Actually," I said, not entirely sure if it was a good idea, "I do still have an interest in detectivey stuff."

He sat forward, his face brightening. "Oh, yeah?"

"Okay, don't think I'm a weirdo or anything, but I started getting interested in true crime about ten or twelve years ago, and then found out there are loads of other people who are too, and lots of them are on a forum called iSleuth."

I stopped to gauge his reaction.

"Go on," he said, leaning closer.

"We read up on real-life cases and we share theories and . . . it probably sounds a bit mad . . ."

Jamie was rapt. "No, that sounds cool! God, what did we do before the Internet, especially out here in the middle of nowhere?"

We sat in my kitchen chatting with Mrs Townsend, I wanted to say, until we didn't anymore.

"I suppose we used to read books," I said instead, "and talked to people on the phone instead of just WhatsApp'ing them."

"Well, you still read books – you always have one with you," he said, nodding towards my bag on the floor. "I just sit staring at the TV with yer man glowering over everything and nothing in the corner, like Victor Meldrew crossed with Jesse James' awkward second cousin."

I snorted a laugh.

"Oh God, you should see him," Jamie went on, warming to his theme, "sitting muttering over everything he sees on his iPad. Grumbling about politicians and banks and foreigners, and everything is *political correctness gone mad*. Then he goes out to take the dog for a walk, which is code for chain-smoking ten cigarettes, only he won't do it in front of me because the doctor told him he has to quit. How he thinks I don't notice the stench off his clothes is beyond me."

"Where does he walk the dog – just around the farm?" I asked, in an Oscar-winningly casual tone.

"Ah no, you don't think it was him, do you?"

Not Oscar-winning then.

"What?"

"You're thinking of the footprints and the drawing. I know he's an eejit and still holding grudges against

143

everyone who's ever crossed him, but his dispute was with Ray, never with you."

I tore a little piece off my napkin and studied it.

"Seriously, Marianne, I'm not defending him because he's my da or anything. I just don't think it's his style."

I looked up. "Ah here, of course it's his style! Remember the dead fox?"

Jamie's face changed. "Remember the dead chickens?"

My eyes dropped again. "I'm not looking to rake over old fights. I'm just saying that creeping up to my house in the middle of the night is not beyond him, you know?"

Jamie sighed. "I know. I don't think it's him though – there's no reason for it. But I'll keep an eye out – how about that?"

I nodded, glad to have someone in my corner.

"About Ray . . . I wanted to ask you about the other day, when you thought you saw him in the bookshop?"

"Yeah, what do you think from the picture – is it him?"

"I think it looks very like him," I said carefully.

"I didn't go over. I just took the photo while he was looking at books. And I didn't hear his voice. But I'd be, like, eighty per cent sure it was him. I wonder what he's doing here?"

I had absolutely no idea. And after what he did, and the way things ended, I needed to believe he'd never make his way back to Carrickderg.

CHAPTER 28

2007

It was just after our second Christmas together, a Saturday night in mid-January, when Ray brought it up. We were on the couch together, me on my laptop, Ray scribbling in his notebook. I sensed he had stopped writing, and looked up from my screen to find him staring at me.

"What?"

"I have a confession."

"Go on?" I said, suddenly chilled.

"I needed to search for something online when you were out this morning and my PC wouldn't connect to the Internet. So I borrowed your laptop."

I swallowed, and shrugged in what I hoped was a *what's mine is yours* way.

"And when I opened Google and started to type, your recent searches came up."

He looked down at his notebook and started to read out loud.

"*Danish serial killers. Dina Karlsen. Unsolved murders + Købæk. Serial killers who drown victims.*" He looked up at me. "Anything I should be worried about?"

I said nothing.

"Is it some kind of project? Who's Dina Karlsen?"

Laying my laptop on the coffee table, I got up to take the photo of my parents from the shelf and sat back down.

"Right, here goes," I said. "I told you my mother died when I was a baby – that's true. But there's more to it. She had gone back to Denmark, and it wasn't for a visit like I always thought. I found out a couple of months ago that she had left my dad and me."

Ray looked up from the photo. "Oh. I'm sorry."

I waved it away.

"But why are you googling serial killers?"

My stomach churned. "That's the other bit I didn't tell you. She didn't just die, she was killed."

His eyes widened.

"See, it's weird, isn't it? It sounds so dramatic. It *is* dramatic. *Urgh*, I don't know how I feel about it."

"Jesus Christ. That's huge. Your mother was *murdered*?"

"Yeah. I found out when I was twelve – Jamie blurted it out after an argument at school, and my dad confirmed it that night. Up until then I thought she had died in her sleep."

"Your dad lied to you all those years?"

I looked at him. "Yes, but to protect me from something absolutely horrific. Anyone would do the same." It came out sounding defensive.

He held up his hands. "Of course. I get that. Do you want to talk about what happened to her? Did they catch the guy?"

"No, but all sorts of cases are being reopened because of advances in forensics, and I'm hoping something new comes up in her case too."

"So what happened to her?" he asked, his eyes wide.

And I told him. Everything about the day she disappeared,

and about Maja and Frederikke, and the similarities, and the differences. And the other cases – the ones from other countries, the paths I'd followed, the virtual snakes and ladders, zigzagging across the continent.

"You don't think the person who killed your mother was also killing people in other parts of the world, do you?" he asked when I stopped.

"No. I mean, maybe. Look, I don't know. It's ridiculous, I get that, but the more I read, the more patterns I see. And if none of the cases are linked at all, in a way that's worse, isn't it – if there aren't just a few killers out there, but literally hundreds, killing for sport. Isn't that terrifying when you think about it?"

"Sure, but in reality the figures are tiny compared to the population of the world. Reading about it compulsively is going to blur your judgement – it feels like it's more prevalent than it is. Right? Maybe you need to cut back and give yourself a break?"

He was right, of course, but I wasn't ready to stop, so instead changed the subject, going for that good old Irish reliable: the weather.

"God, it's freezing, even with this blanket. Is the heat definitely on?" I got up to feel the radiator for good measure, and stopped to look out at the swirling snow. I hugged myself and sat back down. "Wouldn't like to be out in that tonight."

Ray looked at me, a sly expression on his face.

"What?" I asked.

"Did you know Alan has two guys living in his outhouses?"

"Yeah, he does that every winter – lets people stay there if they've nowhere else to stay. Fair play to him. Hell of a lot better than sleeping rough in that weather."

147

"Yes, but he *charges* them. He's not doing it because he's such a philanthropist."

I sat up straighter. "Oh! I didn't realise he was charging them. I thought it was his good deed, to make up for being such a prick most of the time."

"I know, right? I was passing yesterday morning, and met one of them. Young guy, down on his luck, landlord put up the rent and he had nowhere to go. He's still getting welfare he told me, but it's not enough to cover rent anywhere else. He can just about afford what Alan is charging. Imagine taking money off someone to live in a shed. He told me there's another guy too, older than him, and not in great shape health-wise. Doesn't stop Alan squeezing every dime he can get."

I shook my head. Alan really was an asshole. I wondered what Jamie thought of it, or if he knew his dad was charging rent.

"And imagine being so badly off you have to live in a shed," Ray was saying.

"The sheds aren't actually too bad," I said. "We used to play in them when we were kids. They're not like sheds for animals, they're properly insulated – Jamie was planning to use one as a home office, I remember. He had it all worked out – he was going set up his art studio there, with a desk and a phone and a bit of space between him and his dad."

"Sure, but they're not proper living abodes," Ray said, sounding pompous.

He said nothing for a minute, his eyes glazing over. Then he asked if he could borrow my laptop. And unlike me, he knew to clear his search history. Otherwise I would have known exactly what he did that night.

CHAPTER 29

As it turned out, while he was good at hiding his search history, Ray was less accomplished at covering his tracks, which is why Alan came banging on our door one freezing cold morning in early February, shouting about snitches. This time, we didn't let him in. We stood in the kitchen, staring at one another, waiting for him to go away. After a minute, I realised that Ray's confused look wasn't quite as genuine as mine.

"Ray, what's he on about – what did you do?"

"I didn't think he'd get to see our names on the complaint!" Ray whispered, though how Alan would hear us above his own shouting and banging, I don't know.

"What complaint?"

"To the County Council. It's illegal to rent out sheds or outhouses – you can't have people living in them. Did you know that? Completely unsanitary and a risk to public health." There was that pompous voice again.

"*Ray! For fuck's sake! You reported him?* Jesus Christ, he was giving shelter to people who had nowhere else to stay – who cares if it's illegal or if he was making a few quid on it. What is *wrong* with you?"

"The law is the law, and people who break it can't

149

expect sympathy when they're found out." He folded his arms, his mouth set, absolutely certain he was right.

"You know something, I hate to say this, but you can't just waltz in here and go stomping all over people."

"Waltz in here – where's *here*? Your town? Your country? Is that it – because I'm not from here, I need to sit quietly and keep my mouth shut?"

"*That's not what I mean, and you know it*," I hissed. "There are rules and laws everywhere, but there are unwritten rules too, and you know what one of ours is? Don't have a fucking raging feud with your fucking next-door neighbour because guess what? *Nobody fucking wins!*"

I stormed out of the kitchen, through to the bedroom and, ignoring Alan's hammering and Ray's indignation, slammed the door behind me.

And, of course, it wasn't the end of it.

A week later, Alan arrived back at our house, this time carrying a black sack. I was in the kitchen attempting a first-ever roast lamb, so left Ray to deal with it – Ray went outside to talk to him and closed the door behind him, which was what made me curious.

Through the living-room window I could see Ray and Alan on our front lawn. Arguing. I strained to hear but couldn't make out what they were saying. Alan was holding up the black sack, and Ray kept shaking his head, until eventually Alan threw down the bag and stormed off.

Ray stood for a minute, then tipped the contents of the bag on the grass. It looked like old clothes but it was hard to tell. As I watched, he reached into his pocket and pulled something out, then hunkered down at the pile.

Seconds later, I realised he'd set fire to them.

"*Ray, what are you doing?*" I shouted, opening the front door. "*You can't just set a fire in the garden!*"

"It's only a small fire and nobody's going to see it."

"But why are you burning Alan's things? Why did he leave them here?"

"Because he's doing everything he can to piss me off, and because this is the last thing he's expecting me to do."

"What have you done now? Did you damage that stuff? Was he trying to get you to replace it?" None of it made any sense.

He ignored me.

"Ray! if you burn his stuff instead, he's just going to come back at you – why do you keep doing this?"

Ray turned, an odd look on his face.

"Believe me, Alan won't be back for these."

I stood by helplessly while the clothes burnt.

Ray watched until the fire was reduced to a smoking pile, then stood and walked towards the house.

"How's that lamb coming along?" he asked as he passed me and went indoors.

I shook my head. Why on earth would Alan dump his stuff here? As retaliation went, it was hardly in dead fox or dead chicken territory. I walked down to the smouldering heap and stamped on it. The clothes were charred and indistinguishable – it was impossible to tell what they had been five minutes earlier. I kicked at the ashes, looking for signs of flames, annoyed more than anything at the damage to the grass beneath.

Then I spotted a piece of paper – burnt across the top but still in one piece. I picked it up and realised it was part of a photograph. A couple and a baby, sitting on a brown check couch. The baby was on the woman's knee, but the couple were only visible from chest-height down – their heads and shoulders burnt off in the fire. It was eerie to look at. The woman's cream blouse and check skirt were straight from the eighties and the man was dressed in what looked like an army uniform. Jamie's mother holding Jamie as a baby perhaps? I had never heard that Alan had been in the army, but maybe he had?

"*Marianne, I think the lamb's burning!*" Ray called from the front door with no sense of irony. "*Do you want me to take it out?*"

I stamped on the ashes, stuffed the photo in my pocket, and walked back to the house.

Predictably, Alan did not let things go. In May, a few weeks before the second anniversary of my dad's death, Ray and I went out for Sunday brunch in the Carrickderg Arms. The food was usually kind of *meh* there, but it was the one place in town with outdoor tables, and on a sunny Sunday morning that trumped everything. I had a copy of an old Barbara Vine book with me and Ray had his current notebook along with a stack of Sunday newspapers.

"What's the book about?" he asked, picking it up while I read the menu I already knew by heart. Irish breakfast. Smaller Irish breakfast. Hearty Irish breakfast. Vegetarian Irish breakfast.

"It's about a guy who dies, and his family discover all sorts of secrets about him. I read it when I was about sixteen, but I don't remember any of the story. Weird how that happens, isn't it?"

Ray nodded in a way that told me he didn't entirely agree. He only read unforgettable books. And wrote unforgettable books.

"How's the manuscript going?" I asked, nodding towards his notebook. He always used the same ones – brown-leather covers, gold lettering, shipped in from somewhere back home.

"Slower than my agent would like, but getting there," he said, opening the notebook, closing it again, and picking up a newspaper instead.

We read until the food arrived, soaking up the early summer sun, and everything might have been okay if I hadn't decided to go down to the bench in front of the fountain after we'd eaten. Caught in the romance of remembering our first encounter there, Ray came with me. We sat, faces to the sun, talking about that day: the mingling of grief and newness, the end of one stage and the start of another. That was Ray's interpretation. I found it difficult to think beyond the funeral, and wondered if that meant something about our relationship.

"I can picture us here when we're old," he said, as we watched the spray. "I'll be writing books and you'll be reading, and we'll sit on this bench, the two most content people in Ireland."

I said nothing, wondering about the prickling feeling in my stomach.

"Doesn't that sound good?" Ray was saying. "To grow old together here?"

"Absolutely," I said eventually, because really, what else could I say?

But there was something not quite right with the picture, and as I watched the spray fall to the water below, I felt a restlessness that was new and unsettling.

I don't know how long we were there, but when we walked back to our table our breakfast plates had been cleared, and someone had left menus on top of the stack of newspapers.

"There you are now. More coffee? Dessert?" came a voice from behind, and Ray ordered two cappuccinos, no dessert.

"Actually, can I take a mint tea, and I'll try the apple crumble," I said, picking up my book.

It was only when we had paid the bill that Ray realised the notebook was missing. We searched on the ground, and down at the bench, though he was certain he hadn't taken it with him. As the search continued, Ray grew more and more frantic, muttering under his breath.

"Was there a lot in it?" I asked, worried now too.

"It was nearly full," he said curtly. "About five chapters of the book. Jesus Christ."

"Had you typed any of it up?"

"No," he said under his breath, going inside the hotel to ask at the bar.

I followed him in, and said I'd check the car, though we both knew the notebook had been with him at the table.

In the car park, there was just one other car, and beyond it I could see something dark on the ground. A small, smouldering pile. I ran the last steps, knowing then exactly what it was, shouting for Ray. I reached down to pick it up, but it was too hot. I pulled my hand away, jamming it under my arm to quench the sting.

"*Ray!*" I shouted again, pulling off my jacket.

"Did you find it?" His voice floated across the from the hotel doorway.

"*Just come!*" I yelled, throwing my jacket on the pile on the ground, stamping on it.

Ray arrived beside me, realisation spreading across his

face. He lifted the jacket. Underneath, in a charred mess, the cover relatively intact but the pages destroyed, was his notebook. He reached down to grab it, but it was still too hot. He stamped on it and kicked it to the side, out of the ashes. Pulling the sleeve of his jacket down over his hand, he tried again. But it was just a shell now, a cover with no insides. The words were gone.

He sat on the ground, shaking his head.

I tried to think of something to say. Nothing came.

"Five chapters." His voice was a hoarse whisper.

"Oh Ray, I'm so sorry. Maybe you'll remember, if you rewrite it soon?" I tried, knowing it wasn't that simple.

"Weeks and weeks of work. Jesus Christ." He looked up at me. "It was him."

"Who?" Though I knew who.

"*Alan fucking Crowley*. Who else?"

"Did you see him?"

"No, but I bet he was here," he said, getting off the ground, and storming back across the car park into the hotel.

As I picked up my charred jacket, a memory of the pile of smouldering clothes flashed through my mind. Had Alan burnt Ray's notebook in revenge for the impromptu fire? But then if he tipped the contents of the sack in our garden, why did he care what happened to them? None of it made any sense. I followed Ray inside.

In the dark interior of the hotel, Ray had pulled together a smile for the barman.

"I thought I saw our neighbour Alan Crowley here earlier – did I imagine that?"

"No, you didn't – Alan's in every Sunday morning for the fry. Extra pudding, no tomatoes."

155

"Right. Thank you, I'll check with him in case he saw what happened my notebook." Ray turned to me, frozen smile fixed in place. "Will we go check with Alan now, honey?"

"Well, let's chat about it," I said, "before we go rushing off anywhere."

In silence, we walked to the car.

Inside, as he turned the key in the ignition, I put my hand on his arm.

"Ray, let's think about this for a minute. You have no proof Alan did it. You can't start accusing him."

"It didn't stop him accusing me of reporting him to the County Council!"

"Eh, yeah, but he *knew* you did it. And that's kind of the point too. Don't you see that if you keep provoking, he'll keep coming back? You've lost weeks of work now, and you can't even prove it was him. What's to stop him burning something else next time? This has gone way out of hand."

"Marianne, you don't understand. I can't just recreate the words. I'll never get them back. What he's done is *criminal*."

"But you burnt his stuff in our garden – isn't that the same thing?"

"That was different. You can't compare a pile of old clothes to precious weeks of work!"

I tried another tack.

"Okay, you're right, taking your notebook and destroying it is clearly criminal. So let's go down the proper channels – let's report what happened to the guards and let them look into it?"

He sat for a moment, shoulders tight, staring straight ahead. Then he slumped against the seat.

"Fine. Let's report him."

I let out a breath as Ray turned off the engine and we got out of the car to walk to the Garda Station.

Maybe now it would come to an end, I thought, and somewhere high above us, the gods of such things laughed heartily.

CHAPTER 30

After that, things calmed down, or so it seemed. Reporting his suspicions about Alan to the police let some air out for Ray. He was less tense. More focussed. In fact, he was writing faster than ever, spurred on by something more than his ever-patient agent's intermittent emails.

We saw Alan out and about but said nothing. We just carried on as normal. Sometimes I caught Alan looking at Ray, perhaps wondering why he didn't say anything, and that gave me some satisfaction. *Don't react*, my dad had always said when I came home with occasional stories of schoolyard slagging. *That's what they're looking for.* And mostly I didn't – Linda and I put their names in our little black book instead and came up with deadly revenge plots that never made it past our overactive imaginations.

If I'd been less involved in my own world, I might have paid more attention to what Ray was doing, but I was spending every night on my laptop at that point, reading about cold cases and new forensic developments. There was never anything new on Hanne's case, and I'd become tired of futile searches, so I'd set up Google Alerts for key names – Hanne Karlsen, Dina Karlsen, and her husband, my grandfather, Erik Karlsen.

Which is how one Saturday morning in November, I got an automatic email to tell me all three names had shown up in a news article.

Fingers scrabbling across laptop keys, I clicked into the website. It was a feature in a UK newspaper about podcasts and the rising interest in true crime, and it covered famous cold cases from countries throughout Europe. The Danish case referenced was Hanne's. There were up-to-date photos of Hanne's parents – Dina was in her sixties by then but looked ten years older, and Erik, who was seventy, had also been hollowed out by grief and time. They were still living in the same house in Købæk, according to the piece, unable to leave the place they last saw their daughter. Police were reopening the cases, according to the article, retesting evidence from all three Danish crime-scenes, to establish if there was a connection. I sat back on the couch, staring at the screen, at the images of my grandparents' faces. Lined with grief, but maybe hopeful too – perhaps they'd finally get some answers?

And suddenly, more clearly than anything, I knew I wanted to meet them. To find out more about Hanne, to understand why she left. To connect.

Back then, they didn't want to see the grandchild who would remind them of their dead daughter, but maybe now it would help them. Feeling only mildly self-conscious, I stared at their faces, and whispered a message: *"I'm coming."*

Ray, of course, wanted to come too. To look after me, he said.

"I'm not a child," I told him. "I'm twenty-four. It's just a week in Denmark, to get to know my grandparents."

"And look into your mother's murder, right?"

I threw up my hands. "There isn't much I can do, but yeah, of course I'm curious. And it'll be interesting to see where she lived, and where she went for a walk that night."

Ray still wasn't keen. I was his *muse*, he said, he needed me there. I laughed it off, ignoring the uncomfortable twitch in my gut. Ray didn't laugh at all. Nevertheless, within days, I'd negotiated a week off work, and booked a flight to Copenhagen.

The next question was whether or not to contact Dina and Erik – would they find a way to avoid me if they knew I was coming? I decided against forewarning. I booked a room in a hostel in Købæk, two streets away from my grandparents' house, packed a bag, and on a Sunday afternoon in late November I flew to Denmark.

CHAPTER 31

The hostel in Købæk was nicer than the word "hostel" suggests – a sprawling redbrick building with beach access, though with the temperature heading for freezing I didn't expect to spend much time on the strand. Hurrying across the courtyard through early-evening darkness, I let myself into my temporary home. I had a room to myself, small, clean, sparse. The exposed brick walls were painted a shrill white, and I couldn't decide if the overall look was Scandinavian-chic or just a bit too stark for a cold climate. There was an ensuite bathroom, tiny, practical, no frills. Anyway, it wasn't a holiday, I reminded myself as I unpacked into the small, white door-less wardrobe.

I'd had an expensive sandwich in Copenhagen Airport while waiting for my bus to Købæk and, too tired to deal with exploring the rest of the hostel, I climbed into the narrow bed, texted Ray to say I'd arrived, and within minutes fell fast asleep.

When I woke on Monday morning it was still dark, and I wondered when I'd get to see Denmark in daylight. Tentatively, I tested the shower, expecting a lukewarm drip,

161

ANDREA MARA

but a stream of hot water gushed into the tray, forcing me to reassess my opinion of hostels, and this small win lifted my spirits, temporarily at least.

Fifteen minutes later, with a woolly hat clamped down over still-wet hair, I made the short but bitterly cold walk across to the main building. Inside, I found a common area, where groups of backpackers and solo-travellers were chatting or reading, and a dining room with a breakfast buffet. Suddenly starving, I loaded my plate with fresh bread, cold meat, and cheese. Two cups of coffee and a decent breakfast later, the sun had started to creep across the dining-room floor, and I was feeling decidedly better about the trip.

Just after nine, I set off with a map. I knew from news articles that Dina and Erik Karlsen lived on a street called Damtoften, in house Number 42. Following the map, within ten minutes I was at the top of the street. It was quiet at that time of the morning, not a car on the road – perhaps everyone had already left for work and school. Trees lined both sides of the street, and the houses were set back from the road, behind high hedges. It all looked very suburban and normal.

Approaching Number 42, I slowed. My head was full of cotton wool as I took my first look at Hanne's childhood home. Low and wide, deep yellow in colour, a single-storey house, with two front windows – like eyes, hooded by a deeply slanted roof. The front door was solid wood with no glass panels, and no welcome mat outside. The front garden was neat, and through the open garage door, I could see a small red car. Someone was home.

I stood outside the front gate, pulling my scarf over my

162

mouth, with no idea what to do next – not yet ready to approach them but unable to walk away. Then the decision was made for me, in a small action that changed the course of everything to come. The Karlsens' front door opened, and a woman I recognised as Dina stepped outside to sweep her porch. Instinctively I moved back, but there was nowhere to go. She looked at me, eyebrows up in an unspoken *Can I help you?* A wave of nausea churned in my stomach. I'd gone over dozens of ways to introduce myself, but none of them seemed quite right.

She stopped sweeping and stood still, eying me up and down. I tried a smile but she didn't smile back. She said something in Danish, and suddenly I wondered if she could speak English – it hadn't dawned on me that my already awkward introduction would have a language barrier. People were always saying everyone in Scandinavia could speak English, but maybe I shouldn't have taken it so literally.

"I'm sorry, I don't speak Danish. Do you speak English?"

Her eyes narrowed. "Yes. Are you a journalist?"

And before a more sensible answer could come out of my mouth, the word hit the air. "Yes."

She nodded. "I have already spoken to a journalist – you can read everything I have to say in that article – it is on the Internet, I believe," she said in precise, accented English.

She began sweeping again, and I walked towards her.

"I don't need much of your time, but I'd really like to speak to you."

"Why does a journalist who is not from Denmark care about this – where do you come from?"

And without hesitation, the next lie jumped out of my mouth. "New Jersey."

163

She leaned on her brush. "Do you have a card? What is your name?"

"Sorry, I don't have a card but my name is Linda." Where were these words coming from? "I'd really like to include you in the article I'm writing. Maybe a wider audience, outside Denmark, would be a good thing?"

"Why? The killer is here in Denmark, this is where it will be solved, if it is ever solved."

"But what if he's not? There are cases like this all over Europe. Maybe there are links."

"Really? Cases of kidnapping and drowning? I do not know of any."

I shook my head. "No, not the same, but there are similarities. Patterns. Isn't it possible the killer went somewhere else too? If he was here all this time, would he have killed three women in one year, then stopped?"

"Not everyone believes it is a serial killer. You do?"

I nodded.

She stared at me, her blue eyes assessing, deciding. Something seemed to shift.

"Come in. We can talk for thirty minutes, then I must go." She turned to open the door. "I go to her grave every day."

I followed her inside, scrambling to work out how to extract myself from the lie but not ready to tell the truth. She led me through to a bright kitchen, and pointed at a low grey sofa. I sat, while she went to the fridge and took out a bottle.

"Water? Coffee?" she asked.

"Whichever is handiest."

She looked confused.

"Water is good, thanks," I said.

Putting a glass of water on the coffee table in front of me, she sat on the adjacent sofa, with her hands clasped on her lap, and waited.

Jesus, what was I doing here? I opened my handbag and pulled out a tiny notebook I used for shopping lists, hoping it looked like something a journalist might carry. I couldn't find a pen. Watching me, she plucked one from a shelf underneath the coffee table, and handed it to me.

"Thank you. I won't take up much of your time, but could you tell me about Hanne – what was she like growing up?"

Her face changed then, the tightness of her mouth slipped to something lighter.

"Oh! Usually journalists only want to hear of that night – what happened, her last words to us, how we felt. Nobody ever wants to hear about Hanne."

She settled back on the couch and began to reminisce.

As she talked about Hanne in school, her friends, her studies, I took an occasional note, but mostly I just listened in a kind of suspended reality. This woman in front of me was my grandmother. I looked for a resemblance, but could see none. She had poker-straight, very dark grey hair, cut short, just below her ears. Her eyes were a light blue colour, not unlike mine. Her grey blouse was smart and well cut, with a string of pearls nestling in the collar, and a brooch that looked like a little golden dove pinned to her pocket. Other than that, she wore no jewellery. Her trousers were dark grey, and her shoes were flat, black, and sensible. She was wholly unremarkable, and I couldn't take my eyes off her.

"I don't have so much time today but it's good that you take an interest in Hanne as a child – perhaps I can send you something in writing?" she said, looking at her watch.

"That would be wonderful!"

"Do you have an email address?"

Now I was stuck. If I told her my email address, she'd know I was Marianne McShane, not journalist-from-New Jersey but granddaughter-from-Ireland.

"Actually, I'm in the process of moving to a new website and my email address isn't working properly yet – maybe you can give me yours, and I'll contact you when mine is up and running?"

She looked at me for a beat, then nodded, perhaps wondering if I had lost interest in Hanne's story after all. As she wrote her details in my tiny notebook, we heard the front door open, and a male voice said something in Danish.

"In the kitchen, Erik, we have a visitor," Dina said in English.

I swivelled on my seat to see him walk into the room. He was just as he was in the most recent newspaper photo – a man who looked like he had once been taller, once filled the room, but had shrunk on all sides. His blue eyes were bright, taking me in with one glance, but his cheeks were sunken, and his shirt collar looked far too wide for his neck.

"Another journalist. I think we say everything before."

"Linda wants to write about Hanne as a person, her life before . . . before it happened." For the first time, her voice cracked.

He looked at me, then at his wife.

"*Jeg forstår, men det vil ikke bringe hende tilbage*," he said softly to her, then addressed me. "I tell my wife I understand why she wishes to do this, but it will not bring

Hanne back. And perhaps it is not good for us to keep talking about sad things?"

I nodded, swallowing as my throat tightened.

"Of course, I understand. Please excuse me." Blurred by unexpected tears, I stood and half-ran to the front door, wondering what had possessed me to lie to these people, and dredge up their tragic past.

CHAPTER 32

I ran until I got to the end of their street, where I stopped to catch my breath, jamming the heels of my hands into my eyes to stem the tears.

A girl a couple of years younger than me was sitting on the front porch of the last house on the opposite side of the road, smoking a cigarette. She stared at me as I stood there rubbing my eyes and, with no idea what else to do, I turned my back. And then it registered – I was standing at the laneway, the spot where they found the torch. Was this where she was attacked? Or where she left with someone she trusted? Tall trees lined either side of the lane – it seemed to be a walkway through to a parallel street, though when I peered through I couldn't see the other end. And up and down Damtoften, apart from the girl on her porch, there was nobody in sight at all. On a cold Sunday evening, the street would have been deathly quiet – no wonder no-one saw anything. But why her, and why then? An opportunistic killer hovering nearby who took his chance? Or a watcher, learning her routine? But then, she didn't have a routine. The news reports said she hadn't been out much at all, this was a first walk in weeks. That pointed back to an opportunistic killer: wrong place, wrong time. Suddenly spent, I sank against a tree and down to the ice-cold ground, my head in my hands.

Moments later, the sound of footsteps made me look up. The girl from the porch was standing a few feet from me, head tilted to one side, still smoking. A jet-black bob and choppy fringe framed pale features and dark, inquisitive eyes. She was wearing a purple shirt, buttoned up to the neck, skin-tight black jeans with Doc Marten boots, and a heavy black wool coat. As she raised her cigarette to her mouth, a tattoo that looked like a star peeped out from under her sleeve. Her slim fingers bore clunky silver rings, and around her neck hung a camera.

Still she said nothing, and neither did I.

Eventually she held her packet of cigarettes towards me and I found my voice.

"I don't smoke, but thanks for offering." Then I remembered where I was. "Sorry, I don't speak Danish."

"Want to talk about it?" she asked in perfect English, with a slight American twang.

She sat down on the ground opposite me as I shook my head – where would I even start?

"Try me," she went on. "I promise you, nothing will shock me."

It came out in one breath: "My mother was murdered twenty-four years ago, possibly in this exact spot, and I've just met my grandparents for the first time but pretended to be a journalist called Linda."

She nodded, taking an unperturbed drag of her cigarette. Perhaps offspring of murder victims turned up regularly on Damtoften.

"Hanne Karlsen? I know about her. Everyone on this

street does. I didn't know she had a daughter."

"And a husband. Nobody seems to know – neither my dad nor I have ever been mentioned in any news reports. And I've never met my grandparents. At least until just now." I bit my lip. "Have you always lived here?"

"Yes, all my life. I wasn't born when it happened, but we knew about it growing up. We used to play games about bad men and kidnappers here in the laneway. Silly stuff, we didn't understand what it meant – that someone really died."

I nodded. "In a strange way, it's the same for me. I've known for a long time what happened to her, but until I came here today, it didn't really hit me."

"Are you going to tell the Karlsens who you are?"

"I have to. I just need to figure out how." I traced a finger in the cold, sandy dirt and looked over at her again. "What do people say? What do locals think happened?"

"Ah. There are lots of stories." She gazed at me from under her fringe. "Are you sure you want to hear?"

I nodded. "I never knew her. So I'm not as emotionally close to it as a daughter might otherwise be." The words came out sounding cold, but it was enough to convince the girl.

"Okay. So, lots of people believe what the papers were saying – there was a serial killer in Denmark. That he killed three women that year, then stopped – maybe because he died or went to another country."

It fit with what I had read.

"But there are other theories," she continued. "Some say it was a man who used to walk the streets at night – he had a cabin out near the Fugl Sø Lake, and roamed Købæk at night, looking for children and teenagers out on their own."

I raised a sceptical eyebrow. "Hanne wasn't a teenager."

"I know. And I think it came from old stories made up to get small children to go to bed. *Bøhmand* stories – in America they say 'bogeyman'. I never saw this man and I don't know if he was real."

I nodded, remembering a similar story Jamie used to hear from his dad as a kid – the bogeyman collected naughty children who didn't do what they were told. My dad never told bogeyman stories.

"It worked though," she continued. "We were all afraid of him – this shadow person we never actually saw. And brave as we were playing kidnapping games in daylight, nobody ever stayed out after dark. This was the quietest street in Købæk at night."

"Back then too," I said, and she looked confused. "The night she was taken I mean. Nobody saw a thing."

"No, which is what brings in the other popular theory: that she went willingly, to meet someone." She stopped and I waited. "Sorry, this isn't very kind – telling you this when she was married to your father."

"Please go ahead, I want to hear everything. I've read so much but this is the first time I'm hearing the locals' version – you know?"

"Okay. There were rumours that she had met someone, a man. And that she went to meet him that night, and left with him, running away. She had gone away before – gone to America, and to England, or maybe Ireland I think."

I nodded. "Ireland. That's where she met my dad – it's where I'm from."

"Ah, I see. Yes, so some people said there must be a boyfriend, but something went wrong – a fight, and he drowned her in the lake."

She stopped and we both sat looking at the ground and perhaps like me she was trying to bat away the image of Hanne being thrown in a lake like an unwanted kitten.

"Were there other stories?" I asked after a while.

"So many, but most of them silly. Some said she joined a cult, some said it was suicide, and that a woman who lives in the forest in Roskilde found her and tried to give her a burial. We heard too that it was the ice-cream man – some people said they heard the music of the ice-cream truck that night. I think that was to stop us asking for ice-cream. Locals did say they heard creepy music that night – violin music. And people said there were strange men in the area in the days before – one blond, one dark-haired. That story was repeated a lot and I think the police looked into it. There was also a story about a white van but, as my mother says, there are always stories of white vans when people disappear, because there are always white vans even when nobody disappears at all."

"Your mother sounds smart."

The girl shrugged.

"What's your name by the way?" I asked, pulling myself to my feet.

"Asta. And you? Not Linda, I guess?"

"Not Linda." I smiled. "I'm Marianne. And now I need to go buy some supplies, and figure out how to tell those poor people I'm their granddaughter."

I thanked Asta for her time and set off back down Damtoften, with the sense that I knew more than ever before, but still I knew nothing at all.

CHAPTER 33

What next, I wondered, as I sat eating a bowl of microwaved soup in the communal kitchen at the hostel. Flipping the pages of my notebook, I winced at the "journalist" notes I'd taken. "*Chatty*" and "*lots of friends*" and "*a busy child*" scratched on one page, and "*email*" on the next. I didn't even remember writing that. On the following page, Dina had written her email address, and I sat staring at it, eating my too-hot soup, and wondering if I should close the notebook and walk away from all of this.

Dotted around the kitchen, backpackers sat in twos and threes, chattering in different languages. One or two sat alone reading books and maps. My eyes roamed to the far corner where a long-haired man was sitting at a computer. A sign above it advertised Internet access. As I watched, he got up from the terminal, and before I could talk myself out of it, I was out of my seat and over at the computer.

"You have to buy a token at the desk," the man said, packing his books. "And I think they're closed right now."

"Ah, okay," I said, disappointed and relieved all at once.

"My session has seven or eight more minutes – maybe that's enough for you?"

I smiled. "It is, thank you."

He nodded and walked away.

It took less than five minutes to do what I needed to do and as I disconnected an email was winging its way from *LindaKirwan83@gmail.com* to Dina Karlsen.

Unsure about my next steps, and wondering about the wisdom of the trip, I went out for a walk that afternoon. Købæk city centre was compact and easy to stroll around – more of a town really, spotlessly clean and very pretty. Narrow houses in every colour stood shoulder to shoulder – mint green, deep yellow, creamy orange and sunset red, with the occasional grey office block breaking up the rainbow. I rambled aimlessly, thinking about Hanne, imagining her stepping on these same streets, as a child with her parents, as a teen with her friends. I passed what looked like a public library, a two-storey building with burnt-orange walls, and decided to go in – a library seemed like a good place to do some research. But everything was in Danish, and apart from a bank of computers and a stack of today's newspapers, most of what was there was fiction, or so it seemed. Perhaps it was only on TV that people used libraries to find old newspapers and read up on local crime. In fact, I thought, as I ran my finger over a row of hardbacks near the door, the place to go to find out about local crime was almost certainly the police station. Would they accommodate questions from a stranger walking through the door? Maybe not, but it was worth a try.

It took another half an hour to find the police station. In contrast to the picture-postcard buildings that filled the city centre, it was a squat, brown-brick structure that reminded me of so many ill-thought-out buildings back home. At the main reception desk, I blurted out my story – my mother had been murdered, and I wanted to ask some questions about it. I was told to sit in a waiting area and after a while a different person came and asked to see some ID. I gave her my passport and she took it with her. Would they have a record of Marianne McShane? It seemed they did. After thirty minutes, a smallish man with receding strawberry-blond hair approached me, offering his hand. Under his left arm was a brown file.

"Ms McShane? Vicepolitiinspektør Nielsen."

I stood and shook his hand, then followed as he swiped us through to a room at the back of the building. Grey and bare, it felt like the kind of place criminals would be interrogated, and for the briefest moment I wondered if this was all a terrible idea. The man smiled as he sat down, flashing tiny teeth. He put the brown file on the table, then reached into his pockets as though searching for cigarettes before remembering where he was.

"So your mother was Hanne Karlsen?" he asked, though it was clearly a conversation opener rather than a real question.

"Yes. I don't remember her at all. I was a baby. But my father passed away two years ago, and since then I've become more and more interested in finding out about her story. I've read everything there is to read, and it seemed like it was time to come here and see for myself."

He nodded, watching my face intently, saying nothing.

"So could I look at the file, and ask some questions?" I said to fill the silence.

"I can't show you the file, I'm afraid," he said, patting it, "but I can certainly answer questions. I wasn't here when it happened, so it is new to me too, but I have been reading up since we reopened the case. What would you like to know?"

Realising I had no idea where to start, I pulled out my tiny notebook for the second time that day, along with an unfamiliar pen. I turned it over in my hand – it was silver with the letters D.F.K. engraved in gold, and definitely not mine. Then I remembered – Dina Karlsen's pen, I hadn't given it back. D.F.K. – her initials presumably. A twinge of guilt hit when I thought about my journalist-lie and the fake email address, but I pushed it aside, and cleared my throat.

"So, I guess I just want to know what the current theory is. I know there's a suspicion about a serial killer, and that the case is due to be reopened. Can you tell me anything else?"

"You know as much as we do then, Ms McShane. That is precisely correct. There is a general suspicion that the murders were connected, though this is circumstantial. New developments in forensics mean we can investigate this more scientifically now, and many old cases are being reopened."

"When I read about it, it seemed to me there must be a link between the three cases, but it was also strange that it was just that one year, and then he disappeared. Do you think he moved to another country?"

He looked at me again, saying nothing for a moment.

I shifted in my hard chair.

"Maybe."

I tried another tack.

"If the murders are not related, are there other theories about what happened to Hanne? I heard there was a white van in the area, for example," I said, trying to remember everything Asta had said.

"Oh, there is always a white van," he said, with a hint of a smile. "But we never got any concrete reports of a van in the area, not that night."

I looked up from my notebook. "But other nights?"

"*Ha!* I need to choose my words more carefully. On other nights in the lead-up to Hanne's disappearance, there were reports of an unfamiliar vehicle – a black car on the street where the Karlsens live."

"And did you find out who it was?"

"No, we never have, and it may not mean anything."

He paused, and this time I said nothing. "There were also reports of two men in the area – not residents." He looked at me, as though waiting for me to shed some light. "Have you heard this from anyone – from your father maybe?"

I shook my head. "Not from my father, but I did meet a girl this morning who lives on the same street – she said there were strangers around in the days leading up to Hanne's disappearance. It's hard to tell how much is urban myth. And she wasn't born when it happened."

He nodded. "The van is, as you say, urban myth. The two men – seen at separate times – that is less clear."

"One blond, one dark-haired?"

"Yes, your friend from Damtoften is correct. What is her name?"

I hesitated.

"Don't worry, we will interview everyone again as part of the new investigation – your friend will not be pulled in for questioning! Unless as a baby in her mother's womb she committed murder?" He laughed at what seemed to me a fairly off-colour attempt at humour.

"Asta is her name. She lives in the last house on the street, near the laneway."

He made a note, bobbing his head down to look at the page, exposing a bright-pink bald patch.

"So you visited the Karlsens this morning? They were happy to see their granddaughter, yes?"

My cheeks flushed. "I did visit, but I . . . didn't mention who I was."

His eyebrows went up in an unspoken question.

"I was caught off guard and said I was a journalist."

He leaned back on his chair, folding his arms. With his reddish hair and sharp nose, he reminded me suddenly of a fox.

"But they are your grandparents – did they not recognise you?"

"We've never met."

"They never visited you? In all this time? No photos even?"

"No. There's never been any contact. My dad said it was too sad for them. Maybe it was too sad for him too – easier to cut off all contact. Actually – that's something I wondered about. My dad and I aren't mentioned in any of the articles about the case. Do you know why that is?"

He frowned and opened the file, leafing through pages of lined paper and typewritten reports.

"I did see something about that . . . yes, here it is." He read for a moment, then looked up. "Your grandparents requested that you and your father be kept out of all press conferences and statements. The newspapers never knew about you, and the police respected their wishes. Your grandparents didn't want the media to intrude on your father's grief."

As I left the police station ten minutes later that was the part I couldn't get out of my head. Dina and Erik had worried so much about intruding on our grief, but never considered we might actually welcome contact – not from the media, but from them, our only link to Hanne. And walking the short journey back to the hostel, I couldn't shake the sense that something about that side of the story just didn't add up.

CHAPTER 34

On Tuesday morning, I walked back to Damtoften to speak to Asta again. I wondered if she'd be at college or work or whatever she normally did, but there she was, sitting on the porch, smoking a cigarette. As I waved in at her from the road, a car pulled up and a tall woman in her late forties got out. Her skin was sallower than Asta's and her wavy, shoulder-length hair a much lighter brown, but the family resemblance was clear. Asta stubbed her cigarette and kicked the butt into the grass, with an air of what looked like forced nonchalance. The woman glanced at me, and walked up the driveway, carrying a bag of groceries. She sniffed the air around Asta and said something in Danish, then let herself into the house.

Asta stood up and beckoned me in.

"My mother," she said, leading me through to the kitchen, where the woman was unpacking groceries.

"*Mor*, this is Marianne," she said in English. "She's the Karlsens' granddaughter."

Asta's mother turned, her mouth a perfect O.

"They have a *granddaughter*?" Her English was more accented than her daughter's, but only just. I could see her trying to work out who I was. "Hanne was your mother?"

I nodded.

"*Åh Gud*," she said, pulling out a chair and gesturing for me to sit.

Asta sat too.

"I am Rikke. So pleased to meet you. You are not Danish?"

"No, I'm Irish. Hanne went to Ireland and married my dad and had me, but nobody here seems to know about us."

She stared for a moment, perhaps trying to see a resemblance.

"You look a little like her. I notice it now that I know you're her daughter. She was very beautiful."

"You knew her?"

She nodded. "My goodness, poor Hanne," she said, leaning against the counter. "Her parents never recovered. No parent could." She shook her head. "I cannot believe Dina never told me about you! Have you visited before?"

"No, never."

"Dina and Erik must be so pleased to have you here. Your visit will be good for them." She nodded, as though confirming something for herself. "They need it."

My face started to feel warm. "I haven't told them who I am. I bumped into Dina yesterday morning and said my name was Linda, and I was writing an article about Hanne." The words came out in a rush and telling it a third time it sounded even more foolish.

Rikke sat beside me and patted my arm.

"It's a big thing to tell. You will do it when you're ready. And it will help them, to have the child of Hanne in their lives."

"Could you tell me a little about her – about Hanne?"

181

"Oh yes! She was bright, so smart. Kind. Funny. I suppose you might say restless. She went to America when she finished school, and then Ireland after university – you know that of course. It was such a horrible shock for us all when . . . when it happened. Asta's older brother was a baby, and Asta was not born. I remember wondering if we should move to another street, sell this house."

Asta looked up. "I didn't know that!"

Her mother nodded. "We did not consider it in a real way but for a long time we felt uncomfortable here. When we found out it was a – what is that term – serial killer, it was a strange relief. Because it was not someone from here, and we were in no greater danger than anyone else. I don't know if that makes sense? Maybe you have to be a parent to understand how much I think about things like this."

I nodded. "I get it. My dad was quite protective when I was young. I was never left alone."

"Your father – of course he would be worrying," Rikke said. "I can see that. What does he feel about your visit here?"

"Ah." The words got stuck for a moment. "He died unfortunately, so now it's just me." Clearing my throat, I changed the subject. "I was at the police station yesterday, speaking to an inspector who's involved in reopening the cases from back then. He said there were reports of two different men in the area, around the time she disappeared, or shortly before." I looked over at Asta. "And I think you mentioned them too?"

She nodded.

I turned back to her mother. "Do you remember anything about them?"

"Oh yes. One blond, one dark-haired."

It was exactly what Asta had said, and Vicepolitiinspektør Nielsen too. Were they all repeating a story that had been told over and over, taking it as gospel?

"And can I ask, did you see the men yourself?"

She shook her head. "I heard about it from my neighbours who saw them."

"Oh, are they still here? Could I speak with them?"

She waved her hand. "Some are here and some are gone or dead. I do not mean one particular neighbour – it is what everyone said at the time. One blond man, one dark-haired man. The blond man had a red beard, or you might say orange more correctly."

I twisted the ring on my finger. "Do you think it's true? Or something one person said and everyone repeated?"

"Oh, but it must be true – everyone has said it, for many years."

I thought about the men seen near victims' houses in cases all over the world – people acting "suspiciously" who turned out to be delivery men, people who looked like "trouble" but turned out to be perfectly innocent passers-by, often because of a hoodie, cap, or skin-colour that didn't fit with the neighbourhood's definition of "safe".

Asta and Rikke waited as I sat, still turning my ring, wondering how much I could ask.

"Would you like me to introduce you to some of the neighbours?" Rikke asked. "Perhaps they will remember more about Hanne and about what happened?"

"I'd really like that, thank you. I've read so much about the case, this one and the other two Danish women and lots of other cases beyond Denmark."

Rikke's eyes widened.

"I read a lot of true crime – it started with my mother's

183

case and went on from there. But nothing I can read on the Internet compares to a conversation with a real person – I'd love to chat to the neighbours." Then I remembered that I was supposed to be Linda-from-America. "Oh, wait, I need to tell Dina who I really am before I talk to anyone else." My stomach twisted.

"Of course," Rikke said. "She is not there now, however – I saw her leave earlier for her *bridgeklub* – sorry, I do not know 'bridge' in English."

"It's the same, assuming you mean the card game." I smiled.

"Ah good. So. Come to me when you are ready, and I will take you to meet some people. I am here most days." She looked at her daughter. "Asta too, though I am certain she will get a job any moment." Her tone suggested quite the opposite, and Asta rolled her eyes.

"It takes time, *Mor*. I'm still waiting for these companies to see my genius." She grinned, and Rikke sighed.

"Perhaps if you wear that smart jacket I bought you instead of this –" she waved a hand at Asta's long black coat and short purple dress, "and spent less time taking photographs, things might go better."

This time Asta sighed, and I figured it was time to go.

I pushed back my chair.

"Thank you for your time and, if you don't mind, I'd love to take you up on your kind offer to meet some neighbours. I'll call back here as soon as I've spoken to Dina?"

Rikke nodded and said goodbye, while Asta walked me to the front door.

"Mothers," she said, rolling her eyes, then clapped her hand over her mouth. "Oh, I'm so sorry!"

I told her not to worry and launched into my usual

script – *she's gone a long time, I don't remember her, I'm curious more than sad*.

But as I walked down the driveway and along Hanne's childhood street, thinking about her last visit and her final moments, I wondered if that was still true.

CHAPTER 35

Back at the hostel on Tuesday afternoon, I logged into my email account as soon as the terminal was free, and found a message from Dina. Her opening made me squirm. She wanted to thank me – Linda – for taking an interest in her daughter, and hoped I was right, that taking it to a wider audience would help. She gave me her phone-number and I typed it into my mobile phone, feeling sick. I'd have to tell her the truth before it got out of hand. Maybe it was already out of hand.

In her email, she went on to write about Hanne.

At school she was restless, dreaming one minute, chattering the next, never sitting still. She had a crazy imagination and talked without stop. Sometimes she disappeared for hours and we did not know where she was but she always came back with a story – stories of witches and wolves and fairies and the Bøhmand. She promised each time she wouldn't disappear again, but Hanne only ever did what Hanne wanted to do. And then one day, she didn't come back.

My throat tightened. The words on the screen blurred as I swiped at my eye, and sat, staring at nothing.

"Will you need long?" asked a girl who was hovering behind me.

"No, I think I'm done," I said and logged out.

It was time to tell the truth.

Returning to Damtoften for the second time that day, I slowed my pace as I approached the Karlsens' front door. The bell echoed inside the house. There was no other sound. I tried again. Nothing. And no car – she must be still at bridge. Deflated but relieved too, I walked back out, and spotted Asta and her mother about to turn into the house opposite the Karlsens. They waited as I crossed to join them.

"Hello again! She is not back?" Rikke said, looking at her watch. "She volunteers at a school for children from poverty backgrounds sometimes – maybe she went there after bridge. We are calling to Fru Hansen – Mrs Hansen – would you like to meet her? She knew Hanne too."

"I don't want to intrude . . ." I said, cursing my cultural inclination to say no when I meant yes.

"You are not intruding. She will be very happy to have a new visitor – come."

Fru Hansen's house was just like Rikke's on the outside, but inside we went back in time. The hall floor was dark walnut, and the deep-red walls were covered in old black-and-white photographs, at odds with the Danish minimalism I'd seen everywhere else. I trailed behind Asta and Rikke as they followed a tiny, white-haired lady into the dining room. She hadn't seemed remotely surprised to see an extra person with her neighbours – it was almost as though she was expecting me.

In the dining room, a burgundy rug covered the polished floor, and the walls hosted mirrors of every shape. Three places had been laid at a large dining table and Fru Hansen set about adding a fourth, indicating that we should sit.

She tilted her head to one side, regarded me with bright blue eyes, and said something in Danish.

"Fru Hansen, Marianne doesn't speak Danish so we will speak English. Is that okay for you?" Rikke said.

Fru Hansen's eyes never left my face, and she nodded slowly.

"Marianne. So you are Hanne's daughter."

Something flickered inside me.

"You know about me?"

Asta and Rikke looked at one another as Fru Hansen answered.

"Yes. Not so many do. Dina did not want your father to —" she stopped and looked above my head, searching for a word, "*struggle* with the newspaper people."

I had so many questions, I didn't know where to start.

"Did you know Hanne well?"

"I did. Since a small girl. Since *she* was a small girl." She nodded as she corrected herself.

"What was she like?" It came out in a cracked whisper.

"*Vidunderlig*. Wonderful. A lot of stories, all the time." She paused to pour coffee. "Fun. Always in trouble." She smiled at me. "Not big trouble, little things. And then she makes a new start every time – she tries so hard!"

"What kind of things?"

"Oh, for reading the wrong items. She comes to me when her teacher is angry at her for reading *tegneserier* instead of books – Asta, what are *tegneserier*?"

"Comics."

"Yes. She gives me all her comics and tells me to keep them, because she is going to read only 'good' books and make her teacher happy."

"Do you still have them?"

Fru Hansen laughed, her eyes crinkling. "No! Because Hanne comes back always in one week to ask for her comics again – she did not want to read the 'good' books any more. It happens many times. She gives me her summer diary – no, I mean *scrapbog* – Asta?"

"Scrapbook," Asta said.

"Ah, of course. She gives me her scrapbook one time, full of drawings and souvenirs of her summer, because she wishes to concentrate on school. Two weeks after, she calls for her scrapbook. I always take what she gives me, and wait for her *uundgåelige* return. Asta?"

"*Inevitable* return."

"Yes, her inevitable return. She always comes back." Fru Hansen smiled, but just as quickly her face changed. "Until of course this time when she does not." She shook her head, and clasped her tiny hands together, her knuckles white.

"Were you here, when it happened?" I asked.

She nodded slowly, her eyes never leaving mine.

"My husband and I help with the search. Every evening we go out in groups, to the town, to the forest, to the lake. We make posters. We cry and we pray. And mostly we search."

I tried to imagine it, Dina and Erik and Fru Hansen twenty years younger, despairing and hoping.

"And when she was found?"

"I would not wish it for the worst person." Her voice, strong and clear despite her age, shook for the first time.

189

"And after that, Dina and Erik shut themselves away?"

She nodded. "They could not –" she paused again, searching for words, "manage it?"

Asta spoke up. "Deal? They could not deal with it?"

Fru Hansen nodded. "Yes. They are falling in pieces, and cannot speak to anybody. For the first bit of time, not even to me or to my husband. We call to them every day, because we know one day they will open the door. And finally they do, but only to us, and some others here." She swept her hand around, and I couldn't tell if she meant Rikke, or the neighbourhood in general.

"And did you have a feeling about who took her?"

"All the talking was of a dark-haired man and a blond man."

"Did you see them?"

"The dark-haired one, yes. I remember his face very clearly, but the police do not know who he is, and Dina does not either. It is very difficult to have seen this man, to know it is important, but still it is no help."

"Where did you see him?"

"Walking near their house at evenings, two or three times the week before. Always beside the hedges, like he is trying that nobody can see him. Why would a man who does not live here be on this street every night? But then nothing happens. The police do not know who he is, so nothing."

Her frustration filled the air, crackling around us.

"What did he look like?"

"I think . . . plain."

"Ugly, you mean?"

"No, no. Plain – normal, average. Brown hair, pale face, not one to remember. Perhaps this is why nobody does."

"What about the blond man – you saw him too?"

"No," she said, after a beat. "I hear from others that he is there, but nobody can say they see him. It is always heard from someone else, you know? So I am not sure. But I think–" She stopped, an odd look on her face, then seemed to decide against whatever she was about to say. She changed tack completely. "Did you ever hear about Nøkken?"

I shook my head. Asta and Rikke exchanged a look.

"Nøkken are water spirits. They can change shape. Male spirits who take other forms. They can –" She stopped and looked at the others.

"Disguise," Asta said softly.

"Yes. Sometimes he looks like old man, and other times a handsome youth with golden hair. Sometimes he is a white horse, and sometimes he is invisible." She paused, and it was as though the room was holding its breath. "Nøkken live in water. They are bad, bad spirits. They change appearance to call women and children, to make them drown in lakes and streams."

I sat up straighter and leaned towards her, hypnotised.

"To make a child come to a stream, he changes into a beautiful white horse. The child sits on its back, and the horse runs into the water to drown the child. Sometimes Nøkken disguise to look like a tree, to make people think the water edge is far away – to trick them to fall in. And to steal young women, they disguise as handsome young man."

I swallowed, mesmerised and cold all at once.

"How did they steal the women?"

"By playing beautiful music to draw them close. By playing the violin."

191

CHAPTER 36

On Wednesday morning, I took the now familiar route to Damtoften, determined to confess to Dina, but again there was no answer at the door. This time the car was there. Maybe she'd gone out with Erik, perhaps they had two cars? I dug into my backpack for my mobile phone, and searched for her number.

What would I say? "This is Linda, only not Linda"? I waited as the phone rang, distracted and nervous, then suddenly aware of a sound from inside. A ringing.

Was she there after all? The sound seemed to be coming from the hall, but there were no glass panels in the front door, so I walked to the window on the right-hand side. It looked into a living-room area, neat, clean, and empty of humans or ringing phones. I tried the window on the other side, and found myself looking at a bedroom. I could make out a narrow, single divan covered with a white sheet, stark like an empty hospital bed. Two framed prints – seascapes, I think – hung on the wall above a neat white dresser. The other walls were bare. A notebook sat on the dresser top but the room was otherwise devoid of personal touches. Hanne's room? Something shifted inside me as I stood staring, and in my head a distant ghost took shape.

Back at the front door, I tried the phone a second time, and again I could hear it ringing. But no movement. No scurrying steps. Could something have happened to her? I eyed up the path that led to the back of the house and figured I was unlikely to get in trouble for trespassing in my own grandparents' garden. Following the path around to the back, I peered in the kitchen window at the same grey couch I'd sat on two days earlier. No Dina. The other window must be their bedroom. Feeling uncomfortable, but not to the point that it actually stopped me, I tried to look in. The blind was down. Probably a good thing, I thought, as I ducked back to the front of the house and down the driveway. Dina was perhaps out without her phone, or in the shower – there were any number of explanations. I pushed away niggling worries, and headed for the town centre.

Back in the library, armed with a guest pass, I sat at a computer, and logged on to my email. Nothing new from Dina, but then she had no reason to contact me again – I still owed her a reply. I clicked into Google and threw words into the search box: **Hanne Karlsen blonde man dark-haired man ice-cream van white van violin lake**. I was operating on a mud-sticking-to-walls premise and it was far too random to give me anything useful.

I tried it again, using "**Denmark**" instead of her name, because I'd already read every single article that referenced Hanne Karlsen. The results were a mish-mash of disturbing suicide stories and studies on hair-colour around Europe. I tried replacing "**Denmark**" with "**Købæk**" and scrolled through an even more random set of results. Then, on the third page, I found it. Her name jumped out at me from the title: "Frederikke Frandsen", followed by some Danish words I didn't understand.

Frederikke Frandsen – one of the two women killed the same year as Hanne. I clicked into what looked like a Danish newspaper website and copied the text into Google Translate.

In English, the headline read: **Frederikke Frandsen: Witnesses Report to See White Van.** The translation was jerky in parts but the gist of it was clear: a neighbour of the victim had reported seeing a van, light in colour, near the victim's house the day before she died. The neighbour had been interviewed by a reporter from a local newspaper a year after the murder, and said she didn't think the police had taken her seriously. The reporter went on to reference a similar case in Købæk but didn't mention Hanne's name.

I sat staring at the screen. Did Inspector Nielsen know about this? I picked up my backpack and pushed back the chair.

Inspector Nielsen didn't seem at all surprised to see me, and his lack of excitement about my discovery was, in hindsight, predictable.

"As I explained to you yesterday, Ms McShane, there is always a white van. It is what people remember when someone goes missing. In fact, every day, we are surrounded by such vehicles and it means nothing. But as soon as something happens, we get witnesses with these stories. And, of course, we investigate all of the reports but most of the time it is nothing."

I slumped in the hard plastic chair, feeling the air go out of me.

Inspector Nielsen took pity.

"But it's good that you are looking, and please do tell me if you discover anything. Did you speak to your friend Asta again?"

"Yes, and I met her mother too. She told me the same thing as you did about a blond man and a dark-haired man but, when I asked for more details, it turned out she didn't actually see them at all. Their neighbour says *she* saw the dark-haired man but has no idea who saw the blond man."

"Who is this neighbour?" he asked, lifting his pen.

Again I felt guilty bringing their names into it, but then Fru Hansen had said she reported it to the police herself. "Fru Hansen. I don't know her first name."

"Ah yes, Inge Hansen, I saw her name in the reports." He looked up at me, as though trying to decide on something.

I waited, but he didn't say anything further. Nor did he write down her name.

"Is there any chance the blond man is a bit like the white van – it didn't really happen?" I asked.

He lifted his hands and shrugged. "Maybe. One person says they saw something and soon everyone is saying the same. Memory is funny like that – people hear something many times, and it becomes real to them. Memory is adaptable and can be contaminated by hearing the same thing again and again. It gets muddy." He stopped and pushed back his chair and it seemed the meeting was over, then he remembered something else.

"Did you speak to Dina Karlsen again – did you explain that you are Hanne's daughter?"

"I tried, but she wasn't there. It was weird. I was at her door ringing her phone, and I could hear her phone ringing inside the house, but there was no answer. I looked in all the windows in case something happened to her but I couldn't see into the hall . . ."

"Maybe she was out without her phone? Older people are not so attached to their cell phones as we are." He smiled, showing those tiny sharp teeth again.

"I know . . . Still, I couldn't help worrying a tiny bit."

He pulled his own phone out.

"Give me her number and I will try," he said.

I pushed my phone across the table, and he typed in Dina's number. I listened as he put the phone to his ear, though I couldn't hear anything. His face changed, and he spoke in Danish. He laughed, said something else, and disconnected.

"That was Dina – there is no problem. I said it was a wrong number." He tapped the side of his nose and grinned. "Don't tell, okay?"

Walking fast, it took only ten minutes to reach Dina's house. Her car was still there, I noticed, as I rang the bell. But again there was no answer. She'd hardly gone out again so quickly, had she? I stood still, listening.

And suddenly it felt like there was someone on the other side of the door, doing exactly what I was doing – standing still, listening.

I glanced at Fru Hansen's house across the road and a tiny suspicion took hold. Pulling out my phone, I searched for Dina's number and hit *Call*, then pressed my ear to the door. This time the sound of her phone ringing was just inches from me, I was sure of it.

"Dina, can you open the door so we can talk?"

Silence.

"I haven't been quite honest with you, and I'd really like to explain."

Still nothing.

"This isn't how I pictured saying it, but I suspect you already know so I'll just go ahead. I'm Hanne's daughter, your granddaughter."

No response.

"I've never asked anything of you, and never judged you for not staying in contact. But my dad has passed away now, and there's nobody left." I swallowed as the words caught me. "I just want to know more about Hanne, and to get to know you. Please?"

The sound of the latch. The door opening.

Dina looking at me. Her grey blouse, similar to the one she'd worn on Monday. The same pearls, the same golden-bird brooch, the same neatly combed slate-grey hair. But somehow an entirely different person. Her face drawn and pinched, her eyes shiny with tears, her cheeks blotchy. She shook her head, her hand still on the latch. When she spoke, her voice was a tightly pulled string.

"Go, and do not ever come back here, *Linda*." She moved to close the door as she delivered her parting words. "I have no granddaughter."

CHAPTER 37

I held back tears until I was safely inside my hostel bedroom, where I curled in a ball on the scratchy blanket, and cried like I hadn't done in years. This was the furthest outcome from the one I'd pictured when I arrived on Sunday afternoon.

My phone started to ring and, as I groped for it, a speck of hope flickered – maybe Dina had changed her mind?

But it wasn't Dina. It was Ray. I cleared my throat to hide the tears.

"There you are, I was getting worried," he said by way of greeting. "You didn't phone me back last night?"

"Yeah, I got confused about the time difference and then it was a bit late." I lay back on the bed, looking up at the cracked ceiling.

Silence.

"Sorry, Ray, I really did mean to call."

"Right. Anyway, did you find out who killed your mother?"

"No." I tried to think of something else to say, but where to start?

"I hate to say I told you so, but . . . Did you see your grandmother?"

"Yeah . . ."

"And?"

And it all came out in a rush – the lie, the conversations with the neighbours, the confrontation that morning.

"Ah. And how did your grandmother find out who you really are?"

"I don't know, but maybe the neighbour Mrs Hansen said it. I never thought to tell her the Linda story. And now it's such a mess. God, I'm an idiot."

"It doesn't matter though – the police are reopening the case so they'll take care of that side. And you never had a relationship with your grandparents anyway – you can't miss what you don't have. All of my grandparents are dead for years and I turned out okay."

I closed my eyes and covered them with my free hand, pressing the phone to my ear with the other.

"I wanted to find out more about Hanne though, and –"

I paused, staring at blackness and pinpricks of light, looking for the right words.

"And?"

"And I wanted to find out why she left. Why she walked away from my dad and me. The neighbours can tell me all about how funny and kind Hanne was as a child, and all about strange men and white vans and violin music, but nobody can tell me what I really want to know. Why did she walk out on us?"

By the time I got off the phone from Ray, I had talked myself down from booking the next flight back to Dublin, but only just. I had no idea what to do though – Inspector Nielsen would go into hiding if I kept turning up at the police station, there was nothing much in the library, and the idea of going anywhere near Damtoften again made me feel sick.

A soft knock at my bedroom door interrupted my thoughts. There was someone looking to see me, a girl said when I answered. I thanked her and took a quick look in the mirror above the sink – my eyes were red and puffy, my hair a straw-like mess. I splashed water on my face and smoothed down my hair before leaving, locking my bedroom door behind me.

In the common area, curled up in a giant armchair, leafing through a magazine, I found Asta.

I pulled up a chair and sat.

"I guess you saw Dina," she said, closing the magazine.

"Yep," I sighed. "She knows who I am, and she doesn't want to see me ever again, so that went well."

"I'm so sorry. We should have warned Fru Hansen not to say anything. She saw Dina yesterday evening and told her how lovely it was to meet her granddaughter. That was the end of Linda."

"It's not your fault," I said. "I should have thought of it. I was so drawn into her story of Nøkken, I forgot about everything else."

"Ah, Nøkken, yes. Fru Hansen loves her folk tales."

"Do you think there's anything in it?"

"What?" Asta laughed. "Do I think your mother was taken by an evil water spirit?" She stopped laughing almost immediately. "Sorry, it's not funny."

"I don't mean literally," I said, "but there must be a reason Fru Hansen told the story. I keep thinking about what she said – the spirit disguised as a golden-haired man, playing a violin to lure women to drown in a lake. There was all that talk of a blond man, and of violin music, and there's a lake near here, isn't there?"

"Yes, Fugl Sø. It's about 15 kilometres from here. That's not where your mother was found though."

"No, but all the same there's something kind of haunting about it – the spirit and the forest and the lake and the music. I dreamed about it last night."

"That's not surprising," Asta said, uncurling her legs and stretching like a cat. "Fru Hansen has a way of telling stories that gets right in. When we were small, we used to go to her house after school, and she would tell us fairy tales like 'Thumbelina' and 'The Little Match Girl' and 'The Snow Queen', and stories she made up herself about trolls and goblins and the *Bøhmand*. I was convinced I was going to be stolen by a giant toad to be married off to her toad son, like poor Thumbelina. My mother would go crazy because I couldn't sleep without a light on. Still Fru Hansen told her stories."

"But why, if they were frightening for you?"

"I guess she saw them as cautionary tales – don't cross bridges, don't go near open water, don't stray far from home because you never know what's lurking in the forest." She looked up at me, her dark eyes unblinking. "Perhaps the old fairy tales did what reading about true crime does now – cautionary tales, creating distance. It happened to *them*, it won't happen to me."

I opened my mouth to answer, but it wasn't a question.

"People have always made up stories to explain things that are frightening or things they can't understand," she continued. "It's what humans have been doing forever. When bad stuff happens, we don't want to believe we did it to each other or to ourselves. So it was the *Nøkken* or the *Bøhmand* or the bogeyman or Candyman. Have you seen that movie?"

I nodded.

"And did you say '*Candyman*' five times in front of the mirror to see if he'd come?"

I smiled. "Absolutely. My friend Linda and I did it together in the bathroom in her house. We were terrified he'd appear but then it was kind of a let-down when nothing happened."

Asta laughed. "Me too, my brother and me freaking out when we heard a noise behind us after we said it, but it was only my mother coming up the stairs."

"But *Candyman* is just a movie – Fru Hansen sounded so serious talking about Nøkken."

"Sure, but it's the same thing. We like to be scared, but it's more than that – it's a –" she stopped, searching for a word, "a defence mechanism of a kind, don't you think? If we hear the stories about the monster, and tell the stories about the monster, he won't come to us. Cautionary tales, warding off evil." She smiled. "As I said, just like your true crime stories. I think if Fru Hansen had a computer, she'd be like you, reading about all the crazy, scary things in the world, and telling us the Zodiac Killer is from Købæk. Oh!" She paused and reached down to pick up her battered satchel from the floor, pulling it onto her knee. "She sent you something," she said, rummaging inside. "Here it is."

She handed me a white envelope, yellowing at the corners, addressed in blue ink, a postage stamp in the top corner.

"What is it?"

"Open it and see."

Inside there was a postcard, with a picture that was

instantly recognisable to any Irish person – a John Hinde image of a thatched cottage. I flipped to see who it was from, but the tiny, cramped writing was in Danish. It was addressed to "Inge". My eyes skimmed to the end, where one word stood out: Hanne.

"This was written by my mother?"

Asta nodded. "Yes, she sent it to Fru Hansen when she was in Ireland. Look in the envelope, there's more. She translated it for you."

I pulled out a sheet of paper. In neat script, Fru Hansen had indeed translated the postcard.

> *Dear Inge,*
>
> *I hope you are well. Me, I'm not so good. I find myself in a cage of my own making and I may have to leave. It is difficult to explain, but I have a reason – you will understand when I see you. I cannot bear to tell my parents, but soon I fear I will have no choice. They warned me against all of it – coming here, marrying him, having the baby, and I did not listen. I can't swallow the humiliation so easily, but more than that, I cannot stay here. Will you help me tell them?*
>
> *Yours,*
> *Hanne*

I read it again, and a third time.

"Do you know what it says?" I asked Asta, and she nodded.

"I helped translate. Why do you think she needed to leave?"

"I have no idea," I said, shaking my head. "I found a

letter in our attic late last year, from Hanne to my dad. She told him she wasn't coming back to Ireland, and she said something about a cage then too. It read as though she had decided she wasn't bothered with being a wife and mother and wanted her freedom. Maybe there was something else to it though."

Even as I said it, I could feel a surge of something – faint anticipation maybe, a pinhead of hope that she wasn't just a restless, flighty person who abandoned her baby at the first sign of responsibility. I needed to find out the truth.

CHAPTER 38

On Thursday morning, Fru Hansen opened the door as soon as Asta rang, as though she had been just inside waiting. She led us through to her dining room, where the table was again set for three. At each place sat a blue-and-white plate with a picture: Fru Hansen's depicted children in a sleigh, Asta's showed a girl feeding a goose, and mine showed a mother and daughter at a snowy window. Fru Hansen poured coffee and offered us some apple cake, though it was only half past nine in the morning. Out of politeness, I took some but all I could think of was Hanne's message.

"You received the postcard?" Fru Hansen said.

"Yes, thank you. So Hanne sent it to you from Ireland?"

"She send me postcards from all over and at first I am happy to see it. But then I am sad to read she wished to leave." She looked up at me. "I am very sad to think she leaves you."

"But can you tell me why? She said she would explain it to you in person?"

Fru Hansen shook her head, and all the air went out of me.

205

"I do not see her when she came back. She is unwell, and wishes to stay indoors, sleeping much of the time. And then, of course, you know what happens – the first time she goes out, she is gone forever."

Another dead end. And I'd ruined any chance of speaking to the two people who could actually tell me why she left.

"You could try asking Dina and Erik?" Fru Hansen said, reading my mind. "I am sorry for causing this problem with them, but I am sure it can be repaired."

"Oh God no, it's not your fault, you weren't to know! But, judging by yesterday's encounter, I'm not going to be welcome there any time soon."

"Give it time," Fru Hansen said softly. "You are their granddaughter. They will get past the –" she paused, "the deception?"

I cleared my throat. "So, back to the postcard – despite what Hanne said about a 'reason', for all we know it may just be what it seemed – that she was bored and restless and fed up with being a mother?" My voice was harder than intended.

Asta looked surprised. Fru Hansen did not. She reached across the table and put her hand on mine.

"I do not know her reason, but I am certain it was not the easy decision. No mother leaves her child unless she is without choice."

My eyes fixed on her hand, on the age spots and the neatly trimmed nails. Christ. I was an idiot to think I'd get a happy resolution. Sometimes things are just as they seem – no great revelation, no fairy-tale ending – my mother had simply walked away.

"Oh, I have this," Fru Hansen said.

She got up, took a ceramic bowl from the sideboard and brought it to the table. Sitting down again, she took something from the bowl and handed it to me: a small key, silver in colour. The kind of key that fits in a diary. I'd had one like it as a teenager.

"What is it for?" I asked.

"Hanne sent it to me from Ireland. I forget until I search for the postcard – it is with all her letters and cards. You take it."

"But what does it unlock?"

"I am not sure. There is a note," she said, reaching back into the bowl and taking out a sheet of paper. She smoothed it out on the tablecloth and handed it to Asta. "You can translate better."

Asta read it to herself, then out loud in English.

"*Dear Inge, I have decided to move on with my life. I am locking away the past, and will make my life here in Ireland with Michael. A fresh start, with no distractions. So I am sending you the key to my past. If I ask for it back, do not send it! Love always, Hanne.*"

I looked at the date – it was sent exactly a year before I was born. A nagging thought took root. Was it my arrival that sent her fleeing? Was she happy until I came along?

I looked up at Fru Hansen.

"And she never said what is was for or asked for it back?"

She shook her head, her white hair glinting in the early morning sunlight.

"I never see her again," she said softly. "Her next visit is also her final visit."

I looked down, seeing but not seeing the untouched apple cake on my plate, trying to put the pieces together.

ANDREA MARA

She had come to Ireland, met my dad, seemed happy, albeit hanging on to something from the past – at least until she "locked it away". Then a little over a year later, she was running back to Denmark, abandoning us, with no explanation. Or at least nothing more than talk of a "cage". And then came the rest – talk of a blond man and a dark-haired man, and her unsolved murder. None of it made any sense.

"The dark-haired man you saw before Hanne disappeared – did you ever see him again?" I asked.

Fru Hansen shook her head. "No, never again. The blond one – that is less clear."

"What do you mean?"

"Nobody can say who saw the blond one or where the story comes from. But there was a man who helped with the search, and he is *velkendt* – what is the word, *familiar*?"

Asta nodded, and Fru Hansen continued.

"I tell the police, but I do not believe they accept my report seriously. I say it to Dina too and she is very sad with me for saying such things about the man – a good friend to her and to Erik, she said. She did not speak to me for some time."

There was something in her voice that made me look up, but her face gave nothing away.

"Let me tell you more about Nøkken," she went on. "There are different stories about Nøkken all around our country. Here, we have Nøkken who come out of Fugl Sø. This is the lake near to us. In some villages they say Nøkken – look as –" She paused and glanced over at Asta.

"Disguise," Asta said.

"Yes. In some villages they say Nøkken disguise as

208

beautiful animals. A horse, or a deer. Sometimes Nøkken start as soft wind, getting stronger as they push you into the lake. Here, near Fugl Sø, Nøkken always look as a beautiful blond man, playing violin. He is dressed in a white gown, and his face is like heaven. Blue eyes, pink lips, a kind and loving smile. He plays the violin, and the woman or girl – it is only women and girl children he wants – follows the music. The beautiful man moves towards the Fugl Sø lake, and she follows, forgetting there is danger, wishing only to be with him. He reaches the lake and she keeps walking, like she is asleep. When she steps into the water, still she does not wake. It is only when her head goes under, she comprehends and then it is too late. She turns to look up at him, from under the water. And as the last breath leaves her body, she sees that his beautiful white gown is really made of mouths of crying children. And his face has changed – the blue eyes, the pink lips they are gone. The face is empty now, blank and white as snow."

Silence, as Fru Hansen finished her story and the only sound was the clock on the wall. My skin was tingling and I couldn't shake the image of the blank-faced Nøkken peering down at the water's edge.

"Fru Hansen always likes her fairy tales," Asta said, with a laugh that sounded forced.

Fru Hansen nodded. "Yes, you can say fairy tale if you wish. Of course you can."

"What do you mean?" I asked.

"With every story in the world, there is much that is from imagination but at the centre there is always something true. Don't you think?"

I didn't know what to think, so just nodded and broke off a piece of cake with my fork.

"Have you been to her grave?" Fru Hansen asked.

"No. I guess I imagined going there with Dina . . ."

"I can take you now if you like," Asta said. "I can borrow my mother's car."

"Is it far?"

"No, only fifteen minutes. Your mother's not buried in the town cemetery, she's in a small graveyard in the grounds of a little church on the Fuglvej. My mother and I went once with Dina a long time ago."

I hesitated, and Asta misread it.

"Or if you prefer to go alone, I can help you organise a taxi?"

"No, it's not that. If you don't mind taking me, I'd much prefer that to going on my own. It's just a bit daunting to think about seeing her grave."

Fru Hansen put her hand on mine again. "It is good that you go. Maybe a way to connect with Hanne, to understand."

"Understand what?"

She shrugged, her small shoulders moving slowly. "Everything. Or maybe nothing. You will know."

She got up and began to clear the plates, removing them to an unseen kitchen beyond.

"Are you sure about this?" I asked Asta. "Don't you have places you need to be?"

"I'm sure. To my mother's great disappointment, employers are not knocking on my door, and amateur photography does not pay bills. So until one of those changes, I'm free. Will we go?"

I picked up the key and put it carefully in the pocket of my jeans, wondering if I'd ever find the corresponding lock. We said goodbye to Fru Hansen, and walked out into the sunlight and the bitter, hostile cold.

CHAPTER 39

Within minutes of setting out in Asta's mother's car, we'd left the suburban streets of Købæk for a country road with forest on either side. There were no other cars. The forest was popular with hikers in summer, Asta explained, but not so much in November, and certainly not at eleven o'clock on a Thursday morning.

Ten minutes later, when she turned into a small side road, we still hadn't seen any other cars. Tall evergreens blocked out sunlight, and as we drove the road narrowed and became more like a track bordered on both sides by dense forest.

Half a mile further, Asta stopped the car.

"Is something wrong?" I asked.

"No, this is it – we're here," she said, getting out.

I couldn't see anything that looked like a church, but I got out and started after Asta as she made her way down the track. Moments later, she disappeared through a gap between the trees, and I followed.

In the middle of a clearing sat a redbrick church. Small, neat, clearly old, but in good condition despite its isolated location. The deeply sloped black roof showed touches of

211

moss, and at the top stood a steeple – like a chimney wearing a witch's hat. A low stone wall marked the edges of the churchyard, the forest flanking it on three sides. And dotted all over patchy grass, headstones.

Asta had already pushed open the small rusty gate and was making her way across the churchyard, stepping over graves as she did. I followed to the far corner where she'd stopped opposite a headstone of black marble. Bowing her head, she took a step back.

I read the inscription. "*Hanne Karlsen.*"

I stared at the stone until the words swam, waiting for something to hit. What should I be feeling – sadness? Anger? Nothing.

Stepping forward, I hunkered down to look more carefully at the inscription – below her name were some Danish words that looked like a quote.

"What does that mean?" I asked, pointing.

"*If you love something, set it free.*"

I let that sink in for a moment, deciding it was probably a perfect quote for the free-spirited Hanne, uncontained by any one person or place. And still I waited for the lightning bolt of emotion, but all I felt was empty.

Maybe sensing the anti-climax, Asta asked if she should go for a walk and leave me in peace.

"No, that's fine, I don't need to stay," I said, getting to my feet.

"I don't want to rush you," she said. "I can go to the lake. Fugl Sø is just a few minutes north along the road. When the light is right, you can get amazing pictures there. You stay for a while."

She started back through the churchyard gate. I looked down at Hanne's grave, waiting to feel a connection, but as the Baltic wind whipped up across the treetops, all I could feel was her ending – the dark, blank space into which she fell.

"*Asta, wait!*" I called, and followed her out.

We left the car beside the church and continued on foot through the thickening trees. After a few minutes, the dirt track seemed to disappear, and it was hard to see ahead, or imagine we'd be coming to a lake.

"Are you sure this is the right way?" I asked.

"I'm sure. I come out here to take photos," she said with a smile, "despite Fru Hansen's stories of Nøkken and witches."

The trees were so thick now, we couldn't see the sky above, and the only sound was the crunching of twigs as we made our way forward. Asta stopped every now and then to take close-ups of insects and tree bark and I found myself silently willing her to keep walking. Maybe it was the reminder of Fru Hansen's stories, or the eerie silence of the forest, but I desperately wanted to reach the lake.

After another five minutes, I sensed a thinning of trees.

"Is that it – are we nearly at the lake?"

"Yes, that's it," Asta said, stooping to photograph a tree stump.

I found myself breaking into run, rushing towards the clearing, and suddenly there it was.

But the bright, sunlit scene I'd been imagining didn't materialise. The lake was dark green and deathly still, a lifeless body of water. Tall trees shielded it on all sides, keeping the wind at bay. The sunlight was gone, the sky graphite grey. Stony, scrubby soil surrounded the lake, and on the shore reeds made it hard to spot where the water's edge began.

"You see how it would be easy to slip in."

Asta's voice caught me off guard and I jumped.

"Yeah, dangerous spot if you had kids or one too many beers," I replied, forcing a laugh.

"I guess this is how the folk tales came about," she said, hunkering down to take a photo. "Fru Hansen's tale of Nøkken: a warning not to step too close."

I shivered, still trying to locate the water's edge.

"*Argh*, I can't get it out of my head now!" Asta said. "The golden-haired man, playing his violin, and the young girl following with no idea of his evil intent."

She laughed. I didn't.

I stooped to pick up a stone and threw it in the water. The splash was loud in the silence that shrouded us like a cold blanket, the ripples somehow reassuring. But then they were gone, the water still again. Still and waiting.

Asta lifted her camera and framed another shot, but after a couple of clicks she dropped it again.

"Not the best light today," she said. "Usually it's beautiful here."

"Is it?" I asked, pulling my scarf up over my mouth and hugging myself for warmth. "To me it feels dark and cold and . . . unfriendly?"

"You've been spooked by the stories. I'm sorry."

"No, no, it's not just the stories. It feels . . . I don't know, there's something not quite right."

She looked at me, eyebrows up, waiting for more, but I wasn't sure myself what I meant.

"I wonder if my mother ever came here," I said eventually.

"I guess so, local people do. Dina and Erik go to the church we have just been to – that's why Hanne is buried

214

there. No doubt they came here on occasion." She paused. "Or do you mean later, do you mean when she died?"

I wasn't sure – maybe I was still chasing the connection I hadn't felt at the grave.

"Are you thinking she came here that night?" Asta went on. "It's about fifteen kilometres – she couldn't walk that far."

"I don't know what I'm thinking – maybe the stories are just getting to me. Why do you think Fru Hansen talked about Nøkken again this morning?"

"She loves to tell stories, she has always been like this."

"But was there more to it? Do you think there's some link with what really happened?"

Asta shook her head. "No, because Fru Hansen doesn't know what really happened. They're just stories, and I'm sorry that it's made you think there was some deeper meaning." She lifted her camera again. "Come on, cheer up, smile for the photo!"

I smiled mechanically and she clicked the shutter.

The wind whipped up again, racing through treetops like an angry ghost, and the sky loomed darker than before.

"It's going to snow," Asta said, lowering her camera. "We had better go."

And as we turned away from the lake and back towards the forest, the first snowflakes began to fall. On contact with the ground, they disappeared, disguising themselves as something else entirely.

CHAPTER 40

That should have been the end of it, and at the time I thought it was. But I had two more days to kill, so spent Friday wandering around Købæk on my own, and on Saturday morning Asta called by the hostel to take me shopping, insisting I couldn't leave without checking out the local stores. We wandered around the pretty town centre, dipping in and out of jewellery and gift shops, lingering to avoid the cold. In one tiny shop towards the end of the main strip, I found a scarf I knew Ray would like and, as I was waiting to pay, I spotted little clay figurines. There were horses and tiny deer, and one that looked like a man in a long gown, holding a violin.

"Are these Nøkken?" I asked Asta.

"Yes, they are actually. I've never seen something like that."

On a whim, I picked up the man with the violin, and paid for it. For Ray or for me, I wasn't sure.

Shopping done, we wandered on in search of coffee. As we approached a colourful building with murals on the outside wall, a woman who looked like Dina walked out. I squinted as she came down the steps, but she was already walking away in the opposite direction.

"I think that was Dina," I said to Asta, who was still scouting for coffee.

"Oh yes, it may have been. She volunteers with a youth group there."

"Your mother mentioned something about 'children from poverty backgrounds'?"

"Disadvantaged backgrounds, she meant. Yes, Dina helps out. I believe your mother used to go there too, to the Youth Club. I never did. My mother wanted me to go after school when she was working, but Fru Hansen offered to look after me instead."

"But my mother didn't come from a disadvantaged background? Nor do you?"

"No, I don't mean it that way – different groups meet there. Dina volunteers a lot," she said, then darted forward towards a café across the street. "Come on, a free table!"

Inside, the café was dark but cosy – it continued to amaze me how warm Danish buildings were despite the cold outdoors. We picked out pastries and ordered coffees, and settled down with no plan to move anytime soon. Something else I'd learned about Denmark – they know how to do pastries like nowhere else I'd ever been. I put the bag with the scarf and the figurine on the table, and took off my gloves.

"The present is for your boyfriend?" Asta asked, nodding towards the bag.

I laughed. "Yeah. Boyfriend sounds funny. Ray's thirty-seven. A bit old to be a boyfriend, isn't it?"

"*Ja*, maybe, but words don't really matter, do they?"

217

Asta said, taking off her woolly hat and stuffing it in her satchel. "He is your *person*, the other half of you."

Our coffees arrived just then and I took a moment to sip the too-hot drink, thinking about what she'd said. Was Ray my person, the other half of me?

"Do you have anyone?" I asked, pushing away questions I didn't want to answer.

"Not right now. There was someone, but he was bad news."

I waited for more, looking at her over the top of my coffee.

"My parents were super-protective when my brother and I were growing up," she went on, "because of what happened."

"To Hanne?"

"Yes. They were so afraid to let us out of sight, and of course when we were teens, we rebelled. My brother left home as soon as he could, and I found a boyfriend with a motorcycle and an apartment. Anything for freedom!" She smiled brightly, but her eyes looked sad.

"And what happened?"

"What happened was exactly what my mother said would happen – he cheated on me, lied, borrowed money from me, got in trouble with the police. If you tried to draw a picture of the worst boyfriend in the world, it would be that guy."

"So you dumped him?"

She shook her head and laughed. "I wish, but no, he dumped me! I lay in my bed for days, crying about him. My mother brought me food and rubbed my back and never once said 'I told you so'."

"And do you really think it was all down to Hanne's disappearance – her overprotectiveness?"

"Oh yes, no question. Much as she disliked Fru Hansen's stories, she had her own more direct warnings. 'Don't go out after dark, you know what happened to Hanne Karlsen' is something we heard over and over growing up."

"But, logically, there was no reason for the killer to strike again in the same street – the other two victims were from different towns entirely."

Asta shrugged. "I guess if you are a parent, logic doesn't come into it."

"This is the kind of stuff I'm interested in – hearing from people who remember what it was like back then. If you think of anything else, will you email me?" I pulled out a pen to write my contact details on a napkin.

"For sure. You go home tomorrow?"

"Yeah," I sighed. "God, I don't know what I expected, but I feel I'm going home without knowing much about Hanne, and obviously without knowing Dina and Erik at all."

Asta gave me a funny look.

"Sorry, that sounds ungrateful," I said quickly. "You've been very generous with your time."

"That's not it – I just didn't take you for a quitter."

I sat up straighter. "Hey, that's not fair – I did try but she doesn't want to see me."

"She's your *grandmother*. Your only link to your mother. Have you really come all this way to go home without giving it one more shot?"

And that's how I found myself outside Dina and Erik's house yet again that Saturday evening. It was pitch dark on Damtoften and bitterly cold as I rang the bell, and when there was no answer, I wasn't disappointed – just empty.

219

Nothingy. I tried a second time, and though I could see some light in the living room where the blind didn't quite meet the windowsill, still there was no answer. Without stopping to think, I moved sideways along the path at the front of the house and ducked down to peer through the gap under the blind. Inside, a candle flickered on a shelf, but neither Dina nor Erik was there. There wasn't a sound coming from the house, nor out on the street – Damtoften was a ghost-town after dark. I crept past the living-room window, and around to the back of the house. Bending low to make my way along the path, I hunkered beneath the kitchen window. Thin light filtered through on to the grass and as I watched, a shadow flickered across it. Someone was in there. I swallowed, wondering what the Danish penalty for trespassing was, then turned and raised my head so my eyes were just level with the bottom corner of the window. Dina was sitting at the kitchen table and opposite sat a man, his hands on hers. A man with light-coloured hair and a darker, red-tinged beard. A man who wasn't Erik; someone I'd never seen before. While I crouched there, Dina inclined her head, as though listening for something. For what? Then it dawned on me. She was listening for the doorbell, waiting to see if I'd call again. A call she clearly wasn't going to answer.

In the darkness, still unseen, I stood and walked away.

CHAPTER 41

Arriving back in Ireland that Sunday, it felt like I'd been gone for three months, not seven days, and Ray acted as though it was the former, wrapping me in a giant hug at Dublin airport, telling me all the way home to Wicklow how much he missed me. He had the kitchen table set and a slow-roast loin of pork in the oven – I didn't even know Ray could cook. In retrospect, I can see that cooking just didn't fit with the character in his head – the intellectual creative who didn't have time for domesticity. The kitchen was freezing cold, and I suggested we decamp to the living room. Ray resisted – he'd put so much effort into setting the table apparently. But, as sleet began to fall outside, and we sat across from one another still wearing our coats, he had to accept defeat. We carried our plates to the couch, and began to thaw over a bottle of red wine.

Ray was full of questions – what was Denmark like, what did my grandparents look like, did I feel any connection to the country? That last question made me stop and think. The short answer was no, and that made me suddenly sad. Ray had moved on to the next question without waiting for an answer – was the man in the kitchen with Dina the blond man people had seen twenty years earlier? Maybe, I told him, though Denmark is bursting with blond men. Did I ring the bell again, he asked – did I see them before I left? No, I sneaked around to the front of the house, and walked away.

And Ray's last question before we settled down to watch *The Clinic* – would I be going back?

No, I told him. I was done.

And I *was* done, at least until I found the key in my washbag while unpacking the next day. I studied it, wondering. Could something so tiny really open anything of value? There were no diaries of any sort on the shelves in the living room, and nothing but Ray's computer in my dad's old room. If there was something to find, it had to be in the attic.

Ray had gone down to the village to write – he couldn't concentrate when I was in the house, he said, though how being surrounded by other people in the Wooden Spoon was going to be any easier, I wasn't sure.

I pulled down the ladder and climbed into the attic, wrinkling my nose against the musty smell. I hadn't been up in almost a year – not since I'd found Hanne's goodbye letter, and now the smell seemed more pungent. Maybe it was time to clear it out properly, to get rid of Hanne's stuff. Perhaps *that* would be the result of the trip to Denmark – not closure, but a prompt to move on.

At the back of the attic, the box of dresses stood where I'd left it, the silver dress near the top. The blue and jade dresses hung in my wardrobe, destined for a life almost as lonely as they'd had up here, wishing no doubt for an owner with more social obligations. I turned to a box of books and removed them, one by one, searching for a diary. Underneath were some journals, but none had a lock. The next box contained only sketchpads. I set it aside, deflated. No locked diary, no locked anything. Maybe the key was just a symbol, Hanne speaking metaphorically when she told Fru Hansen she wanted to lock away the past.

I sat back, turning the key over in my hand. This was the problem with growing up on mystery novels – everything was supposed to have *meaning*. Yet since I'd started getting to know Hanne and her story, I'd found only dead ends.

I pulled out the silver dress. Did she ever wear it? It didn't seem like Købæk would offer any more opportunities for glamour than Wicklow did. Carefully I folded it and put it back, brushing against something solid as I did. I pulled it out – the wooden jewellery box with no jewellery inside. There was something so lonely about that.

The lower drawer was still stuck and I wondered where the handle was or if I could attach something to replace it. I held it towards the light to see better, and that's when it struck me: I wasn't looking at a missing handle, but rather, a keyhole.

The key slid in and turned easily, allowing the drawer to open. The inside was crammed with paper. With a glow of excitement, I crawled back to sit directly under the light bulb and pulled out what looked like four or five folded drawings. The first showed a deer, nuzzling a small girl. Drawn beautifully in pencil, the attention to detail was stunning. The second page showed a white horse, with a child on its back. In the third sketch, a child was being blown forward by an unseen wind. In the fourth, a man in robes was playing a violin while a young girl trailed behind, her face lit up. It was the final sketch that stopped my breath. Water, and a young girl's face just below the surface, eyes wide in terror. Looking down at her was the man with the violin, only now his robe was covered with faces of crying children. And his own face was gone – in its place, just emptiness, as blank as the new-fallen snow.

CHAPTER 42

2018

Thoughts of footprints and chalk letters were still ricocheting around my head when I got back to the house on Sunday after coffee with Jamie. He was certain Alan couldn't be responsible for any of it, but I wasn't so sure. People we are close to do all sorts of things that are out of character, I reminded him, I knew that better than most. Look at Ray, I'd said, and what he was doing, under my roof. But as Jamie gently pointed out, I only knew Ray for a couple of years – he'd known Alan all his life. I wanted to say more – to remind him of all the things my dad didn't tell me about Hanne, and what Hanne did to my dad, but I just nodded and agreed that Alan probably wasn't the guy.

As we were draining our coffees, I told him I'd reported the chalk letter to the police that morning, and found myself watching his face for a reaction. But he just nodded and agreed it was the right thing to do. And then the weirdest thing of all happened. Jamie, the guy I've known since I was four years old, asked me if I wanted to grab a drink some night. *To talk it through a bit more,* he blurted, as soon as he'd made the suggestion, his face colouring. I could feel my cheeks heating up too as I nodded yes, and agreed it would be good to talk it through. Whatever *it* was.

And that was that. At the grand old age of thirty-five, life-long neighbours Jamie Crowley and Marianne McShane were going for a drink. Linda would have a field-day.

Parking the jeep at the side of the cottage, I walked around to the front door, my eyes combing the ground for more chalk letters. There were none, and no trace of yesterday evening's R. R for what? R for "Ray"? I shivered. That made no sense. I scanned the front of the house. Everything looked just as it had this morning, nothing out of place. Bedroom curtains closed, living-room curtains open. Windows tightly shut.

Standing outside my bedroom, I slipped my fingers under the lower part of the sash window and tried to lift it. A fraction of an inch but nothing more. You could slip a piece of paper through at most. I thought about what Jamie had said – about putting sticky tape around the frame. Did I even have any tape? I couldn't remember the last time I'd needed it. Christmas presents aren't a big thing when you have no family. I unlocked the door and stepped inside. The house felt quieter than usual, though I couldn't pinpoint what sounds I was expecting to hear. I stood in the living room, listening, my skin prickling. Would I know if someone had been here while I was out? Maybe I *should* put a piece of thread across the doorway. Or even easier, something in front of the door, something innocuous that would slide away if the door was pushed open. Like a book, I thought, glancing over at my Julia Land paperback on the coffee table.

I shivered. The living room was ice-cold. Sooner or later I'd have to invest in some kind of insulation, but the burglar alarm was going to eat up a chunk of savings. And the motion-sensor lights. What else had the security consultant said? Close the front gate – so simple, and yet I'd left the bloody thing open again. Sighing, I pulled on my jacket and walked down the driveway to close it. As I was about to turn towards the house, I spotted someone in the distance, standing in the middle of the road. Squinting into the afternoon glare, I could just about make out the black-brimmed hat. Alan. What was he doing? As my eyes adjusted, I realised he was staring in my direction. What the hell was up with him now? I shook my head and stalked back to the house, cursing Ray for getting me into this situation in the first place.

That night, with Ray and the bookshop sighting still on my mind, I googled him again. Still no news of a book tour in Ireland. So what was he doing here? I tried Facebook – we weren't Facebook friends but Ray had no idea how to fix his privacy settings so I could pretty much see everything he posted. Back when he lived here, Facebook was the new shiny thing we were all trying, but he dismissed it, announcing it would never take off. He shook his head in mock dismay when I set up my account, and at the time I thought it was somehow cute – part of our relationship dynamic: the older, cultured writer, and the younger, tech-savvy girl. Now I could see it for what it was – a constant need to make pronouncements about anything and everything, whether he knew what he was talking about or not.

But his Facebook account gave me no clues. Photos of his books, his book signings, his pug, and his house –

nothing about Ireland. Good. Maybe it was a fleeting visit. Maybe he was gone. Maybe it was never him.

There were new notifications in the Armchair Detective group. Judith and Barry both had updates on the footprint cases they'd been researching. Barry had taken four cases and had suggested I take just two, because I had my day-job to do as well. Barry didn't have a job – something to do with a tech business he sold off in his thirties. He never struck me as the tech-entrepreneur type – according to Facebook, he was forty-two, but in his profile picture, courtesy of his receding hairline and 1980's style gold-rimmed glasses, he looked older. He could be needy and obsessive about the group but, to be fair to him, he was extraordinarily good at research, and had come back with a whole heap of extra information on his cases. He'd typed up all his findings in a Word document and added the file to the Facebook group. It was brilliantly put together, but there were so many details – some similar to the Blackwood Strangler's profile, some not at all – it made the whole thing muddier.

I'm way behind, sorry, guys, I typed, after a quick read of Barry's document. **The real world sucked me out of things for a bit. And I don't know if I'll ever manage such a detailed executive summary – fair play, Barry.**

Barry replied with a hugging emoji. **Thanks, Marianne, that means a lot. I can help with your cases if you like?**

No, don't worry – I have time tonight and could do with distraction.

Judith joined the conversation: **Nothing wrong with being sucked out of the internet and into the real world, Marianne.**

Yeah, it wasn't anything good in the real world though . . . it was a bit weird actually. I woke up this morning to

find someone had drawn a letter R in chalk just outside my front door.

I stopped, wondering if they'd think I was overreacting.

Oh my God, you mean like the woman in Denmark who found the hangman in chalk drawn in her front yard and ended up dead? That was Neil, lurking until there was a bit of drama.

Judith was quick to jump in. **That's not quite the same thing, Neil – you'll be worrying poor Marianne.**

It did make me think of that though, I typed. **The chalk hangman and the initials scratched in the windowsill of another victim. And I didn't tell you guys this but I may as well now – on Monday morning, there were footprints in my garden, and I thought I saw a face at the window in the middle of the night. And someone left a doll in my jeep.**

Good Lord, but you surely don't think the Blackwood Strangler is in Ireland stalking you? Judith said.

Before I could reply, Barry jumped in.

If I may say, there are strong links between the cases around Europe – there's every possibility these were Blackwood Strangler, or copy-cat.

I realised then I'd told them my story so they could reassure me there was absolutely no way it had anything to do with a serial killer. On that front, things were not working out as planned.

I suppose if he's gone to other countries, there's no reason he wouldn't go to Ireland.

That was Neil again. Thanks, Neil.

Isn't it more likely it's a child playing a prank? Especially the doll? Judith wrote, and I couldn't tell if she was trying to make me feel better or saying what she really believed.

229

Yeah, a prank or someone local with a grudge. Anyway, I'm getting an alarm and going to pay more attention to security, I replied.

That never stopped the Blackwood Strangler!

Neil again. Fuck off, Neil.

That sounds smart, Judith typed, ignoring Neil, and it's not surprising that you'd feel a little worried when you think about the kinds of cases we're looking at. Not everyone's ideal bedtime story.

Indeed it wasn't, and I did wonder about the wisdom of it all as I settled down to read about stalkers and footprints and unsolved murders.

CHAPTER 43

On Wednesday morning, as I was leaving for work, I grabbed a book from the living-room bookshelf and placed it just inside the front door. I rolled my eyes to show the universe I knew it was silly – but what harm could it do? And just because I'd had three uninterrupted nights didn't mean he was gone for good.

My phone pinged with a private Facebook message from Barry.

Hi Marianne, just wondering how you're getting on with the footprint cases and thinking since two heads are better than one, it might help to meet up and swap notes? Always easier to go through things in person, instead of typing everything out on FB ☺ And I'm only up the road from you in Dun Laoghaire – we could meet in my flat on your way home from work some evening? If it suits ☺ Let me know? Barry

Oh good Lord. This was the last thing I needed. I swiped at my phone, pushing the message away, and braced myself for the icy road to Dublin.

Sifting through work emails ninety minutes later, I found one from Asta, with bad news about Fru Hansen.

She's been very ill, and now seems to have given in, Asta wrote, **she's even found religion which is a sign, I guess – my mom told me she asked to see a pastor. I called in to her yesterday and she was so frail, it was sad to see.**

I did a quick calculation in my head – I reckoned Fru Hansen was in her mid-eighties when I met her, so mid-nineties by now. Our encounter had been brief, but it was sad to think I'd probably never see her again. And another connection to Hanne would be lost.

I replied, asking Asta to send my love to Fru Hansen, but it felt empty and redundant and lonely.

Still brooding an hour later, I decided to try phoning Linda. I'd caught her at a bad time last week, maybe now she'd be able to chat. She picked up after two rings – a good sign, I figured – until I heard the unmistakable sound of irritation.

"Hi. Marianne? Sorry, one sec."

Muffled sounds of children and TV drifted into the phone. Then she was back.

"Sorry. Everything okay?"

"Oh, yeah – all good here, I was just ringing to say hi."

"Right. Sure."

Silence.

"So how are you?" I tried.

"Oh you know, the usual. *Sadie! Get down!* Sorry. Jesus, she's a nightmare at the moment, climbing on everything."

"I can imagine," I said, with a small laugh.

Linda didn't join in. "How's work?" she said mechanically, and suddenly all my plans to tell her about Jamie's sort-of-invitation for drinks disappeared.

"Grand – actually, I'm calling from work and my boss has just given me a look – I'd better go."

"No worries, I'll give you a call at some stage," she said, and that was that.

I put down my mobile, and sat staring at it. How had we come to this?

Traffic was worse than usual as I crawled from the city centre towards the motorway that evening, and that was why I decided to detour into Stillorgan Shopping Centre to pick up dinner – or, at least, that's what I told myself. It took no more than ten minutes to choose a steak from the butcher's along with some salads from the deli and then, like a moth to a flame, I was inside the warm glow of the bookshop. In crime, I picked up an old Jeffery Deaver novel I'd read as a teen, and a newer book about a woman whose husband has just murdered someone.

"That one's very good," said the lady behind the till. "Brilliant opening line. You like the darker stuff, I see!"

I laughed. "Yeah, I don't know why I keep doing it to myself – I should probably try something light or funny or just less bloody at some point."

"Ah, I like crime too," she said, scanning my purchases. "If it's happening in a book, it's less likely to be happening in my life, that's my theory anyway. You know the author's doing a talk in the library in Dun Laoghaire in a few weeks?"

"Is she? I must keep an eye out. I'm going there this Friday to see Julia Land being interviewed."

"*Love* her books. Especially the early detective ones. Now, do you need anything else today?"

"I'll take this too," I said, picking up a roll of Sellotape from a stationary stand by the counter. I cleared my throat. "Actually, do you stock *The Sophisticate* by Ray Sedgwick?"

"We do, and that's funny, because there was someone else looking for it last week. It's been out for years and we only have one copy, but the other customer just wanted to see it, so you're in luck!"

She came out from behind the counter and moved to the A to Z Fiction section, returning moments later with the book. I took it from her, because that's what she expected me to do, and stared at the familiar image on the front cover.

"Have you read his other books?"

I shook my head. I had read some of his earlier books, back when we were first together, but I found it hard to connect with them, and Ray never seemed to mind that I didn't read them all. In fact, he'd told me not to at one point, saying I'd probably found them boring. For the first time, it struck me that what I took to be self-deprecation was in fact a snobbery of sorts – it wasn't that he didn't think his books were good enough for me – I wasn't good enough for his books.

The lady was behind the till again, waiting, as I continued staring at *The Sophisticate*.

"Will I ring it up for you?"

"I might leave it for now, and come back," I said, putting it aside. "The other person who was asking about it – I don't suppose you remember what he looked like?"

She gave me a curious glance, and I rushed on.

"I'm buying it as a present for my uncle – he mentioned he liked it and I'm wondering now if that was actually him looking at it in here – maybe he didn't like it after all!"

"Ah, I see. Well, the man who asked about it was probably a bit young to be your uncle – he was in his late forties, I'd say." Then she laughed. "Sorry, that's very rude, I'm making assumptions about your age!"

I brushed it away. "No, not at all, I get you. And yeah, my uncle is much older than that," I said, conjuring up an imaginary, white-haired relative.

"Also, the man who came in had an American accent – is your uncle American?"

My stomach gave a small lurch. "No, definitely not him then. I'll leave the book till another time."

I paid and walked into the cold evening chill, certain now that Ray was back, but none the wiser why. Would he come looking for me? My stomach lurched again. I wouldn't be hard to find.

As I slid into the jeep, my phone pinged with another message from Barry:

Just to say, no hard feelings at all if it doesn't suit to meet – it was just a thought. I'm not offended! I probably wouldn't want to meet with me either ☺

Argh, awkward. I clicked into the message to reply, but the right words didn't spring to mind. Instead I put the phone on the passenger seat and pulled out into traffic.

Nothing stirred in the dark garden or the road beyond. The only sounds came from me, as I pulled strips of tape from the roll. It wasn't wide enough to properly cover the window frame, but it was enough. If someone opened the window while I was out, I'd know. *What if he spots the tape and replaces it?* I shook the thought away. There were only so many *What ifs* I could cover. The tape was a precaution. Sensible.

But that night, as I lay awake, alert to every creak and rustle, I couldn't help wondering about the line between knowing and not knowing, and if perhaps it was better before I knew. Before the snow.

235

CHAPTER 44

Thursday morning's alarm pulled me from a deep, dreamless sleep with a suddenness that left me dizzy and confused. I lay, blinking at the ceiling, assessing, testing how I was feeling. Glad. Definitely glad of another uninterrupted night. No knocking, no noise, no face. But low and gloomy too, I realised, because I wasn't going into the office. On edge, facing a day on my own.

With no reason to get dressed, I made coffee, and stood for a while looking out the kitchen window, the lino cold under my feet. The sky was a giant blanket of grey nothing – the kind of day that wasn't going to brighten up, and before I was halfway through my coffee, the chill in the kitchen had soaked through my skin, right to my bones. I moved into the living room, switching on the light and sitting down with a heavy sigh to open my laptop. That's when I realised my folder of work notes wasn't in its usual spot on the coffee table – I'd left it in the jeep when I brought in the groceries and books the night before. And the Sellotape. I should probably check the tape was still in place. Pulling on an oversized cardigan and a pair of boots, bracing myself for the rush of cold air, I opened the front door.

But something stopped me from stepping forward: on the doorstep sat an apple. Peering down, I could see it was on top of what looked like an old book – perched like a stock image of an apple on a teacher's desk. Only not shiny and red like the ones in the pictures – wizened, brown skin encased shrunken flesh, and tiny holes told of insect-foraging. Hunkering down, I tried to read the title of the book beneath. An old brown hardback cover, frayed at the edges, faded gold lettering on the spine spelling out *Hansel and Gretel*.

I reached towards the rotting apple, to move it aside and see the book better, but the top half came away in my hand, separated from the lower part along an incision I hadn't seen. Inside the half still resting on the book, there was movement. Fat brown maggots slipped and slid where fruit flesh used to be, shiny and pulsating, disturbed by sudden light. Jerking back, nausea swilling through my stomach and up my throat, I stood. And as I stared, as my fingers gripped the other half, too late I felt the slippery movement against my skin. Dropping the infested fruit, I screamed, loud and unrestrained into the grey morning emptiness. Loud and unrestrained and unheard.

Fuck. Sweating now, breathing fast. Where was my phone? I needed a photo. In my bedroom, as I scooped my mobile off the nightstand, every inch of me wanted to climb back into bed and pull the covers over my head, like I used to as a kid, when Hanne's story got too much. But that's the shitty thing about being a grown-up, no more hiding under the covers.

The morning sky was still too dark for a proper shot – I turned on the porch light and tried again, and imagined showing it to Patrick and Geraldine. They were going to think I was losing it. My breathing slowed. I forced myself to focus the screen on the still-squirming maggots and the fruit carcass on which they feasted. But what the hell did it mean? A jumble of images rushed through my mind – Snow White's poisoned apple, Eve and the forbidden fruit, silver apples and moons – something from a poem we'd learned in school. And the book – a children's fairy story, but not one that featured apples, as far as I remembered. Hansel and Gretel, lost in the woods. Witches and cages and bones flickered through my mind. Was it random, intended to confuse and freak me out, or was it some kind of message?

Having taken four or five photos, and certain I wasn't going to touch the rotten fruit again, I left it there, on top of the book. My work file was still in the jeep, but as I looked across the shadowy garden, I decided I could manage without it.

At lunchtime, still unsettled, the need for escape and for human contact clanged too loud to ignore. Plus I had no fresh food in the fridge – there was something ironic about an apple on the doorstep when I had no fruit of any kind in my kitchen, I thought, as I opened the front door.

Only the apple wasn't there any more, nor was the book. I stood and stared at the empty space they had occupied just hours earlier. Could the wind have blown them across the garden? My eyes scanned the grass and the driveway. It was gusty out, enough to blow half a rotting apple away, but not a hardcover book surely? If it wasn't the wind, there was only one other possibility. Someone had been here while I was inside working. Heart thumping loudly in my chest, I stepped across to my bedroom window and made myself check the tape. Still in place. I let out a jagged breath, and ran to the jeep.

Wrapped in worry, I didn't see Jamie until I'd driven past him. He half lifted his hand in salute, and I pulled in to offer him a lift. My voice sounded shaky and Jamie gave me a funny look as he hopped into the passenger seat, but he didn't comment. Alan had taken the Land Rover, he said, and the car they shared was being serviced – he was on his way to pick it up. The thumping in my chest began to subside. It was a relief to have company.

"So Alan was gone somewhere all morning?" I asked in what I hoped was a casual tone. I stared straight ahead, focusing on the road, conscious Jamie was looking at me.

"About an hour ago, himself and the dog – why?"

"Just that it must be a pain for you, stuck there with no transport."

"Oh listen, story of my life. You know my da – he does what suits him, and wouldn't think about whether or not I need a lift now any more than he did when I was ten."

It was true – Alan had somehow managed to be an absentee father, despite literally working on the grounds of their farmhouse and being the only parent Jamie had. If it wasn't for Mrs Townsend, I don't know if he'd ever have had a hot meal after school.

"Yeah, true," I said. "I guess he was always so caught up in the farm, he didn't think beyond it."

Jamie laughed, but it was hollow. "You're being kind. Most of the time, he just didn't care all that much, and he was as caught up in whiskey as he was in the farm. Remember the time I went home from yours and the house was all locked up?"

I did. Jamie had waited in the freezing cold for over an hour, and eventually shut himself into a shed Alan used for storing old furniture and animal feed. We found out about it when Alan came banging on our door at ten o'clock that night, shouting for Jamie to get home. When my dad explained Jamie had left hours earlier, Alan looked irritated, not worried, and it was my dad who instigated the search. They found Jamie asleep in the storage shed, on an old mattress. And instead of showing relief or remorse, Alan berated him for not coming when he was called.

"But surely things have improved over the years?" I asked, indicating to turn onto the main road to Carrickderg.

"Oh absolutely," Jamie said, smiling. "I have my own key now." He paused. "So, c'mere, it's good to reminisce about the bad old days – are you on for that drink we were talking about?"

Still looking straight ahead, I nodded. "Sure – I think this is the bit where I'm supposed to make it sound like I'm really busy most nights, but I'll skip all that – when suits?"

"Tonight?"

And suddenly, as I nodded yes again, I found my mind rushing through my wardrobe and my fingers rushing through my hair, and I wondered if this was really just two old friends catching up and, more than anything, I wanted to talk to Linda.

CHAPTER 45

Still not sure what they'd make of my imminent report, I called into the Garda Station and asked to speak to Patrick or Geraldine. They were both there, and both came to the front desk at the same time. It was obviously a slow morning for crime in Carrickderg.

Two expectant faces and two sets of folded arms waited for my latest instalment, and I got ready to be humoured.

"What's up, Marianne, is it more footprints?" Geraldine said. "Did you get that curtain I told you to get?"

"I did, thanks, Geraldine," I said, like a schoolgirl eager to please the teacher.

"Right. So what is it now?"

"Well, I was here on Sunday to tell Garda Maguire about a chalk letter R that someone drew outside my house . . ."

She nodded, slowly and deliberately, making it clear in one movement that Patrick had filled her in, and that she wasn't about to call in the nearest SWAT team over my chalk letter.

"Then this morning I woke to find someone had left an apple and a book on my doormat, and later they both disappeared."

Two sets of eyebrows went up simultaneously.

"I know it sounds silly," I went on, "but the apple was rotten, full of maggots." Remembering their touch against my fingers, I shuddered. "On top of the chalk letter at the weekend and the other stuff last week, it's freaking me out."

"Well, yes . . . but what does it mean? And why does it have to be something *bad*?" Geraldine asked. "Maybe whoever left it didn't realise the apple was rotten? Were they just trying to leave you a present? What was the book?"

"*Hansel and Gretel*."

"The story of the kids left in the forest by their stepmother and father? Witch, gingerbread house, all that?"

"Yes." I could feel my face colouring. It sounded silly.

"Hang on," Geraldine said, "could it be someone with a crush?"

"Sorry?"

"Hear me out. Someone came to your house the night of the snow, but chickened out of knocking on the door. So he tried to leave you a message – the doll, the chalk letter, and now the book as a gift!"

She was so pleased with her deduction she was almost hugging herself. Patrick looked sceptical but said nothing.

"I see where you're coming from," I said carefully, "but the footprints were under my bedroom window, not at my front door. And look, here's a photo of the apple – nobody could have mistaken it for anything other than rotten."

I held out my phone, but Geraldine was too caught up in her new theory to pay any attention.

"People do strange things when they're in love, believe

me – I could tell some stories," she said. "Watch now, you'll go home and find flowers on your doorstep next time – I bet I'm right!"

A sudden image flashed through my mind – a single pink rose on a doorstep, and the woman in Austria who thought she had a Peeping Tom. Until she wound up dead. I shivered.

"Are you alright?" Patrick asked. "Marianne?"

"I'm fine. Just spooked. I get that it doesn't sound worrying or serious, but for me waking up to find that someone was sneaking around outside my house at night, it's not nothing. I need to know who it is, and I need them to stop. That's all." My voice broke on the last words and I could feel tears threatening.

"Ah Marianne, I'm sorry, I didn't mean to belittle the story," Geraldine said in a soft voice I hadn't heard before. "I was just trying to reassure you that there's probably nothing to worry about. We'll look into it, of course we will. In the meantime, is there anyone who could come and stay with you?"

With a watery smile, I shook my head, and turned to leave, not trusting myself to speak.

I got home in time for my afternoon conference call, and was in the middle of giving an update when I heard Bert's knock. Opening the door with my phone still to my ear, I pointed at it to indicate I couldn't talk.

"Don't worry," he mouthed, placing a package just inside my front door and stepping back to go.

"One sec!" I mouthed, holding up a finger. "That's everything from my side," I said into the phone, and put it on mute.

"How're you, Marianne?" Bert asked.

"I'm okay . . . I was wondering, were you up this way this morning on your route? I know I didn't have any letters, but maybe you had some for houses further up the road towards Ramolin?"

"No, nothing this morning – but I don't pass your house to get to Ramolin, I go round the other way. Why do you ask?"

"Ah, someone's been creeping around at night, and they left something here this morning. I was hoping maybe you'd been past and seen. Doesn't matter."

He tilted his head. "You're not okay, are you, love?"

"I'll be fine," I said, my throat tight. "It's probably just kids messing."

"Well, look, I'm around this way at least every second day, so I'll keep an eye out, okay?"

I was about to say I was fine again, but who was I fooling?

"I'd appreciate that," I said quietly. "Thank you, Bert."

Jamie was picking me up at eight, and at quarter to I was still rummaging through my wardrobe, cursing my year-round jeans-and-jumper uniform. Then again, for a Thursday night in Delaneys', maybe jeans-and-jumper was exactly right? I hadn't gone out with anyone in over a year, and that was a blind date Linda organised with one of her husband's friends. I'd listened to him talking about investment banking and rugby all night, then told him Zorian were sending me on sabbatical to the Limerick office. Zorian don't have a Limerick office, and a quick Google would have caught me out, but the guy was so busy talking about himself, he wasn't going to remember a thing

I'd said. In fact, in the years since Ray and I split, I hadn't gone out with anyone more than two or three times, and I'd never cared enough to worry about how I looked. Why did this feel so different, I wondered, and why on earth didn't I own proper make-up?

In the end, I went for black jeans and a black long-sleeved top, brightened up with a silver pendant and my one and only pair of heels. Then I decided heels were ridiculous for a Thursday night in Delaneys', and changed back into my boots, just as Jamie knocked on the door.

"You got the car back then?" I said by way of greeting, forestalling any chance of awkward hugs or references to the unusual circumstances of our encounter.

"Yeah – otherwise you'd be in a Land Rover that smells distinctly of pigfeed," Jamie said as he opened the passenger door for me. "Though knowing my da, you'd be sitting at home going nowhere – he'd have said no to me using it out of spite."

"Well, we could have booked a cab – and I meant to say, if you want to leave your car down the village and have a drink, I'll drop you down tomorrow to pick it up?"

Jamie nodded thanks, and something in his face told me he was as much in need of Dutch courage for this not-really-a-date date as I was.

"And about Alan – does he, um, know?"

Jamie looked sideways at me as he pulled out of the driveway.

"Know we're going for a drink together?"

"Yeah . . ." This was weird. But not bad weird.

"No – I just said I was going out. Can you imagine his face? I might save telling him for some time when I really want to piss him off."

245

He grinned at me, and I grinned back, and settled in the seat, wondering where all of this was going.

In Delaneys' we got quizzical looks from the sprinkling of customers, most of whom had known both of us all our lives but had never seen us come into the pub together. Jamie led the way to a small table near the fireplace and went up to order drinks. I could see John behind the bar saying something to Jamie, and smirking in my direction, as Jamie shook his head. What did that mean? Jesus, I needed to stop overthinking everything – it was Jamie Crowley for God's sake. We'd picked blackberries and climbed trees and swapped books – we could surely handle a drink together without analysing it to the nth degree.

"Good to see John's as big an arsehole as always anyway," Jamie said in a low voice as he arrived back with two pints of Guinness.

"Ha! What did he say?"

"You don't want to know," he said, his brown eyes meeting mine. "His mind is in the gutter."

I could feel my face colouring, and picked up my pint to take a sip.

"He hasn't changed a bit." I said. "He was like that when I was working here, twenty years ago. It was gross then, and it's even worse now that he's older."

"I know. And the thing he did with my da – spiking Ray's drinks that time, that was shitty. He's a gobshite."

"Did you know about that?"

"Of course. My da came home bragging about it. I never got to apologise for it at the time – I should have."

"God, no. It wasn't your fault, sure you weren't even here. And let's face it, Ray was as bad as Alan in the end."

"Any news on that front – do you reckon he's definitely back?"

I filled him in on my stop-off in Stillorgan, and the conversation with the bookseller.

"So he *is* back. I wonder what he wants?"

There was something odd about the way he said it.

"What do you mean? I guess he could be in Ireland for all sorts of reasons."

"Sure, but is he really going to travel all this way and not come back to Carrickderg?"

"Ah look, why would he come back here?" I said with a laugh that sounded high and artificial. "Sure everyone else rushes off as soon as they can. Actually, out of our whole class in school, I think you and I are the only ones left?"

Jamie nodded. "Believe me, I'm *very* aware of that fact. At least you escaped to Dublin for a few years. Did you ever see Sorcha Riordan when you were there – she's in Grand Canal too, isn't she? One of the big US tech companies?"

I hadn't realised that – I couldn't imagine Sorcha Riordan as an adult. In my mind, she was still the whiny bigmouth she was when we were eight.

"And Linda scarpered as soon as she could," Jamie continued. "God, you two were like glue when we were in primary – you must miss having her around."

"I guess."

"Oh – I'm detecting a distinct lack of enthusiasm – what's up?"

"Ah, nothing new – same as I was saying before – we've drifted apart recently. I'm the one doing all the calling, and she's not making any effort at all. I'm fed up to be honest."

It came out sounding bitter. "I think I'll back off a bit. She knows where I am if she wants me."

Jamie looked at me for a moment, and I couldn't read his expression.

"Do you remember the time Linda stuffed her lunch down the back of the radiator in school," he said after a moment, "and then you and me did it as well?"

I laughed. I'd forgotten all about it. Nobody knew until the heating went on the following morning and the smell of warm tuna filled the classroom.

"Oh yes! Ms Brown went mad at us – remember?"

"Nope, she went mad at me and Linda – she didn't say a word to you – you were always teacher's pet."

"Hey! I was not!" But thinking back, he was right – Ms Brown had sent Jamie and Linda out of the class to stand in the corridor, but not me. "Well, maybe a little," I conceded. "I think she always felt bad about that Mother's Day card thing – remember it led to a whole discussion about how my mother died? She was mortified."

Jamie nodded, his eyes searching my face. "Did you ever find out more?"

"More?" I knew what he meant though.

"About your mother – sorry, you might not want to talk about it."

I took a big swallow of Guinness. "I don't mind. Things were bottled up in our house for long enough, and it all happened so long ago."

"I remember Da saying you went to Denmark once, back when Ray was still here – did you get to meet your grandparents?"

"Yeah . . . but I messed up and it didn't work out."

"Ah."

Jamie wasn't going to push me into saying anything further, but suddenly I wanted to talk.

"I wound up fibbing about who I was, then they found out, and refused to see me."

Jamie put down his drink. "Ah, I'm sorry to hear that. That's shitty of them in fairness."

I shrugged. "I get it. They were still grieving for Hanne, then I came along disrupting everything." I paused. "Basically I panicked and said I was a journalist from New Jersey called Linda." I smiled and shook my head. "So. Dumb."

"But you had good intentions. Did you ever try again?"

"I called back another day to apologise and Dina – that's Hanne's mother – turned me away at the door and told me never to come back. I tried one last time the night before I left, and ended up sneaking around to the back of the house, peeking in the kitchen window at her and some guy."

Jamie burst out laughing. "See, you did become Nancy Drew after all! Who was the guy? Was she having an affair?"

"Jesus, no! If you met Dina – she doesn't look like . . . Anyway, I don't know who the man was. They seemed close, just not in an affair-having way."

"So you never tried getting in touch after you came home?"

"No."

Jamie looked at me for a moment, soft eyes soaking me up. "Would it be worth a try again? Even a letter?"

"What's the point? There's only so much rejection a girl can take!" I laughed, as tears sprang to my eyes.

"But –" He paused, as though choosing his words.

"Well, I'm assuming they're getting on a bit now – not to be morbid or anything, but what if they die before you have the chance to meet them?"

I picked up a beer mat and studied it, blinking to clear the blur of tears. "I stayed in touch with Asta – a girl I met while I was there. She sends me snippets about the case whenever there are local articles and keeps me posted on the ins and outs of Damtoften, where Hanne's parents live. If something happened, she'd tell me."

"But, Marianne –"

"Yes?" I looked up at him.

"If something happens your grandmother, it doesn't matter how many people you have sending you news – won't it be too late?"

CHAPTER 46

It was only when John pointedly began switching off lights behind the bar that we realised how late it was. We still had unfinished pints in front of us, and an unfinished conversation – about marriage of all things. An outdated concept, we agreed, though an onlooker might have wondered at our mutually earnest conviction. Jamie swallowed the rest of his pint, I pushed mine aside, and we wandered out to the quiet street towards the minicab office. We spent twenty minutes rubbing our hands in front of a storage heater before Mick O'Shea, the only driver working that night, made it back to pick us up. Jamie tried to get him to drop me first but I insisted it was ridiculous – his house was on the way to mine, I pointed out, as I slid into the passenger seat.

When we stopped at the Crowley farmhouse, Jamie tried to pay the fare, but I told him he could pay next time, surprising myself with how much I wanted there to *be* a next time. I told him I'd message him in the morning about going down to pick up his car and said a breezy goodbye. Jamie hesitated, but then the front door of the farmhouse opened, and there was Alan, scowling out at the two of us.

Jamie muttered something under his breath and got out. As the cab turned in the front yard, I watched them in the doorway, framed by the light behind. Alan was blocking the way, his hands on each side of the doorframe. Jamie was shaking his head, then pushing past to go inside. Jesus, it was like being school kids again, coming home to disappointed parents. Except there would be nobody waiting for me, I thought, as the cab turned into my driveway, and a long-suppressed trickle of loneliness welled up inside. Something else hit me too, though I couldn't put my finger on it.

"Fierce cold tonight," said Mick as I searched through my wallet. "You wouldn't want to be out walking in that. They say it's the global warming, but it feels awful cold for global warming."

"At least the snow is gone," I said, handing him a fifty-euro note. "Sorry, I don't have anything smaller."

"You're grand," he said, going through his money-pouch for change. There was no hurry on him, and I could feel him settling in for a chat. Mick was the longest-serving cab driver in Carrickderg, and a gent who'd never see you stuck, but God he could talk for Ireland. "You had some trouble here with the snow, didn't you?"

"Oh, nothing much," I mumbled, wondering how he knew.

"The missus was filling me in," he said, reading my mind. "The morning she had the brick through the Post Office window – you were telling Patrick Maguire about someone trespassing here. Same fella maybe?"

"It seems not – that guy is long gone, so it couldn't be him."

"Oh – you mean you've had more trouble since?" His voice was kind.

I swallowed. "Ah, nothing really, I'll be fine."

"Well, look, I'll stay here till you're inside," he said, handing me my change. "Have you a torch on your phone to see the keyhole? It's fierce dark here – do you not have a porch light you could leave on?"

I looked over at the door and realised that was what had seemed odd as we drove up. I always left the porch light on.

"I do, I think I just forgot it tonight."

"You'd be as well getting a few more lights around the place – good deterrent, you know? I'm always telling the missus to be more security-conscious. She'd leave doors unlocked all over the place during the day, thinks nothing bad could ever happen in a town like Carrickderg. Well, she did anyway, until that bloody brick through the window. She never stops talking about it. You'd think Russian spies were sending her a message to hear her go on. And she's some woman for talking, there's never a minute's quiet."

There's a pair of you in it, I thought, as I smiled and said goodbye. Good as his word, Mick stayed in the driveway, headlights trained on my front door, until I was safely inside with my living-room light on and the door locked. I gave him a thumbs-up from the window and dropped to the couch, eyeing up my closed bedroom door. It was late and I had work in the morning but sleep held little appeal. What if he was out there already, planning his next surprise? My skin prickled, recalling the touch of the maggots' fat bodies. And after all my trouble taping the windows, I'd forgotten to bloody check them. Well, there was no way I was going out there to do it now.

On my phone, a sudden glut of notifications from the

Armchair Detective group pinged through, providing a tempting and timely alternative to sleep. I opened my laptop.

The flurry of chat centred around a newspaper article on the Blackwood Strangler, speculating that he was responsible for crimes in other countries too.

So annoying when we've been saying that all along! That was Neil.

Hmm, I don't really see it that way, Judith replied. **I like it when our theories get some validation. It means we're on the right track and should keep digging.**

I know but that guy who wrote the article gets all the credit! Neil replied.

It's not about credit, is it? said Judith. **Surely we're just a group of curious minds with a hobby?**

I didn't care about validation or credit, I just wanted someone to tell me there was no way in the world the Blackwood Strangler was in Ireland.

Anyone got something new on the footprint cases? I asked.

Judith said she'd taken a longer look at the Danish murder – the one with the chalk hangman – and the more she read, the more convinced she was it was the Blackwood Strangler.

I don't suppose there were any cases where he left an apple at someone's doorstep? I asked.

Not that I've seen – there was a rose left at someone's I think, Judith replied. **Why do you ask?**

You know the stuff I was saying about footprints and a chalk letter – someone left an apple on my doorstep.

Maybe just a random apple that blew there? Judith suggested. **Do you have an apple tree in your garden?**

No, I replied, but can't help thinking about the rose in Austrian case. Not the same, but similar …

Judith came back quickly. Yes, but it's human nature to see patterns, apohenia (sp?) or something? The more I read about the cases, the more similarities I spot, while handily ignoring the bits that don't fit and the other explanations – like an ex-husband who got the life insurance or a son with a heroin habit.

Good point, Neil typed, and as we all know, while serial killers mostly kill for sport, the vast majority of murders are committed by people we know.

On that cheery note, I logged out.

I stood, catching my reflection in the mirror above the couch. The lipstick I'd touched up in Delaneys' mocked me. What was I getting all worked up about? It was just a drink with an old friend. I rubbed my eyes, itching from the late hour and the drinks and the laptop screen, belatedly remembering I was wearing mascara. I took my hands away to inspect the damage, squinting through the blur. As my vision cleared, my eyes were drawn to something else.

A shadow.

A white face.

At the window behind me.

Someone outside, looking in.

I whirled, turning to face the window, to see who was there though I really didn't want to see who was there. He was gone. It was gone. The window was blank and empty, nothing but coal-black sky beyond. I stood staring, frozen. My breath came fast, out of control. Like a panic attack. I'd never had a panic attack, I couldn't tell. *Slow down. Breathe slowly. Panic won't help*. I needed to close the curtains, but I couldn't make myself walk to the window. *Slow down. Breathe.*

I turned back to the mirror. In it, the window reflected the living-room light. Was that what I had seen? But it was so like the white mask at my bedroom window. Wasn't it? Or had I superimposed it, blurred by beer, rattled by talk of the Blackwood Strangler?

Still I couldn't make myself go to the window and close the curtains. Instead, I walked to the light switches beside the front door and pressed the one for the porch.

Nothing.

No comforting glimmer from outside. I hadn't forgotten to switch it on – the bulb must have blown while I was out. *Or something else*, said a little voice inside my head. *Someone else*. I pushed it away. The bulb had blown, that was all – I couldn't remember the last time I'd had to put a new one in. And there was no way in hell I was going out there to change it tonight.

Still shaky, still pushing away other explanations, I checked the door was locked, and went to bed.

CHAPTER 47

On Friday morning, groggy after pints and the late-night scare, it took me longer than usual to open my eyes. Sunlight drifted in under bedroom curtains, promising, reassuring, and the face in the mirror was a blurry memory, seeming ever more like a trick of the light. Rubbing my eyes, I squinted at my phone. I could make out a Google alert, and a message from Barry. Shit. I still hadn't replied to him. I waited until I had a first cup of coffee before opening it.

Marianne, I wish I hadn't sent the message, sorry if I've annoyed you. If we could wipe the slate clean, that would be great. There was no pressure intended. In my circle of friends, it's customary to reply to invitations, even when the answer is 'no'. I guess that's just the bubble I live in – we are all different.

Oh, for the love of God.

I started to type, to tell him I had friends who go weeks without replying to messages, but I stopped. That wasn't going to help – knowing Barry, it would lead to a protracted discussion about manners and society in the social-media age. Instead I went for the age-old balm of apology.

Barry, I'm so sorry. Up to my eyes in work and both times I saw your msgs I was about to drive so couldn't reply, then it slipped my mind. Sorry! Anyway, I'd love to meet at some stage but am just crazy busy with work right now. Can I get back in touch with you on it?

Moments later, a little tick showed me he'd seen the message. I sipped my coffee, waiting for a reply, but nothing popped through. I opened the Google Alert – articles had come up about Ray. A flicker of unease uncurled in my stomach as I clicked into the first one, a piece in TheDailyByte.ie.

Renowned US author Ray Sedgwick is back on our shores and will be signing copies of *The Sophisticate* in a number of bookshops around Dublin this week. The author, who wrote much of the book during his time in Ireland, returned to his native New Jersey ten years ago.

"I'm excited to be back on the old sod," Sedgwick says. "There's something about the Island of Saints and Scholars that inspires me like nowhere else. The warmest people, the best stout, the most beautiful scenery anywhere in the world."

The next article was exactly the same, word for word – a press release sent out to all the papers. This one had a list of the bookshops he was due to visit though, including Seven-Storey Books in Dun Laoghaire that evening. Ray, after all this time, just thirty kilometres away. Fuck, actually just minutes away – I'd be in Dun Laoghaire library at the same time, at the Julia Land interview. Minutes away and far too close. Maybe I should stay home.

All day Friday it lurched around inside me. The easiest option would be to stay put. But why should I, just because

Ray was in town? He'd be busy with his signing, nowhere near the library. What if I bumped into him before or after? Doesn't matter, I thought, as I scrubbed the bathroom, cleaning the already spotless bath. It was a lifetime ago. He'd probably walk right past without recognising me. Could I park on the outskirts of town and avoid going anywhere near the bookshop, I wondered, watching the clock creep towards six, the empty evening stretching ahead. Fuck it. I wasn't going to let Ray's reappearance keep me hiding at home.

The café in Lexicon, Dun Laoghaire's flagship library, was pulsing with jostling Julia Land fans, eager to get into the auditorium. Most of us arrived wrapped in huge padded jackets and woolly scarves, and these now unnecessary accoutrements made the space even tighter. A queue was forming and I joined it.

Feeling fidgety and wound up, I shuffled forward, wishing suddenly I hadn't come on my own. Ray wasn't going to show up here, I knew that, but too much time in my own head was proving unhelpful.

"Marianne?"

I turned and found myself staring into the face of someone I'd never met in my life. A balding man, a little shorter than me, was looking up at me expectantly.

"It *is* you, isn't it?"

"Oh, hi," I said, grasping desperately for clues, "Zorian, right?"

Confusion washed over the man's face.

"Zorian? No, I'm Barry!"

Oh my God. Barry from Facebook. In the flesh. He was shorter than I'd realised, and had a lot less hair on top than his profile picture showed, but the glasses were the same and, now that he said it, of course it was Barry.

"Oh, hi, lovely to meet you in real life! What are you doing here?" I planted what I hoped was a welcoming smile on my face.

"I live nearby, so I come to a lot of the author talks. I was actually going to go to the Ray Sedgwick signing but I decided against it." He sniffed. "I reckon he's a bit up himself. I tweeted him to say I was coming and he didn't reply. I hate that – why do celebrities even have Twitter if they're not going to reply?"

I was pretty sure whoever was operating Ray's Twitter account, it wasn't Ray – unless he'd done a huge about-turn on his anti-technology stance in recent years.

"I didn't know you went to things like this – did you come in from Carrickderg?" he asked.

It was odd to be standing here with this person I'd never met and to realise how much he knew about me – and how much I knew about him.

"Yep. So you live nearby?" I said, plucking for something to talk about.

"Yeah, an apartment down near the DART station. Small but perfectly formed." He grinned as if making a joke I didn't quite get. "Like me," he explained.

"Ah, of course," I nodded, then wondered if I should have agreed less readily. He really was unexpectedly short. Then again, it's not like Facebook profile pictures tell you much about a person's height.

"Actually – if you're not rushing off after, why don't we get a cup of tea and chat through some of our cases?"

I groaned inwardly, at the "our cases", at the awkwardness of it, at the mean part of me that just wanted to escape.

"Sorry, that's probably the last thing you want to do, don't mind me." He raised his hands and bowed his head like a surrendering martyr.

"Of course we can go for a cup of tea – I have to get back to Carrickderg before the supermarket closes at nine, but that'll give me half an hour maybe?"

His face lit up and I felt bad for how much I was resenting it – thirty minutes wouldn't hurt.

As soon as the wonderfully distracting interview with Julia Land ended, a smiling Barry was at my elbow, escorting me out of the library. We made small talk as we walked along Queen's Road, past the sea-facing cafés, all now firmly shut. Within minutes, we found ourselves opposite the DART station, out of tea options. Or not, as it turned out.

"This is my apartment actually," Barry said, as we stopped outside an upmarket modern block across from the station. "Sure we'll just go in here instead."

I couldn't think of a good reason to say no.

Inside his building, as the soft-close door shut behind us, the noise of traffic disappeared instantly. Deep carpets muffled the sound of our footsteps on the way to the lift, and the shiny doors and polished buttons spoke of good cleaning staff and high management fees. Barry's apartment was on the third floor, and surprisingly spacious, with floor-to-ceiling windows looking out over the train line and Dublin Bay beyond.

"Oh wow, the view must be amazing on a sunny day!" I said, looking out, while Barry walked through to what I assumed was a kitchen.

Moments later, there was a tap on my shoulder.

"*Jesus!*" I yelled, spinning around.

261

"Sorry! I didn't mean to give you a fright."

"Oh my God, I didn't hear you at all!" I laughed, though my heart was still thumping. Poor Barry, I wasn't turning out to be the most gracious guest.

"Sorry, the carpet absorbs all the sound. Do you want to give me your jacket – it's warm in here – the insulation is almost too good at times."

"Sure, thanks." I shrugged off my jacket. "I have the opposite problem – no insulation at all, especially in the kitchen."

"Ah, but your kitchen is an extension, isn't it – they're always a bit colder in those old cottages."

I must have looked surprised, because he rushed to explain.

"You said it in the group once – that you were moving into the sitting room because it was too cold in the kitchen. Sorry, that makes it sound like I memorise details about you! I just have a weirdly good memory for details. I remember picturing you picking up your laptop and moving into the living room." He looked at me, his eyes magnified behind his glasses and I tried again to imagine him as a tech entrepreneur but couldn't quite get there.

"So, I don't have long – will we chat through one of the cases before I have to head?" I said, pushing up the cuff of my jumper to check my imaginary watch.

"Of course. The kettle is on for tea. Take a seat," he gestured to the black leather L-shaped couch, "and I'll grab my notes."

His "notes" consisted of four archive boxes filled with printouts and clippings – he placed them one by one on the sitting room floor, while I silently cursed myself for agreeing to it.

"That's a lot of work you've put in!" I said, reaching over to open the first box.

He sat down right beside me and looked at me, owl-like from behind his glasses. I could smell onions on his breath.

"I believe in it, Marianne," he said simply.

My eyebrows went up in an unspoken question.

"I believe that we'll be the ones to find him – with enough time and effort, we can succeed where the police have failed, and the Blackwood Strangler will be stopped, one way or another." This was delivered in full-on not-remotely-ironic superhero mode.

Part of me wanted to laugh, but mostly I wanted to move just a few inches away from the onion smell.

I knelt on the floor to pick a random file from a box marked "Sweden" and when I sat back I chose a spot a little further to his right, putting about a foot between us. I thought I'd done a good job of being discreet, but Barry looked at the newly created space and back at me, unblinking.

"Will we take a look at the Swedish case, since we've both read up on that?" I said.

That – the tangible plan – seemed to relax him. He pulled the Sweden box towards him and from inside took a folder of handwritten notes.

"So, the facts." He began to read. "*A woman murdered in her remote house outside Malmo, husband at a conference.*" Barry glanced up at me. "His alibi checks out."

I nodded and resisted the urge to ask him how he knew that – fewer interruptions meant I could get out of there sooner.

He carried on reading. "*Wife phoned husband because*

someone had tidied their shed – laid out all the contents in a neat line – and she'd seen a set of footprints. They couldn't make any sense of it on the call, but weren't too worried. It seemed like a prank rather than something menacing, the husband said afterwards."

A prank. A thread of unease wound its way through me. So many so-called pranks.

"Now, here's the bit I researched most recently." He looked up at me again.

In spite of myself, I was curious.

"The timeframe makes it *possible* that it was the Blackwood Strangler. The Swedish murder happened about four months after the last UK killing, and it was another twelve months before the next UK case, I think." He flipped some pages forward. "Yes, the next one was over a year later."

I opened my mouth to respond, but he held up a hand to stop me. I closed my mouth.

"I know, I know. Just because it *could* be him, doesn't mean it *was* him. But look at it this way. There was no known serial killer in Sweden at that time. So the murder was either personal, or a burglary gone wrong. But burglars don't tidy sheds, and the police found nothing in her personal life to suggest she had an affair or a jealous ex or anything like that. TV would have us believe there are serial killers up and down the country but, in real life, cases are few and far between. Thank goodness!"

He grinned at me. I shifted on the couch and smiled back.

"So if it *was* a serial killer, it had to be one operational in another location during that time."

He waited for a response.

I murmured agreement and checked my imaginary watch again.

"And the thing is, the Blackwood Strangler had enough gaps between kills – he may have gone to other countries around Europe."

An image of Hanne flitted suddenly into my mind and I shook it away.

"Are you alright?"

"Yes, sorry, just thinking about what you said. Do you think the police have ever considered the possibility he travelled to other countries? Did you find any articles suggesting they have?"

He shook his head, a wise and knowing owl, disappointed – or perhaps secretly pleased – with the ineptitude of the police.

"I don't believe they have, Marianne. Which is why, crazy as it sounds, I think we've a good chance of cracking this case and nailing the guy."

Nailing this guy. Oh, sweet divine Mother of God.

We spent another twenty minutes reading files and sharing theories, before I told him I really had to go. He insisted on walking me to my car, though I wondered what he'd actually do if we were confronted by some kind of danger – he was an unlikely bodyguard.

I slid into the Jeep as soon as we reached it, avoiding any awkward decisions about handshakes or hugs and, waving goodbye, I pulled onto the long, dark road home.

CHAPTER 48

I made it to the supermarket just before they stopped letting people in, though there were meagre pickings at the deli counter at almost nine o'clock on a Friday night.

"I'd go for the fish cakes if I were you," came a voice from behind, and I turned to find Jamie grinning at me. "I tried to talk my da into getting them but no chance –if it's not meat and potatoes, is it even a dinner?"

I laughed. "Okay, I'll get the fish cakes and you can live vicariously through me since you're not allowed to get them yourself."

I wondered – and perhaps he did too – if this was a cue to invite him over. It hung between us for a moment, before I turned to put in my order.

"What are you doing here this late anyway," I asked as I waited. "Don't you and Alan usually go to the Wooden Spoon for dinner in the afternoon?"

"We did, and then yer man insisted I go with him for a pint, and that turned into two, and sure you know yourself what he's like once he starts going on about the politicians and the roads and the cost of everything. There's no getting him out of the pub when he's mid-flow. What has *you* here so late?"

"Oh God, long story. Right, I was at a book event and I bumped into a guy I know online – he's in a Facebook group I'm in – and he recognised me. He ended up convincing me to go back to his apartment to look at his notes on some cases he's researching."

Jamie nodded slowly. "To look at his *notes . . . hmm*?"

"Oh Jesus, nothing like that!" My face reddened. "He's sweet and means well, but kind of intense. Not my type."

Again, the words hovered between us, said but not said.

"Is this your detective group?"

"Yeah, it sounds silly, I know. But we've found a whole heap of links between this serial killer in the UK and some other European cases, and –" I paused, searching for the right words. "It's a rabbit hole. Once you start reading up on this stuff, it's hard to stop. Barry is one of our more enthusiastic members – sometime takes it to a whole other level."

"And did this guy Barry know you were going to be the book event?"

"No, not at all, it was just a coincidence. I think he goes to a lot of events. Speaking of which, Ray was doing a book signing in Dun Laoghaire tonight too. You don't think he'll come out this way, do you?"

"God, I hope not," he said, grinning. "My da would have a heart attack."

I was worried about more than Alan's hypothetical heart attack, but then Jamie didn't know the full story.

His grin suddenly disappeared as his attention was caught by something over my shoulder.

"This is fierce cosy – what are you two prattling on about?" came Alan's voice from behind me.

"Books," Jamie said quickly.

"Yeah, we might start a book club," I said.

Alan looked from his son to me and back to Jamie again, all the while scowling beneath his ridiculous hat. The smell of stout wafted towards us.

"Jaysus, ye've little to be worrying about. I'm going now, so you'd better come if you want a lift." He looked at me and added with a sneer, "Unless you have a better offer?" He walked off, muttering something about keys and patting his pockets.

Jamie rolled his eyes and showed me the car keys in his hand. "Let the battle commence . . . I'll see you soon, Marianne, take care." He touched my shoulder as he passed, and followed Alan out of the shop.

A pointed look from the manager prompted me to hurry up with my shopping – at that stage, there was only one other customer left in the supermarket. Walking towards the till, I realised it was Geraldine – all muffled up in a giant navy padded jacket and a pink bobble hat.

"Gone to weigh my salads," she said, nodding at the empty cashier chair. "I always forget to weigh the salads. So, Alan still causing trouble?"

"Ah, he's a harmless old eejit. Never happy unless he's giving out about something."

Geraldine said nothing for a moment, focussing on lining up a rolling grapefruit behind a rolling bottle of wine. She looked at me.

"Yeah, he comes across as the gormless eejit alright, but don't be fooled. There's a cruel streak to Alan."

"What do you mean?"

"Just what I said. Nothing criminal, mind, he's always been careful about that. But he wouldn't hesitate to leave you out in the cold. If you were on fire and he had a bucket of water, he'd try to charge you for it. You know?"

Her metaphors sounded mixed though the message was clear. But then Alan wasn't the only one who caused trouble while skating on the right side of the law. I wondered how much Geraldine knew about what Ray did, before he stepped over the line.

"Anyway," she continued, "that's all – don't underestimate him. The biggest troublemakers I see in my line of business aren't the ones who signpost it all over themselves – it's the sneaky ones, the ones hiding in corners and under beds, pretending to be harmless." She lowered her voice as the salad-laden cashier returned to the till. "Or pretending to be nice."

We switched to weather-talk as she paid for her groceries, and she waited while I paid for mine. Together we walked outside and were about to go our separate ways when a noise from across the street, down outside Delaneys', stopped us.

We looked over to see Alan, half–in, half–out of the driver's seat of the Land Rover, and Jamie trying to physically pull him out.

Geraldine shook her head. "Jesus, I'm tempted to let Alan start the engine," she muttered. "He'd be sorry then."

She started down the street, and I followed, curious to see how this would end. But before we got there, Patrick arrived, coming from the other direction. Geraldine and I stopped, still across the street, and watched as Patrick took over from Jamie. He didn't touch Alan, but whatever he said seemed to work – Alan got out of the Land Rover, flung the keys in the gutter, and stalked off to stand outside Delaneys', searching for a cigarette. Jamie bent to pick up the keys, and stood to talk to Patrick.

"How does he put up with him?" I said to Geraldine, or maybe to myself.

"I don't know. My own father had a thing for the drink, God rest him. And God forgive me, but sometimes it's a relief he's gone." She turned to me then. "Sorry, Marianne, that was insensitive – I know you still miss your dad."

I made a no-worries gesture.

"At least he was a good dad to you," she went on. "I sometimes think losing a good parent might be better than only ever having a bad one – is that a terrible thing to say?"

I wasn't sure how to respond – was she talking about her own dad or Alan?

"I suppose," I said after a moment. "I guess people who have tough upbringings have a much harder road in life." It was a nothingy answer, but she didn't seem to mind.

"Then again, he had a rotten time of it by all accounts," she said, lowering her voice and nodding over to where Jamie was still talking to Patrick, "and he turned out okay, didn't he?"

"True. I wonder why his dad ended up the way he did though."

She looked at me, as though weighing up how much I knew.

"I don't know the full story and it's probably not my place to say, but I know you won't repeat it, Marianne." She lowered her voice further, though there was no way anyone could hear us. "I believe he was in the army at one point and got discharged for some fairly serious infraction. It hit him hard, and he turned to drink. And, sure, it was all downhill after that. Then the mother – as far as I know anyway – thought what happened was all her fault, and it spiralled even further downhill. Depression, social services,

270

care home, the works. He doesn't know I know about it."

I hadn't known anything about a care home, or the army, or *any* of it, but suddenly I remembered the charred photo – Jamie on his mother's knee, and Alan in his army uniform. But why dump the clothes in our garden? I still had no idea. Ray had remained tight-lipped, not responding to my few tentative enquiries. And was there some link with the army jacket I found in my garden last week?

I watched Alan across the street, sucking on his cigarette, and now I could picture him so easily as the wounded soldier, frustrated and humiliated at being discharged. No doubt losing his wife so young had a huge impact too. Then again, my dad lost Hanne, but was still a good father. Unexpected tears welled up and Geraldine squeezed my arm.

"Ah, sorry, Marianne. Listen, you head on home – looks like Patrick has this sorted, so I will too."

I nodded and walked to my car, as Patrick joined Geraldine, and Alan, a great big sulky face on him, got into the Land Rover with Jamie.

Back home, with *The Late Late Show* on TV and fish cakes in the oven, I poured a glass of wine and opened Facebook to read a message from Judith.

I hear you and Barry met up to discuss the case! He is very fired up about it and hopes to meet again – I thought I'd warn you!

Oh God, he was broadcasting it already.

How did you know – did he say it in the group?

Yes, in the group, she replied, **and he messaged me privately to tell me too – that's how excited he is. Best of luck, Marianne, you've got yourself an admirer!!**

I clicked into the group to see what he was saying and found an entire post dedicated to telling the others we'd spent time going through cases in his apartment and both felt it was the best way to move the research along.

I messaged Judith again.

Oh my God, talk about two ways of looking at a story! It was pure chance we met, and I wasn't in his apartment for more than half an hour. We never said we'd do it again either, at least I don't think we did. Damn, what have I done!

As Judith typed her reply, I got my fish cakes out of the oven.

He means well, she said. **He seems a nice man, a little needy perhaps, and doesn't seem to have many friends. You made him very happy – it can be your good deed for the day!**

True. I'd just have to use work as an excuse to avoid future requests to meet.

And exactly at that moment, a message from Barry pinged through.

Great night, Marianne, we make a good team! Same again next Friday?

Oh God, this was going to hurt.

Another message came through then, but on text this time, from Linda.

Hey, if you're in Dublin in next few days, could you go to Petit Pois on Grafton Street and collect something for me? Sadie lost the teddy you bought her when she was born – they have them in stock and they're holding one for you. She's distraught! I'll Paypal you the money xx

I stared at it. Was she for real? Tears pricked my eyes as I closed the message. After months of next to no contact, she was back in touch when she needed something, like my only purpose in life was to be the handy godmother, available to pick up in an emergency, unnecessary beyond that. A thousand responses came to mind but, in the end, I put the phone aside and didn't reply at all.

CHAPTER 49

The alarm installation wasn't scheduled for another fortnight, but if I wanted lights and cameras they needed to know which ones and how many. So on Saturday morning, I found myself outside my house, looking for suitable spots for cameras. The corner above my dad's old bedroom would be ideal, I figured – it would show me if someone was standing at the front door. Or crouched at my bedroom window. My stomach lurched as a memory of the white, staring face flashed up. I pushed it away. It was a reflection, a trick of the light. Nothing more.

The consultant had recommended one motion-sensor light for the back of the house and one for the front. With the brochure tucked under my arm, I looked up at the eaves and wondered where the best spot would be – the corner above my bedroom maybe? Or would it be too bright when I was trying to sleep? But then it wasn't supposed to be on all the time – only if someone was moving around outside. I shivered. What the hell would I do if the light suddenly came on in the middle of the night?

I stepped forward to get a better look at the spot, putting my hands on my bedroom windowsill. As I stepped back again, I noticed something scratched in the paint. My breath quickened as I took it in. Etched into the windowsill, was the distinct outline of a hangman.

I stared until it started to blur. How long had it been there? Was it there when I'd put the tape on the windows? Or the morning of the footprints? I tried to remember if there had been snow on the windowsill, but I couldn't. Was the hangman old or fresh? I had no idea how to tell. *Fuck*. I took three quick photos, moved inside, locked the door, and phoned the Garda Station.

Patrick picked up, sounding sleepy, reminding me it was just after eight.

"Hey, it's Marianne. Again."

"Hi, Marianne, what's up?"

"I need to caveat this by saying it's going to sound like kids again."

"Okay – what is it?"

"Someone's scratched a hangman on my bedroom windowsill."

Silence on the other end of the phone, and I pictured him shaking his head at the madwoman from the cottage on the hill.

"I know that it's not the crime of the century. But taken in context with the footprints, the chalk letter, the apple, it all goes back to the same thing – someone is coming into my garden when I'm asleep."

"Did it happen last night?"

"I don't know when it happened. It's not very big so you wouldn't see it unless you were looking at the windowsill."

"So could it be there a long time – like even years?"

"I suppose . . ."

275

"I remember once me and my pals scratched our names into the paintwork on the wall at the end of the garden at home – my ma went nuts! Could it have been something you did yourself years ago when you were a kid?"

"No, definitely not. I'd remember."

Even as I said it, I wondered. Would I remember?

"But I suppose the cottage would have been painted since then?" he went on. "When was the last time, do you know?"

I paced up and down the living room, trying to recall.

"Not since my dad died, so not in the last thirteen years." Silence again. "Look, I get that it could have been done any time, but it's just a bit weird along with all the other things. And–" I paused.

"Yes?"

"Well, it's back to these serial killer stories, about the Blackwood Strangler." I could hear a muffled sigh, but I ploughed on. "There was that case in Denmark where a chalk hangman was drawn in a woman's driveway and she wound up dead – remember I told you that when I found the letter R?"

"*Mmm.*"

"And then there was this other case in Poland, where a couple found random letters scratched in the paintwork of a windowsill. They were murdered . . ." My voice trailed off on the last words.

"So let me get this straight," Patrick said. "Someone found a hangman in chalk, someone else found letters scratched in paint. You have it the other way around – a letter in chalk and a hangman scratched in paint?"

"Yes."

"So it's similar, but not quite the same."

"Well, yes, but kind of scarily similar, don't you think?"

"Or are you seeing connections because you've read so much about the cases?"

I closed my eyes. "I know how it sounds, and I see that there are differences," I dug my nails into my palm, wondering how many times I'd have to say it before I'd be taken seriously, "but even putting aside the other cases, the bottom line is someone has been coming into my garden and someone has been looking in my bedroom window while I sleep."

"You got the new curtain, right?"

Oh, sweet Jesus.

"Yes. I got the curtain."

He must have heard something in my voice.

"Okay, one of us will pop up later to take photos and have a look around, and obviously we have a log of everything you've reported, so we'll keep adding to that, and we're still looking into the army jacket. We'll send a car tonight too, to drive past. That should put him off. Does that sound okay?"

I nodded.

"Marianne?"

"Yes, I'm here."

"Don't worry, we'll get it sorted. Okay?"

"Okay. Thank you."

Driving down to the village that afternoon, I spotted Jamie walking in the same direction and pulled in beside him.

"Is the car gone again?" I asked through the window. "Do you need a lift?" Then I clapped my hand over my mouth. "Oh my God, I was supposed to drop you down yesterday to pick it up! Please don't tell me it's still there?"

Jamie stuck his hands in his pockets and grinned at me, for all the world the same kid he was when we were ten.

"It's grand – sure you were busy in your detective buddy's apartment. And it's not like my da couldn't have taken me down this morning if he'd wanted to. The walk gives me a break from him."

"I'm so sorry. Here, get in and I'll drop you down."

He walked around and sat in beside me, still grinning.

"What are you smiling at?"

"The irony of it – we both know there's no love lost between your family and mine, and Da's a bit rattled about our drink the other night, but if he'd just given me a lift, or stayed off the pints yesterday, I wouldn't be here now."

I smiled too. There was something very appealing about giving the middle finger to Alan. And something nice about being in it together with Jamie. Like the old days, but different.

"So what's new, Nancy Drew?" he asked as we snaked down towards the village on roads still sparkling with overnight frost.

"You mean with the whole footprints thing or just generally?"

"Either or."

"I found a hangman scratched into the paint on my windowsill."

"What do you mean a hangman? A guy who executes people?"

"No, I mean like the word game we used to play on the blackboard in school – technically I suppose it's the *hanged* man not the hangman, since it's the guy who's dangling from the gallows."

"Nice."

"I know."

"And I didn't mention this before but someone left a maggoty apple on my doorstep on Thursday morning. Well, Wednesday night, I guess."

Silence.

"What do you think?"

"How come you didn't mention the apple when I saw you on Thursday?"

I glanced over at him then back to the road.

"I don't know, I guess it didn't come up."

"You still think this is something to do with Alan," he said flatly.

"I don't know what to think. He's my nearest neighbour and he's done it before."

"But, Marianne, the stuff with the dead fox and burning the notebook – that was all to get at Ray. Once Ray left, it was over. Why would my da suddenly start picking on you?"

Why indeed, I thought as I drove down Main Street looking for parking. Nothing had changed – I hadn't done anything to antagonise him, at least as far as I knew. But then, Alan had never been the most rational person.

"What if it's because he's annoyed that we're . . . spending time together?" Oh Christ, what an awkward way to put it.

More silence. I couldn't tell if it was because we were discussing whether or not his dad was stalking me, or the fact that Jamie and I had sort of gone on a date. Suddenly I really wanted to get out of the car, but I still couldn't find somewhere to park.

"Well, yeah," Jamie said eventually. "As I said, he was unimpressed by our trip to Delaneys' the other night. But the footprints at your house came before that, right? So that doesn't make sense. And my da, difficult though he may be, is not a *stalker*."

There was an edge to the last words, a reasonable reminder to rein it in. Jamie could slag off his dad, but they were father and son at the end of the day. The complexity of relationships between adult children and their parents was not my area of expertise.

I nodded and drove on past the library, still looking for parking. As I did, something caught my eye. A poster on the library door, with a familiar book cover.

I parked and as Jamie went off to pick up his car, I walked back to the library to read the cheery announcement on the poster: **Coming soon to do a talk about his most famous book on its ten-year anniversary – Ray Sedgwick, author of *The Sophisticate*.**

A chill settled across my skin. Ray was coming back.

CHAPTER 50

At home that night, I checked the doors three times before making myself sit down with a glass of wine and a book, but I couldn't concentrate. Was he already out there, watching? Planning his next visit? Geraldine had come up to take photos of the hangman, and a police car had driven by twice since, but still – they couldn't be there all night, and then what? Meanwhile, I'd pissed Jamie off by making only the slightest suggestion Alan was responsible, and now Ray was coming back. I felt sick.

After an hour of disjointed reading, I got up to make sure the front door was locked, and suddenly remembered the sticky tape. I hadn't checked it when I came in from town. Dammit anyway, I'd have to go outside. I slid back the bolt, unhooked the chain, and turned the key. Outside, I could see my breath, but I didn't bother putting on a jacket. It would only take a few seconds. Hugging myself for warmth, I ran to the window and began the familiar ritual, tracing my fingers around the frame.

The tape wasn't there.

Hands scrabbling over the woodwork, sure I was wrong, I kept searching. It was cold, pitch dark, I'd missed it, that was all. *Slow down and try again.*

But I wasn't wrong. I hadn't missed it. It was gone.

Back inside, I slammed the door and turned the key, and didn't stop to check the time as I hit the number for the Garda Station. Patrick picked up, sounding weary. Saturday night. He was probably expecting a call about drunks.

"It's Marianne," I said, out of breath. "I think someone tried to break in. I hate making a fuss but please can you or Geraldine come up?"

Within ten minutes, Patrick had pulled up at the house, and ten minutes later he had checked all the rooms and done a thorough search of the front and back gardens. I showed him the window and told him about the sticky tape.

He looked confused as we moved back into the house.

"But, Marianne, how would Sellotape keep someone out?"

Jesus, no wonder he was confused.

"No, of course not, it's not to keep anyone out – it's so I know if someone tried to get in. Tried to open the window. And now the tape is gone, so that means someone did."

"Ah, I see. Is it okay if I look in your bedroom again?"

I led him through and watched as he examined the window from the inside, and the floor underneath.

"It doesn't look like anything has been broken or tampered with, and there's nothing on the floor – no bits of muck or dirt like you might get if someone climbed in. I reckon it's safe to assume someone removed the tape but didn't do anything else?"

I nodded. Partly because it made sense and partly

because it was a lot better than believing someone had been in the house.

"Do you change the tape every day or leave the same one there?"

"I leave it there unless it rains. It loses its stickiness if it's wet – then I change it."

"Well, it rained earlier this afternoon, maybe it fell off and blew away, I'll have another look at the ground outside."

"Maybe . . ." I conceded.

"And I know it's not cheap, but the best way to make sure someone doesn't try to break in is a burglar alarm. Better than Sellotape." He smiled at me.

I didn't smile back.

When he left, satisfied that the tape had blown away despite not finding any on the ground, I sat back down to read, but it was no good, I couldn't concentrate. Every creak, every rattle was amplified, and every dark story I'd ever read was coming back now, a tangle of faceless monsters and creeping fingers clawing through my jittered mind.

My phone beeped and I grabbed it, realising I was hoping to see Jamie's name. But it was Linda.

Did you see my text – any chance you can pick it up in next few days? Sadie won't sleep without it, total nightmare.

Seriously? Without stopping to think, I hit the call button.

"Oh, hi," she whispered when she picked up, "I texted instead of phoning because I didn't want to risk waking the kids." A hint of reproach. "Is it about the teddy?"

"No, it's not about the bloody teddy."

Silence.

"Marianne?"

"Yes, I'm still here. Not that you bloody care." My throat was tight with anger and threatening tears, but I couldn't stop now. Months of hurt came tumbling out. "All you think about is you and your kids, and you never bother with me anymore, not until you need something. You're a walking cliché – all those stories you hear of women who have kids and dump their friends – I never thought it would be you, Linda."

Another silence. I carried on.

"I matter too, you know? Just because I don't have four kids doesn't make me less of a person. I have stuff going on that you know absolutely nothing about, because you haven't bothered to call me, much less visit, in I don't know how long. And I'm so hurt and so upset but, most of all, I'm so bloody angry right now."

"Marianne."

She said it so quietly I almost didn't hear.

"Marianne, I'm so sorry. I should have explained but there was never a good moment and I suppose I was in denial for a long time."

I heard her take a breath.

"I haven't been myself since Harry was born. I'm on antidepressants but –" her voice cracked and then she was crying, "I'm struggling. Every day, just getting out of bed and looking after them is a struggle. I feel like a shitty mother, I feel like they'd be better off with anyone but me. But there's nobody else – Dónal is busy with the surgery, and my mam is in Arklow. So it's just me, trapped with four kids who need every ounce of my energy. And I know that's not your fault and not your concern and I should have been a better friend but I'm just in a really, really shitty place right now."

"Oh Linda." It came out as a whisper. "Linda, I'm so sorry."

"No, I'm sorry – there's no way you could have known, and there I am sending you stupid messages about stupid teddy bears. Only she won't sleep without it and I'm just broken – I'm completely and utterly broken."

"And . . . and are you getting help? I mean, besides the medication?"

"Yes, I'm seeing a therapist. I had postnatal depression with the other three but nothing as bad as this – it's completely blindsided me. My mam was able to come down to help out in the past but she's getting on now and couldn't come this time. Dónal's been brilliant though – he noticed pretty quickly that things were worse this time."

"Oh Linda, I'm so sorry. I should have realised."

"How could you? I didn't even realise myself at first. That's the irony, I suppose – I was so overwhelmed by it I couldn't see the wood for the trees. I'll get there, but it's slow. Now, you must tell me what's going on with you."

I switched the phone to my other ear and stood up.

"God no, don't worry about me – I wouldn't have said a word if I'd known."

"Please, Marianne, I could do with the distraction – even if I can't help, a listener couldn't hurt, right?"

She was right. So I told her – all of it. The footprints, the bizarre souvenirs, the Armchair Detective group, Ray. And Jamie – I told her about our not-quite-date and she said it was best news she'd heard in years.

We talked for over an hour and when we finally said

goodbye, I felt better than I had done in months.

I got up to go to bed, checking the door one last time. Soon I'd have cameras and an alarm to keep the stranger out, and then it would be over.

CHAPTER 51

When I opened my work email on Monday morning and spotted Asta's message, it gave me a jolt – the "bad news" subject line jumping out among more mundane correspondence about projects and meetings.

> Hey, Marianne,
>
> As per my previous email, I'm afraid Fru Hansen isn't getting any better. She has seen a pastor and also a solicitor about her will – she said she is determined to be organised in death. She is very direct! When I got upset during our visit, she told me not to be silly. She talked about your mother, and said it was a privilege to live to such an age when poor Hanne had so little time.
>
> But then something happened and this is why I am writing to you.
>
> There was a Bible on her nightstand and she picked it up – I thought maybe her last wish was to convert me to God now that she'd found him! But something slipped out of the Bible and onto the floor. I picked it up and saw it was a photograph –

ANDREA MARA

an old Polaroid of a man in front of a church, the one we visited near Fugl Sø, you remember? I asked if it was her son. She looked confused and took the photo from me.

She stared at it for a long time. Then she passed it to me and said in the strangest voice that I must take it to the police. I wondered if her mind was going but she got agitated so I promised I would do as she asked. Then she became very specific. She said I must explain that it's connected to Hanne's death, and tell them the man in the photo is the one she saw near the house in the time before Hanne disappeared. Still I wondered if she was imagining things or trying to fix all of it before she dies. I guess she could see my scepticism because she took my hand and said: "You must go straight to the police, not to Dina. That is important. You tell them he is the man who was there before Hanne died."

I asked why not Dina, though I didn't intend to go to Dina anyway – I would not be comfortable showing up at her door with a photo of a stranger and talking about her daughter's death.

"Because he is the dark-haired man nobody seemed to know," she said, "and this Bible is not mine – it was given to me this week. This Bible belongs to Dina."

I stopped reading and stared at Asta's email, trying to make sense of it. If Dina had a photo of the dark-haired man, she must have known him – so why didn't she tell the police? I thought back to the man in her kitchen that night ten years ago – should I have said something to the police back

288

then? But what could I have said – I was snooping around my estranged grandmother's back garden and saw her talking to a *man*? It was hardly a crime.

I started to read again.

> She was so agitated, I promised I would go to the police and I wouldn't speak to Dina about it. I didn't see any harm – if the police want to dismiss it as the unravelling of an old lady, that will be their decision. But I thought of you also, and your search for the truth. I wondered if you would want to see the photo. So I stopped on my way to the police station, and scanned a copy. See attached. Good luck with your detecting!
>
> Asta xx

I clicked on the attachment and a photo appeared on screen. The church in the grainy black-and-white image was instantly recognisable as the one Asta and I had visited – the graveyard in which Hanne was buried.

But I wasn't looking at the church.

I was looking at the man.

As I stared at his face, a sickening dread slipped across my skin. And I knew nothing would ever be the same again.

CHAPTER 52

In a blur, I started to type a reply to Asta.

> **The man in the photo is my dad. Can you tell Fru**
> **Hansen and see if she knew he went to Denmark?**

I deleted it immediately. If my dad was in Denmark back then – if he was the dark-haired man – would the police think of him as some kind of suspect? And what the hell was he doing over there? He had never said anything about it. In fact, I could remember asking him if he went to Denmark and he said no – he stayed here to look after me. Why would he lie? I made another attempt at the email.

> **Hi Asta,**
> **I missed your email over the weekend, just saw it**
> **now. How is Fru Hansen? If she's well enough, do**
> **you think you could ask her again about the man in**
> **the photo, to see if she knows anything at all?**
> **Marianne xx**

Her reply arrived minutes later.

> **Dear Marianne,**
> **I'm so sorry to tell you this but Fru Hansen died**
> **sometime on Saturday night. My mother went in to**

bring some food yesterday morning but she had passed away. She was of course very elderly and ill, but it is sad to think of her dying alone. I am more upset than I expected to be.

I sat back on the couch, feeling something much like Asta – sadder than I expected for a woman I'd met just twice, a long time ago. Another link with Hanne gone – one of the last people who could help solve what happened. I started typing again.

> Asta, I'm so sorry. I understand your sadness – it doesn't matter how old someone is when they go – death has a finality that's hard to process. I am sad too, and I hardly knew her. Is your mum ok?
>
> Mxx

As I waited, I clicked into the photo again, and stared at my father's face. There was no doubt about it, it was him. The dark hair, the sad eyes I knew so well, the forced half-smile. Why was he there? And who took the photo? Could it have been something to do with her funeral? He'd told me he hadn't gone to it but maybe he did and kept it from me for some reason? Though funerals weren't photo opportunities, even in the most bizarre circumstances, I couldn't imagine someone asking my dad to pose for a photo beside his dead wife's grave. My eyes wandered to the left of the photo, to the headstones around where Hanne was buried. Was hers there? I couldn't make out the inscriptions – the copy was too grainy.

I typed another email to Asta.

> PS about the photo – did you give it to the police and what did they say? Did they keep it?

It felt like an eternity before she replied.

> Yes, they took it. The person on the desk didn't

seem very excited but I guess once it gets to the right person, they will know what to do with it.

I typed again.

Did you happen to look at the headstones before you handed it in? Do you know if it was taken after Hanne's burial or not?

This time her reply came through quickly.

I did, yes, and I couldn't see Hanne's headstone. I can't be certain, but I think it was taken before she was buried.

The words swam a little as I read them again, trying to make sense of it. Had my dad gone over to help with the search? Then where was I when he went, and why did he never tell me? Or was it before she went missing? A buzzing behind my eyes was starting to hurt.

I picked up my phone. Asta answered after one ring.

"Hey, Marianne, it's good to talk to you. Are you okay?"

"I'm okay. I'm so sorry about Fru Hansen."

"I'm sorry for you too, I know she was important to your search."

"Yeah, my search – how I wish I'd done something about it in the last ten years, instead of leaving it until it's too late."

"It's not too late. You can still try. Does the photo mean anything?"

I hesitated.

"Marianne? Are you still there?"

"Asta, you can't say this to the police – you promise?"

"Sure. What is it?"

"The man in the photo is my dad. I have no idea why he's there – he told me he never went to Denmark."

Silence.

"I don't know what it means," I went on. "Maybe he had a good reason for not telling me."

"Was he there before or after she went missing?"

"I have no idea. Maybe after, to help with the search?"

"But then why would he be posing for a photo like this – I don't know if you can make it out so well from the copy, but it looks like a tourist photo. You know what I mean?"

I did. It didn't tie in with a search at all.

"And Fru Hansen –" She stopped.

"What is it?"

"Fru Hansen was certain she saw the man there in the week before Hanne went missing. A few times that week, and never after. She was very much involved in the search, so if your dad was there to help, she would have mentioned it I think?"

True. But if he wasn't there for the search or the funeral, then what?

"God, Asta, I just don't get it. And now I'll never bloody know because Fru Hansen is gone."

"There is someone you could ask . . . your grandmother."

"I think those bridges are well and truly burnt."

"Marianne, time has passed – isn't it worth trying again?"

"It's not up to me – Dina is the one who pushed me away."

"Of course. And you can sit there in Ireland and do nothing. Absolutely. And then just like Fru Hansen, Dina will die, and it will be another link lost. But that is up to you."

I closed my eyes, pressing the phone to my ear.

293

"Are you still there?"

"When is the funeral?"

More than ten years had passed since I'd walked the pavements of Købæk, but nothing had changed. The streets were as clean and picturesque as I remembered, and the March wind was every bit as cold as the November one. I planned to book a hotel but Asta insisted I stay with her – she was renting an apartment in the town centre, with a second bedroom she used as a darkroom. The flat was littered with prints – photographs of buildings and spires and people and skies – some framed and hung on walls, most in messy piles scattered around the wooden floor.

"You really made it as a photographer, despite your mother's warnings," I said, picking up a black-and-white photograph of Rikke.

"I don't know if I *made it* – there's not much money coming in, but I'm happy. I sell some prints online, and I give classes to teens at the Youth Club. And yes, even my mother has accepted that I'll never get a 'proper' job."

"Good! I'm looking forward to seeing her. I guess she'll be at the funeral tomorrow?"

"Yes. But tonight we're invited for dinner – will you come?"

I nodded, though the idea of being back in Damtoften made me uneasy.

"I promise she won't interrogate you about your love life. Or perhaps just a little." She grinned. "Is there someone?"

"No, though someone from back then is on his way towards Carrickderg . . ."

My stomach twisted as I filled her in on Ray's upcoming

visit, and on the footprints too. She listened without comment, her eyes growing wider as I talked.

"So, in a way, coming here seemed like an escape from all that," I finished, "but now I'm getting apprehensive – do you think Dina will be at the funeral?"

"Yes." Asta looked at me, her dark eyes wide beneath her heavy fringe. "You can do this. Ten years have gone by – it's time to get to know her, isn't it?"

I opened my mouth to answer, but was cut off by a loud thump from the window above Asta's head. I jumped, blood rushing to my ears, though I could already see what it was.

"Oh no, poor bird," Asta said, getting up to look out the window. "It's dead, I think."

The blood in my ears began to subside but a sense of malevolence had taken hold. Nothing good would come of this visit.

Dinner at Rikke's was a quiet affair with just the three of us. Asta's father would be home in an hour, hungry and tired after travelling from Malmo, Rikke explained, and Asta's older brother might drop by later. They would all go together to the funeral in the morning.

"It is so good to see you, Marianne," she said as we began to eat. "You look just the same as before. How are you? And – I'm sorry, I forgot his name – the man friend?"

"Ray? Ray is long gone." *If only*, I added, though not out loud.

"Ah, I'm sorry. You have a new man?"

Asta rolled her eyes. "*Mor!* Having a man isn't everything!"

Rikke pursed her lips. "Don't be rude, Asta. I am allowed to ask our guest simple questions."

I smiled. "It's okay – I don't mind. But no, there's no man, and I'm very happy on my own." An unexpected image of Jamie flashed into my mind – hands in pockets, kicking stones, grinning at me from under his curls.

Rikke looked at me for a moment, then her face broke into a wide smile.

"I believe you," she said, nodding with exaggerated emphasis, and poured wine for all of us.

I coughed and took a sip.

"So, will Dina be at the funeral tomorrow?"

"Of course. I think she feels especially proud – maybe proud is not the right word – responsible? Responsible that Fru Hansen discovered God again before she died. She even gave her a Bible."

Asta kicked me under the table and I shot her a look.

"*Mor*, did Fru Hansen say anything in the last days about the Bible, or anything she found in it?"

"What do you mean?"

Asta shrugged. "She said something to me about a photo in the Bible, but I don't know what she meant."

"No, she did not say something about this. But she was very confused at the end. She thought that I was you. She called me Asta sometimes, and she asked me if I talked to the police. I thought maybe she was going back in her mind – back to when Hanne disappeared." She glanced at me. "Did you hear anything from the police in all these years?"

I shook my head. "Nothing much, until this week when I told them I was coming over. I contacted Inspector Nielsen after I came home last time and he replied to say there was nothing new – reopening the case didn't lead to anything. I wrote again but didn't hear back. Last year I emailed him a photo of the letter Hanne wrote my dad and some of her more unusual sketches in case they had any bearing, but he didn't acknowledge receipt. I look online all the time – I have Google Alerts set up for Hanne's name, but it's rare that anything comes up."

"And now with Fru Hansen gone, another door is closed," Asta said. "Did she say anything else, *Mor*?"

"Oh, many things in the last two days, but I could not follow – the nurse gave her more morphine and told me it might make her confused. She was speaking about *lys* and *mørk* – light and dark – and being wrong. She said 'the wrong path' many times. Maybe she was worried that she was not religious and turned back to God too late."

"What exactly did she say about light and dark?" I asked.

"It was hard to tell. She was not making great sense."

"*Lyshåret* and *mørkhåret*," Asta said quietly. "Light-haired and dark-haired."

"Yes," Rikke said, "I did wonder if she was thinking back to Hanne and the men seen back then. But I do not know. Will you speak to the police while you are here, Marianne?"

I nodded. "Yes, Inspector Nielsen is still in charge – I have an appointment. I'm sure he'll be delighted to see me turning up again . . . "

"And Dina?" Rikke asked, passing me a dish of red cabbage. "Will you try to speak to her?"

"Yes," I said, with confidence I didn't feel. "Even if she pushes me away, I have to try. Life's too short for grudges."

CHAPTER 53

I wasn't sure what to expect at Fru Hansen's funeral but in the end it wasn't so different to funeral services at home. The church, smelling of incense, leather, and rain, was crowded, and everyone wore grey or black, though I couldn't tell if this was standard Danish uniform for the time of year, or specific to funerals. Rikke and Asta sat either side of me, and further along the pew were Asta's father and brother. On the other side of the aisle, a few rows back, I saw Dina and Erik. Dina looked remarkably similar to how I remembered – she hadn't aged at all in ten years it seemed. Or maybe she did all her aging in the time following Hanne's death, and life had eased off on her. She was wearing a light-blue blouse, neat and demure, very like the grey blouse she'd been wearing when we first met. Her haircut hadn't changed in a decade and even the pearls were still in place. I wondered if there was comfort in her routine, her rituals. Erik looked older and smaller than I remembered, his black suit hanging off bony shoulders and down over unseen wrists. His hands were clasped in front of him and his mouth moved in response to the prayers being said from the altar. Dina held what looked like a prayer book in her hands, but her mouth was tightly closed.

I never intended to approach her at the funeral but, as we walked out of the service into the pouring rain, I spotted her standing alone under a tree. Erik was shuffling his way to the gate – to get their car perhaps. Dina was fumbling with a small black umbrella and didn't notice me as I walked over. She looked up, ready to smile, then her face changed.

"You."

"Yes."

"Why?"

I swallowed, regretting approaching her already.

"I wanted to see you – to apologise for lying to you back then, and to make peace. You're my grandmother, and . . . I couldn't come all this way and not try."

Her light blue eyes scanned my face.

"I wish you no ill-will, but this is very difficult for Erik and for me. You understand?"

"I do. But maybe we can help each other? What happened to you all – it was awful. The worst. But I didn't do it. I was the baby left without a mother, and without grandparents too."

She flinched.

"I just mean I'd like to get to you know you," I said softly, as the rain poured down around us.

Her eyes ran over my face again – perhaps looking for a resemblance to her daughter, or maybe trying to come to a decision. And I knew that I shouldn't have to beg, but that with every inch of me I would.

"Maybe we can talk. We will be home tonight at six if you wish to call by?"

The formality of the invitation jarred but I pushed that aside.

"I'd love to."

She inclined her head. A restrained nod to seal the plan. "I must go."

And with that she walked away. There was no smile, but I knew we'd come further in two minutes than we had in ten years.

Asta and her family were going to a nearby hotel for food after the burial, but I had an appointment with Inspector Nielsen, so we went our separate ways.

The police station hadn't changed, but Inspector Nielsen had – he was completely bald on top, and had developed a beer belly that sat awkwardly on his wiry frame. His greeting indicated he remembered me, though perhaps he'd just refreshed his memory by rereading the file.

He looked at his watch as we sat opposite one another in a small, stuffy office.

"I'm afraid I have only a few minutes, Ms McShane, but there is also not a lot to tell unfortunately."

"Oh. Across the three cases?" I asked. "Nothing new to confirm they're definitely related or definitely not?"

"Nothing is for certain." He paused. "But in the Maja Pedersen case, there is a . . . strong suggestion someone known to the victim may not be excluded after all. There is a reasonable chance it was a domestic dispute, in which case her death is not linked to your mother's."

I stared at him, taking it in.

"So if Maja Pedersen was killed by someone she knew, that greatly reduces the likelihood it's a serial killer, doesn't it?"

He looked at me, not nodding, but not shaking his head either. It was as close to a confirmation as I was going to get.

I took a deep breath. "Do you believe Hanne was also killed by someone she knew?"

"It is not possible to say anything with certainty, but we know that statistically most murder victims are killed by persons they know."

"Right." I paused to choose my words. "And can I ask about the photo that Asta dropped in to you last week – she told me that Fru Hansen wanted you to see it for some reason?"

He scanned my face and I held his gaze, digging my nails into my palm. Did he know?

"She told you of this?"

"Yes, Asta and I have stayed in touch. She gets why I'm keen to know what's going on with the case." A mild dig.

"And what did she tell you?"

"That the photo fell out of a Bible that Dina had given to Fru Hansen, and she wanted Asta to bring it here, without telling Dina." Still I held his gaze. "Do you know who it is?"

A thousand years went by.

"No."

Out of sight, my hands went slack on my lap.

"What do you think it means?" I asked.

Again, he said nothing at first. He seemed to be considering how much he could say.

"I am sure your friend Asta has already told you the same as she told me: Fru Hansen makes the claim that the man in the photo is this famous dark-haired man she saw near the Karlsens' house before their daughter disappeared."

301

I nodded vigorously, eager for him to know he was on safe ground, not telling me anything I didn't already know.

"Of course Fru Hansen was elderly and on her dying bed. We do not know if she was correct."

"Of course. But does it tie in with what you already know – I mean, reports from back then, from Fru Hansen and others? Could he be the dark-haired man?"

A brief nod.

"And what about the blond man?"

"We do not believe there was a blond man."

"Really?"

"Your friend Fru Hansen came to the station many years ago to tell my colleagues she had seen a blond man with the Karlsens and had concerns. But he was a family friend. There was no connection to the case. And nobody ever said they actually saw a blond man when she disappeared. They just repeated what other people said. And in all these years, we never found someone who saw him. It is like stories on top of stories becoming facts, but incorrect facts. You see?"

I did, sort of.

"I remember Fru Hansen mentioned that the first time I came here," I said. "She'd gone to the police and also said it to Dina. I think they fell out for a while over it."

Inspector Nielsen shrugged. Neighbourhood quarrels didn't concern him.

"I'm afraid that is all I have, Ms McShane. I wish I had more. I have your email address, and I can contact you if something changes."

I smiled and thanked him as if we both believed this was true, and left the police station wondering which was worse – not knowing why my dad came here, or finding out the truth.

CHAPTER 54

As the digits on my phone clicked over to 18:00, I pressed the bell and stood back to wait, wondering if Dina would have changed her mind. She hadn't. The door was opened almost immediately, and she pulled it back to invite me in. There was no smile but her eyes held none of the hostility I'd seen earlier. That was something.

Without speaking, she led me through to the kitchen where I took a seat on the same grey couch I'd sat on the first time round. She lowered herself into an armchair opposite, a small coffee table the bridge between us.

"So we start over. Marianne, not Linda."

"I'm sorry about that. I panicked."

"I am sorry too. I overreacted. If I am honest, it was not the lie. It was the shock of meeting you after all this time. It brought it all up again. My husband and I had tried to move on and –" She stopped, her voice shaking.

"Oh Dina, I'm so sorry." Instinctively I leaned forward. "I can't even begin to imagine what you've gone through."

"And you!" she said, and it came out like a gasp of air from someone close to going under water. "You lost your mother. I could not think of that – I thought only of myself.

I am sorry." Her eyes were shiny.

"Thank you. But losing a mother I never knew pales in comparison to losing your only child."

Briefly, she closed her eyes. "Thank you for understanding, and I hope we can start over. If it is not too late."

"It's not too late," I said softly, putting my hand on the coffee table.

She looked at it but didn't move. She cleared her throat.

"Erik – he is not so ready I am afraid. He has gone for a walk."

A sting, but smaller. One step at a time.

"I understand."

"It has been a terrible time for so many years. We don't see too many people. Mostly it is just Erik and me."

I thought back to the man in her kitchen that night ten years earlier – the blond man who helped with the search? The man Fru Hansen turned into something he wasn't. Or was.

"And Fru Hansen, I guess?"

A pause.

"Yes. Inge's passing will be felt. We did not see one another so much in the last years, but she was a good woman. She had good meanings. Good intentions."

My turn to pause. How much could I ask without saying the wrong thing and undoing all of it?

"She was one of the people involved in the search?"

"Yes, many people helped."

Jesus, I'd never make an actual detective. I had no idea how to get on to the subject of the blond man or my dad.

"What was Hanne like when she came here that last time," I tried, "when she visited you before she disappeared?"

Dina looked down at her hands, clasped on her neat

grey skirt. A plain gold band was the only ring she wore, and her wrists were free of any jewellery. The ever-present pearls hung around her neck, grazing the top of her neatly buttoned blouse, and the bird brooch clung as always to her breast pocket. It was like a uniform, I realised, and wondered if this how she had always looked, or if it stemmed from losing her child.

"She was unwell," Dina said eventually. "She had pains in the head and stomach, and she was always tired but could not sleep. She was broken," she sighed, "but we were helping her. If it had not happened," she looked up at me, both of us clear what "it" meant, "I think she would have recovered."

"Do you mean she would have come back to us in Ireland? Was it because she was unwell that she came here?" I could hear the scratchy hope in my voice.

"I am sorry, but that I cannot say. Hanne was a trapped bird in Ireland, and coming here set her free again." She leaned forward, and placed her hand on mine. "Perhaps, in time, she would have gone back." There was no certainty in her words, only the kindness that comes with not telling the truth.

We sat, taking in the enormity of the shared tragedy. I was reluctant to break the spell and the physical contact, but I had one more important question.

"I wanted to ask about this," I said, using my free hand to pull a printout of the photo from my bag. "I just found out this week that my dad was here in Købæk back then. I had no idea he came over. Can you tell me about that?"

And too late, far too late, I saw her face transform, and I knew I'd undone all of it.

Dina snapped her hand back as though my skin had burnt her. She stood.

"You need to leave now," she said, her voice cold. The compassion I'd seen moments before was gone, and I couldn't tell what I was seeing in its place.

"But why? What's wrong?" I tried, scrambling to my feet, still holding the photo.

"This was a mistake. Do not come back here." She stood there, her arms folded, her eyes boring into me. Lips tightly closed now. She'd said all she was going to say.

Hurt and confused and fighting tears, I walked out of the room, through her front door, and out into Damtoften's cold night air.

CHAPTER 55

Back in Asta's apartment, as we sat cross-legged on the floor eating Thai food straight from cartons, it all came pouring out. I thought I'd be more upset – to have come so far only to have it all fall apart again – but mostly I was numb.

"She is truly the world's most hypersensitive person," Asta said. "I mean, that's a big overreaction, just like the last time, right?"

"Yeah, she does seem to blow hot and cold. One minute she had her hand on mine and we were really talking, the next she was throwing me out of the house."

"So let me understand this – it was all going good until you showed her the photo of your dad, and then she freaked out?"

"Yep."

"So it's something about your dad, perhaps something he did before Hanne's disappearance or during the search or after she was found – maybe at the funeral?"

"He didn't go to the funeral," I said flatly, twisting noodles around my fork.

"Oh yes, you said that." She paused. "Isn't that odd?"

I put down the fork. "I guess he was so distraught by all of it and he had me to look after . . ."

"But surely he could have found someone to look after you?"

"Yeah . . . now that I think about it, I can see how it seems strange. But right from the first time he told me what happened, I knew he didn't go to the funeral so I just accepted that as normal. I was only twelve when I heard the story."

Asta nodded but didn't look convinced. "Don't forget, you didn't hear the full story that time, right? He told you she had gone to Denmark for a visit, not that she had left him. Maybe there are other things he didn't tell?"

"Maybe."

"Not maybe – definitely. I don't think there was Photoshop in the 1980's, so if we believe this photo is real and you are sure it is your father, then we know he was here in Denmark, in the church near Fugl Sø at some point. But he never told you this."

True. I wondered if anyone else would be able to tell me more – would Alan know something? Or Mrs O'Shea or Bert or Mrs Townsend? I took a sip from my bottle of beer, and made a decision.

Pulling out my phone, I typed a message to Jamie.

This is going to sound odd, but can you do me a favour – could you ask your dad if my dad ever went to Denmark around the time Hanne disappeared? Before it happened, or during the search? I thought he wasn't here, but it seems maybe he was. Just trying to piece things together. Thanks, Marianne x

The "x" was added and the message sent before I thought too much about it – I wondered briefly if we were at the kisses-in-messages stage but Asta was asking me something.

"Did Dina say anything else before she freaked out – anything about your mother?"

"She said she was ill when she came back here – headaches and stomach aches and difficulty sleeping. She said she was liked a trapped bird, but I don't know what exactly she meant by that."

Asta uncrossed her legs and stood up to get two more beers from the fridge.

"Like the inscription on her headstone maybe?" she said as she sat back down. "Remember – *if you love something set it free.*"

"That's right, I'd forgotten." Something clicked in my memory. "Asta, do you remember the postcard you transcribed for Fru Hansen – the one Hanne sent to from Ireland. Wasn't there something about being in a 'cage' in that?"

Asta looked up at the ceiling, her forehead creased in a frown.

"That sounds familiar but it's a long time since I saw it. Do you have it with you?"

I didn't. Then I remembered something else.

"I emailed Inspector Nielsen last year with a copy of the letter Hanne wrote my dad – that'll be in my Sent Items, and I think she said something about being caged there too."

It took a few minutes searching two different email accounts on my phone, but I found it.

"Got it."

Asta came and sat by me. I held the phone as we both read the letter.

> *Michael,*
>
> *I am so sorry to do this to you and to the baby, but I know it is best for you and for her and for me.*
>
> *I never meant for any of it to happen. I came to Ireland for all the best reasons but instead I found myself in a cage.*
>
> *I can't live the way I was living. I'm not the person I know. I need to escape from the cage. I'm back where I belong and it won't be a visit. I need to stay now. I trust that in time you'll explain this to the child, and I hope you will eventually forgive me. I will understand if you can't.*
>
> *Yours,*
> *Hanne*

"When I read it first, I thought she meant she just didn't like the responsibility of being married and having a child. But I wonder . . ."

I pulled up another number on my phone and hit *Call*.

"Dónal Kirwan."

"Hey, Dónal, it's Marianne."

"Ah hello, Marianne. Linda's gone out for a walk – do you want to try her mobile?"

"No, actually it's you I wanted to talk to – but how's she doing?"

"She's getting there, though it'll take time. She told me you two talked last weekend and it seems to have done her good. Everything okay with you?"

"Yes, I'm just looking into something and you might be able to help. I was wondering, are there ever physical symptoms with postnatal depression?"

"Well, yes, there can be but Linda didn't have them –

why do you ask?"

"Could you let me know what they are?"

"Not everyone gets them, but you can have tiredness all the time, headaches, stomach pain, loss of appetite – the kind of symptoms that are often associated with anxiety. Why?"

I let out a shaky breath. God, poor Hanne.

"I can't be certain, but I think my mother may have had postnatal depression after I was born. She left my dad and me to go back to Denmark, and my grandmother told me she was in bed a lot but not sleeping and had headaches and stomach pain. She also referred to her being a 'trapped bird' – I remember Linda told me she felt trapped."

"Well, obviously I can't say with any certainty but it might well have been PND. It was far less understood back then, so she may not have got the support she needed. And lots of people didn't think it was something to worry about – people were expected to just get on with things. Look, I have to go here – the kids are jumping on beds and I've just heard a thump that doesn't sound good. But give me a shout if you need more information, okay?"

I said goodbye and sat back, leaning against the couch.

Asta reached out and touched my hand but said nothing.

Poor Hanne. What hope did she have in the middle of nowhere, with no support? And my father beside her, with no idea what was going on. It still didn't explain why he was in Denmark, or why he never told me, or what happened to Hanne. But as I sat, staring at the far wall of Asta's living room, at a framed photo of a glassy lake, I sensed the answers were close.

CHAPTER 56

The following morning, there were three messages waiting for me when I woke in Asta's spare room. The first was from Jamie.

Hey there,

I asked my da, and he took ages to reply – kept asking me why I wanted to know. I think because he knew the request was from you and he's desperate to figure out if we're seeing each other.

I smiled at that, and my stomach did a weird flip.

He says your dad did go over for a visit, a while after your mam went. He made air quotes when he said 'visit' and sniggered. I told him to cop on and just say what he meant. So he told me he suspected your mam was gone for good and your dad was trying to get her back. Only Alan could think that was something to laugh about. Hope that helps, Jamie

No kiss. Did men do kisses? I had no idea – the only men I messaged were work colleagues, and kisses definitely weren't a thing in Zorian.

I typed a reply.

Cheers for that, would you mind asking one more

thing? Could you ask who looked after me while he was gone? It's a bit weird my dad never said anything about it – I'm curious now.

His answer came back immediately.

Will do, Jx

I grinned at the "x" and, feeling like a schoolgirl with a crush, I opened the second message – this one was from Inspector Nielson and was simply a link to a news story. I clicked in, and found a report on the Maja Pederson case – police had arrested a man in his fifties. He was unnamed, but a source close to the family said the man had been dating Maja and they'd broken up shortly before her death.

One small article that potentially changed everything – if there was no link between Maja's death and those of Hanne and Frederikke. Did that mean there was no serial killer at all back then? Did three becoming two make a material difference?

I clicked into the last message – this one was from Dónal.

Marianne, am emailing you some info on PND and more severe version – postpartum psychosis. Latter very rare, but have a read and come back if you have questions. Linda says hi. Dónal.

Asta knocked on my door just then, to say she was going out to pick up breakfast. I said I'd go too but she told me to stay put and make coffee. So I did as she suggested, and sat in the sun-filled living room to read Dónal's information on PND. It was eye-opening and upsetting to think of Hanne going through this, virtually alone and so far from home. The document mentioned that sufferers experience one or more of a long list of symptoms

– feeling lonely, feeling a lack of interest in the baby, feeling overwhelmed, and physical symptoms too, like "exhaustion, headaches, stomach pains, or blurred vision". Halfway down the list, I spotted "panic attacks or feeling trapped in your life". I sat back. From what she'd written in her letter and told her mother, this was it to a tee. Yet nobody knew to get her the help she needed. Did Dina even call a doctor? The second document Dónal sent was on postpartum psychosis – a serious mental illness to be treated as a medical emergency, according to the information. Symptoms included hallucinations, delusions, and behaving out of character. Was Hanne behaving out of character? That was something only Dina and Erik could answer. I went back to reading the list of PND symptoms, all of which seemed to suddenly slot into place. Or was I seeing connections where there were none – forcing the pieces to fit? I needed a more analytical approach, a list of reasonably concrete facts.

Grabbing a notebook from my bag, I rummaged for a pen, but came up empty-handed. I glanced around the room. Maybe Asta would have one in the kitchen – I got up to look. None there either. Perhaps in a drawer. The first one I opened contained cutlery, and the one below that, a mishmash of photos and receipts. The third drawer had rolls of film and charging cables, and finally, a pen.

I grabbed it and sat to make notes.

As I started to write, I realised the pen had the letters D.F.K. inscribed on it. Suddenly I was transported back ten years to the first time I met Dina. The pen looked very like the one she'd loaned me – the one I'd inadvertently taken with me when I left. Why would Asta have a pen belonging to Dina?

Just then, I heard a key in the door, and Asta walked in with a brown-paper bag.

"Ah good, you found the coffee," she said, walking over to pour herself a cup.

"Yes," I said, "and this." I held up the pen. "Did Dina give it to you?"

"Dina?"

"Yes – I think it's her pen?"

Asta came over to look at it, and shook her head.

"No, I think it's one I picked up at the Youth Club when I was teaching there. What made you think it was Dina's?"

I pointed to the inscription. "D.F.K. – her initials. Well, D and K are her initials – I don't know about the F. I accidentally took a pen with me when I first met her. I'd forgotten all about it till I saw this one."

Asta laughed. "They're not her initials! D.F.K. is Den Første Kirke. It translates as 'The First Church'. They run classes in the Youth Club for underprivileged children – I guess that's how I picked up the pen."

"Oh! I assumed they were her initials. And yeah, I remember now, you told me she volunteers at the Youth Club."

"She's a member of Den Første Kirke. They are a little – what's the word – *evangelical* about getting new members, but they know me now and don't try anymore. They do lots of good things for the community."

"Dina never mentioned it," I said, turning the pen over in my hand.

"Why would she mention it? You haven't had much chance to know each other, and also church isn't something people here talk about much. Maybe in Ireland it's different?"

315

"No, same at home . . . What kind of church is it – are they part of the Church of Denmark?"

Asta shrugged. "I'm not sure, my mother would know. I think they're like Church of Denmark but more strict."

"Do they have a website?" I asked.

"I have no idea." She opened her Mac and swivelled it towards me. "Have a look if you like?"

I typed in **Den Første Kirke + Denmark**, and the top result seemed to be their official website. Beside the banner at the top of the screen, was a logo: a golden bird, just like the one on Dina's brooch. The home page showed pictures of children sitting at small tables – it looked like a classroom setting, but I had no idea what the accompanying text said. I turned the screen to Asta.

"Is that photo from the Youth Club?"

She tilted her head for a better look. "Not ours, but very similar. I think there are branches of the church in different towns around Denmark."

I turned the laptop back. Under a menu option called "Resources" I found links to YouTube videos with various speakers, but again everything was in Danish.

Asta sat beside me. "They're talking about getting new members and letting Jesus Christ into your life, being saved – that kind of thing."

I clicked into the FAQ section, and Asta leaned over to translate.

"The first question is 'Can I be saved?' and the second one is 'How can I donate?' The next one means 'Why is it called The First Church?'"

I rolled my eyes. "I'm immediately sceptical if the second question is about money! Could that be what it is – a moneymaking racket?"

"I don't think so . . . Dina *volunteers* there, she doesn't make money from it if I've understood correctly from my mother."

"Well, sure, *she* volunteers, but someone is making money if donations are a key feature. Who is the founder?"

Asta shook her head. "No idea. I've never thought about any of it. We always knew that Dina volunteered there and didn't think anything strange about it. Don't people volunteer for church activities in Ireland?"

"They do, but usually mainstream religions we're all familiar with. This 'First Church' seems more . . . niche?"

"We can ask my mother – she would know more about it. But I think they're simply a harmless group who feel we are not taking our church seriously any more."

I scrolled to the bottom of the Home page and found an "About" menu in the footer. Again, the text was in Danish, but I wasn't interested in the words. It was the photograph that caught my attention – a picture of someone I'd seen before.

"Who is this?" I asked Asta.

"It says his name is Rasmus Abraham, and he founded Den Første Kirke when he became disillusioned with the Church of Denmark. Wow, nearly forty years ago."

"Is he from Købæk?"

She continued to read, her eyes moving over and back across the screen, scanning words that meant nothing to me.

"Yes, he is – how did you guess?"

"It's not a guess – I'm pretty sure I saw him, sitting in Dina's kitchen when I was here ten years ago."

"Are you certain?"

"Not one hundred per cent but it looks really like him."

"I guess that's not so strange though," Asta said, getting up to pour more coffee for both of us. "If she's a volunteer, and he's from here too."

"What if it's more than that?" I said.

She laughed. "You mean an affair?"

"God, no! I'm wondering if he was the 'blond man'?"

Asta sat back down, putting fresh coffee in front of me.

"Maybe. But couldn't it be anyone?" She laughed. "There are lots of blond men in Denmark!"

"I know . . . but there's something – the stories of the blond man, the stories of Nøkken, the man I saw in her kitchen . . ."

Asta looked at me, her eyes wide with sympathy. "And if there is something about the blond man, it means we don't have to worry so much about the dark-haired man, right? About why your dad was here?"

Slumping back on the couch, I nodded. Whatever was going on with Rasmus Abraham, I still had no idea what my father was doing in Denmark.

318

CHAPTER 57

We were due over to Rikke for lunch, so while Asta took a shower in the apartment's small bathroom, I sat on her couch with her Mac, googling Den Første Kirke and Rasmus Abraham, and copying text into Google Translate. The top results were all either on the Church's own website or on YouTube, and my eyes hurt from rolling so hard at the earnest plan to save the people of Denmark. But other than the ubiquitous "donate now" button, and some slightly inflammatory language about "fighting" to save people, I didn't see anything of great concern. Maybe it really was what it seemed – a harmless spin-off of the more established church.

As I paused to pour a third cup of coffee, my phone beeped with a message from Jamie – Alan had gone out so he couldn't check who looked after me while my dad was in Denmark – he'd ask later.

No rush, I replied, then added **Hope all good with you.**

All fine, checked your house last night just to keep an eye while you're gone, esp as your new alarm not in yet, but all good.

My new alarm – as if anyone would hear it anyway in the middle of nowhere. But I liked the idea that Jamie had taken the time to check the house. There was something unexpectedly appealing about someone other than me taking an interest in my security.

Thanks a mill. Any more news on Ray? I asked.

Nothing new on Ray. But my da saw the poster on the library door – the one about the talk. He nearly crashed the Land Rover. Cue thirty minute of ranting and raving.

I typed a reply: **Should we let the guards know?**

Jamie's response was succinct. **I think Alan can take care of himself.**

I wasn't worried about Alan.

Another message pinged through before I had a chance to reply: **But yeah, I might mention in passing to Patrick or Geraldine, so Alan doesn't get himself arrested. I'll keep you posted.**

I put down the phone. What the hell was Ray doing, coming back to Carrickderg? He surely couldn't be that desperate to sell books that he needed to add our remote library to his tour, and he must know he wouldn't be welcomed by the local constabulary. Geraldine wasn't there that final night, but she'd read the report – she knew the side of Ray he didn't show at book signings and author dinners.

I stuck his name into the search box on Asta's Mac, and clicked into the "News" tab. The first search result was an interview he'd done with *The Irish Times Weekend Magazine*. It was all very *Ray* – gushing about how much he'd enjoyed his time living in Wicklow, and how the Irish are the warmest people in the world. This from the guy who discovered a dead fox in the driveway, courtesy of the neighbour he'd reported to the County Council. I shook my head and clicked back out, then keyed "**Den Første Kirke**" into the search box again.

But this time I clicked into "News". And this time, I struck gold.

Article after article on news websites in Denmark and around Europe – including some from Ireland – and the results were very different from the posts on the church's own website. The headlines were mostly in Danish but there were some in English, including "**Concerns Over Visit from 'Cult' Leader**" and "**Rasmus Abraham – the Man Who Says He Can Cast Out Demons.**"

Jesus. So this was the real story. I started with the first of the English-language links, and began to read.

Ten minutes and four articles later, Asta came out to tell me the shower was free.

"Thanks – I've gone down a rabbit hole of information about the church here – want to take a look?"

She sat beside me and I showed her the article I was reading – a group in France warning people against Rasmus Abraham and his brand of religion.

"Oh wow, I didn't know any of this – what are they warning against?" she asked.

"He preaches that with prayer, true belief and financial donations, anything can be 'cured' – including autism, depression, schizophrenia . . . Basically he says these are all 'demons' and can be cast out – by him, or by his *Stjerner* who are his appointed disciples."

"And Dina is part of this?"

"She must be. I mean, even if she's just volunteering at the Youth Club, she must know what the church is really about, right?"

Asta nodded slowly. Then her face changed. "Click into that one," she said, pointing at the screen.

The thumbnail photo beside the article showed a

woman submerged in water, and a hand resting on her head. The headline read: **Local Groups Raise Concerns as Danish 'Church' Leader Carries Out Mass Baptism.**

The article was from a UK website – the reporter had found out about a planned baptism in a remote part of the Lake District and had gone along to see what it was all about.

There were about thirty people there, some to be baptised, others accompanying those who needed 'curing'. Among the former were children, and I couldn't tell what their supposed ailments were. At the beginning of the lakeside ceremony, Abraham played music on a violin, and spoke to the crowd – in faultless English he preached about cures and demons and making space in the soul for Jesus Christ.

I spoke to people around me, though none were willing to be named in this article. One woman had brought her daughter, because she had a schizophrenia diagnosis. She had read up on the teachings of Rasmus Abraham and believed that what her daughter actually had was a demon inside her. According to the woman, Abraham had cured others with similar diagnoses.

Abraham had a list of names, and one by one people were called forward. In each case, the 'afflicted' person was asked to walk into the lake, to about waist height, and Abraham placed a hand on his or her head. The person was then submerged in water for around ten seconds, as Abraham closed his eyes and mouthed something. Some of the children were reluctant to go under the water, but their parents were allowed to stay with them, to coax them. In at least three cases, people visibly resisted going under but were pushed down by Abraham. Nobody complained.

When I asked a woman beside me if she thought it was okay, she simply replied, "God knows best."

"But it's not God, it's a man," I pointed out.

She smiled and replied, "Blessed are the believers," and walked away.

The article ended with quotes from a number of UK mental health organisations, advising people to steer clear of "cures" offered by anyone who was not a medical professional.

Asta and I stopped reading at the same time.

"Oh my God," Asta said after a moment.

I couldn't find any words at all.

She got up to get me a glass of water, and on autopilot I took it, still staring at the laptop screen.

"Marianne, where was your mother found?"

"A wooded area of Roskilde," I whispered, "more than likely drowned."

Asta got up and began to pace.

"Okay, we need to slow down and think about this. Maybe we're getting carried away." She looked at me.

I blinked but said nothing.

"Your mother drowned, but we don't know where. This man Rasmus Abraham is the head of Den Første Kirke and he carries out baptisms. And Dina is a member of the church. But we don't know if there is any link at all between Abraham and Dina, or if he really carried out a baptism on your mother. We can't be certain he was the blond man you saw in her kitchen, right?"

"I'm certain."

She opened her mouth but closed it again and resumed pacing.

"Even if he was the man you saw in the kitchen," she

323

said after a minute, "there's no certainty he was the blond man from the time Hanne disappeared. And no reason to think she was baptised."

"But there is," I said. "There is every reason. If she had postnatal depression, or maybe postpartum psychosis, there is every reason to think Dina and Abraham believed it was a demon to be cast out. That's what Abraham does – baptises people with mental health issues and behavioural disorders, to 'cure' them."

Asta stopped pacing. "What are you going to do?"

"I need to talk to Dina," I said. "And either she goes to the police, or I do."

CHAPTER 58

When we turned up at Rikke's an hour early, she was flustered, until we explained I wanted to see Dina before lunch. Dina wasn't home, she said. She'd gone to the cemetery to visit Hanne's grave, just as she did every morning.

Asta nodded back towards the car and, without speaking, we got in to drive to the small churchyard near Fugl Sø.

Dina's car was parked on the side of the narrow road just before the gateway to the church. Asta pulled in behind it and said she'd wait there. As I walked towards the gate, my stomach lurched – I had no idea how Dina would take what I was going to say. But I wasn't leaving without answers.

I pushed through the gate, and there she was. The only person in the graveyard, her tall frame and short grey hair instantly recognisable even with her back turned. She was standing at Hanne's grave, her head bowed. I stopped, my resolve shrinking. She'd been through so much, and now I was going to turn everything upside down again. I watched as she blessed herself. Then her shoulders hunched together and her hand went to her face. I sucked in a shaky breath. It needed to come to an end, for her sanity as well as for mine.

When she stood up straight again, I cleared my throat. She swung around to look at me, her eyes red from crying.

"*You*. Why cannot you leave us alone?"

I stepped towards her.

"I know about Abraham Rasmus and the baptisms," I said softly.

She stood rod-like, a grey spectre against the white sky.

"And? He is the Head of our Church, yes, and he carries out baptisms. Why have you come to this holy place to tell me something I know?"

"He baptised Hanne, didn't he. To rid of her of her 'demon'."

A flash of anger crossed her face. "*Do not come here with such stories!*" she said, in a low hiss. "Hanne was murdered by a serial killer."

"But she wasn't murdered by a serial killer," I said gently. "You didn't read the paper today, I guess, but when you do you'll see – Maja Pedersen was killed by her ex-boyfriend."

Dina stared at me and shook her head.

I kept talking, "There is no serial killer, Dina. Maja was killed by someone she knew. Like most victims. An ex-husband, a boyfriend. A family friend."

She shook her head again but some of the fight had gone out of her.

"Dina, I've seen photographs of baptisms online. Rasmus Abraham said Hanne had a demon, didn't he?"

She closed her eyes, and her shoulders sagged. The nod was so tiny it was almost imperceptible.

"Oh Dina." I reached my hand towards her, but she didn't move. My hand dropped to my side.

"Rasmus Abraham is a good man. A man of God."

Something bubbled up inside me, and my resolve to stay calm evaporated.

"How can you defend him? She came home looking for help, and you handed her to a monster!"

"Help?" Dina said, eyes wide. "She did not look for help, she did not care about anything. The old Hanne was gone, the demon took her and gave me a *heks* – a witch – in her place. She cared for nothing and for nobody. She hurt people."

"Do you even hear yourself? She was ill! So what if she didn't seem like the perfect daughter, so what if she didn't care about you – she needed help and support! If she hurt you it was because she was terribly ill!"

"I don't mean she hurt *me*," she said, "I mean she hurt *you*."

A cold sick feeling spread through my stomach. "What are you talking about?"

"That photo of your father? It was taken here at this church. He came to Denmark to talk to her, to ask her to go to Ireland, and he brought you with him. You were a baby. We thought it would help Hanne to have time with you. So we left you with her, and we took your father to be tourist in Købæk. It was so cold, and your father's coat was no good, like wearing paper in snow. I think he hated it. But we all believed it was a good idea. And it was just a few hours."

"What happened?" I whispered.

"When we arrived back, Hanne was sitting at the kitchen table with a coffee. Your father asked if you were

327

ANDREA MARA

asleep, and she answered him in Danish. He did not know what she said – I had to tell him. She said you were in a 'better place' but would not say more. She was like in a dream. You understand?"

I nodded, the sick feeling spreading.

"Erik and I began to look in all the rooms, and your father stayed with Hanne, asking her again and again, 'Where is the baby?' but she stared at nothing and did not answer. It was evening by then, and dark outside, and very, very cold – below zero. We took torches and went outside, praying we would find you there, but also, praying we would not – it was really so cold, too cold for small baby. Erik and I searched the garden and up and down the street, but nothing. Then I heard a small cry – I remember so well – it was from Inge Hansen's house. I ran to her doorstep and there you were, wrapped in blankets, blue with cold, eyes closed."

My legs loosened. I lowered myself to sit on the ground.

Dina nodded, and continued with her story. "I screamed and called for Erik and reached to pick you up. I pulled you inside my coat, and ran to the house. I pulled off the cold blankets and wrapped you in warm ones and told Erik to build up the fire. Your father – he stood looking at me and I think not really breathing, in shock. I held you to me and it seemed like the longest time, but finally you opened your eyes. Your father, he took you and he cried."

"And Hanne?" I said in a whisper, looking up from my place on the ice-cold ground.

"Hanne stayed at the kitchen table, drinking cold coffee."

"Did my father talk to her?"

"No. He was very upset. He left the next day, taking

328

you home. He did not say goodbye to Hanne. She did not notice or care." Her expression hardened. "She was like a doll with no feeling on her face, she did not care that she had almost killed her own child. That was not my Hanne, that was the demon in her. She was a *heks*. You see now, I think?"

And I realised then that she thought I'd understand – that I'd see the baptism was necessary. That as the victim, I'd somehow view things differently.

"Dina, there was no demon – don't you see she had some kind of postnatal psychosis? She wasn't trying to *kill* me – she obviously thought I'd be better off with Fru Hansen. She was severely *ill*, not possessed! And you handed her over to that delusional man with the God-complex, and he killed her. And you let it happen. Were you there? Did it happen in the lake, here in Fugl Sø?"

She ignored my question. "Her death was God's will. Hanne was not for this world – she is happier in the afterlife, I am certain."

"You need to go to the police."

"Why?"

"Why? Because you need to stop covering for him – what if he does it to someone else?"

"He is a strong man."

"You don't need to be frightened of him – the police will arrest him, he can't get you then." Even as I said it, I wondered if it was true – would the police be able to arrest him so quickly?

"He is a strong man and a good man."

"Dina, you have to stop. If you won't go to the police, I'll do it."

She sat down heavily on a step behind her.

"Then do so. I will not stop you."

Cramped and dizzy, I pulled myself to my feet, and turned to walk away. But something in her tone nagged at me. I stopped.

"Hang on – will you tell them what you've told me though? They're going to need a statement from you."

"I will not speak to the police."

"Dina, you have to stop covering for him!"

"Covering – what does this mean?"

"Telling lies to hide what he did."

"Ah. Yes. But, Marianne, you do not understand. I am not covering for him. He is covering for me."

CHAPTER 59

I stared at Dina as the pieces slipped into place.

"*You* did it? You drowned Hanne?"

"Not drowned. Baptised. It was God's will that she be taken. The demon was too strong. The real Hanne was gone." She held up her hands, as though telling me about a bird that had died.

"Where did you do it?"

She nodded to her left. "At the lake. I am a *Stjerne* of the church and have the authority to carry out baptisms. She was not getting better, so I brought her here to baptise. But when she came up from the water after the first prayer, there was no light in her eyes – her face was just like a doll, and I knew then the demon was still inside. I tried again, for longer, but still she looked the same. Dead inside, existing, not living. I did a third prayer, for longer now, holding her under, begging the demon to go, to give me back my Hanne. I could feel it. I could feel the demon fighting against me, pushing back against my hand, kicking. But I was stronger, and eventually it stopped fighting – it was gone."

"But Hanne was gone too."

"Yes. God's will. The demon was too strong."

"Oh Dina. Is that truly what you believe?"

"Of course. It is the truth of Jesus Christ. Only the believers of the truth will be saved."

Out of the corner of my eye, I could see Asta hovering behind the gate. With my hand by my side, I motioned for her to stay where she was.

"What did you do then?"

"I pulled her to the dry land and laid her there. She looked so peaceful. Then I drove to the house, and Erik called Rasmus to tell him. Rasmus explained to us that people would not understand that it was God's will, and we must hide Hanne. He said he would do it. Erik and I are forever grateful to him."

"He buried her in Roskilde?"

She nodded.

"And you allowed people to search for her for months, never admitting what you'd done or that you knew where she was?"

For the first time, she looked uneasy.

"It was the only way."

"And when I turned up ten years ago, all this faux rage about me lying to you – you let me believe I'd done something wrong."

"Even if it was God's will that Hanne left us that night, I am sad that I lost her to the demon. I did not want any reminders."

That last word was the one that tipped me from incredulity to white-hot rage.

"*Reminders?* That's what you had to worry about? Me, the child left without a mother, because you're a deranged psychopath, and my poor father, left without his wife, cut

completely from your life. Because we *remind* you of her?
Sorry, but *go fuck yourself*, Dina."

She recoiled, and a small part of me remembered she
was an elderly woman not in her right mind, but I didn't
care. I was too angry to care.

"I did not want your father's sadness interrupted by the
newspapers," she said.

"That's *bullshit*! There's nothing in any of what you've
said that suggests you even once thought of anyone but
yourself. You kept him out of things because you didn't
want people to know about the so-called demon, and to
work out what you'd done."

She threw up her hands and shook her head. "I did not
want people to know what she did."

"What *she* did?"

"To you. Leaving you to die in the cold."

"Is that what mattered most? Hiding what she did? She
was *ill* for God's sake – she didn't know what she was
doing! She thought I'd be better off without her, that's why
she put me at Fru Hansen's door. Not to die, but to go to
a better home. If you'd got professional help for her instead
of hiding her away, you'd have known that. *Jesus Christ*."

"But, Marianne, you forget one thing," she said in a
quiet voice, still sitting on the step.

"What?"

"I saved you. Without me, you would have died. Like a
winter leaf."

I walked away then, because there was nothing to else
to say – no way to make her see.

Asta was just outside the gate, her face pale, her eyes huge.

"You heard all that?" I asked, reaching for her shoulder
to steady myself.

"Most of it." She put her arm around my waist. "Oh, Marianne, I don't know what to say."

"Let's just go."

Inspector Nielsen wasn't there when we arrived, but I said we'd wait.

Asta and I sat together, going over everything Dina had said.

"I guess the blond man was Rasmus Abraham," Asta said. "People saw him around the Karlsens' house over the years, and during the search. You were right."

I sighed. Being right didn't feel good.

"My mother must have known him when she was growing up. And judging by the sketches of the Nøkken, she obviously knew something wasn't right with what he was doing."

"All that talk of locking away the past," Asta said, shaking her head. "I guess she was trying to escape her upbringing? Escape the control of the church?"

"I think so. It all seems obvious now, but only because we know who the blond man is. And the dark-haired man was my dad. No wonder he never told me about the trip to Denmark." I shivered. "Poor Dad, living all those years with the belief that Hanne tried to harm me."

"You think he also didn't understand it was postnatal depression?"

"I don't know, but it seems like it." I threw up my hands. "I mean, I'm only guessing – I'm not exactly qualified to diagnose an illness in someone who's been dead all this time, but everything points to it."

Asta nodded, and slumped back in the chair. "I don't know what my mother will say. All those people helping with the search, and Dina knew the whole time where Hanne was." She sat up again. "You know, it sounds bad to say this, but I'm glad Fru Hansen died without knowing this truth."

"I think she did know."

"What?"

"Not the whole truth – not that Dina did it, but I think she suspected there was something not right. You remember those Nøkken stories she told us during my first visit? The ones about the man playing the violin to lead women and children into water?"

Asta nodded.

"I think she was talking about Rasmus Abraham. She had gone to the police but nobody took her seriously. So she wove it into a fairy tale."

"And she fell out with Dina for some time – it makes sense now," Asta said.

"I think Hanne felt the same way. You remember that key Fru Hansen gave me? It unlocked a jewellery box in our attic, and inside I found sketches in a jewellery box that belonged to her, showing Nøkken in various forms. She must have known exactly what Rasmus Abraham was doing."

"And perhaps her mother too . . ." Asta said.

And yet she had gone home for help, because that's what people do – turn to their mothers, trusting they'll do what's best for them. Did she understand what was happening to her, as her mother held her under the water? Did she know she was going to die? I had no idea, but I hoped she could rest better now the truth was out.

CHAPTER 60

When we eventually finished at the police station, we'd lost all track of time, but knew we were hours late for Rikke's lunch. Asta had called her with a garbled message about Dina and the graveyard, so when we finally arrived back there, cold and hungry and exhausted, Rikke was ready with soup and bread and a pot of coffee. Between us, we filled her in on the story, and she sat open-mouthed until we got to the last word.

"I do not know what to think," she said, shaking her head. "Poor Inge. I am glad she does not know this."

"I think Fru Hansen knew there was something up with Rasmus Abraham but nobody was listening to her," I said.

"The blond man, yes?" Rikke said. "The '*lyshåret*' one she spoke of?"

"Yes, and the dark-haired man was my dad. When the photo fell out of the Bible, Fru Hansen realised that Dina must have known the dark-haired man all this time but said nothing to the police or anyone else. Fru Hansen didn't know it was my dad of course, she was just worried about why Dina had never said anything."

Rikke took our soup bowls to the kitchen and came

back with cake.

"Sorry, cake does not seem appropriate now, but I did not know all this would happen today."

I smiled a sad smile. "Me neither. I've been trying to work out what happened to Hanne for so long, and now that I have I wonder if it was better not knowing."

"What will you do now, Marianne?" Rikke asked, cutting into the cake.

"I have to go to the police station tomorrow morning for another interview, and if it goes to court I will have to fly back here, but for now I will go home, go back to work, get on with life, I guess."

"And hopefully no more footprints in the snow," Asta said, "unless you were enjoying the mystery?"

"God no, I could do without that."

Rikke looked puzzled.

"Asta, maybe you can explain it to Rikke," I said. "I'm going to pop out to make a quick call to Inspector Nielsen."

As I walked through the living-room door into Rikke's hallway, I didn't immediately register that the blue lights were out of the ordinary. From outside, through the glass, scattering across the dark floor. Blinking. Warning. In a fog, I opened the front door. Across the way, a bright yellow van. An ambulance. Outside the Karlsens' house.

Running down the driveway, I could see a stretcher being lifted into the back of the ambulance. The doors slammed shut before I could see who it was. Farther along the street, a second stretcher was being wheeled towards another ambulance. A sheet covered the patient's head.

"Who is it – what happened?" I asked a young woman in a high-vis jacket. She said something in Danish and turned to walk away. "I don't speak Danish, but this is my grandparents' house – can you tell me what happened?"

She turned back, sympathy and something else on her face.

"I cannot say, but police are there," she said, pointing to a small group of police officers.

In their midst, I spotted Inspector Nielsen.

"*What's happened?*" I shouted, rushing over.

He broke free from the group to steer me down the street, his hand gentle on my back. We stopped under a streetlamp.

"What's happened?" I asked again, whispering now.

He pulled out a packet of cigarettes and offered me one. I shook my head, and waited as he lit his.

"We arrested Rasmus Abraham this afternoon, and then we came here, to take Dina Karlsen into custody. We found Dina and Erik sitting together on the living-room sofa." He paused.

"What happened to them?" I said, my voice barely audible.

"They had both passed away, I'm afraid."

"I don't understand."

He took a deep drag of his cigarette, and exhaled blue smoke into the night sky. He looked at me again.

"There will be an investigation, but it seems as if Dina tied a plastic bag over Erik's head and one over her own. His hands were tied. Hers were not."

That's when I threw up.

CHAPTER 61

It was late on Sunday night when I finally pulled into the driveway. I parked around the side, and picked my way through the darkness, back to the front of the house. At the living-room window, I drew in a shaky breath and traced my fingers around the frame. Smooth. No disruption. The sticky tape was still in place. The front doorstep was empty, no new souvenirs.

Now the bedroom window. My fingers worked their way across the tape at the bottom, up the left side, and then the right. Halfway up, I felt a bump. The tape was twisted, not smooth. I had left it perfectly smooth, I always did. Had someone taken it off and put it back on? My mind went back to Thursday morning, rushing to leave for the airport. Could I have made a mistake? I couldn't even remember putting on the tape. I'd done it on autopilot. And surely if someone had been in the house, the tape would be broken, not tangled.

Nerves frayed, I turned the key in the front door and pushed it just two inches. I slid my hand in and felt for the book. Still there, where I left it, just inside the door. No-one had been here. No-one had been inside the house.

I reached for the living-room light-switch.

The bulb flickered to life.

And then I saw.

At my bedroom door, neatly placed on the floor, a book.

At the kitchen door lay another one.

At my dad's old bedroom door, a book there too.

I stood staring, my heart hammering in my chest.

He'd been inside my house.

It took three goes for me to explain to the young garda who answered the phone what I meant and in the end I think I may have been shouting, but, within half an hour, he was in my house. He checked every inch and outside too, returning twice to look at the back door.

"It's hard to tell for sure but with those old doors you'd need nothing more than a credit card break in." He looked up at me. "Are you certain nothing was taken? Someone broke in and just left books on the floor?"

"I don't think anything was taken. I reckon whoever did it wanted to show me that my security is pointless. And it bloody worked."

"You said you're getting an alarm?"

"Yes, but it's not due for another week."

"I'd say get a locksmith tomorrow to fit a deadbolt to this," he nodded towards the backdoor, "and maybe call the alarm people to see if they can speed things up? We're always at the end of a phone too. Call anytime."

It was the kindness in his last words that undid me. My eyes were suddenly wet, my throat choked. I ushered him out, utterly mortified, and locked the door. Whatever good that might do.

As the heating clanked slowly to life, I wrapped myself in

a blanket and huddled on the couch with my laptop and a bowl of microwaved soup. I couldn't get warm. I didn't think I could ever feel warm again. Or safe. Not here. Maybe it was time to go. Tears sprang up again. My childhood home. My parents' home. Only it didn't feel like home anymore. I got up to check the front door and the back door. I'd get a better lock tomorrow, but what about tonight? What if he came back? I went to my bedroom, picked up the shotgun, and sat back down on the couch. Ready.

Facebook was hopping with notifications from the Armchair Detective group – I clicked in on autopilot, my mind still on locks and shotguns, and the books he'd laid out to mock me. So it took a few minutes to focus, to make sense of all the posts and comments, but it seemed police investigating the Blackwood Strangler case had made an arrest. A man in his sixties, unnamed, was being held in custody. Details were scant but rumour was rife. The story with most traction was that the man's wife had found a box of jewellery and trinkets in the attic, and thought her husband was having an affair. She showed a friend, who recognised one of the necklaces – a distinctive gold pendant with an inscription. The friend searched online, and the pendant turned up in a newspaper report about a murder in Bournemouth. The two women trawled the Internet searching for other Blackwood Strangler stories and were able to match up two more pieces of jewellery before they decided to go to the police.

Back in our Facebook group, Neil was sceptical.

I'm just not convinced. A woman finds jewellery in the attic? Who says she didn't plant it there to get her husband in trouble – I read that she was about to look for a divorce.

341

I'd read the same – she was on the verge of kicking him out. Not because she had any idea of what he'd allegedly done, but because she realised she was happier when he was away on his many business trips than when he was home.

Judith replied to Neil: **I suppose it's a little anti-climactic but that's how it goes in the real world – are you upset because it wasn't us who caught him, Neil?** ☺

Neil got predictably defensive: **Of course not. I'm just not altogether certain this is the guy. Why would he leave the box of souvenirs in the attic for a start, and why didn't the wife find them sooner?**

Cheryl jumped in: **I read about that on iSleuth – apparently the wife is quite short, and can't reach the hatch to the attic, even standing on a chair. So she left it to her husband to deal with getting things up and down. But then there was a leak and he was away on business, so she got a stepladder and climbed up. That's when she found the box and took a look inside. Amazing how it was such an everyday thing that got him caught in the end – a leaking pipe!**

I put my empty soup bowl aside and started to type. Only I didn't know what to say. Somehow, after all this time, I didn't care much about how the Blackwood Strangler was caught.

So, if this is really him, what do we do next? Judith typed. **We need a new case! Who wants to choose? Barry and Marianne, anything interesting going on over in Ireland?**

Barry was quick to reply: **It'll be interesting to see if this man they've arrested is responsible for the other cases we found – the ones in Germany, Poland, Sweden etc. They're** saying on iSleuth he is but, if not, maybe we could keep looking into those? What do you think, Marianne?

My fingers were on the keyboard, but I couldn't will them to type. I sat back on the couch and shook my head, silently acknowledging that I just didn't care.

The conversation went on, Barry's question hanging in the air. Different people put forward different cases, some well known, some less so. The conversation kept going back to the Blackwood Strangler and the rumours that were flying around the Internet. It would be a while before it died down, Judith said after a bit, maybe there was no rush to find something new.

A little later, a private message from Barry popped through.

Are you ok? Very quiet tonight?

I told him I was fine, just back from a trip to Denmark and tired from the journey.

What took you to Denmark? he asked.

A funeral, I typed. **Bit wrecked, need to go to bed now, chat soon.**

Oh no, who died? he asked, not getting the hint.

I read the message without clicking into it, hoping he'd think I'd logged out for the night. I could deal with Barry more easily after a sleep.

Judith messaged too, also wondering about how quiet I was. I told her the same. She sent me her condolences and didn't ask any further questions.

Relieved, I logged out, and went to bed.

On Monday morning, I woke with a jolt, disoriented. I'd slept through the night, I realised, and while this should have been a relief, it was quite the opposite. What had I

missed, had he been here? It took over an hour to search
every inch of the house looking for signs of disturbance.
Nothing. Nothing that I could see.

The house was too quiet. I switched on the radio. The
morning papers were under discussion, and there was only
one topic: more heavy snow on the way. *Why does the
country shut down every time there's an inch of snow?* one
texter complained, followed by another announcing he'd
be refusing to cooperate with any curfew this time.

I glanced over at the living-room window but outside
the sky was bright blue and clear, no sign of any snow. I
took my coffee to the front door and opened it, turning my
face to the weak sun, closing my eyes, breathing in the crisp
air, willing it to clear my cluttered head.

A shadow passed and I opened my eyes. A grey cloud
had appeared out of nowhere, blocking the sun – maybe
the forecast was right after all.

Suddenly my eye was drawn to something at my feet –
a rolled-up newspaper. Only I didn't have any newspapers
delivered – I read everything online. Picking it up, I
unfolded it, wondering if perhaps the local free paper was
being delivered everywhere now, even to those of us in the
sticks. But it wasn't a freebie, it was *The Irish Times*, and
someone had circled the main headline in thick black
marker: **Weather Alert Warns of Heaviest Snow in 10
Years.**

I pulled out my phone to message Jamie.

Did you drop me a copy of the paper?

I already knew the answer – of course he didn't – why
would he leave a paper on my doorstep when he could text
me instead? Perhaps it was another well-meaning
neighbour. Or Bert – maybe the Post Office was delivering

papers as some kind of one-off promotion? I rang O'Shea's and Mick picked up. He hadn't heard of any newspaper promotion, he told me, but then they wouldn't know – they didn't have anything to do with outgoing post. He said he'd ask Bert who had just walked in. Bert hadn't heard anything either, Mick confirmed after a pause, and hadn't dropped any newspaper on my doorstep.

"Is she alright?" I could hear Bert saying in the background as I disconnected the call. Good question.

Jamie's reply came through – he hadn't left a newspaper on my doorstep.

Are you ok – someone spooking you out again?

Maybe, I replied. **Kind of a weird way to do it though. A newspaper?**

No weirder than a chalk letter, Jamie replied.

I brought the paper inside and took a photo of it, anticipating the reaction I'd get from Patrick and Geraldine. *Sure isn't it nice that one of your neighbours left you a paper – aren't they only looking out for you?*

It was time for my first conference call. I dialled in but afterwards, if my life depended on it, I couldn't say what was discussed. My head was buzzing with Dina and Hanne and the Blackwood Strangler and Ray and Alan and Jamie and snow, and most of all, the faceless person who was coming into my garden at night. And now my house. My own *Bøhmand*. And I realised that somehow the uncovering of Hanne's death and the arrest in the UK had lulled me into believing the footprints were over. Not because there was any real link, but because it would be just one of those things – a weird time in my life, now over. Only not over. And the snow was coming back.

CHAPTER 62

By one o'clock, the sky had completely clouded over and it was noticeably dark. It was impossible to concentrate on work, and I took time out to call the Garda Station about the latest drop.

Patrick picked up, and I filled him in.

"Okay . . ." he said, after I'd explained it, and my heart sank as I waited for another dismissal. "It doesn't sound like anything to worry about, but I know that's easy for me to say – it's different when you're the one on the receiving end."

I would have hugged him through the phone-line if I could. "That's it – I just want to know who's doing it and why."

"Is it today's paper?" he asked.

I said it was.

"So someone dropped it very early this morning, I suppose. It wouldn't have been available before that, certainly not out here in Carrickderg."

A valid point, but not one that clarified things any further.

"Jamie Crowley mentioned something about this author

fella Ray Sedgwick who's doing a talk in the library – said he's an ex of yours and there was some trouble with Alan Crowley way back?"

I sighed. "Yeah, a rift that got out of control."

"And could that have anything to do with this?"

I traced my finger on the newspaper, following the arc of the circle.

"Marianne, are you still there?"

"Yeah. Just thinking. I honestly don't know. I'm not sure it's Ray's style and Jamie is certain it's not Alan. I trust Jamie's judgement."

Now it was his turn to go quiet.

"What is it?" I asked.

"No, nothing," he said, "just thinking too."

With nothing more to say, I promised I'd email through a photo of the newspaper, and he said he'd send a car later that night. If nothing else, it might deter someone who was watching. I disconnected the call, and got up to close the curtains, though it was still only lunchtime.

A knock at the door minutes later made me jump. I peeped out through the curtains before answering but it was just Jamie, and some shopping bags.

"Hope you don't mind me calling unannounced," he said, "but I knew you'd say no if I offered, so here you go!" He held up two bags of groceries.

"What's this?" I asked, pulling the door wide.

"There's a big freeze coming tonight, and the shops are going to run out of everything again like they did three weeks ago, and you're the only person I know who won't have stocked up on provisions. Am I right?"

I smiled. "The cupboards are bare. I could have gone down this afternoon though."

Jamie tilted his head to one side. "And would you have?"

"Okay, you win – here, hand me those and I'll put the stuff away. Will you stay for a sandwich?"

"Absolutely. I bought the fancy bread – the one with the dates and walnuts – I'm not missing out on that. So how was Denmark?"

He followed me through to the kitchen.

I filled him in, watching his eyes go wide at each revelation. When I told him about Dina and Erik's deaths, he shook his head.

"My God, Marianne, that's horrendous. Are you going to go to counselling?"

"I don't think so. It's over now."

He looked like he wanted to say more, but I took the sandwiches through to the sitting room and, side by side on the couch, we sat to eat.

"So do you think Ray's talk will go ahead?" I asked, nodding towards the curtained window. "He'll hardly be able to drive down here tomorrow if the weather forecast is right?"

"No harm if it's cancelled," Jamie said. "My da is still ranting and muttering about 'that gobshite' and God only knows what he's got planned. I can't see him letting what Ray did go by without confronting him."

"Are you worried?"

"A bit. I did tell the guards. It was Maguire I spoke to, and he didn't know anything about what happened – Geraldine would know, she'd remember, but I'm not sure if he passed on the message."

"I'd say he did – he mentioned it to me today anyway."

"Oh, were you on to them today?"

I reminded him about the newspaper.

"Maybe it's a do-gooder – someone like me who thinks you don't look after yourself and could do with supplies!" he said, laughing.

I didn't join in. "Ah sorry, I didn't mean it like that." His expression changed and he looked at me more closely. "Marianne, you're really worried about this, aren't you?"

He reached over and put his hand on my shoulder, his eyes full of concern and suddenly more than anything I wanted to bury my head in his chest and have a good old-fashioned cry. Instead I looked at the floor, and nodded.

"Anyway, I'd better eat this and get back to work," I said when I could trust my voice again.

Jamie changed the subject – we talked about safe topics like TV and books and whether or not Danish pastries are called Danish pastries in Denmark.

Just before two o'clock, I opened my laptop and told him I'd need to log on for a call. He nodded and got up to leave.

Outside, the sky was a slate-grey cauldron and the first swirls of snow had started to fall.

"Will you be alright tonight – do you want me to –" he said, looking up at the sky and back at me, but he didn't finish what he was going to say.

"You go on now," I said. "Quick before it gets too heavy!"

And he did, with a small wave and a smile that looked sad, or wistful perhaps. I shut the door and leaned against it, realising too late that I wanted him to finish his sentence.

At six, I finished my final call, and stood to stretch my legs. Outside, the snow was coming down heavily, no longer melting on contact with the ground. *I hope it sticks!* we used to say when we were kids. *It bloody better not*, I thought now. The snow should keep everyone at home – it should keep me safer. But I couldn't help feeling it was drawing him out again, drawing him back to me.

Nerves jangling, I locked the doors, and checked the windows. Desperate for distraction, I clicked into Facebook but even that didn't work – there was a further barrage of notifications about the Blackwood Strangler arrest and I ignored them all. Barry had tagged me in a post about a case in France that looked like the Swedish one we'd researched but I ignored that too. If you look hard enough, you can find patterns and links between anything and everything, I thought, shutting down Facebook and opening my personal email.

And there, amid the usual slew of newsletters and LinkedIn requests, one email stood out. *"Hello there"* was the simple subject line, and the sender was Ray Sedgwick.

CHAPTER 63

2008

The night it all fell apart had started out so perfectly. We were in the Yacht Club in Dun Laoghaire for the launch of Ray's new book, in a beautiful high-ceilinged room, looking out over the marina. The sun was just beginning to set, casting an orange glow on the guests inside. There were readers and authors and local politicians, all helping themselves to wine and canapés and waiting for a glimpse of the man himself. He and I arrived a little late – and as we exited our taxi to go into the club, he stopped to check some important messages. There were no important messages, but he needed to be sure there were people at his launch before he made his entrance. When we did arrive, he was greeted with cheers and applause. No doubt there were many genuine fans in the room but, also, I suspect, a good smattering of people who had never read any of his books. And who doesn't like a free glass of wine on an unseasonably warm Thursday night in March?

There were stacks and stacks of his new book, *The Sophisticate*, lined up on tables around a podium, and staff of Seven-Storey Books on hand with a till to facilitate purchases. I hadn't seen the finished version of the book at that point. Ray had insisted I wait until the launch. The cover depicted a silhouette of a man in what looked like a cowboy hat and, thinking back, that's when I felt the first tiny pang of concern.

A local councillor took to the podium to make a speech about Ray and his writing. "An important book," he said. "One that paints a picture of an Ireland we all know well."

I had no idea what the book was about and my curiosity was piqued. Ray had been writing furiously for over a year, but said it was bad luck to tell me anything about the book. That was fine with me – anything that distracted him from his ridiculous feud with Alan was a good thing.

The councillor was still talking about *The Sophisticate*. "When you scratch the surface," he was saying, "unfortunately the underbelly is not pretty. It is often grotesque, in real life as well as in fiction."

Ray nodded along, hands in pockets, looking at his feet. This was humble Ray, a part he played well when people were watching.

He looked up when the applause started and smiled bashfully as he thanked the councillor and took his place at the podium.

He thanked me, the people of Carrickderg and, rather majestically, the population of Ireland. Then he said something that caused the little pang of concern to swell.

"And there's one person in particular I want to thank but he's not here tonight – he was the inspiration behind the character of Ned in *The Sophisticate*." A little "*ooh*" from the crowd made me wish I'd had the opportunity to know who Ned was. "Don't worry, there's no chance this person will ever find out – he's not the book-reading type!" Ray continued, to what seemed like nervous laughter.

He went on to talk in glowing terms about his three years in our beautiful country of saints and scholars, then finished with an invitation eat, drink, and be merry.

"Have you read it?" a voice beside me asked, as I picked up a copy of the book.

"Not yet," I said, "have you?"

The lady, a curly-haired woman in her forties, nodded. "I wouldn't like to be that man he mentioned – the one who inspired Ned. It's a good book, but I didn't realise it was based on real life."

I ran my hand over the glossy cover, and the silhouette of the man in the cowboy hat.

"What happens to Ned?"

"Ah, I won't spoil it – you read it yourself and find out. Let's just say it's not what happens to *Ned*." She raised her eyebrows knowingly, but I had no idea what she meant. "I'd better go find my husband – we only paid the parking for an hour," she said, and whirled off into the crowd.

"So what's it about?" I asked Ray, three hours and many glasses of wine later, as we sat in the back of the taxi to go home.

He winked at me. "Nice try but you're going to have to put down your laptop and actually read it!"

"Ray . . . is it about someone we know?"

"Just read it, and you'll find out!"

"But you can't write about someone you know – surely that's libel or slander or one of those?"

"Not if it's fiction. I didn't say it's about someone, I said it was *inspired by*. And look," he said, opening the book, "it says it right there – 'All characters and events in this publication are fictitious'."

"What if Alan reads it?"

"How did you know it was Alan?"

I made an 'Ah, come on' face but I don't know if he could see it in the dark.

"Marianne, it's fine." There was an edge to his voice now. "Do you really think Alan reads anything other than tabloid newspapers?"

I shook my head. Three years in Carrickderg and Ray still didn't understand how small towns work. Alan didn't have to read the book. As long as people around him did, he'd know exactly what was going on.

It was after ten when we got home, and lightheaded from too much wine and too few canapés, I made toast, and sat to start the book. Ray poured himself a whiskey and got out his laptop to look for new reviews. I could feel him looking over at me every now and then, and there was something heightened in the air, thick and tense and blurred with wine.

The book started with scenes from a small town in Ireland, and a local man called Ned who seemed to think a lot of himself. Behind his back, people laughed at Ned, and the early chapters were devoted to lampooning him – the 'man about town' who walked with a swagger, but had no idea people saw him as a bit of a buffoon. Alan wouldn't like it at all if he recognised himself, though it was possible he wouldn't – he probably had no idea what people in Carrickderg really thought of him. And the details were a little different – Ned had a wife, and two young sons, John and Paul.

An hour later, I was about a fifth of the way through the book and thinking of going to bed.

Then I got to Chapter Twelve. My half-closed eyes sprang open and I sat upright on the couch. With a knot in my stomach, I made it halfway through the chapter before I had to stop – the scene unfolding between Ned and his small son Paul was too stark, too graphic, and far too disturbing.

"Ray?"

He looked up, eyes innocent but knowing.

"Yes?"

"How could you do this?"

"What?"

"It's so very clearly Alan in the book, and then you make out that he's abusing his son? What the hell were you thinking?"

"I didn't. I wrote a work of fiction. It's about a character called Ned."

"Who is very clearly based on Alan – you even alluded to it in your speech."

He shrugged.

I stood.

"You need to fix this – it reads as though Alan is some kind of monster, who abuses his son. People will think the Paul character is Jamie. Ray, what have you done?"

"*Relax*, Marianne, my publisher's legal people gave me the OK. There are enough differences – Alan can't sue."

"But it doesn't *matter* whether he can sue or not! For fuck's sake, Ray, what matters is that people around here will think it's Alan! Don't you get that? It's not about what's *legally* right or wrong – it's about what's morally or ethically right or wrong. Jesus, I'm so mad right now I can't bear to look at you!"

He stood too, arms by his sides.

"It's art, Marianne, I don't expect you to understand."

"It's not fucking *art*," I spat. "It's just the latest cheap shot in a ridiculous, childish feud. I can't believe your publisher ran with it. *Jesus, Ray!*"

"Oh, it's not 'fucking art', is it not?" He took a step closer. "And what would you know about that?"

Looking back, I can see the warning signs were there. But at the time, I was too mad to see anything.

"What would *I* know? What, because I work in IT and don't write books, I'm some kind of philistine? I don't have to be an artist to understand that this excuse for a book is nothing more than another lame attempt to get back at Alan. *Jesus, it's not even well written. It's a vehicle to attack Alan, nothing more!*" I could see little bits of spit flying out of my mouth and I was shouting, but I couldn't stop now even if I wanted to. "*I may not write books but I read a hell of a lot of them, and this – as you might say yourself – is trash!*"

I flung it across the room so hard it knocked a picture off the wall. The crash of breaking glass stopped us both momentarily.

Slowly, Ray walked over and picked up the book. Then a shard of glass from the broken picture. He straightened up and looked at me. His eyes hard. He walked towards me, book in one hand, shard of glass in the other. The atmosphere in the room, so charged one second, so high with emotion, slipped to something else entirely. Something cold. I opened my mouth but my voice was stuck in my throat. My legs felt as though weights were pulling them down, my feet rooted to the floor. Ray took another step towards me. Stranger's eyes, a face I barely recognised. The glass glinted in the overhead light and, as I watched, it nicked his skin, blood trickling along his palm. He looked down at it, and back at me. And took another step closer.

I needed to move, but I was frozen. There was no moving. There was nowhere to go.

He looked down at the blood again, and dropped the glass shard. It clattered to the floor, loud in the silence. Relief washed over me.

Too soon.

Far too soon.

Ray took another step towards me, so close now I could feel his breath, hot and whiskey-soaked. Before I worked out what was happening, he'd done it. The pain, when it came, when his fist connected with my cheekbone, was like nothing I'd ever imagined. Suddenly I was on the floor, holding my face. Staring up. Shocked. Not making a sound. A scream stuck in my throat. A scream that nobody would hear.

His face was coming towards me. His arms reaching. He took both of my hands in his, and pulled me to my feet. He put his forehead against mine, his breathing heavy.

"You can't talk to me like that, Marianne," he whispered. "You just can't."

He pulled me into a hug, my head on his shoulder. Like a rag doll. A voiceless rag doll. As he crushed me to him, I stared at the wall behind. At the bookshelves, at the photo of my parents. At my dad, who in all the years had never raised a hand to me. At my mother, smiling, unaware of the violent death to come. I closed my eyes.

"You understand, don't you?" he said into my ear, pleading.

"I do. It's okay. But I need to lie down," I whispered, my cheek still throbbing.

"I'll make tea, and bring it in to you," Ray said, tears

in his eyes now. "Marianne, I swear to you, it'll never happen again."

"Okay."

"You believe me, don't you?"

"Yes, Ray."

His face softened into a familiar smile. "You lie down, I'll make that tea."

In my bedroom, I turned the key in the lock. And, as Ray boiled the kettle. I called the police.

When he realised the door was locked, he tried everything. Begging, cajoling. Shouting, banging. At one point, he tried to shoulder the door in, but it held fast. I sat on the floor, my phone in my hand, praying he wouldn't go outside to break the window.

"I've called the guards, Ray, they're coming."

That's all I said. And in the end, that's all I had to say. Maybe back home in New Jersey, he could have talked his away out of it. But not here. Not as the interloper the locals didn't trust. Not in a town where everyone knew everyone and he was the outsider. I knew it and Ray knew it. By the time the guards pulled into the driveway, Ray was gone.

The fallout from the book was exactly as I anticipated. Locals read it, and whispers went back to Alan. He came banging on my door two days later, and I told him Ray was gone. Alan was almost foaming at the mouth and I couldn't blame him. Even the sight of my horribly bruised and swollen face didn't quell his anger. Rumours had already started around the village. *There's no smoke without a fire*, someone said. *You never know what's going on behind closed doors*, someone else chimed in.

Jamie did his best – kept his head held high, dispelling rumours whenever he could. But of course nobody said anything to him directly, it was always behind his back. Alan didn't help himself – upset, he ranted and raved and argued over anything and everything, drinking more and more, giving people the excuse to nod knowingly. *I always knew there was something not quite right with him*, they said to one another.

Time passed and memories faded, but the stench of suspicion never quite left Alan. And he never stopped ranting about Ray. Or what he'd do if he ever saw him again.

CHAPTER 64

2018

And now, ten years later, an email from Ray. Just like that.

Hey Marianne,

It's been a while!

I wanted to tell you I'll be in town tomorrow evening, to do a talk in your local library. Maybe we could catch a drink after?

Or if you're in Dublin when you get this, look me up – I'm staying at The M Hotel on Leeson Street.

Best,

Ray

I stared. No apology, no excuse, no defence, no reference at all to what he did. Just "hey" as though we were simply old friends who hadn't been in touch for some time.

In a flash, my fingers were flying over the keys, lashing out the reply that had been running through my head for a decade. All the 'how dare you's' and 'what were you thinking's' and a promise that I'd press charges if he came back, though I had no idea if I could actually do that, so many years later.

But, in the end, I deleted it. What was the point? The

Ray I remembered would never see it any way but his own – I was wasting my time.

Distracted and unfocused, I clicked back into Facebook. There were two messages waiting for me, the first was from Barry.

Hiya, are you ok with the snow? I know you're deep in the countryside, hope you have supplies. Let me know if I can do anything?

I wondered what would happen if I said, "Yes, please, could you call out with a pizza?" then felt mean – he was only trying to be nice.

The second message was from Judith.

Marianne, I noticed you were quiet online the last while – is everything alright?

For a second, I thought about telling her all of it – Hanne's death, what Dina did – but I couldn't. It was too much, and I wasn't ready to go through all the details so soon.

I'm fine, thanks for asking, I typed instead, **just anxious cos there's more snow here and am thinking about those bloody footprints again.**

You poor thing, she replied, **but if the weather is going to be really bad, I suppose even your footprint-maker will stay away.**

Exactly, I thought, getting up to look out the window. The snow was about three inches deep – not a lot by international standards, but enough to hamper travel around here. I thought about Jamie, half a mile away – his house just as remote, but at least he had company. I thought about Ray in his hotel room on Leeson Street, too close for comfort. And I thought about footprints and faceless monsters and Nøkken. And then I closed the curtains.

CHAPTER 65

The knock made Ray jump, even though he'd ordered room service. Maybe it was because the hotel was so quiet tonight, or perhaps it was the eerie atmosphere outside, the snow casting a strange pink-grey light on the empty street below.

He rolled off the bed, searching for the remote control to lower the TV volume, but it had disappeared somewhere under the covers. Giving in, he opened the door and at first he didn't register that the man wasn't wearing the hotel uniform, only that he had a baseball cap pulled low over his face and didn't appear to have any food with him.

"Is there something wrong with my order?" Ray asked, raising his voice above the noise of the TV.

"Nothing wrong with it at all," the man said, coming into the room.

He closed the door behind him, and that's when Ray began to feel alarmed.

"What's going on?" he asked, taking a step back.

"Let's just say I'm here to fix things."

Ray took another step back and folded his arms.

"I don't know what's going on," he said. "Maybe

you're mixing me up with someone else, but you need to leave."

The man laughed, but Ray's attention was drawn away from his mouth – he watched, first with disbelief, then bone-deep terror, as the man calmly raised a gun. Not the kind of gun you see in a toy store, but a heavy, black, very real-looking gun. The man began to explain, but Ray couldn't hear a word over the whirr of white noise and ice-cold fear.

"I *said*, on your knees," the man instructed after what seemed like a long time but was probably only half a minute.

Ray tried to take it in but the buzzing noise in his head wouldn't let him think straight.

"I won't tell you a third time," the man said, moving the gun closer to Ray's head.

Ray dropped to his knees.

"Please," he begged, as the man screwed something on to the end of the gun.

"Actions have consequences," the man said, pointing the gun towards Ray's forehead.

Ray put his head in his hands, covering his face.

"Please!" he said, louder now, panicked.

"Look up at me."

Ray kept his head down.

"I said look up at me."

Ray didn't move. Couldn't move.

"You have to understand. I'm not doing this until you look up at me."

Still Ray didn't move.

Neither did the man.

Ray stayed stock still, kneeling on the ground, his face

ANDREA MARA

in his hands. Silently begging the man to leave. *He would not look up. He would not make this easy.* He had only this small power left, and he would not give in.

The man stopped asking.

Time ticked by. Ray heard the blare of TV but nothing else. The political show came to an end, and a new show began. Still he stayed, face in hands. His knees cramping, his neck stiff, but he would not give in, he would not look up.

After what felt like forever, he heard the click of the hotel-room door. Opening. Then closing.

A breath, let out. It was over.

He lifted his face. He opened his eyes. To the barrel of the gun.

364

CHAPTER 66

The blare of my clock radio jolted me awake. My eyes snapped open, scanning the room. Senses heightened, on edge. The light was different. The snow was back.

The morning news confirmed it – the big freeze had set in. I stared across at my bedroom window as I slipped out of bed, but nothing could make me go over there and pull the curtain aside. What if he was back? What if he was standing there, looking in?

Instead, I padded through to the living-room window. Distance. At least a little. With one finger, I lifted the edge of the curtain and peered through the narrow gap.

Nothing.

I opened the curtains fully, squinting to look more closely. No footprints. Nobody. Just six inches of undisturbed snow.

Back in my bedroom, the news was still on – a report on a man who'd been shot in Dublin 2, and a story about the homeless crisis. I switched on the heating and looked up the forecast – no thaw due until tonight or tomorrow morning. Ray's talk would surely be cancelled but, still, I felt uneasy.

A message from Jamie popped up on my phone.

Did you make it through the night without turning to ice?

A now familiar warm feeling fizzed up inside as I typed a reply.

Still in one piece, won't be driving anywhere today though. All ok at urs?

He replied to say they were fine, then a second message came through.

I could walk up later if you fancy some company? You'd be doing me a favour tbh to get away from yer man. The cabin fever is REAL.

Then a third message:

I can bring wine. This was followed by wine and beer emojis.

Let's see how the weather is later, I replied. **I don't want you getting yourself frozen to death trying to escape Alan – it's NEARLY but not quite worth it.**

Then it was back to the world of work, and meetings with people in places where six inches of snow didn't make news headlines.

By five o'clock, it was almost dark and, although it had stopped snowing, it was bitterly, bone-numbingly cold. The thaw wouldn't be coming any time soon, I thought, standing at the window looking out. And Ray's talk couldn't possibly be going ahead, could it? I checked the website and found an announcement. Cancelled. So that was that. And yet, there was no relief.

I checked the doors and windows, and was heating up ravioli for dinner when my phone rang. The number came up on screen: **Garda Station.** I answered with one hand while tipping ravioli into a colander with the other.

366

It was Patrick.

"Something new on the footprints?" I asked, stepping back from rising steam.

"No, it's something else, Marianne. Is there anyone you could call to be with you maybe?"

"No, what's happened?" I asked, slightly panicky, though there was no reason for it – the usual fears for parents, siblings, or children didn't apply to me.

"Don't worry, everything is fine, but either Geraldine or myself will call in to tell you in person. If we can't get up tonight, it'll be the morning. Don't be reading the papers maybe."

"*What?*"

"Look, just –" he paused, "we'll tell you when we see you, try not to worry."

Obviously, the first thing I did when he ended the call was go online to see what was in the headlines. Most of the stories were weather-related – cancelled weddings and empty supermarket shelves. There was a story about a car accident, and one about a shooting in a Dublin hotel. Other than that, it was stories from around the world, including one about the Blackwood Strangler – surely that's not what Patrick meant? That would be ridiculous. I went back through the stories again, but nothing jumped out. I'd have to wait till Patrick or Geraldine told me in person.

I took my ravioli to the sitting room, opened my laptop, and switched on the TV for company. Would Jamie call in? The snow was deep in my garden though probably not as bad on the roads. He hadn't texted but then again, he might not, he might just turn up. I looked down at the pasta sauce stain on my shirt and decided to change.

In my bedroom, I didn't bother switching on the light.

Unbuttoning my shirt, I threw it in the laundry and grabbed a jumper from the wardrobe. The light-blue one that someone once said matched my eyes. Oh, for goodness sake! He probably wouldn't call anyway. I checked my bedroom window, and drew the curtains tighter.

Back at my laptop, Facebook was hopping with Armchair Detective notifications as the nightly Blackwood Strangler discussion took hold.

Neil was hanging on to his theory that the arrest was a mistake, but sounding less sure, now that all the major news outlets were reporting the same story about the wife and the souvenirs.

Anne and Cheryl were chatting about other cases – a missing woman from a small town in Wales, and a murder in Leeds.

Judith shared a link about a teen missing from her own housing estate, and wondered if we might take a look.

Barry pointed out that it might be just a runaway, and shouldn't we stick to cases that were definitely crimes?

It seemed nobody was quite sure what direction to take now that the Blackwood Strangler was caught. He was the reason for our existence and we were rudderless without him.

I felt bad for Judith though, and slightly – admittedly unfairly – irritated by Barry.

I think we should take a look at Judith's case – no harm in it, and it's not like we have urgent plans. I'm snowed in here anyway.

Oh really, Marianne? Barry replied. **It's not bad here in Dun Laoghaire at all now, road outside my apartment is totally clear. Are you ok there?**

A private message came through from Judith.

Thanks for jumping in to champion my missing person case. Everything alright this morning – no footprints or apples or newspapers? Though I think I'd quite like someone to leave me apples and newspapers!

All good here, I replied. Nothing outside my door this morning. And no worries re the missing person case – we may as well be doing that as anything else.

A beep from my phone interrupted me – a message from Jamie. Only it wasn't to tell me he was calling in – it was to ask if I'd seen Alan.

He went out for a walk an hour ago, without the dog though, and I'm worried he's slipped or something. He'd normally be 10 mins max having a sneaky fag. No sign of him up by you?

No, I haven't seen him, I typed, standing to look out the window. The ground was a blanket of glistening white – the snow soft, almost welcoming, with a deceptive innocence. Pretty, with no hint of the havoc it could wreak.

Would he come tonight? The circle drawn on the newspaper must mean something. I picked it up from the coffee table and looked again.

Weather Alert Warns of Heaviest Snow in 10 Years.

Was it a warning that he'd be back with the snow? Or something else entirely?

Something flashed into my mind, then slipped away as I tried to catch it. Something about the headline? I shook my head and sat back down.

I'll let you know if I see him, I typed to Jamie, but I can't imagine him coming up this way on a night like this.

No reply. And no more talk of visits and wine. I changed the TV channel and picked up my book; a murder mystery set on a remote farmhouse in the Australian

ANDREA MARA

outback. Maybe not ideal reading material tonight. What I would have given for a light, frothy magazine right at that moment. The thought that had been hovering flashed closer. Something about the newspaper. I picked it up and looked again, paging through, searching for notes. Scanning each page, sure I'd find something, but no. Nothing. I sat back. What was it? I picked up my laptop to check the weather forecast, and spotted the message from Judith still open.

That's when it hit me.

The newspaper. I'd told the group about the footprints and the chalk drawing and the apple. But not the newspaper. They were full of the Blackwood Strangler arrest, I was just back from Denmark, and I never got around to telling them.

So how did Judith know?

Hey, just curious – how did you know about the newspaper by the way? I typed.

I waited, watching for the notification that she'd read it. There it was. Still I waited. No reply. I refreshed the browser, and now the message disappeared completely.

What the hell was going on?

In my Facebook search bar, I typed her name. Nothing. Had she deleted her account?

I clicked into the Armchair Detective group – maybe Facebook was being glitchy. But Judith's name was greyed out – she'd left.

Guys, did Judith just leave and delete her FB account??? I posted.

Moments later, a flurry of replies in a cloud of confusion.

No! Anne said. **Judith can't go – she's the Mum of the group!**

370

Maybe she clicked "leave group" by accident, I've done that before – I'll go message her, Cheryl said

No, she's gone from FB. Her whole account is gone, Neil said. I don't get it – did someone upset her? Were there some private messages going on? An argument behind the scenes?

Sometimes when people left the group, it was for exactly that – an argument the rest of us weren't privy to, followed by a dramatic flounce. But Judith and I hadn't argued, had we? I just asked her how she knew about the newspaper.

Guys, I typed, you know the stuff I told you about, the footprints and all that? Can you remember the details about what I said was left on my doorstep?

As they were answering, I searched and scrolled back through what I'd posted – footprints, doll, chalk letter R, apple. No newspaper. I checked their answers and they tallied – everyone remembered the details I'd shared, and nobody mentioned a newspaper. It wasn't my imagination. The only way Judith could know about it is if she was in contact with the person who did it.

Ok, I typed. Here's what happened. Judith messaged me earlier and mentioned the footprints and the apple but also mentioned a newspaper. Yesterday morning, there was a newspaper on my doorstep, with a circle around the forecast for snow. Only I hadn't posted about it here or mentioned it to Judith. When I realised, I msgd her to ask how she knew and that's when her account disappeared.

Silence. Then the flurry of responses. Surprise, shock, some doubt, but more than anything, a wave of excitement trickled through the group. Drama of the best kind. Just not so much for me, sitting at its epicentre.

Theories flowed in. Judith was feeding information to

someone in the UK who had now come over here to Ireland. Judith was giving details to someone who already lived here in Ireland. Judith had come over here herself – that one generated laughter.

Maybe Judith has been here all along, Barry said.

More virtual laughter.

I love a good theory as much as the next person but I don't think an elderly retired schoolteacher is tramping around Marianne's garden at night, Barry! Anne said.

But how do we know she's an elderly retired schoolteacher? Barry asked.

Silence again, no laughter this time.

Between us, we started to rake over it: searching, scrolling, trading thoughts. I'd met her on iSleuth three years ago, which is where we'd all met, and at that stage all any of us knew was her username, same as for everyone on the site. Judith didn't have any convoluted Internet-age type username, she was simply Judith Hill and her avatar was a photo of a bicycle in the snow. Very few people had personal photos on iSleuth, everyone used fairly anonymous avatars. When we moved over to Facebook to set up our group, we all got to know one another better – now we could see what one another looked like. Profile pictures changed over time but Judith's never did – it always showed her sitting on a chair in a garden, her white hair in a tidy bun, a smile on her face, and her baby granddaughter on her knee. Now that she'd left Facebook, the photo was gone too.

Would anyone have a screen shot of anything that would still have her photo? I asked.

Barry did – he'd taken a screen shot of the thread where we doled out the "footprint" cases we suspected were linked to the Blackwood Strangler, and he shared it in the group now.

I zoomed in, took a screen shot, and put it into a reverse-image search tool – it came up on a Pinterest account of someone called Becky O. I clicked through to her blog, where she talked about her grandmother and the sweet relationship she had with her. Her grandmother, the elderly lady in the photo, was called Doris, and lived in Cleveland, Ohio. She'd died six years ago.

Jesus. So Judith, the person we'd been chatting to for the last three years, didn't exist. Then who the hell was behind the account?

My phone beeped. Jamie.

Alan not back, am out searching up your direction. Can you keep an eye out too?

I walked to the window, pulling the curtain back. The blanket of snow sat undisturbed, eerily bright under the night sky. Ethereal. Squinting, I tried to see out as far as the road. Was that something moving? I closed my eyes and opened them again, adjusting to the ghostly dark-light. There was definitely something moving out there. Not some*thing*, but some*one*. Alan? There was no way to tell in the darkness, but unease snaked through me as I stood staring. Stepping towards the front door, I flicked the switch for the porch light. Nothing happened, and I remembered now that I hadn't changed it after the night Mick drove me back from drinks with Jamie. Did I have a spare somewhere? Swallowing, I opened the front door and reached up to remove the old bulb.

Only there was nothing there. Someone had removed it.

Shit. I stepped back and slammed the front door. *Shit.*

373

Is that you I just saw on the road near my house? I typed to Jamie. **Or maybe it's Alan? I saw someone outside.**

Shaking, I sat back down to wait, but there was no reply. On my laptop, a Facebook message from Barry flashed up.

Marianne, are you ok? I'm worried about this – if Judith is not Judith, it could be someone you know. Can you think of anyone it might be? Someone close to you?

The unease ticked louder. I went to my room, and picked up the shotgun. Scared and ridiculous, I slid it behind the couch. I couldn't tell if it was loaded and it would probably make any situation worse. But still. Maybe it would frighten him off. I sat down to wait for Jamie's reply.

CHAPTER 67

Tonight

When the knock comes, I freeze. Every limb goes numb and all I can hear is white noise. The knock comes a second time, then a voice.

"*Marianne? It's Patrick. Are you okay?*"

Jesus. I stand, and make my way to the door – it's like walking through quicksand. I open it and let him in, closing it quickly behind him.

"Was that you outside on the road a few minutes ago?"

"Eh, I guess? Like just now?"

Was it just now? Or ten minutes ago? I can't tell.

"Marianne, are you alright?"

"When I was looking out the window, I saw someone down on the road. Was it you?" I feel like I'm shouting, but I can't tell.

"Oh God, sorry, yeah, it probably was – I didn't mean to scare you. I had to leave the car half a mile down the road, outside Alan Crowley's, too slippery to come up the hill in it. Nearly turned back. But I'd promised you that Geraldine or myself would come by. So I walked. Christ, I'm definitely not as fit as I thought I was."

I let out a breath. "Sorry, I'm just a bit rattled tonight.

So what is it – what's the thing you wanted to tell me? I looked at the papers online and didn't see anything."

"Maybe you should sit down," he says gently.

Shit. I sit down on the couch and he does too.

"Did you see a story about a man who was shot in a Dublin hotel?" he asks.

I nod, my throat tight, though I have no idea why or where this is going.

"Marianne, I'm so sorry, but it was Ray Sedgwick."

Jesus. Ray. A million things go through my head.

I stare at Patrick, trying to take it in.

"Ray? Why? What happened?"

He shakes his head. "There aren't a lot of details yet, but it seems he opened the door to someone and that person shot him. Do you have any idea who might do something like that? Someone with a grudge?"

I'm still staring, processing what he's just said. What he's just asked. Does he think I had something to do with it?

"Marianne?"

"I . . . I suppose there were grudges, yes, but nobody who would kill him."

"I know about the feud with Alan."

It's a statement, but one that commands an answer.

"I can't imagine . . . You surely don't think Alan had anything to do with it, do you?"

"At the moment we have no idea at all, so we're going to talk to everyone and anyone with a link to Ray, past and present."

A beat.

"Is that why you're talking to me?" I can hear the defensive tone but I can't stop it. "You think I had something to do with it?"

Patrick puts his hands up, placating.

"We just need to speak to everyone and gather as much information as we can. That's all. I called into Alan's house on the way, but there was nobody there. I'll try him on the way back. And Jamie." There's something about the way he says the last two words. An afterthought that's not really an afterthought at all.

"Alan's gone AWOL, and Jamie's searching for him," I tell him. "Up this direction I think – you didn't see either of them?"

Patrick writes something in a notebook.

"What – why are you writing something?"

He hesitates. He's holding something back, I'm sure of it.

"No need for alarm, but it's worth considering there may be a link between Ray's death and your footprint thing," he says eventually.

"*What*?"

"We have to investigate everything, and it's just one avenue."

Which tells me precisely nothing.

I pull my laptop onto my knee and google Ray's name. Nothing under "News", but then there wouldn't be if he hasn't been named yet. Across the various stories about the murder in the Dublin hotel, there are some differing details, but for the most part, the reports are the same – a man, believed to be visiting from the United States, had been found dead in his room in a Dublin 2 hotel. Nobody heard anything when it happened, and the body wasn't discovered until housekeeping came by this morning. Jesus.

"Is there any doubt?" I ask. "Any possibility it's a mistake and it's someone else? They don't name him here . . ."

Patrick shakes his head. "I'm so, so sorry, Marianne," he says, perhaps reading my horror as grief. "There's no doubt. His publicist identified the body, and we're in the process of informing friends and family. Nobody needs to find out something like this in the papers."

I click into another report, a more up-to-date one that says the victim was due to travel to Wicklow today. God. I feel sick. A message from Barry pops through – asking if I'm okay after the whole Judith-is-not-Judith thing.

Am all over the place tbh, I reply. **Have just found out the guy murdered in the hotel (maybe u saw news story) is someone I know.**

Patrick clears his throat.

"Sorry, just reading the news reports about Ray. I'm still reeling. Do you need to go?"

"No, no rush, I just need to ask you a few more questions and the lads in Pearse Street Station – they're the ones dealing with it – they're trying to gather contacts for Sedgwick, other people we need to inform. Would you –" He stops as his phone rings and stands up to fish it out of his pocket.

"The station," he mouths at me as he answers, and turns away.

I stick my head in my laptop but it's impossible not to hear his side of the conversation.

"Yeah. When did he last see him? Jesus, not a great night to be out. I'll have a look around near the farmhouse and either side. No bother. Right."

He disconnects the call, puts his phone on the arm of the couch, and sits back down.

"That was Geraldine. Jamie called the station about his dad, still no sign of him. Have you had any interactions with him recently?"

"No. But I was away for a few days. I'm only back since Sunday night."

"He'll turn up, like a bad penny," Patrick says, but he sounds worried.

That's when we hear it.

A grating sound, like someone slipping. Coming from just outside the front door. I jump, and look over at Patrick. He gets up suddenly and puts his finger to his lips, then makes a stay-there motion with his hands. Quietly, he goes to the window, and peers through a tiny crack in the curtains.

Like lightning, he moves to the door and pulls it open. A blast of cold air comes in as he goes out, and the door shuts behind him. I am frozen to the couch, laptop sill on my knee, every cell of my body ice cold. Listening. The sound of one voice, then another. Shouting, but I can't make out the words above the wind. Alan's voice? Or Jamie's? Louder now but still not clear. A bang, something hard against the door. And again. Jesus, I need to do something. Can I reach the shotgun? But my body won't move. Shouting still, louder again. Then sudden quiet as the voices stop. Why? Too late I understand why.

The sound of a gun going off. Then silence.

CHAPTER 68

I will my legs to move, to get me off the couch and somewhere safe or anywhere else at all, but I'm paralysed, staring at the door.

As I watch, the handle turns.

I push myself back against the couch, closing my eyes.

"Marianne, it's okay."

Patrick. I let out a breath but still can't move or find words.

"Marianne, it's okay, he's gone."

Please say it wasn't Jamie. Please say it wasn't Jamie.

"Who?" I whisper.

"He had a shotgun." His voice is shaking. "When I tried to get it from him, it went off. Jesus, what the hell was he thinking?"

"*Patrick, who was it?*"

"Alan. Marianne, there was nothing I could do – I had to try to get the gun. *Jesus.*"

"Oh my God. Will . . . will I call an ambulance?"

Patrick shakes his head. "There's no need, it's too late."

I hear what he's saying but it still doesn't make sense.

"Alan's dead?"

"Yeah. Jesus, why didn't he just give me the gun?" He runs his hand across his head, pacing. "I phoned the station and Geraldine's going to get the boys from Wicklow to come up. They'll have to take a statement from me and from you. Christ. I've never . . . Christ!" He looks like a little boy.

I nod because that seems like the only possible response.

Patrick is still pacing, pale and sweating. "He must be the one behind your footprints. And Ray's murder."

I can't tell if he really believes that, or if he needs it to be true, to justify what's just happened. He lifts the curtain and looks out. I'm still glued to the couch under my laptop, too numb and shaky to offer him tea or brandy or whatever you might give a person who's just shot someone.

And then I see it.

The faintest, tiniest light. Small but unmistakable. Half hidden by a cushion, having slipped off the arm of the couch. A phone. Patrick's phone.

A sick feeling takes hold, twisting and coiling, spreading like lava. Didn't he just say he called the station outside? How, if his phone was here all the time? Maybe he has a second phone?

I replay what happened, and it starts to feel like he arrived back inside just seconds after the shot was fired. How could he have made a call in that time? And shouldn't he have stayed with the body? As I sit looking at him, he reaches up to wipe condensation from the window, and his jacket rides up a little. Underneath, the briefest glimpse of something black and metallic before the jacket covers it again. A gun? Alan's maybe? But Patrick had said Alan had a shotgun, so that doesn't make sense. And Patrick is just a regular garda – they didn't carry guns. Maybe I imagined it . . . maybe it wasn't a gun.

"I'll try to get those contacts you needed – for Ray," I say, my voice sounding scratchy.

"Thanks, Marianne," Patrick says, turning to look at me, then back to the window. I shift so I'm sideways, my back to the arm of the couch, my screen turned as far away from Patrick as possible.

On my laptop, I click into Google and search "**Patrick Maguire Garda Carrickderg**", mis-typing the words three times before getting them right. My breathing speeds up. I need to slow it down or he'll notice. The search results are swimming in front of my eyes and nothing is useful but I don't even know what I'm looking for.

A message.

I'm so sorry about your friend's death – is there anything I can do?

Barry.

Barry, I need your help, urgent, might be in trouble. Can you search Garda Patrick Maguire, see if any link to Ray Sedgwick or Alan Crowley or me? Garda based here in Carrickderg but city centre before.

I hit send and open a second browser to hide the message.

Patrick turns and walks towards the couch – I open my email and scroll through my contacts, though he can't see my screen. He sits, frowns, looks down at the couch, then picks up his phone. My stomach clenches in a tight ball. Does he realise his mistake? My eyes stay firmly on the screen, and the only sound is his breathing. Is he still looking at me? I don't know and I can't look up.

"Any luck with the contacts?"

"Not yet," I try to say, but the words catch in my throat. I cough to cover up, and try again. "Not yet, still looking."

He goes back to the window, phone in hand this time. I flip my browsers, and find replies from Barry – short, staccato replies, he's typing as he reads.

Patrick Maguire, from Bray, college in Templemore, stationed in Store Street.

Transferred to Bray then on to Carrickderg.

?? This any help?

I type back: **Link to me, Ray, Alan??**

I flick to my email again just as Patrick steps away from the window and comes to sit on the couch. He seems jumpy but then anyone would be after a shooting.

"It's starting to snow again," he says. "In that wind it'll be a real blizzard. We're not cut out for this."

I nod and keep my head down.

"Were you and Ray still in touch?" he asks.

"No, I haven't seen him since the night he left, ten years ago."

"Really?"

Again I nod, and brave a look at Barry's messages.

No link yet, sorry, will keep looking. What 's going on?

I answer: **He is in my house, have bad feeling. He is a guard but I think might be the one – the footprints.**

Barry asks: **Will I call the police?**

He IS the police, I reply.

He says: **Ok then I call police and say there's a man in your house. Right? I'll take blame – all my fault, if you're wrong.**

Yes. Do it, thank you.

Relief spins around me like a cloak but only for a second before it slips away again – how soon will the police get here in this weather?

"Do you mind if I make tea?" Patrick asks after a few minutes.

"Sure, I can do it!" If I'm in the kitchen, I can get out the back door while the kettle boils. Is the backdoor locked? I think yes, but the key is in the keyhole. And there are boots beside the door.

"No, you keep going with that, I need the distraction anyway."

Is there something in the way he says it? Does he know what I was thinking? I can't tell. He gets up and goes to the kitchen. Barry has sent new messages.

Have called police, they will send car as best can in snow. Still searching re Patrick Maguire

Through the open kitchen door comes the sound of cups and spoons. I look at the front door – if I'm quiet, I can make it across the room without him seeing me. He'll hear the door, but then I'll be gone. Gently, I push the laptop off my knee and unfold my legs, touching my bare feet to the floor. I don't know how far I'll get in the snow without shoes, but I have to try.

I stand, just as Patrick comes back into the room with two teas.

"All okay, Marianne?" he asks, and there's something harder in his voice now. Something pointed.

"Pins and needles." I stretch, calculating quickly in my head – if I can't get out, I need the laptop and access to Barry. I sit and pull the laptop onto my knee in one fluid movement that I hope looks relaxed.

Patrick stands watching for a second longer than necessary. Then he sits too, putting the teas on the coffee table.

"Oh crap, I put milk in yours," he says. "Sorry, I should have asked!"

"That's grand," I say. "I take milk."

He sounds exactly as he always does, Patrick Maguire,

local garda in nothing-ever-happens Carrickderg. Jesus, he probably has two phones, he's probably allowed to carry a gun, and I'm letting years of true crime creep into real life.

Barry's next message comes through.

His dad Robert Maguire, in the army, dishonourable discharge after a random drug test.

Patrick's dad was in the army? But wasn't it Alan who was discharged from the army?

Arrest for drunk and disorderly afterwards, suggestion he took discharge badly.

But this is Alan's story – *Alan* was in the army, at least according to Geraldine. And what about that photo I'd found – the burnt picture of Alan in an army uniform? I think back to the conversation with Geraldine at the side of the street, as we watched Patrick and Jamie talk and Alan look sullenly on. Had Geraldine been confused? My mind goes over it, trying to remember and make sense. She'd said he'd had a "rotten time of it" and had "turned out okay". I picture us standing there, Geraldine lowering her voice, telling me about the army, nodding over at where Jamie and Patrick were talking.

And then it hits me.

She was never talking about Jamie. She never said his name. I just assumed that's who she meant.

He had a rotten time of it and turned out okay.

She meant Patrick.

Only he didn't turn out okay.

Dad died in unusual circs, Barry types, **about 12 years ago, am still digging. U ok? Any sign of police?**

I reply: **No but the snow isn't helping.**

"Jesus, that snow is coming down heavy now – that's

going to slow the team from Wicklow," Patrick is saying. "God, Marianne, this is all a lot for you to be dealing with – are you okay with me staying here till they get here? Only I can't leave the body unattended."

"No problem."

"Are you sure you're okay? You look pale."

I swallow, willing my voice to cooperate. "Yes, just still thinking about Ray."

"I can imagine. Why did you two break up?"

I look over at him.

"Sorry, that's a bit intrusive, don't answer if you'd rather not."

"No, that's fine." There's an unmistakeable shake in my voice. "Ray and Alan had been at each other on and off for years and it came to a head when Ray published a book that all but named the fictional character as Alan Crowley."

"Is that so bad?"

"It's what was in it. A suggestion that Alan – well, if you believe it's based on Alan – was abusing his children."

"Oh God."

"Yes."

"What did Jamie think of it?"

Jamie. Jesus, his dad is lying dead outside, and no doubt he's still out looking for him. I look at my mobile on the coffee table. It's worth a try. Not too quickly, not too slowly, I pick it up.

"What are you doing?" Patrick asks.

"I'm going to call Jamie about his dad – he could come up this way and find him lying there."

"No, don't, Marianne. He'll need to formally notified. It can't come from you." There's an edge to his voice.

"Right." I put the phone down and bury my head in my laptop screen again.

Barry has come back – another staccato message.

I've got it. Dad in and out of trouble after army, couldn't hold job, lost home. Died sleeping rough in freezing temperatures, in place called Ramolin. Inquest found had been living in farmhouse shed but asked to leave – died few nights later.

Oh Jesus. I remember that story on the news at the time.

I type: **Where was farmhouse?**

He replies: **Carrickderg. Farmer Alan Crowley. Maguire evicted by Crowley, not clear why.**

I know why.

And now I know why Alan dumped a bag of old clothes in our garden after Ray reported him to the County Council. Deadman's clothes. I know why Ray burned those clothes. Guilt he couldn't or wouldn't accept. I know who was in the charred photo of the couple with the baby. It was never Jamie with his parents. It was Patrick.

And now I know why Ray and Alan are dead.

Call police again, definitely in trouble. Please, Barry.

Can you get out of there? he asks.

I look over at Patrick who is drinking tea and watching me. His phone in his hand, mine on the coffee table. I think about Dad's shotgun, down behind the couch. Patrick's side of the couch, too far to reach from here. If I can find a reason to go to the kitchen, I can reach in and pull it out.

"I'm just going to the bathroom," I tell him, closing the laptop and standing up.

He watches me as I walk around the coffee table. I need to get past him to go through to the kitchen and on to the bathroom. My breath is speeding up. I can't slow it down. He's going to know. Stay calm. Walk slowly. Don't look at him. Keep going. Nearly at the kitchen door. Do I run or grab the gun? Does he know?

I turn and risk a glance.

We lock eyes.

He knows.

CHAPTER 69

In that split second, the decision is made. I duck and reach to grab the gun from behind the couch, and stumble into the kitchen.

Patrick appears in the doorway.

"Oh Marianne, don't kid yourself. You don't know how to use it."

"I do. My dad taught me."

"I can see it in the shake of your hand and the frightened-rabbit look in your eyes. You're not even holding it right." He smiles calmly, looking nothing like the lost, scared boy he was a few minutes ago.

"What do you want? Why are you doing this? I had nothing to do with what happened to your dad."

"But you did, Marianne – your name is on the complaint to the County Council – there's no point in lying about it now."

"It wasn't me. He used my name, but it wasn't me."

Patrick shakes his head. "Easy to say now Ray is dead, isn't it? But it's there in black and white in the records." He pauses, licks his lips. "I was twelve. Can you imagine what that was like? My dad, dead in a ditch. My mother, crying and wailing and blaming herself for kicking him out, before she lost it completely. I got taken into care then. Do you have any idea what that was like? And I blamed them, blamed my parents for being weak, for leaving me to fend for myself. A twelve-year-old boy, lost and alone in the world, betrayed by his mother and father. Hansel with no Gretel." He grins. "Did you like that touch? Did you enjoy trying to guess what it meant?" His face changes again. "Then I found out it wasn't really my parents' fault at all. It was you and Alan and Ray. Your fucking stupid feud and your fucking stupid complaints to the Council." A cold smile flashes across his face. "Poor old Ray. I don't think he understood a word I said to him last night. And Alan had no idea either."

He takes a step towards me. I take one step back, still pointing the gun at him.

I force myself to speak. "Your dad, Alan, and Ray are all dead." It comes out in a hoarse whisper. "Isn't that enough death?"

"I thought it might be. I thought when I walked away from the hotel last night that I'd feel it was over. That there was justice. But I just felt empty."

"Because killing isn't the answer," I whispered.

"Ah, wouldn't it be nice for you if that was why? But no, that's not it, Marianne. It was too quick. Too easy. Ray didn't even take in what I was saying. I should have made him listen, made it last longer. If I wasn't worried about hotel staff hearing me, I could have started with a shot to the knee. Then one to the hand. Slow and painful, like it was for my dad, lying in the ditch, freezing to death, limb by limb." He takes another step towards me. "I should have done it somewhere like this, where there's no-one to hear. Where there's time to play, all night long. To take things slowly." He grins. "You've been sitting here petrified since the shot went off, haven't you?"

I can't speak. I think I'm going to throw up. The barrel of the gun is just inches from his chest. He's not afraid. He knows I can't use it. Can I?

In a flash, he reaches and grabs the barrel. I shove it forward at the same time and run for the back door. The key turns and I pull it open, running into the snow, darting for the undergrowth at the side of the garden. I can hear Patrick coming out of the house, calling my name. There's nothing frantic, nothing panicked about it, and that scares me more than anything. We both know a barefoot woman is no match for a man with a gun.

Crashing through trees, I reach the wall at the end of the garden. Is there something I can stand on to get up and over? Stone slabs have fallen off the top of the wall but they won't give me the height I need.

And there's no time.

Behind me, Patrick's approach is steady, not rushed. He's still calling my name. There is no way out. Jesus Christ, this is *not* how it ends. Frantic, my eyes scan left and right and then I see it.

The den.

Against the wall, in the furthest corner of the undergrowth, hard to make out in the dark, but still there. I drop to my hands and knees and lift the branches that hide the opening. I slither through and pull the branches down again. The old tin roof has rusted through in places and our once clear floor is covered in leaves and muck, but there's room enough for me to hunker down. And stay out of sight.

"Marianne, there's nowhere to go. Believe me, I know your garden. I've visited you on so many nights, not just the times I left gifts for you."

He's still about thirty feet away, but I can't breathe in case he hears.

"Did you like my gifts? Were you starting to solve the clues?"

A pause. He stops speaking and I think he's stopped moving. Then he starts again, the sound of crisp snow and twigs crunching getting louder.

"That apple I left for you? That's what my da resorted to eating when he was kicked out of Alan's shed – apples that were meant for the pigs. You and Ray – you never stopped to think about the consequences of that report to the Council, did you? Too busy playing God. You didn't give a shit about the collateral damage – that's all my da was to you, collateral damage."

I didn't know! I want to scream, as I huddle against the back wall of the den. But what does it matter, he doesn't care who knew what back then – there's no getting away from what I know now, about Alan and about Ray.

"Playing God, and playing executioner. Because that's what you did. When you put in that complaint, you signed my da's death warrant."

The sound of his steps comes closer and moves away. He's checking the other side of the undergrowth. Soon he'll find the den. I need to do something. Behind me, I feel the tin where we used to keep the Blacklist notebook and biscuits and the torch. And scissors. Would they still be there? Fumbling, I prise off the lid and feel inside. My fingers close around the metal blades.

"And now the roles are reversed," comes Patrick's voice.

I hear bushes and branches rustling as he pokes. Nearer now.

"I get to play hangman. Think of the tragic newspaper reports – me getting here just too late to save you from Alan, too late to stop him grabbing your shotgun and shooting you in the head. But at least I got him before he could hurt anyone else, right?"

More rustling, closer now.

"Poor old Alan. He was in to me twice in the station to say he was worried someone was on your property at night – asked me to keep an eye on you. That's what he was doing tonight – checking on you, Marianne. And you, like a scuttling mouse, hiding from him."

He laughs. The rustling is closer.

"And I want to thank you, Marianne, because you've made the last few weeks so enjoyable. All your little discoveries in Armchair Detectives, so easy to replicate. I'm going to miss being Judith. Maybe I'll re-open her Facebook account and join the group again, to tell them the sad news of your murder. And Barry – he carries a torch for you, doesn't he? I'm going to especially enjoy telling Barry."

His voice is right outside the den now and, as my eyes adjust, I can make out the shape of his legs. If he ducks down, he'll find it. And me.

"So sad, Marianne, and ironic. Murdered. Like mother, like daughter."

I have to get out of here. I crawl to the entrance of the den. He's just inches away. I don't dare breathe. Between us, nothing but overhanging twigs. I can't do it. What if I miss? I have to try. I close my eyes, beg my mother to guide my hand, and plunge the scissors into the back of his leg.

CHAPTER 70

He roars and reaches to grab his leg, dropping the shotgun. He falls sideways, still clutching his leg. I have no idea how badly injured he is, but surely after the initial shock, he'll be back on his feet. I crawl out, grab the shotgun, and stand up straight, taking a step back.

"*You bitch!*" he roars.

It's hard to see but the moonlit snow casts some light – I can tell he's still on the ground. Now he's pulling himself to his feet and moving towards me. *Fuck.* I step back, but he's faster, and suddenly he's hurtling towards me, reaching. At the last second, I turn the shotgun and push the butt with everything I have into his face. I wait for a scream but hear only crunching bone. He stumbles back against a tree, then slips sideways onto the snow. Rolls over and is still. A crumpled, silent heap, face down in a mound of snow. I take three steps backwards, point the gun at him again and wait, but there is no movement.

In the distance, I hear a siren, but I can't tell how far away it is. Part of me wants to get back inside the house and lock all the doors, but then I'll never know if he gets up again. If he's coming for me. I need to wait here, to keep watch. To know if he's dead or alive.

Something clicks in my mind – something about my mother, about her death. Her drowning. And slowly I realise Patrick will drown. Or suffocate. Face down in the snow.

If he's not already dead. I creep closer, trying to see.

I don't know what a dead body looks like. I've seen them in coffins in tidy funeral homes, but not like this – not in this maybe-state, flat on the frozen ground.

Dead. Or not dead, just waiting for me to come closer.

One or the other.

It's still too dark to see, and I understand now that it's always been too dark – for me, and for Hanne. Spinning blindly in the wind while other people pulled the strings.

And I feel it even now, the snap of the string, pulling me forward. Towards the body.

Dead. Or not dead.

One or the other.

My breath comes fast. Another step. A closer look.

A movement. Slight, but enough.

And I think about all of it, all of the deaths and all of the accidents and all of the pain. And it's not dark anymore. I know what I need to do.

I take another step forward, my heart in my mouth, and reach the barrel of the gun towards him. I push it against his shoulder, but it isn't enough. Fuck it. I put down the gun, kneel on the snow, and reach to turn his head. No longer buried in snow.

CHAPTER 71

After

The two of us sit together on the couch in my living room, while Geraldine makes tea. The ambulance has gone, taking Patrick under armed escort to hospital. A blanket covers me to my neck but still I shiver, cold to the bone, and I wonder if I'll ever feel warm again. Beside me, Jamie sits poker-straight, clutching a brandy someone put in his hands.

"It's about forty years old," I tell him after a while.

"What?"

"The brandy. I didn't even know we had it."

Jamie nods but I don't think he registered what I said.

"Do you think he was coming to do something bad?" he asks. "Alan, I mean?"

"No," I say gently. "He was coming to check on me. He had his faults, but he's not the bad guy in this."

Geraldine comes through with tea and sets it in front of us.

"Marianne," she says, perching on the edge of the armchair, "I don't know what to say. Officially, I can't say anything of course. So this is off the record, but I'm so, so sorry. If I'd had any idea . . ."

"None of us had any idea. I was reporting things to him – the footprints, the chalk letter – and he was laughing up his sleeve at me the whole time because he'd done them himself. There's no way you could have known."

"Well," she says, slumping back in the chair, "at the very least I could have taken you more seriously."

Instead of answering, I reach out over the blanket to pick up the tea and hug the cup in my hands.

"Don't they do background checks on guards?" Jamie asks.

Geraldine sighs. "The fact that his father died in tragic circumstances wouldn't have raised any flags, Jamie. He put in a request for an inter-divisional transfer from Bray to here, and nobody knew about the connection with the area. It just never came up."

"So he killed Ray," I say, "and came here planning to kill me. Alan's arrival wasn't in the plan."

Geraldine looks at me. "Alan was the spanner in the works."

Jamie winces. I take his hand.

"But so easy then to make it look like Alan killed me and Patrick killed Alan in self-defence or an attempt to save me."

"Yes." That was all Geraldine was going to say about it.

"Either way, I'd be dead, just like my mother."

Geraldine says nothing.

Jamie squeezes my hand. "It's over."

Of course, it wasn't really over. There was Ray's funeral in New Jersey and Alan's funeral in Carrickderg, and Patrick's trial. There was his refusal to admit he'd done anything wrong. There was the psychiatric assessment, as we waited, worrying he'd be treated as ill rather than guilty. There were the nightmares about Dina and Erik, their distorted faces and warped minds. There were the thoughts that wouldn't go away – did Hanne know what was coming that night, when her mother held her under the water? What would have happened if my dad had stayed and listened, or if even one person had given her the help she needed? And was it all for nothing – all our locked doors and security systems and motion-sensor lights, all the avoiding strangers and white vans – if the monster is not the stranger outside, but the one we let in the door, the one inside the house? The mother, the father, the husband, the trusted friend, the pillar of the community in his reassuring uniform?

But, in the end, Patrick wasn't ill, they said – he was guilty. He was going to prison for life, or whatever life might mean. And as Jamie and I sat in the courtroom, holding hands, then, finally, the story was over. Not a happy ever after. Not a fairy-tale ending. But for us, a new beginning.

THE END

ACKNOWLEDGEMENTS

First and foremost, thank you to Paula Campbell, Gaye Shortland, and all at Poolbeg – third time round, you made this even easier than ever – it has been a joy from start to finish.

Thank you to my agent Diana Beaumont. I'm so glad we had our serendipitous meeting!

To my sisters, Nicola, Elaine, and Dee – thank you for being my first readers and constant entertainers. Dad, you were off the hook for proofreading this time, but only because you went to South East Asia at the critical point, a fairly extreme attempt to avoid being roped in. Also, this one's for you, to say thank you for everything.

To my early readers, Karen Mulreid, Elizabeth McDonnell, Naomi Lavelle, Emmet Driver, Gavin Driver-O'Donnell, Lorna Sixsmith, Tric Kearney, Noeleen Rooney and Denise Slevin – thank you so much, I know it's not easy to read pdf! Particular thanks to Naomi who swooped in at the last minute and saved the day.

Sincere thanks to Darragh, Stephen and Allen, for making sure my officers are stationed in the correct stations and ranked in the correct ranks. (Stephen, I think you should be writing a crime series.)

ANDREA MARA

Thank you to the Denmark gang: to Melanie Hayes of DejligeDays.com, for answering my big Danish questions; to Zoe Healy and to Rachael's friend Aoife for the little bits and pieces along the way, and especially to Nanna Kock Johansen for always being at the end of the line when I needed a translation. Any remaining errors, as they say, are mine.

Special thanks to Theodor Hans Helsengren Gøgsig and his dad, Johnny, for inventing the town-name Købæk.

Thank you to Tricia Griffith of WebSleuths, and to the Lurvers Armchair Detectives – so many rabbit holes, so little time.

Thank you to dlr Lexicon and The Mellow Fig, where chunks of this book were written.

Thank you to my oldest friends from my own school and my newest friends from my kids' schools, and everyone else in between – you have been so incredibly supportive throughout all of this.

Thank you to my blogger pals – the parent bloggers and book bloggers, for all the reading and sharing and advising and turning up – you are all more brilliant than you know.

Thank you to the Irish writers I've come to know – for the honest insights and inspirational chats in the backs of taxis and in the pubs of Listowel and in the beer tent in Harrogate and on WhatsApp and Facebook – you make a sometimes lonely pursuit far less lonely.

And a huge thank you to the OfficeMum.ie readers, because that's where it all started.

A side note for any Danish readers or Myths and Legends aficionados: I've taken some liberties with Nøkken (though I still wouldn't like to meet one).

More liberties: *The Sleeper Lies* is set during the big

snow of March 2018, but in my fictional version, the curfews and red weather warnings and fresh snow don't occur on exactly the same days as they did in real life.

It was while I was hunkered down, snowed in with my husband and kids for three days, that it struck me how eerie and sometimes sinister the snow looks, especially at night. Then there was the cabin fever side of things – three days in an upside-down world of closed schools, depleting food stocks, and no escape. It was a time that brought out the worst in my fictional characters but the best in real-life people, banding together to shovel snow, clear roads, and share information about when Tesco was *really* opening again. Particular thanks to my friend and neighbour Rachael Barry, who gave me half a sliced pan when she had one and I had none – that's how I remember the snow.

It was during this suspended reality that the idea for the *The Sleeper Lies* came about, so thank you to Elissa, Nia, and Matthew for muddling along so admirably during the snow, for brainstorming plots with me, and for helping to find cake recipes that didn't require butter, when we ran out of that too.

Thank you to Damien for trudging through the snow to bring home supplies, and for your unfailing support of this new and sometimes erratic career. I couldn't do any of it without you.

And finally, thank you to *you*, the reader, for reading this book!

Now that you're hooked why not try
ONE CLICK
also published by Poolbeg

Here's a sneak preview of
Chapter 1

CHAPTER 1

One Click

The woman is where she is every day. Her eyes closed, her face turned to the sun, and she has no idea I'm here. Turquoise waves lap around her feet and the low frame of her deckchair. Dark-red hair glints in the morning light and her book hangs loosely in her hand. It's Utopia wrapped up in a single square shot and I can't resist.

My phone is on silent, and there's no tell-tale click when I take the photo, but still she glances up. Does she know? She looks at me for a moment, then down to her book.

I turn and take some more shots, out to sea this time. My arms drop to my sides and I stand for a moment, breathing in the sea air, letting the babble of accents wash over me. Then a wave splashes across my feet and the spell is broken.

My wet trainers squelch on the sand on the way back to the campsite. I should run, but it's too hot now, and I'm tired. Or maybe old. Older than yesterday when I'm sure I ran for longer.

"*Caffè? Pasticcini?*" comes the familiar call from the kiosk.

"*Cappuccino, per favore,*" I say, feeling only slightly guilty that I don't have enough money with me to take pastries back to the girls. I'll drink my coffee on the walk back so they don't get cranky. Especially Rebecca, I think, picturing the raised-eyebrow look she's been perfecting since we arrived in Italy. The coffee is strong and hot as it hits the back of my throat, and the morning ritual is complete.

"Mum, did you bring us anything?" Rebecca asks as I walk up to the deck, not looking up from her phone. Her hand hovers absentmindedly over a plate of toast.

"Are you on Snapchat again? It's going to cost a fortune, Rebecca."

Now she looks up, and there's the raised eyebrow. "Did you bring us pastries?" she asks, and takes a bite of toast.

"Nope, I didn't have any money with me," I tell her. "Where's Ava?"

"Still in bed," she says, going back to her phone.

Pulling up a chair beside her, I scan through my photos. Fourteen taken this morning – the girls will have a field day. They never take photos of the sea, or anything that doesn't have a pouting human in the foreground, and they can't understand why I do. I stop when I get to the girl with the dark-red hair. There's something about her expression that radiates an easy indifference to the sunbathers and paddlers around her. The way the book hangs from her hand, the tilt of her wrist. Her upturned unlined face. The blush-coloured dress against nutmeg skin, a turquoise bracelet the only flash of colour. A sun goddess dressed up as a carefree millennial. Clicking into Instagram, I upload the photo. It doesn't need a filter – the girl on the beach speaks for herself. I type a caption.

All the envy on my morning run – this is #howIwishIspentmytwenties

I hit share, and put down my phone as Ava pads out of the mobile home and flops into a chair.

"I'm starving – did you bring us anything? Hey! Rebecca, did you eat all the bread?"

And just like that, I'm back to the real world of ever-hungry teens and bickering siblings.

It's after lunch before I check into Instagram. 354 likes already. I share it on Facebook and Twitter too, and Rebecca catches me smiling.

"Mum, are you obsessing over your blog again? *You're never off that phone*," she says, mimicking me.

"It's not my blog, it's Instagram, and I'm just checking it. *I haven't been on in hours actually*," I say, mimicking her back.

She leans in to have a look.

"Who's that in the pic?"

"I don't know – just a woman I saw on my run this morning. Doesn't she look so happy and chilled?"

"Yeah . . . does she know you took her photo though? Did you ask her?"

"No, but it's just a photo of the beach – people take pictures like that all the time. With strangers in them, I mean."

"Sure, but this picture is very much about her, and now you've put it online. Like, you can see her really clearly – she's not just one of the crowd. Ha – you're constantly telling us not to post photos without permission, and now you've just gone and done it!"

"Excuse me, it's not the same thing – photographers take pictures like this all the time. It's a candid shot – a study of a person having a moment in time, that's all." I'm aware of how defensive I sound and, watching my daughter do her perfect eyebrow-raise, I see she is too.

"Whatever, Mum, but maybe practise what you preach?" she says, picking up her plate and walking inside.

I can hear her telling Ava about it and I can picture the eye-rolls. Shutting out their voices, I look down again at my phone. It's just a good photo. That's all. And the woman will never know I took it. Even if she did, she'd surely be flattered. She's beautiful, and she has 354 likes now too.

At the pool, the girls jump straight in the water while I stay on a sunlounger with my book. It's odd to think of all those times I wished for this when they were small – now they don't need me any more, and I miss it. I watch as Rebecca stands under a fountain of water, shrieking that it's cold. Memories of a similar pool in another campsite surface – a much smaller Rebecca standing under a stream of water while Dave held her, the two of them laughing hysterically. I close my eyes to block it out but it doesn't work. Dave did all the holiday bookings – he was rubbish at lots of things, but great at finding just the right campsite in just the right part of France. That's why we're in Italy now – because I needed it to be different.

Still thinking about Dave, my eyes move across to the next pool and that's when I see her – the woman from the beach is lying on a lounger, reading her book. Shit. I had no idea she was staying on the campsite. Then again, what does it matter? She's hardly going to see the photo. I wonder where she's from? At the beach I assumed she was Italian, but now I'm not sure. I squint to see the name of her book but I can't. Did it show up in the photo? I click into Instagram to check. *The Goldfinch* by Donna Tartt – so she's an English-speaker, or at least someone who can read books in English. A splinter of unease digs into the pit of my stomach. Maybe I should take down the photo . . . But it has over 600 likes on Instagram now and almost a hundred between Facebook and Twitter. I'm being silly – it's not doing any harm. There are dozens of new comments about what people wish they'd done in their twenties too and, as I scroll, I spot one from Rebecca.

So much for 'don't post pics online without permission', Mum.

She's followed it with a smiley face but it still makes me defensive.

It's a candid shot of a beach, smarty-pants, I reply before scrolling on.

A message interrupts my browsing – Dave wants to know if he can let himself into the house to collect some more stuff. He's thinking of booking a week in the sun, he says. With Nadine, of course. Closing my eyes, I take some deep breaths and only start to type when I know I can say the right thing.

Of course, any time. Weather great here.

I hit send, and stuff my phone in my bag. My book is on the ground beside me but I don't feel like reading any more. How ironic, after all those years wishing I could do just this. I close my eyes.

One Click and *The Other Side of the Wall*
is also available on poolbeg.com

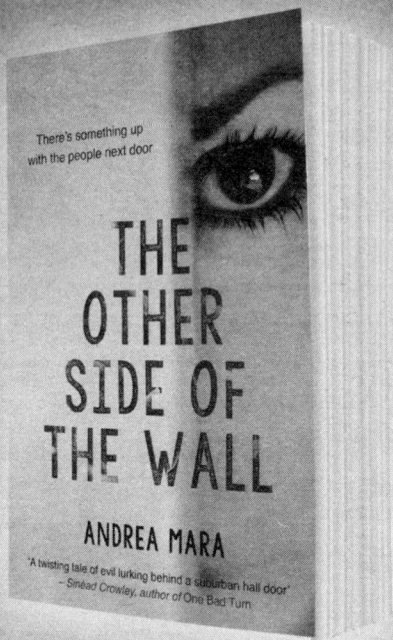